HOSTILE TAKEOVER

ARCANE CASEBOOK 8

DAN WILLIS

Print Edition – 2022

This version copyright © 2021 by Dan Willis.

All rights reserved. No part of this book may be reproduced or transmitted in any form or by any electronic or mechanical means, including photocopying, recording or by any information storage and retrieval system, without the express written permission of the copyright holder, except where permitted by law.

This novel is a work of fiction. Names, characters, places and incidents are either the product of the author's imagination, or, if real, used fictitiously.

Edited by Stephanie Osborn
Supplemental Edits by Barbara Davis

Cover by Mihaela Voicu

Published by

Runeblade Entertainment
Spanish Fork, Utah.

1

THE FEATHERED SERPENT

The office of accountant Willie Faust was opulent but tasteful, as befitted a professional of his status. The desk that occupied the center of the room was white oak, stained slightly darker than its natural color, with inlays of glistening cherry wood. The fixtures were from Tiffany, the fountain pens had gold nibs, and the carpet was Persia's finest. A bank of bookshelves stood behind the desk, filled with sumptuous, leather-bound books, mementos from a lifetime of travel, and a salt-water tank filled with tropical fish.

Despite the confident air of elegant certainty the office inspired, Alex could see a few cracks in the veneer. None of the books in the bookshelf had even the slightest crack in their spines — they were for show, much like the Tiffany lamps and the colorful fish.

Behind the desk Willie sat in a leather chair, leaning sideways with his feet up on the top. He was a man of middle years, perhaps forty, perhaps a bit more, with a long, narrow face, a downturned nose, and sharp, dark eyes. Like his office, Willie's suit was expensive and well-tailored, accenting his thin frame and padding out his shoulders so he would cut a more heroic appearance when he stood or walked.

"I know you didn't find anything at my house," Willie said with the air of a fighter who was assured of victory. "So if there's nothing more, I've got clients who expect me to be working."

"Save it," a gruff voice replied before Alex could speak. "We found plenty at your apartment."

This last came from New York Police Detective Derek Nicholson.

Nicholson worked for Lieutenant Detweiler of division three, and Alex had worked with him a few times before. From Alex's perspective, the detective was a slob, always showing up in a rumpled suit, and he wasn't really very bright. That said, he was smart enough to work with Alex whenever he got the chance, which forced Alex to raise his opinion of the man.

"Do tell," Willie said, an easy, confident smile ghosting across his face.

"I'm glad you asked," Alex replied, returning the accountant's grin as he plunked down a paper shopping bag on Willie's immaculate desk. "Let me show you what we found."

Willie's expression changed, but instead of alarm, it slid toward boredom.

"I'll tell you what you didn't find," he said, stifling a theatric yawn. "You didn't find a solid-gold bookend."

The retort hit a nerve, but Alex stifled any reaction. It had already taken far too long for him to figure out that Willie had taken the museum's missing exhibit.

"First," Alex said, reaching into the paper bag, "there's this." He pulled out a large, rectangular battery that weighed about two pounds. Alex set it gently on the desk.

"What's that supposed to be?" Willie asked.

"This is a lantern battery," Alex said. "We found it in the bottom of your pantry. Curiously, we didn't find a lantern to go with it."

"I broke the lantern," Willie said. "No sense getting rid of the battery."

"Then there's this," Alex said, pulling out a jar of green liquid and setting it next to the battery.

"Cleaning fluid?" Willie chuckled. He looked from Alex to Nicholson. "You're really getting desperate, Detective."

"This isn't cleaning fluid, Mr. Faust," Nicholson said as Alex pulled a white, button-up shirt from the bag. "In fact, it stained your shirt right here."

He pointed to a small green dot next to one of the shirt buttons.

"In fact," Alex repeated, "it's actually nickel sulfide."

"Is that something illegal?" Willie drawled.

"No," Alex said, stepping around the large desk and moving to the bookshelf. He picked up a shiny, chrome statuette and held it up. "Nickel sulfide is also known as electrolytic nickel, and you use it to make things like this."

The statuette had a blocky snake head sitting atop a plain square pedestal. It was, in fact, the exact item stolen from the museum, only rendered in chrome instead of gold.

"That's a replica," Willie said. "I bought it from the museum gift shop. It's interesting to look at, which is why the museum sells hundreds of them every month."

"I imagine people like the history," Alex said, putting the heavy figure down next to the stained shirt. "It's from the museum's Mesoamerican collection and represents a feathered serpent, also known as the Aztec god, Quetzalcoatl. But that's not why you were interested in it; you wanted the money it would bring."

Willie sighed and sat up in his chair.

"Let's get down to brass tacks," he said. "If I stole this mezzo-coat-tail thing, then where is it?"

Alex smiled down at him.

"You remember that I told you this green liquid of yours is also called electrolytic nickel? Well, that's because it's used in a process called electroplating. You take something like this," he picked up the statue again, "and you submerge it in your electrolytic-nickel solution. Then you add electricity," Alex indicated the battery, "a sacrificial piece of nickel, and in a few minutes, you've chromed the object."

"So you think I did that to the original and then put it on my shelf for all to see?"

Alex gave him a knowing smile and reached into the paper bag again. This time he pulled out a stoppered glass container full of clear liquid and then an open-topped beaker.

"What say we find out," Alex said, removing the stopper from the bottle and carefully pouring the liquid into the beaker. "This is hydrochloric acid. Funny thing about hydrochloric acid; it dissolves nickel plating... but not gold."

Willie Faust laughed in Alex's face.

"First of all," he said, "if you get any of that on my desk, I'll sue. And secondly," he pulled open his desk drawer and reached inside, "you're going to be here a while." When he withdrew his hand, he held another of the Quetzalcoatl figurines. "You see, I figured you'd come to some conclusion like that when you saw that I had a replica on my shelves, so I decided to buy a few more.

He set the second replica on the desk, then dipped back into his drawer and added a third, then a fourth, fifth, and sixth. When he finished, he closed the drawer and picked up his desk phone.

"Have fun with your little science experiment," he said, holding the receiver to his ear. "Hello, Marge?" he said, "I think this is going to take some time; would you send out for lunch, please."

While he spoke, Alex took off his suit coat, then unbuttoned the cuff of his right sleeve and began to roll it up.

"Oh, I don't think it will take all that long, Mr. Faust," he said, moving around the far side of the desk. "I want to start with this one."

Willie Faust hung the phone up as Alex lifted the lid on the tropical fish tank and reached down inside. When Faust saw what Alex was doing, he started out of his chair but didn't make it far, as Detective Nicholson was there to push him back down again.

Gotcha, Alex thought, not bothering to hide the smile spreading across his face.

He reached down to the bottom where a squarish bit of what looked like stone lay beside a model sandcastle. Picking it up with his fingers, he tugged it free of the gravel that made up the bottom of the tank. As he lifted, his fingers wiped away the algae from the tank, revealing another chrome replica of the figurine.

"Gee, Willie," Alex said, shaking it off as he pulled it from the water. "This one feels a bit heavier than the others."

Willie glared at Alex, but he kept his mouth shut.

Alex carefully lowered the figurine into the beaker of acid, releasing it before his fingers contacted the caustic liquid. Willie watched, transfixed, as it sank to the bottom and began to bubble.

"Give that a few minutes and it should take care of your evidence problem, Detective," Alex said to Nicholson as he picked up his suit coat and headed for the door.

The offices of Faust Accounting were in the inner ring but still too far away from Empire Tower for Alex to walk back to his office, so he stopped by a newsstand to buy a paper before catching a cab.

Stocks Plunge! Second Crash Around the Corner?, the banner headline screamed. Despite the provocative nature of the headline, Alex shrugged and skipped the story. Ever since the big crash in twenty-nine, headlines predicting a second crash had become commonplace. Every time a sufficiently large company took a stock dip, the papers recycled their headlines.

The rest of the front page was filled up with war rumblings from Europe. Hitler had been calling on Germany to reunite, by which he meant that Austria should be part of the Third Reich. There was even a companion story on page three about German armor and troops massing on the Austrian border.

Alex shook his head and suppressed a shiver. Despite his best efforts to just be a private detective and make a living, his work had brought him to the attention of powerful people. All of them had told him that another war was coming in Europe, coming from Nazi Germany.

He hadn't wanted to think about it, actively putting it out of his mind. Now every day the papers conspired to drag it back into his consciousness. The World War had killed some forty-million people when all was said and done, and the financial repercussions had been staggering. Now the stage was set for it to happen all over again.

"Except now we have weaponized magic to contend with," Alex muttered.

Falling back into his pattern, Alex turned the page, desperately seeking something positive. He finally settled on a story of heroism by the Manhattan twenty-second fire brigade who had arrived at a burning house so quickly they were able to save most of the structure. The mayor announced he would be giving the brigade captain the key to the city.

"Empire Tower," the cabbie's voice broke through Alex's musings. "That'll be two bits."

Alex extracted a quarter and a dime tip out of his pocket and handed them over before getting out.

"Thanks, Mac," the cabbie called as he shut the door. "Have a great day."

"Doing my best," Alex replied as the cab drove away. "Doing my best."

Fifteen minutes later, Alex stepped off the elevator on the twelfth floor and turned left. He'd stopped in the terminal below to grab a cup of coffee and ended up chatting with Marnie the whole time he drank it. As the queen of coffee for Empire Station, Marnie always had a smile and a good word, something Alex needed in these darkening times.

When he opened the door to his office, he found his secretary, Sherry Knox, sitting behind her desk going through a stack of papers and making notes on a small pad of paper. She looked up as the door opened, broke out into a wide smile, and her dark eyes sparkled. Her black hair was piled up on her head in an ornate style and she wore bright red lipstick that matched her blouse.

"There you are," a gruff voice said. "It's about time."

Alex stepped around the door and found a blocky man in an expensive suit sitting on his leather waiting couch. He had bushy eyebrows, a thick neck, and calloused hands that meant he was no stranger to physical work. All in all, he looked more like a nightclub bouncer rather than the leading property recovery agent for Callahan Brothers Property.

"Mr. Wilks," Alex said, pasting a smile on his face. "What brings you to my office?"

Wilks stood up, seeming to be at a momentary loss for words.

"I can't believe I'm going to say this, but I need your help," he managed.

Alex glanced at Sherry, and she shrugged almost imperceptibly.

"Let's go into my office," Alex said, indicating the door in the right-hand wall.

"No time for that," Wilks said. "I need you to look at a body for me."

Alex was taken aback for a moment. Wilks was Callahan Brothers' property recovery expert, he shouldn't need Alex to look at a body.

"This isn't a personal problem," Alex asked, "is it?"

Wilks expression turned from earnest to irritated.

"Of course not," he growled. "I used to be a cop. I know how to get rid of a body."

Alex hadn't thought of that, but the man had a point.

"When companies depend on certain people in order to stay in business, it's customary to take out insurance on them. It's called a key man policy."

"And one of your key men turned up dead?" Alex guessed.

"Exactly. Now the cops think it was an accidental death," Wilks began.

"In which case your company would have to pay out on the policy," Alex interjected.

Wilks gave him a sour look and nodded.

"I think there's something funny about the whole thing," he said, "but I can't put my finger on it."

"And you want me to take a look and see if there was any foul play," Alex finished.

Wilks nodded and put on his hat.

"I got the police to hold the crime scene for me, but they're getting antsy. I need you to take a look and give me your read on the situation."

Alex glanced at Sherry, wondering if she had anything pressing for him. Anticipating his question, she shook her head and went back to her notes.

"All right, Mr. Wilks," Alex said, opening the door again. "Let's go look at your ex key man."

Wilks' car was a 1937 Chrysler Imperial, painted a light cream color with a convertible top. As the insurance man eased it through traffic, Alex couldn't help but be impressed. He'd been flirting with the idea of buying his own car and the Imperial made an elegant case for such an expense.

"You ever hear of Waverly radios?" Wilks asked as they drove.

"Who hasn't?" Alex replied. "They make the best tabletop radio on the market. I've got one in my apartment."

That was true, but Alex never used it on account of the fact he spent most nights at the brownstone. It was probably a good thing where the radio was concerned, since Waverly radios had casings made out of some fancy material that looked great, but tended to crack if they got too hot.

"Well, what makes them so good is a secret process they use when they manufacture the tuner," Wilks explained. "They use a proprietary rune to make it work."

Alex was starting to see why Wilks had thought of him.

"I'm guessing your key man was the runewright who made this secret, proprietary rune."

Wilks nodded.

"His name was Fredrick Chance and he was found dead in his office this morning," Wilks said. "With him gone, it could seriously compromise the company. The stock took a nosedive as soon as word leaked out."

Alex remembered the story in the paper about some companies losing big in the markets. He hadn't looked at the story, but he'd bet Waverly Radio was on the list.

"So, how did Mr. Chance supposedly die?"

"Nope," Wilks said, easing the car off the road and into the parking field of a large, industrial building. "I don't want you going in with any preconceived notions."

That seemed a little severe, but Alex just shrugged and got out of the car.

Wilks led him across the field and through a heavy door in the side of the building. Inside was a large, intricate assembly line with men and women sitting along it, building radios.

"This way," Wilks said, leading Alex along the periphery of the workspace to a metal stair along the back wall.

The stair ran up to a door that led into a reception area, complete with a young woman at a desk. She looked up with a smile when Alex came in but, on seeing Wilks, her smile faded. For his part Wilks ignored her and led Alex to the left, to a short hallway and then to a door with the name *Fredrick Chance* painted on it in gold letters. Beneath the name was the title; *Rune Specialist*.

Fancy, Alex thought. Most runewrights just called themselves runewrights.

A tired-looking cop sat in a chair next to the door and he only looked up for a moment before going back to dozing.

Wilks opened the door, revealing a large office that was almost the size of Alex's waiting room. It had a slanted drafting table like Alex's, with a tall shelf on the left side fitted with slots for various papers and slots for ink pots. A well-worn carpet covered the floor and Alex could see it was becoming a bit threadbare under the high stool where Fredrick Chance sat to do his work.

The afternoon light was streaming in through several large, southerly windows, giving the room a warm, cheery feel despite the chill in the March air. A timeworn couch stood against the back wall and a small writing desk sat by the large windows. Alex could tell by the shape of the couch cushions that Fredrick Chance was in the habit of sleeping there.

The writing desk was neat and orderly with a light coating of dust, which suggested Fredrick didn't use it much. The only other furniture in the room were two square tables about three feet on a side, and a portable gas heater sitting under a metal chimney by the window. One of the tables stood by the door and had two wire baskets on it labeled "In" and "Out." The other table stood on the right hand of the drafting table and held a bottle of Scotch, a bottle of bourbon, and a mostly empty bottle of something clear. A short tumbler glass sat in front of the bottles on a coaster made of cork.

Alex took all of this in for a moment, then looked at Wilks.

"The police think he didn't open the flue," Alex said, pointing to the gas heater. "That explains why someone opened the window earlier today."

Wilks gave him an incredulous look and Alex moved to the windows.

"You can see where the dust on the latch has been disturbed," he said, pointing to the clear spot on the otherwise dusty frame. "Did they find any sign that the heater or the flue was tampered with?"

"All in good working order," Wilks said.

Alex nodded at that. He'd seen this kind of thing before. When the weather got cold, people would use portable heaters, but when you burn anything, you produce carbon monoxide, and that had to be vented outside. Inevitably someone would forget to open the chimney flue and would die from carbon monoxide poisoning.

"What makes you think this wasn't an accident?" Alex asked.

"The body was found here," Wilks said, pointing to a spot between the writing desk and the window.

Alex raised an eyebrow at that. Most carbon monoxide poisonings were people who fell asleep. People who were awake could usually feel themselves getting light-headed in time to escape.

He walked over to the table with the liquor and picked up the nearly-empty bottle.

"Vodka," he said, reading the label. He put it back and turned to Wilks.

"Your instincts are very good, Mr. Wilks. Fredrick Chance was murdered."

2

THE GORDIAN AFTERMATH

Alex flipped open his pocketwatch as he ascended the granite stairs of the brownstone's stoop. He felt the runes inside flare to life, reaching out to their companions keeping the front door shut, and he made a face. Since the first time Iggy taught him to inscribe the runes inside the watch cover, it always felt the same. Runes working in conjunction had a harmony about them; it wasn't audible, but to Alex it was musical. He'd come to associate that feeling with home.

Now however, the sound set his teeth on edge. A few months ago, when Alex had gone to Washington D.C. with Andrew, Iggy had taken the opportunity to upgrade the protective wards on the building. To be fair, Alex's adversary and fellow initiate into the circle of Moriarty's immortals, Paschal Randolph, had attempted to gain entry by putting a magical bomb on the stoop.

And he almost managed it, Alex thought as he pulled the new door open.

That was another sore spot for Alex. The original front door had been white with an oval, stained-glass window in the center. Now the door was a heavy oak number with brass accents and a much smaller, round window at head height. The only saving grace, in Alex's opinion, was that the window was stained glass, depicting a compass face around the outside edge and with a tall ship listing on the waves in the center. It reminded Alex of the Mary Celeste, the merchant ship that first led Iggy to the Archimedean Monograph.

Stepping inside and shutting the door, Alex couldn't shake the alien feeling that gripped him. The vestibule was exactly as it had been, with polished wooden boards surrounding a tile mosaic of Manhattan Island. Something felt off to him.

"You're home early," Iggy's voice came from the kitchen as Alex shut the inner vestibule door and hung up his hat on the row of pegs just beyond.

"It's five-thirty," he said as he headed toward the back of the house. "I'd say I'm right on time."

He entered the kitchen and found Iggy in his shirtsleeves with a heavy cooking apron tied over his front. He stood in front of the stove tending several steaming pots at once.

"Based on when you usually drag yourself in here," Iggy said, giving him a sly look under a raised eyebrow, "I'd say you're at least an hour early."

"Very funny," Alex said, still in a bit of a sour mood from his encounter with the new front door. He did have to admit it had been a while since he'd managed to sit down with his mentor at a meal, so instead of complaining further, he began setting the table.

"Anything interesting happen today?" Iggy asked as he pulled what appeared to be an entire chicken from a pot of boiling water.

As Iggy plated up a dinner of boiled chicken, dumplings, and thinly sliced potatoes au gratin, Alex told him about finding the museum's missing Mayan statuette and about Arthur Wilks' case of the murdered runewright.

"How did you know it was murder and not just an accident?" Iggy asked as they sat down to the meal. Once grace had been said and the plates were passed around, he continued. "I mean, there are several dozen deaths from carbon monoxide every year. It's not an uncommon accident."

"It was the vodka," Alex said. "It had been cut with something really strong, like moonshine."

Iggy nodded and grinned.

"You smelled the alcohol," he declared.

"Vodka has a very slight alcohol odor, but when I sniffed this, it almost curled my hair."

"So your theory is that Mr. Chance was too drunk to get to the window and open it once he realized what was happening."

"If he realized it," Alex said. "His body was on the floor right by his chair. It's possible he'd passed out without ever figuring out that his flue was closed."

Iggy nodded at that.

"Did you see anything interesting in the paper?"

Alex grinned. It was a wry expression.

"Apparently there's another market crash around the corner."

"Tosh," Iggy growled. "That's a stock headline they bring out every time the market dips. Don't waste my time with such nonsense."

"How about that story about the fire brigade putting out a house fire in record time?"

"More fluff and nonsense," Iggy declared. "Did you even read the paper?"

Alex chuckled at his mentor's indignant tone. He was very particular about what he considered real news. For the next half-hour they discussed the major stories of the day. There was a bank manager suspected of embezzling that Iggy declared was guilty with only the facts in the paper. Another story covered possible mob interference with horse racing, and the theft of a fishing boat. None of it was terribly exciting, but it kept their wits sharp.

"Charles Grier is coming over tonight," Iggy declared as they gathered up the dishes. "He's going to help me restock my surgery, then we'll play some pinochle. Do you have plans?"

"I'm going out with Sorsha," he said in an unamused voice. He'd had these plans for a week and Iggy well knew it.

"Do you think that's wise?"

The question hung in the air for a moment before Alex answered.

"We're just going to a club to listen to the music and have a quiet drink," he said. "Nothing demanding."

Alex's trip down to Washington had been a rounding success in every way but one. When he'd stumbled into a plot by the elusive Legion to steal books of rune lore from the government's magical research lab, Sorsha had insisted on coming along. That decision had left her the subject of a runic curse. Something called a Gordian rune was slowly leeching away her magic and, as the days and weeks went by, it was getting worse.

"Any word from your new friends in the underworld?" Iggy asked, keeping his voice neutral and judgement free.

Alex knew how Iggy felt about Alex's new deal with "Lucky" Tony Casetti. He simply didn't believe in the idea of a reformed gangster. Truth be told, Alex wasn't sure about that himself, but his deal with the ex-mobster was simply to provide him with preservation runes once a month, so he wasn't too worried. What did concern him was that "Lucky" Tony and his pals were supposed to get a very specific rune book for Alex and, thus far, they had failed to deliver.

"No news on that front," Alex said, keeping his irritation out of his voice.

"I'm shocked," Iggy said in a complete deadpan.

Alex made a mental note to call Connie Firenze in the morning for an update and let the matter drop. Neither he nor Iggy would be changing their minds about this arrangement so there was no sense discussing it further.

An awkward silence descended as Alex washed the dinner dishes and, before he was done, there was a knock at the front door.

"That'll be Charles," Iggy said, heading for the door. "Tell the sorceress hello for me."

"Will do," he called after Iggy.

When he finished the dishes, Iggy and Charles Grier were taking inventory in Iggy's vault, so Alex headed upstairs. Since his plan was to take Sorsha out to a swanky place, he'd need his tuxedo and that was in his vault. Iggy's reworking of the protection runes on the brownstone had cut the connection between Alex's third floor bedroom and the vault, but that was one thing Alex was able to restore exactly as it had been.

Using his pocket watch, Alex opened the cover door and entered his vault. The hallway that led to the brownstone door passed his little kitchen and the bedroom on the way to the main area. Stopping in the bedroom, Alex changed into his tux, then headed out into the main room. The drafting table he used for his rune writing was covered in photographs that he'd stuck to the board with tape. They each showed the same thing, an illegible squiggle of magical symbols written over each other in a crude circle.

This was the Gordian rune. The twisted construct that was stealing away Sorsha Kincaid's magic power and weakening her by the day. The mere sight of the photographs made Alex clench his jaw. He'd spent most of his spare time trying to figure it out, to somehow see the runes that made up the insidious construct. The only problem was that with them all jumbled up atop one another, it was impossible to tell what might be part of any specific rune.

When Iggy saw it, he declared that the rune was written that way specifically to prevent anyone from understanding or countering it. Alex was certain he was right.

Checking his watch, he hesitated. He didn't have to meet Sorsha for fifteen minutes, so he had time to work on the rune a bit.

"No," he said out loud to himself. He knew from experience that once he started in on the devilish construct, he'd lose all track of time. That was something he couldn't risk tonight. Sorsha was counting on him, and he would not let her down.

Turning away from his desk, Alex turned toward the front of his vault where his original vault door would open whenever he summoned it. To the left of the place where the door would appear was his gun cabinet, and he pulled it open once he reached it. Inside was his personal collection of weapons. A Browning A-5 shotgun, a Thompson sub-machine gun, a snub nose .38 and a 1911. Alex had lost both of his handguns in recent adventures so both of them were shiny and new.

Despite the display of firepower before him, Alex picked up his rune-covered knuckle-duster from the peg where it hung. He wasn't too worried about appearing with the sorceress in public, but both of them had a way of attracting trouble, and Alex didn't want to be completely unarmed.

He checked his flash ring to be sure its four charges were still intact and, satisfied that they were, Alex closed the gun cabinet, snapping the latch closed.

There were still a few minutes until he was supposed to meet Sorsha, but he was as ready as he'd ever be, so he decided that being a few minutes early wasn't bad. Turning, he walked to the back of his vault, past his drafting table and workbenches to a formerly bare patch of wall. Now there were two new doors covering two new openings into his vault. The right had the word, "Office," painted on it and on the other read, "Home."

Stepping up to the one labeled "Home," he took out his pocket watch and released the runes that kept it closed. He turned the handle and knocked as he pushed it open.

"Alex," Sorsha's voice greeted him. "I had a feeling you'd be early."

Beyond the door was the enormous foyer of Sorsha Kincaid's flying castle. With her magic getting weaker, Alex had used his vault to connect between the castle foyer and her private office in the Chrysler Building. Every morning he would meet her in her foyer and escort her the few feet through his vault to her office. Since his schedule in the evenings wasn't reliable, she'd use her sleek, black floater to return home.

This evening, Sorsha was seated on a divan to the right of the vault door. She gave him a radiant smile, then stood so he could admire her. Alex had seen her that morning, but now she was dressed to the nines. Usually Sorsha favored evening gowns for outings to a nightclub, but this time she wore a close fitting blue dress of some sparkly material that only went down to her knees. She'd swapped out her usual burgundy lipstick for a very dark blue color that matched the dress, and a fur stole adorned her shoulders.

As much as Sorsha's look reflected her style, that wasn't reflected in her face. She looked tired and careworn, with slumped shoulders and heavy makeup to hide the dark circles under her eyes.

"You look great," he said, pasting a smile on his face.

She looked at him hard, as if trying to detect any falsehood in his declaration, then gave him a warm smile and offered her arm.

Alex escorted Sorsha back into his vault and past his drafting table to the other hallway. They went past his little first-aid room and down to the doors that led to his office and his apartment in Empire Tower. Since it would be unseemly for Sorsha to be seen emerging from his apartment, Alex opened the door to his office, and several minutes later they emerged on the ground floor, where they could catch a taxi.

Wherever Sorsha went in the city, her arrival was an event. It was no different at the Rainbow Room, where the maître d' immediately escorted her to their best table. After that, Alex knew, a long train of important well-wishers would stop by for a quick chat, hoping one of the news photographers would snap their picture with the sorceress. During this obligatory parade, Alex would engage in polite conversation but say nothing of importance.

"Now you understand why I don't usually go out," Sorsha said when the last of the attention-seekers left.

She'd maintained her poise during all this, but it left her looking drained, and she slumped a bit in her chair.

"You all right?" Alex asked.

"Yes, Alex," she snapped, then her look softened. "I know you're worried about me, but I'm an adult. I can take care of myself."

"Yes," Alex admitted. "But you don't have to."

She looked like she was going to be cross with him but instead she smiled.

"Come sit next to me," she said. "I'm cold."

Alex knew very well that Sorsha didn't get cold, at least she never had as long as he'd known her.

Her magic must be getting very weak.

Not offering any commentary, Alex picked up his chair and moved it beside Sorsha so she could lean against him. They stayed that way while the band played and through the floor show. Finally Sorsha sighed and looked up at him.

"You haven't asked about my day," she said, a note of challenge in her voice.

"You always tell me to mind my own business," he said, mustering a smile.

"It's not your fault, you know," she said, lifting up her head to give him a hard look. "So stop blaming yourself."

Alex had to stifle an angry response, so it was a moment before he spoke.

"You wouldn't have been at that raid if it weren't for me," he said.

"As if you could have stopped me from coming," she scoffed. "I'm actually doing a bit better today. I might have turned a corner."

Alex wasn't sure if Sorsha was lying for his benefit or if she was lying to herself, but she was lying.

"Shall we dance, then?" he asked, offering her his hand.

Sorsha glared at him for a moment, then took his hand.

"If it will make you stop treating me as if I'm made of glass," she groused.

Alex led her to the dance floor and took her in his arms. It was the only part of the evening thus far that felt right. Sorsha smiled up at him as they weaved their way across the floor, and it was like nothing had changed between them.

But it only lasted for a few precious moments.

As the band struck up a livelier number, Sorsha stumbled and sagged against Alex, forcing him to hold her upright.

"I think," she said, her breath coming in short gasps. "I think I'd like to go home now."

Alex was tempted to say something, to tell her that he'd been right about her getting weaker, but there was nothing left to say. He was losing her day by day and inch by inch, and she simply wouldn't admit it. It was a battle she was bound and determined to face alone.

"Of course," Alex said. He deposited her in a chair on the periphery of the dance floor, then collected her handbag and stole.

Helping her to her feet, they rode the elevator down to a random floor, then Alex opened his vault and escorted her home. By the time they reached her castle foyer, Alex had to carry her up the stairs to her bedroom, where her ladies' maid helped her into bed.

Since there was nothing more he could do, Alex headed back to his vault. Once the door to Sorsha's home was safely shut and the wards were back in place, he turned and shouted a swear word at his vault. Once the echoes died away, he moved to his drafting table and poured himself a double Scotch from the bottle on top of the roll-away cabinet.

"You have to do something," he growled.

He'd been through the Archimedean Monograph three times looking for anything that would be useful, but thus far he'd found nothing. What he needed was that book Lucky Tony had promised him. All he'd gotten out of Connie was that there had been complications getting it.

Alex looked at the photographs of the Gordian rune on his desk. He knew there wasn't anything there he hadn't seen already, but he downed his Scotch and climbed up on his tall chair to spend a few hours looking anyway.

3

BOOK LEARNING

It was after eight when Alex finally dragged himself downstairs to the brownstone's kitchen. He had no idea when he'd actually made it to bed, but he was fairly certain it wasn't 'late' so much as 'early.'

"You look wrung out," Iggy commented from the kitchen table. He was sitting behind what remained of a plate of eggs and sausage, reading the paper. "I take it things went better with Sorsha or you'd have been home earlier. That's a good sign."

"Not really," Alex said as he poured a cup of coffee from the pot. "Her maid called just now to say she didn't need me to help her to her office."

Iggy raised an eyebrow, then folded his paper and set it aside. "You'd better tell me what happened."

Alex set his coffee on the table, then filled a plate with cold scrambled eggs and a few sausages.

"She's weaker," Alex said, sitting down with his breakfast. "Last night she barely had the strength to dance with me for about ten minutes. I had to carry her up to her room once I got her home."

"This isn't exactly unexpected," Iggy pointed out. "Last month she didn't have enough magic to teleport, then two weeks ago she couldn't enchant more than a few of the iron bars she uses for cold disks."

"But that's magic," Alex protested with a mouthful of eggs. "We know the Gordian rune is sapping her power, but now it seems like…"

Alex let the sentence go, not daring to finish it.

"Like it's draining her very life," Iggy finished.

Alex looked at him and nodded.

"I admit," Iggy went on, "I was concerned this would happen. We know that runes can be used to convert life energy into magic. That's what got you in trouble, if you recall."

Alex nodded again, more slowly this time.

"That damned construct must contain a life rune," he growled.

"It makes sense. Whoever did this to Miss Kincaid intended to sap her strength until she has no more to give."

Alex squeezed the fork in his hand till his knuckles went white. Between Iggy and himself, they knew more about rune lore than anyone in the city, maybe more than anyone outside the Legion, or Moriarty and his voyeur clan of immortals. The problem was that Moriarty only showed up when he wanted to, and the Legion were the ones who had cursed Sorsha in the first place.

"I don't get it," Alex said after the silence had stretched out into minutes. "How are the Legion smart enough, skilled enough, to pull off something like this? We know they don't have the Monograph."

Iggy sighed, then shrugged.

"The Archimedean Monograph isn't the only source of powerful rune lore in the world," he said.

Alex growled at that, and Iggy went on.

"I have been giving that some thought as well," he admitted. "When you foiled their plans to rob the rune research lab, they were looking for a book on lore on these Gordian runes. That suggests, to me anyway, that they don't know as much about those runes as you might think."

"Explain," Alex said as he continued to eat. He was tired and cranky, but Iggy had that twinkle in his eyes that meant he'd figured something out.

"Remember when you learned your first runes?" Iggy said.

"Sure." Alex's first rune had been a minor mending rune, followed by a minor barrier rune, both taught to him by his father.

"In the beginning, you didn't know what the symbols meant, did you? You simply copied them off a master diagram."

Alex remembered. He still had that diagram in his lore book, one of the few things that remained from his father.

"The way I figure it," Iggy went on, "if these Legion fellows really understood the Gordian rune, they wouldn't have been looking for a book explaining it at that lab."

"You think they found this draining curse by itself," Alex said, catching Iggy's train of thought.

"Or rather, they found instructions on how to make it."

"But they don't understand how to make original ones of their own," Alex guessed. "They only know how to make that one, because it's the only one they have a recipe for."

"That's why they need the book," Iggy finished. He reached out and grabbed Alex's wrist. "I know your new friends have been promising you they can get it for you, but it's been three months. I think it might be time to pursue another course of action."

Usually Alex could catch up to Iggy when his mentor was explaining things, but this time he literally had no idea what the old man meant. If there were another way to get hold of the elusive Gordian rune book, he would have taken it before now.

"Andrew Barton," Iggy said, reading the confusion on Alex's face.

Alex wanted to reject that idea. The fewer people who knew about Sorsha's condition, the better. There was also her privacy to consider. Still, she was literally dying, and thus far, there wasn't anything he or Iggy could do about it.

"Andrew has a lot of pull," Alex admitted. "What makes you think he'd help?"

Iggy scoffed at that.

"If you tell the Lightning Lord that there's a cabal of runewrights that can magically bleed a sorcerer to death, he wouldn't stop until he'd found a way to prevent it."

Alex nodded. Andrew was no coward, but neither was he a fool. If he knew that he could be attacked by a rune, he'd take measures to prevent it, or to stop it if someone managed to successfully use it on him.

The other side of that coin, of course, was that telling Andrew would make the world's most powerful sorcerer aware of just how capable and dangerous rune magic could really be. It wouldn't be much of a leap for him to conclude that Alex and Iggy had the Archimedean Monograph. Andrew Barton was a good man, but he was also clever and ambitious. He had a habit of launching new projects without having thought through the ramifications all the way. If Alex had his druthers, he'd rather Andrew remained ignorant of what he and Iggy could do.

Sorsha's life might depend on him knowing, he chided himself.

"All right," he said, making up his mind. "I'm going to call Tony when I get to my office. If he doesn't have the book yet, I'll go to Andrew."

Iggy held his gaze for a long moment, then nodded approval.

"I should get going," Alex said, picking up his dishes and depositing them in the sink. "And thanks."

"You know," Iggy said, stroking his bottle-brush mustache. "Something you said has tickled my imagination."

Alex gave him a penetrating look. Iggy only stroked his mustache when he was on to something.

"What is it?"

"You said that you were surprised that this Gordian rune drained life once it had drained magic."

"And you pointed out that we know runes can drain life," Alex replied.

"But we also know that runes can replenish life," he said. "I'll wager that's something the Legion doesn't know."

Alex was dumbstruck. It was such an obvious idea he couldn't believe he hadn't seen it.

"We can give Sorsha more time by giving her more life energy," he said. "Iggy, that's brilliant."

Instead of smiling, Iggy cocked his head to one side in a gesture of hesitancy.

"What?" Alex asked.

"I'm thinking we might not be able to give the sorceress as much time as all that," he said. "She's not like a runewright; her magic is a part of her, it's always with her. As far as we can tell, sorcerers have access to tremendous amounts of magical power, and this rune has stripped Sorsha down to nothing."

"What are you saying?" Alex asked, certain he wouldn't like the answer.

"Somehow this rune has managed to siphon away Sorsha's magic faster than she can replenish it." Iggy gave Alex a hard look. "The only explanation is that this Gordian rune is accelerating, growing geometrically. Every day the construct is bound to her, it takes more and more from her."

"Until it has everything," Alex said, his voice barely a whisper.

"Even with our help, Sorsha may not have much time."

Alex felt numb. He had to do something, but right now he had no idea what that was.

"How long will it take you to prepare a life transference construct?" he asked.

"About three days," Iggy said, rising from the table. "I'll start right away."

"Thank you," Alex said, then he turned toward the stairs. "I'll go get that book."

Since his office was only a quick trip through his vault away, Alex arrived before nine. Moving straight to his desk, he ignored the stack of files Sherry had left for him. He did tap the key on the intercom twice to let her know he was in the office before he reached for his telephone.

"What number?" the operator asked. Before Alex could answer, Sherry's voice came over the intercom.

"Alex, there's a Connie Firenze here to see you," she said.

Alex thanked the operator and hung up the phone. He sat for a long moment with his eyes closed, focusing on his breathing.

"Alex?" Sherry's voice came again.

"Send him back," he said after keying the intercom's microphone.

Alex stood, but resisted the urge to pace. There were several possible reasons Connie could be stopping by, but since Alex had already given him this month's supply of preservation runes, this might be good news.

There was a knock at the door and then a bouncer with a flat face, blue eyes, and a crooked smile came in.

"Connie," Alex said with a nod. "I was about to call you."

An abashed look crossed the big man's face for a moment, and he shrugged.

"About the book," he said, "I know." His face brightened into his crooked grin and he pulled a package wrapped in brown paper from the pocket of his suit coat. "But that's why I came over."

He dropped the package on Alex's desk with a thump and stood back.

Alex had to keep his hand from shaking as he picked up the paper-wrapped object and began peeling the wrapping away. Inside was a small book, about an inch thick with a dark blue leather cover. Opening it, Alex read the title on the page just inside.

"A Treatise on the Gordian Method of Rune Craft." He looked up and found Connie grinning like the cat that ate the canary. "This is the book?"

"The very one," Connie assured him. "The boss wanted me to express his apologies for taking so long to get it. Apparently the Feds knew that your bad guys were looking for it, too. They locked all the books down and searched everyone going in and out of the place where they were stored. It took some time, but we got it."

Alex went to his liquor cabinet and poured some of his best whiskey into two shot glasses.

"Tell Tony I'm grateful," he said, passing one of the glasses to Connie. "And thanks for bringing this over."

"Salute," Connie said, clinking his glass against Alex's.

When both men downed their liquor, Connie set the glass on Alex's desk and picked up his hat.

"I guess you've got a lot to do, so I'll make myself scarce," he said.

Alex thanked him again as he turned to go, but Connie stopped before he reached the door.

"You know," he said, nodding at the cabinets along the back wall, "you should put a cooler in there. Keep a few Homestead beers handy. You know, for clients and such. The boss says it never hurts to advertise."

Alex wasn't really a beer drinker, but the idea wasn't bad, and he said so. After Connie left, Alex sat down with the book in the middle of his desk and stared at it. Everything he'd been trying to understand for the last three months should be in there. All the answers he'd struggled to find, the knowledge of how to save Sorsha, all of it.

But what if it isn't?

The Legion didn't want that book because they *knew* what was in it, they wanted it because they *suspected* what was in it. If they knew, after all, they wouldn't actually need the book.

"Enough," Alex said aloud, quieting his doubts.

He picked up the book and opened it past the title page. The first few pages were a description of Gordian runes and how they had been created to prevent other runewrights from countering or tampering with them.

Satisfied he was on the right track, he keyed his intercom and instructed Sherry not to bother him unless it was important. Thus secured against frivolous interruption, Alex poured himself another two fingers of Scotch, set a notebook and pencil on his desk, and settled down to read.

Sometime later, the intercom buzzed. The sound tickled Alex's awareness, as if he heard it from a great distance. At first, he dismissed it as having imagined the sound, but a few moments later it came again, pulling Alex's mind from the place of intense focus it had occupied.

Slowly, as if the lights were being turned up, his mind returned to his office and he became aware of Sherry's voice on the intercom.

"Boss? You with me?"

"What is it?" he asked, keeping any note of annoyance from his voice. He'd told her not to interrupt him unless it was important, ergo, this was important.

"Mr. Wilks is here to see you again," she said. "He says it's a matter of some urgency."

Alex sighed, looking down at the Gordian rune book and the pages of notes he'd made. Already he'd learned a great deal about the history of the rune and the basic principles behind it, but he was nowhere near understanding it. Still, he had a business to run.

"Send him back," Alex said as he closed the book and put it and his notes into the center drawer of his desk for safekeeping.

A moment later the door opened, and Arthur Wilks entered. He wore a sour look, like he hadn't had a very good morning, and he was looking for someone to share it with.

"Don't tell me the autopsy didn't show a high blood alcohol level," Alex said as Wilks sat down.

"No, it did," Wilks said. "They just didn't think it was evidence of murder."

"Someone spiked his vodka," Alex protested.

"Yes, but there's no evidence he didn't do that himself. People mix their drinks all the time."

Alex blew out an exasperated breath as he sat back in his chair.

"I'm guessing that since you're here," he went on, "you don't intend to pay out the claim yet."

Wilks sneered, then shrugged.

"This thing stinks," he said. "If it comes down to it, Callahan Brothers will pay the claim, but I want this thing properly investigated before I do."

"And you want me to do that investigation," Alex guessed.

"You owe me, Lockerby," Wilks growled. "I'll pay your rate, but you'll take this case because you owe me for all the times you and your buddies came to me for help."

Alex considered telling Wilks to get out, but the man had a point. He had helped Alex on several occasions and his help had been valuable.

"What is it you need me to do?" he asked.

"The cops don't want to mess with this for some reason," Wilks said. "The only way they're going to reopen this case is if I've got evidence of an actual crime."

"Which means that not only do I have to find evidence of murder, I need to find motive and the actual killer as well."

Wilks nodded.

"Got it in one," he said. "And I can only give you a week. After that, I'll have to pay off the policy."

Alex pulled the notebook from his shirt pocket and flipped it open.

"As I understand a key man policy," he began, "the only way you don't pay is if someone at Waverly Radio killed Fredrick Chance. If his wife killed him, or a jealous lover, or pretty much anyone else, the policy is valid."

"Not necessarily," Wilks said. "If he was killed by someone else who wanted to hurt Waverly's business, or if his murder was related to his work in any way, the policy would pay."

"So I need to find out who killed him, and why," Alex summed up.

"And you have to do it in a week," Wilks said. "If you don't have anything definitive by then, I'll have to pay out on the policy."

"And you're going to be paying my bill no matter what I find," Alex pushed, "right?"

Wilks chuckled at that.

"You know I pay my bills, scribbler," he said, using the slur as a term of affection. "But I've got a great big carrot for you. If you prove that Fredrick Chance's death was insurance fraud, you get ten percent of the payout just for saving us the money. That's twenty grand."

Alex whistled. Since he was getting paid as a consultant for Barton Electric and as a partner in Homestead Breweries in addition to his clients, he wasn't hurting for money. That said, twenty G's was nothing to sneeze at.

"That'd pay for a few years' rent in this fancy pad of yours," Wilks went on.

"All right," Alex said. "I'll find out who killed Fredrick Chance for you."

Wilks seemed to relax, as if he thought Alex would turn him down.

He'd been right in the beginning, Alex owed him, and Alex paid his debts too.

"Where will you start?" Wilks asked as Alex stood up.

"I need to get a handle on Fredrick," he said. "Find out what kind of man he was, if he had any enemies, that kind of thing. He was married, right?"

Wilks tore a page out of his notebook and handed it over.

"Her name is Katrina," Wilks said. "Address is on there."

Alex glanced at it, then tucked the paper into his pocket.

"I'll start with Katrina, then," he said.

4

HATHAWAY HOUSE

Fredrick and Katrina Chance lived in a new, modern apartment building in the inner ring. It was the kind of place Alex used to dream of living in back in the days of his basement office in Harlem. As he rode the elevator, he marveled at how his life had changed since those days.

When Alex knocked on the door of apartment 1221, the door was opened by a slim, attractive woman in a black dress. She had sharp, angular features with blue eyes and dark hair that was tied behind so that it hung straight down her back.

"Mrs. Chance?" he asked. "I'm Alex Lockerby." He handed her one of his cards. "I've been hired by Waverly Radio's insurance company to investigate your husband's death. Do you have a minute?"

Katrina Chance stared at the card for a long minute before finally registering what Alex had said.

"I...," she stuttered. "I don't understand. Fredrick's death was an accident, wasn't it?" She looked up with genuine fear in her eyes, like the wrong word from Alex could send her world crashing down.

"That's what it looks like," Alex replied in his most comforting tone. "The insurance company just wants to make sure. Waverly Radio held a policy on your husband."

She seemed to waver in the door as if she didn't know what to do. Alex figured that had very little to do with his visit. Katrina Chance was still reeling from the death of her husband. Despite that, Alex had a job to do.

"I'll only be a minute, Mrs. Chance," he said.

"All right," she said, stepping back from the door to let Alex enter. For modesty's sake, she left the door open, then ushered Alex to the kitchen table. The apartment was much larger than his room in Iggy's brownstone, but still smaller than his suite at Empire Tower. The front room and the kitchen were one long room, with a large bank of windows along the back wall that lit up the space with a view of Empire Tower and the Chrysler Building in the distance.

The furniture was tasteful, and it was clear Mrs. Chance had an eye for decorating. The front room looked like something out of a fashion magazine and the kitchen positively gleamed.

"Would you like something to drink?" Mrs. Chance asked before she sat down. "I'm sorry, I should have asked before, but I'm not a very good hostess today."

"No, thank you," Alex said, waiting for her to sit. When she did, he offered her a cigarette from his case, and lit it for her before seating himself.

"Tell me about your husband," he said, flipping open his notebook.

"He was a good man, Mr. Lockerby," she said, taking a drag on the cigarette. "I know I had my problems with him, but we were good together."

"What kind of problems?"

Katrina shrugged.

"He worked too hard," she said in a wistful voice. "He was always at work making his runes, then when he came home, he would study his lore book and his notes, sometimes while his dinner got cold."

There was an edge in Mrs. Chance's voice that told Alex this was one of her major complaints.

"Some days he wouldn't come home at all," she went on. "He would call me and tell me he would be working late and that he'd sleep on his couch."

Alex remembered the couch from Fredrick Chance's office and

how it had worn in the shape of a recumbent person. Based on the wear, Alex assumed Fredrick was in the habit of sleeping in his office at least once a week.

"Did you think he was having an affair?" he asked.

Katrina looked away, then wrapped her arms around her body and shivered.

"I did at first," she admitted. "But Lillian is more man than woman. Fred would never have taken up with the likes of her."

"Lillian?"

"Lillian Waverly," she scoffed. "She's the president of Waverly Radio. She's...she was Fredrick's boss."

Alex made a note of that. It wasn't unheard of for the daughters of industrialists to take over the family business, but it wasn't common by any means. Katrina clearly thought that Lillian Waverly wouldn't tempt her husband, but Alex had followed enough cheaters to know that men stepped out with inexplicable women all the time. Lillian could be a dwarf with a hunchback and there would still be some men attracted to her.

The fact that she's the heiress to a profitable company doesn't hurt either.

"You said you believed your husband was having an affair at first," Alex pressed on, "so what made you change your mind?"

"I went to see him at work," she said. "The only pretty girl in the office is Lillian's secretary, and Lillian doesn't let any of the men near her. I knew then that my husband wasn't sleeping with someone at his office."

Alex didn't know if he believed that, but it was clear that Katrina did.

"As I understand it, your husband had a special rune he wrote for Waverly. Do you know anything about that?"

Katrina shook her head.

"He kept his rune work to himself," she said.

"Who will inherit his rune book?" Alex asked. He couldn't see Fredrick willing it to Waverly, but if he had, that would certainly be motive.

"He has a brother in New Jersey," Katrina said. "He's not as skilled as Fred was, but he is a runewright. I guess I can give Fred's lore book to him."

Alex suppressed a sigh. So far Fredrick Chance seemed to be an average workaholic who should have paid more attention to his attractive wife.

"Did your husband have any enemies?" he asked. "Anyone who might want to do him harm?"

Katrina chuckled at that, but a sad smile crossed her lips.

"No," she said. "He didn't have any friends outside work. Waverly was his whole life."

"Was he acting strange in the last few weeks?"

Katrina shook her head.

"No more than usual," she said in a wistful voice. "I'm feeling tired, Mr. Lockerby." She crushed out her cigarette in the ashtray on the table. "I need to rest."

"Of course," he said, rising.

He let Mrs. Chance show him out, then waited in the hall until she'd shut and locked the door. It didn't seem like he was any farther along toward proving that Fredrick had been murdered, but that was only because Katrina Chance didn't know anything. It was sad how she was an outsider in her own marriage, with a husband that had given his life to his work before her.

Unbidden, Alex's thoughts drifted to Sorsha. He should have asked to talk to her when the maid called, just to see how she was doing. The maid said that Sorsha didn't need him to open his vault to get her to work, but that might be Sorsha's pride at work. She might have been embarrassed that he had to carry her up to her room and decided that she'd get to work on her own. He resolved to call Miss Burnside, Sorsha's Southern personal secretary, and discreetly find out. If Sorsha was in, he'd send her a bouquet of roses; if not, he'd swing by her flying castle after dinner with a doggie bag from Iggy.

Satisfied that he had a plan, Alex turned his thoughts back to the task at hand. Fredrick Chance had been killed in his office, the very same office where he wrote a secret and proprietary rune that was the backbone of Waverly's business. Given the importance of his office, it didn't seem likely that someone off the street could just waltz in and tamper with the flue for his heater. If someone he didn't know entered his office, he wouldn't have turned his back on them. There was no way a stranger could have closed the flue or spiked Fredrick's vodka.

That means it was probably an inside job, he told himself with a sigh. Given the critical nature of Fredrick's work, that didn't make a lot of sense. It would mean someone at Waverly Radio wanted to destroy the company.

At that moment, his stomach complained, throwing off his train of thought. He wanted to go straight over to Waverly Radio and have a word with Lillian Waverly, but he checked his watch and saw it was almost one-thirty. Resolving to stop someplace where he could check in with Sherry and get a sandwich, Alex pushed the call button for the elevator.

"Lockerby Investigations," Sherry's voice greeted Alex once he'd located an automat with a phone booth.

"It's me," he said. "I just talked to Fredrick Chance's wife."

"You think she killed him?"

"No," he admitted. "He was married to his work and didn't pay enough attention to her, but she didn't hate him. I'm on my way over to Waverly Radio to talk to the president of the company."

There was a pregnant pause on the line.

"What is it?" Alex asked when Sherry didn't speak.

"Well," she said, lowering her voice. "There are some clients here to see you and...and I think it's...important for you to talk to them."

Alex knew that tone. Sherry was an augur, someone who could, on rare occasions, glimpse the future. Clearly she'd seen something in these clients she thought Alex needed to hear.

He took a deep breath, then sighed. With his deadline to solve Fredrick Chance's murder, now wasn't a good time for a distraction. On top of that, it was Friday. That meant that many businesses would be closed tomorrow.

"All right," he said, resolving to play the cards he'd been dealt. "Tell them I'll be there in twenty minutes."

"Thanks, boss," she said and hung up.

Alex hung up the phone, then dug his change purse out of his pocket so he could buy a stale egg salad sandwich that he'd have to eat in a cab.

Ten minutes later a very surprised Alex exited the Empire Tower business elevator and turned toward his office door. Not only did the cab ride take half the time it should have, but the pickle bits in his egg salad sandwich had actually been crunchy.

He shouldn't have been too surprised. On the few occasions Sherry got specific instructions from her magic, the universe seemed to go out of its way to reward Alex for following her hunches. Of course, fast cab rides and tasty automat sandwiches weren't exactly big things, but Alex would take whatever he could get.

When he opened his office door, he found Sherry leaning on her desk smoking a cigarette. Sitting on the corner of his waiting room couch was a young colored couple. The man wore a stylish, well-made suit and had a walking stick with a silver handle hung over his arm. His hair was cut close to his head and he had a neatly trimmed pencil mustache. The woman wore a silk dress that looked similar in color to Sorsha's burgundy lipstick, with a matching hat dressed with peacock feathers.

"This is Alex," Sherry said as he shut the door.

The couple turned toward Alex and stood. The man had a slim build but broad shoulders despite it. A nervous look crossed his face as his eyes met Alex's. The woman, on the other hand, flashed him a broad smile, as if she and Alex were old friends. She had pearly white teeth which contrasted with the darkness of her complexion, accenting her pretty face.

"Mr. Lockerby?" the man said, sticking out his hand. "I need to speak to you about an important matter."

Alex took his hand and shook it. He had a firm grip, and looked Alex in the eye. Based on what he could see, these people came from money and had been well educated. If their matching rings were an indication, they were also husband and wife.

"Mr..." Alex left it hanging.

"Briggs," he said. "Lucius Briggs, and this is my wife, Ethel."

"Delighted to meet you," Alex said, inclining his head to Ethel. "Why don't we go to my office and you can tell me why you're here?"

Both of them looked relieved by Alex's response. Despite their obvious wealth and upbringing, there were still people who wouldn't work for colored clients. Alex found the very notion of race to be foolish. He'd known Danny for almost two decades and had never found him different from anyone else in any substantive way. Only his looks set him apart. Iggy had taught him that judging a person by how they looked was a great way to get yourself killed. You'd end up overlooking someone dangerous because you categorized them without really seeing them.

Alex led the way down the short hallway to his office, then ushered his potential clients into the overstuffed chairs that sat in front of his desk.

"Now, Mr. Briggs," he said, taking his seat behind the desk. "How can I help you?"

"Someone's trying to steal our house," Ethel blurted out before Lucius could answer.

That was a new one. Alex had never heard of anyone stealing a house. He knew they could be swindled away from their owners, but outright theft seemed unlikely.

"What my wife means," Lucius said, "is that there are some very aggressive people trying to buy our house from us. We've told them we weren't interested, but they won't take 'no' for an answer."

"They keep coming around," Ethel said. "It makes me nervous."

"What's so special about this house?" Alex asked.

"The building is historic," Lucius said. "It's called the Hathaway House and it's one of the oldest buildings in Manhattan. It was a tavern before the civil war, then it became a hotel. Both Abraham Lincoln and Ulysses S. Grant stayed there. Later it was a bordello, and it was a speakeasy during prohibition."

"What is it now?" Alex asked.

"Until recently it was a boarding house," Ethel said. "Lucius' uncle ran it, but he got too old and the place fell into disrepair."

"He died a few months ago," Lucius picked up the story. "I inherited the place and I decided to turn it back into a hotel."

"But if we're going to make it a going concern," Ethel said, "we need to have the place declared a legitimate historical site."

Alex scribbled in his notebook, then looked up when the pair stopped speaking.

"So why do these people you mentioned want to buy the place?" he asked. "Are they in the historic hotel business?"

"That's the problem, Mr. Lockerby," Lucius said. "I can't find out what business they're in. All they ever say is that they want to buy Hathaway House. They even offered me more than it's worth."

That startled Alex.

"Why not sell?" he asked.

"My family has run Hathaway House since the day it was built," Lucius said with the fire of pride burning in his voice. "That place is my legacy and I'm not going to sell it, not at any price."

Alex could understand that. The lore book he'd gotten from his father only had a handful of basic runes in it, but Alex would never have sold it. It was a part of his past and therefore, part of who he had become.

"I don't see how these people, whoever they are, could force you to sell if you don't want to," he said.

"That's the problem," Ethel said. "The house needs work before it will be ready to go back into service. It's a big enough job that we'll need to take out a loan to get it all done."

So far that didn't sound unusual or out of place.

"The loan is contingent on Hathaway House being recognized by the city as a legitimate historical site," Lucius said, reading the confusion on Alex's face. "That was supposed to happen on Monday."

"We had it all arranged," Ethel added.

"Then two of the board members on the New York Historical Commission changed their votes," Lucius finished.

Now it was making sense. Whoever the mystery buyers were, they must have pressured or bought off the two commissioners.

"How do these buyers contact you?" he asked.

"Usually someone comes by the house," Lucius said. "It's never the same person, though."

"They did send us a letter once," Ethel said, "but it didn't have a name on it, only a phone number."

"Did you keep it?" Alex asked.

Lucius looked at Ethel, who wore an expression of uncertainty.

"I don't know," she replied, her voice contorted with worry.

"That's all right," he said, giving her a reassuring smile. "Look for it when you get home. In the meantime," he continued, consulting his notebook, "you want me to find out who these persistent people are, find out how they changed those votes, and get the commissioners to reconsider."

"That's exactly what we want," Ethel said, looking relieved that Alex understood.

"All right," he said, pushing his notebook across the desk. "Put the address of Hathaway House down there along with a phone number where I can reach you. I charge twenty-five dollars a day, plus expenses."

"That will be fine," Lucius said as he picked up the notepad.

Once he'd finished with the notepad, Lucius handed it back and Alex walked them out to the front office. Lucius gave Sherry a fifty-dollar bill as a retainer and then the young couple left.

"What did they want?" Sherry asked as she pulled out the heavy steel cashbox. Alex started to explain but she interrupted. "Damn this thing," she cursed. She knocked on the lid again, but nothing happened. "It still doesn't like me."

Alex rolled his eyes. There was absolutely no precedent for runes that only worked for some people, either they did or they didn't.

"It's me," he said, knocking on the cashbox's lid. A ringing clang sounded and the lid of the box popped up a bit.

Sherry gave him a dirty look as she pushed up the lid and counted the fifty in with the other bills. As she worked, Alex told her the story of Hathaway House, its strangely insistent buyers, and the historical commission.

"So what are you going to do?" she asked once she'd put the

cashbox away. "I mean how can you make the commissioners change their votes?"

"That depends on whether the mysterious buyers bribed them or blackmailed them," Alex explained. "If they were bribed, I'll threaten to expose them. If they were blackmailed, I'll have to find out how, then I can lean on them."

Sherry gave him a skeptical look and he grinned.

"Before I can do any of that, however, I need to know who the vote changers are, and why anyone would want to buy Hathaway House."

"I take it you want me to pull the records of the historical commission vote and get the names of the 'no' votes, then head to the library and look up Hathaway House."

Alex's grin grew wider.

"You really are a mind reader."

She gave him a sour look, then laughed.

"I don't have to be a mind reader to see you coming a mile away, Alex Lockerby," she said. "And what will you be doing while I'm getting dust on my new blouse?"

"I need to talk to a woman about a radio," he said.

5

RECEPTION

The offices of Waverly Radio were in an industrial building in Brooklyn, so Alex rode the express crawler north, then caught a cab. Once inside the structure, Alex found himself in a large waiting area filled with tasteful displays of various tabletop radios. Each section of the room had been decorated to represent the kinds of places someone might use a radio; a kitchen, a living room, an office, and even an outdoor patio.

A perky brunette sat behind a large desk and greeted Alex with a smile as he entered. She looked to be in her mid-twenties with a pretty face and a bit too much makeup. Her dress was modest but flattered her roundish figure.

"Can I help you?" she asked, rising from her desk and walking around to where Alex stood.

Alex produced one of his business cards and handed it to her.

"I've been sent over by Callahan Brothers," he said. "Your insurance company. I need to speak to Mrs. Waverly."

The girl's permanent smile slipped for a moment as she processed the request.

"Let me make a call," she said, her smile back in place.

She went back to her desk and dialed her desk phone. While she had a hushed conversation, Alex walked among the radio displays. Waverly made its name with tabletop radios that had superior reception to their competition. Within a year of announcing their Clarity line of radios, people from every walk of life wanted one.

The radio in the kitchen display was an amber color and gleamed like a piece of hard candy. Alex didn't have a lot of time to listen to the radio, but the stylish little box made him consider moving the one in his apartment to his brownstone bedroom. Waverly was clearly doing very well and he wondered what would happen now that Fredrick Chance was gone.

"Mr. Lockerby?" the secretary said from behind him.

He turned and found her standing next to her desk, beside an opening in the wall that was obviously an elevator.

"Mrs. Waverly will see you now," she continued. "Top floor on the left."

Alex thanked her and rode up the elevator to the fourth floor. It was a sign that Waverly was doing well that they had an elevator just to go up four floors. Most places didn't bother unless they had five stories or more.

The elevator door opened on a brightly lit hallway lined with office doors. Turning left, Alex passed the door on the right side with the name Fredrick Chance stenciled on a frosted glass panel. Testing the knob, he found it locked, so he continued on to the lone door at the end of the hall with the name Lillian Waverly on it. He was about to knock when a woman's voice came through the door.

"Come in."

Alex did as instructed and found himself in an office that was only slightly smaller than Andrew Barton's. The main difference was that while Andrew's office was three stories tall, this office was only one. After a moment, Alex realized it had been laid out in a similar fashion to the waiting room downstairs. Instead of differently decorated zones intended to mimic different rooms, however, Lillian Waverly's office was set up for the differing tasks she performed as the president of the company.

In the center of the room was an elegant mahogany desk with a leather insert taking up most of the top. The insert was a blood red color and it stood out against the dark wood. A couch stood in front of the desk, where visitors could sit, and there were couches to either side, framing the space. Around this central work zone was a lounge with an enormous hearth, a work area with a disassembled radio, a display wall that seemed to show the history of the company, and an area with a conference table and several roll-away blackboards.

What Alex didn't see when he entered was Lillian Waverly.

"Around here," the voice called from behind the open door.

Alex shut it, revealing an actual bar along the wall. It reminded him of the one in Andrew Barton's waiting room, though this one didn't have a uniformed bartender waiting to take his order. Instead, a tall, shapely woman in a deep red dress was pouring clear liquor into a glass. When the glass was three-quarters full, she set the bottle aside and added a scoop of sugar and a splash of some fruit juice from a bottle, then finished it with a shot of soda water.

"It's a gin fizz," she said, looking up at Alex at last. She had blue eyes that sparkled, and her mouth was turned into a sly smile, as if she were privy to a secret no one else knew. Her skin was flawless and her dark hair framed her face perfectly, both calling attention and accentuating her beauty. "Would you like one, Mr. Lockerby?"

Alex pulled his wandering attention back to his task and put on his pleasant smile.

"Yes, thank you," he said. He'd never been much for cocktails, but he'd try anything once.

She took out a second glass and repeated the process, handing it to Alex once she finished.

"Arthur called and said you'd be coming," she said, picking up her drink and moving around the bar. "Come join me by the fire and you can tell me why dear Arthur is holding up my insurance payment."

"With all due respect, Mrs. Waverly, a man is dead," Alex said, following her past the inky black desk to the couches that flanked the hearth. "A man you presumably knew well, since you worked with him every day."

"Don't mistake me, Mr. Lockerby," she said, sitting on the far couch. "Fredrick was a friend, a dear friend. His death wasn't just a blow to the company, it was a blow to me, personally." She motioned for Alex to sit in the couch across from her. "That said, you aren't here to commiserate, you're here for business. So let's do business."

She crossed her legs as she brought her drink to her lips, revealing a long, smooth, pale leg up to mid-calf. Alex felt himself starting to sweat. Not only had she shown that she could play hardball in business, but she was reminding him that she was a woman.

I'm glad I don't have to negotiate a contract with her, he thought.

"Well, Mrs. Waverly," Alex began.

"Call me Lillian," she interrupted, picking up an ornate cigarette case and popping the lid open.

"Lillian," Alex went on, "Mr. Wilks wanted to make sure all the I's are dotted and the T's crossed, so he asked me to look into Mr. Chance's death."

Lillian held his eyes for a long moment, then lit the cigarette she'd slipped between her lips.

"I was under the impression that the police ruled Frank's death an accident," she said, blowing out a long train of smoke.

"That's true," he admitted. "But the police have a lot on their plates and they're motivated to close cases quickly, when they can."

"So Arthur sent you to poke around," Lillian said with an exasperated sigh. "Very well, let's get this over with." She took another drag on her cigarette as Alex pulled out his notebook. Before he could speak, however, she went on, "To answer your questions; No, Frank didn't have any problems at work, he had no enemies, he was happy and well paid, and no," her face split into a sardonic smile, "I was not sleeping with him."

Alex hesitated for a minute, then he wrote down everything Lillian had said. Clearly she'd been asked these questions by the police.

"Be that as it may," Alex said with a half-smile, "can you account for your whereabouts the night Mr. Chance was killed?"

"I went to the opera, to see Die Walküre," she said. "I have a private box, but I'm quite certain dozens of people saw me."

Alex wrote that down as well.

"What kind of work did Mr. Chance do for you, Lillian?" he asked. "I know he had some secret, proprietary rune, but how does that rune relate to your manufacturing of radios?"

Lillian raised an eyebrow at that and her knowing smirk turned into a full-blown smile.

"That's a very good question, Mr. Lockerby."

"Call me Alex."

"Well, Alex," she said, setting her empty glass aside and standing. "Why don't I show you."

Alex expected the Waverly factory to look like any number of other factories he'd seen. Since the invention of the assembly line, most factories had gone that way. Waverly, on the other hand, was a series of stations where men worked on complex boards filled with tubes and wires. Once they were done, the completed boards were picked up by runners and moved to other stations where other men installed the finished boards into sleek, stylish radio bodies.

"What makes them look like they're wet?" Alex asked as he and Lillian moved among the workstations. "The finished radios, I mean."

"Bakelite," she said, the heels of her pumps clicking on the cement floor. "It's a kind of plastic so we can mold it into any shape we want. And, as you pointed out, they look fantastic."

Alex didn't have such a high opinion of plastic. To be fair, the last time he'd come up against it was in Dr. Burnham's fog machine, and at that time it was threatening to burn down the city.

"Didn't I read somewhere that Bakelite cracks if it gets too hot?" he wondered, pushing the image of the fog machine from his mind. "That can't be good in a radio."

To her credit, Lillian's easy smile didn't slip at all.

"It is a problem," she admitted. "Right now we have to build them a bit bigger and add vents over the tubes, but we are looking into ways to make the finished product more heat resistant. Some of them are very promising."

Alex nodded sagely at that comment, as if he'd been expecting it.

"Through here," Lillian said, pushing thoughts of plastics from his mind. She opened a door set into the back wall, revealing a large office inside. A man with a vest and a cigar sat at an angled desk, much like Alex's drafting table. The only differences were that this table wasn't adjustable like his and the surface of this table was riddled with holes. On the right side of the table, a wooden box had been mounted in place with a hinged lid. To the left of the table was an open packing box with paper dividers inside, making around thirty square cells. A board, similar to the angled top of the table, had been stacked against the wall, but it had grooves in it that formed a roughly rectangular shape rather than holes.

"This is the secret of Waverly Radios, Alex," Lillian said, reaching into the box and extracting a round glass tube with five metal prongs on the bottom. "This is a receiver amplifier," she said. "RCA makes them for us. And this," she said, pointing to the man in the vest, "is George Wilcox. He's the man that turns these," she held up the amplifier tube, "into the magic behind Waverly." She turned to George and handed him the vacuum tube. "George, this is Alex Lockerby. Show him what you do."

George nodded at Alex, then stood up and carefully fitted the five metal prongs on the bottom of the vacuum tube into the holes in the slanted table. Moving quickly, he extracted another dozen and filled up the top right corner of the table. From there, he moved around, counter-clockwise, until he had ninety-six of the tubes fitted into slots. Now that they were filled up, Alex could see that there was a square metal plate in the center of the pattern.

With the tubes in place, George pressed a large button on the side of the desk and a green light mounted on top lit up.

"The tubes are mounted in series," Lillian said. "When the light is green, it means they're all in place correctly."

George reached into the box with the pivoting lid and pulled out a square piece of paper the exact size as the plate in the middle of the angled board full of vacuum tubes. As he placed the paper on the table, Alex could see a fairly complex rune written on it. Before he got a good look, however, George Wilcox touched his cigar to the paper and it vanished in a puff of fire and smoke.

Alex may not have known what the rune did, but he felt it activate. It had a warm, electric feeling, like Alex had shuffled across a carpet in winter. After a moment, the rune faded and he felt the magic dissipate into the array of vacuum tubes.

"And that's it," Lillian said, reaching out and plucking one of the tubes from its slot. "Now this little beauty is three times stronger than it was a minute ago."

"How?" Alex asked.

Lillian's smile soured.

"I have no idea," she admitted. "That's what Fredrick's rune did. We're got about forty more of his runes, but after that..." she sighed and handed the enchanted vacuum tube to George. "After that, Waverly radios will be just the same as any other radio."

"You don't have any idea how his rune worked?"

She shook her head.

"That was part of the deal we had. Waverly bought the rights to use Fredrick's rune, but he kept it a secret. No one but Fredrick knew how the rune was made. So, as you can see, no one here would dare to kill Fredrick, because they'd be killing the company and their jobs."

Alex had to admit, it was a good argument, one he'd thought of himself. Waverly radios were known for their crystal-clear reception, and without Fredrick Chance's rune, they'd lose their edge.

"If you're satisfied here," Lillian said, "let's go back to my office."

She led the way back across the factory floor, exchanging pleasantries with some of the men as she went. From what Alex could tell, she was well liked, and no one gave her a cross look.

Back in her office, she moved back to the lounge by the hearth and they resumed their seats. Alex could tell there was something she wanted to discuss, but she didn't speak right away.

"Alex," she said, finally, "when Arthur called and said he was sending you over, I called around to find out what I could about you."

"Oh?" Alex said. He was used to digging up other people's past, but very few people ever returned the favor. "And what did you learn?"

Lillian's sly smile returned and she crossed her legs again.

"I learned that you aren't just a celebrated private detective, you're also a runewright. From what I hear, a very good one."

"Guilty as charged, I'm afraid," he said.

"As I pointed out, without Fredrick and his enhancement rune, Waverly is finished."

"And you want to know if I'm good enough to deconstruct Mr. Chance's rune before it's too late for you," Alex guessed.

"Got it in one."

Alex didn't have any idea how Fredrick Chance's rune worked, but all he would need to figure it out is one or two of the remaining rune papers and some time.

"I could take a look at what Fredrick did," he said. "But not until I wrap up my investigation for Mr. Wilks."

"Or you could tell Arthur that no one here killed Fredrick and then work for me," she said. "If you can figure out Fredrick's rune, I will make it worth your while."

Alex already had his runes working in two side businesses and he wasn't keen to add another.

"Let's not get ahead of ourselves," he said. "I think you're right that no one here had an obvious motive to kill Fredrick Chance, but what if he was killed by someone who wanted to destroy your company?"

Lillian's face clouded over for a moment.

"You mean killing Fredrick might be some act of industrial sabotage?"

"I mean exactly that," Alex said. "You said it yourself, without Fredrick's runes, Waverly Radio is over and done with."

"I confess I hadn't thought about it that way," Lillian admitted.

"So," Alex said, opening his notebook again. "Is there anyone you can think of who would want to ruin your company?"

Lillian scoffed and shook her head.

"You mean besides all our competitors in the radio business?"

"Anyone with enough of a grudge to commit murder," Alex said.

"The only one I can think of is my good-for-nothing, cheating husband."

Alex was taken aback by her answer.

"Why would your husband want to ruin his family's company?"

Lillian took a deep breath, then let it out slowly.

"He's cheating on me," she explained through clenched teeth. "If he knows that I know, then he wouldn't want me to get Waverly Radio in the inevitable divorce."

That actually made sense. Alex had been involved in more than his share of contentious divorces and he knew how petty people could be. Alex did wonder if a judge would award Lillian the business, though. Even though she was running it, it belonged to the Waverly family.

"Tell me about your husband," he asked.

"Tommy is a spoiled little brat," Lillian said. "Of course I didn't know that when I married him." She paused and seemed to contemplate for a moment. "Maybe he wasn't that bad when we got married," she finally admitted. "Anyway, that was before I was running Waverly Radio."

"Why are you running it?" Alex pressed. He knew some women ran companies, like Sorsha, but it was hardly the norm.

Lillian flashed him a mocking smile.

"You don't approve?" she said in a sickly-sweet voice.

Alex shrugged.

"It doesn't bother me, but since you married into the family, I would have expected your husband's father to groom him for the job."

"He did," she said. "Everything was going according to plan until Tommy got sick. Polio," she answered Alex's questioning look. "When the doctors gave him the bad news, we knew things had to change."

"And that's when you became president of Waverly Radio," Alex guessed.

"At first, we came to work together, and he'd show me the ropes. Eventually, the polio landed him in a wheelchair."

That explains the elevator, Alex thought.

"After that I was mostly on my own here," Lillian continued. "I had to learn to swim with the sharks while Tommy tried to advise me from home. That was twelve years ago. I've been here ever since."

Alex glanced up at the woman opposite him once he finished making notes. She sat, contemplating him right back, the picture of poise and grace. Initially, he'd been put off by her businesslike manner, but now he saw it for what it was, a defense mechanism. It was her way of telling a man who might think her an easy mark that she knew how to play the game.

"It looks like you've done well, both for yourself and for the company," he said.

"Thank you." She grinned at him with a raised eyebrow. "That's always nice to hear."

Alex had to admit, Lillian was an impressive woman. She looked to be about his age, maybe a bit older, but she was beautiful and confident – and that was sexy.

"You said your husband was in a wheelchair," Alex said, pulling his wandering mind back to the task at hand. "That makes me wonder who he's having an affair with."

Lillian's basking smile evaporated into a look of irritation and disgust.

"About three years ago, his condition got worse," she said. "We needed to hire a full-time nurse for him and naturally he picked some buxom young bimbo."

"Why did you put up with that?"

Lillian sighed.

"I didn't think Tommy could…perform any more," she admitted. "He hasn't in years as far as I'm aware."

"What's this nurse's name?"

"Irene Masterson."

Alex jotted that down, then closed his notebook.

"I think I've got all I need for now," he said, rising.

"How long is your investigation going to go on?" Lillian asked, shifting her shoulders back to better display her figure.

She definitely knew how keep a man off balance.

"Mr. Wilks gave me a week," Alex said. "If I haven't found anything new by then, the police report will stand."

Lillian sighed as a look of irritation crawled across her beautiful face.

"All right," she said, rising. "You'll tell me if you finish your investigation early?"

"Of course," he said.

6

CIRCLES

It was after four when Alex got off the south-bound express at Empire Station and made his way up to his office. If Sherry was back from her fact-finding trip, he would go over what she found out about the New York Historical Commission, and if not, he had the Gordian rune book to read.

As he rode the elevator up to the twelfth floor, he reviewed his two cases. He'd have to check Lillian Waverly's alibi, but he didn't like her for Fredrick Chance's murder. She had far too much to lose and nothing to gain by it, nothing he could see, anyway. The husband seemed a good prospect, assuming he really was stepping out on Lillian with his nurse – metaphorically, at least. Alex would go see him in the morning.

As far as the Hathaway House was concerned, Alex just needed to figure out who wanted to buy it so badly that they'd bribe a city official. That might prove a problem if the offer was made through an attorney, since he wouldn't have any leverage to entice them to name their client. There were other avenues, though. If he could dig up a money trail proving that one of the vote-changing bureaucrats had been bribed, he could use that to apply pressure of his own. All he wanted was a name, after all. It was a crude, but very effective tactic, especially with politicians who didn't want their dirty laundry all over the front page of the Times.

When Alex reached his door, he found the office locked and the lights off. Usually, when Sherry went to do research, Alex's protégé Mike Fitzgerald would fill in. Since the office was locked, Alex could only assume that Mike was out on a case.

Pulling his key ring from his pocket, Alex unlocked the door and went inside. He was tempted to leave the door unlocked and fill in for Sherry himself, but he wanted to spend some time with the Gordian rune book before dinner and he didn't want to be interrupted. Resolving to close the office early, he shut the door behind him and turned the lock.

Once back at his desk, Alex switched on his desk lamp and pulled the small, blue book inside the circle of its light. With a silent prayer that he'd find the book more informative than he had that morning, Alex opened its cover and began to read.

The grandfather clock in the brownstone's downstairs hallway chimed six as Alex descended the stairs from his bedroom. When he reached the kitchen, he unceremoniously threw the Gordian rune book on the table and slumped down in one of the kitchen chairs.

"Rough day, lad?" Iggy asked, his voice tinged with a layer of judgement regarding Alex's behavior. Iggy had opinions regarding the treatment of books. He stood at his usual place by the stove wearing a cooking apron over his shirt and vest.

"It's this cursed book," Alex growled, snatching it up off the table and holding it up in his fist.

Iggy raised an appraising eyebrow.

"Is that the Gordian rune book?"

Alex nodded and tossed it on the table again, this time in Iggy's direction.

"I thought you'd be happy about that," Iggy remarked as he stepped to the table and picked up the thin blue volume.

"I would if it made any damn sense," Alex growled.

DAN WILLIS

"Language, lad," Iggy admonished. He opened the Gordian rune book and paged through the first section. "Give me the Reader's Digest version."

Alex sighed and rubbed his temples while he gathered his thoughts. He was finding it difficult to talk about the book without cursing.

"Based on what's in there," he began, "a Gordian rune is just a special kind of construct. Like a regular construct, you build the Gordian rune from smaller runes and constructs designed to work together."

"Then what's so special about it?" Iggy asked.

"It's the way you lay the runes down," Alex explained. "In a Gordian rune, you start with whatever your foundational construct is. Once that's done, you write a linking rune on the last bit of the base, then you use a thin coat of flammable lacquer to seal over everything but the linking rune. Once the lacquer is dry, you write another linking rune on top of the first one, then start the next construct, repeating for as many constructs as you need, and then ending with a special cap rune that they detail in the book."

"Sounds excessively complex," Iggy commented.

"Actually, it's fairly simple," Alec countered. "But, the process is full of fiddly details."

"No doubt about that," Iggy chuckled. "Did the book mention why someone came up with this method?"

Alex sighed and nodded.

"It's so that runewrights could put down runes that other runewrights couldn't destroy or alter later," he said. "The book doesn't say, but I imagine it wasn't very long before someone adapted this to military uses."

"And curses, apparently."

"Those too."

Iggy paged through the book slowly while Alex sat and stewed.

"Does the author list any way to counter these constructs," he asked, "or maybe a way to identify the runes used to build them?"

"No," Alex said. "The whole point was to build constructs that resisted attempts to disarm or circumvent them."

"Have you finished it?" Iggy asked, setting the book back on the table.

Alex nodded.

"Have at it," he said. "But if you're wondering if there is any hidden text that can only be seen by ghostlight, don't bother. I already looked."

Iggy gave him a compassionate smile.

"Don't worry," he said, stirring something in a large pot. "Sometimes a fresh set of eyes is all you need."

"Let's hope so," Alex said, cradling his head in his hands.

Silence stretched out between them as Iggy busied himself with his cooking. After a few minutes, Alex got up and set the table.

"How is the life transference rune coming?" he asked, more as a way to make small talk than any desire to know.

"Right on schedule," Iggy said. "I'll be done on Sunday, but we'll have to wait till Monday to use the slaughterhouse; that's when their next shipment of hogs comes in."

"Are you going to make the rune more potent?" Alex asked. "Sorsha's losing energy fast."

"I don't think that would be wise," Iggy said. "She's already in a weakened state and even though she can channel large amounts of magical energy, we're dealing with life energy. If we give her too much it could overwhelm her."

Alex's mind raced back to a solitary mayfly in a bell jar. When Iggy had given it too much life energy, the poor creature had burst from the inside. The thought of that happening to Sorsha gave him the shivers.

Taking his pocketwatch from his vest, Alex flipped it open. He hadn't considered the extra clock hand made of blue energy for some time. Ever since they'd used Iggy's construct to transfer life back into him, the hand had pointed resolutely to the number two, stubbornly refusing to move. Iggy told him that once his life energy fell below one year, the hand would change back to red and begin to move backwards.

"Iggy," Alex said, sitting up suddenly. "Can you make one of these for Sorsha?" He held up the pocketwatch so his mentor could see the blue clock hand.

Iggy considered the watch, then nodded slowly.

"I could," he said, "but that construct is very complicated. It will take a solid week of work just to write it."

"Could I do it?"

"Of course," Iggy said, "but I'd have to be there with you the first couple of times and that would negate the purpose of having you do it."

Alex ground his teeth. Everything seemed to be conspiring to slow him down, to make him wait while Sorsha wasted away in front of him. He wanted to hit something. Instead, he took a deep breath and let it out slowly.

Iggy declared that dinner was ready, so Alex loaded a plate with rice topped with some kind of meat stew, and a bit of hard bread. They ate in relative silence, each man contemplating the problems before them. For his part, Alex got more and more frustrated until finally he sat back in his chair and rubbed his temples.

"It's not as bad as all that, lad," Iggy said after a moment. "We've got our wits and we still have some time. We'll figure this out."

"What if we need more time?" Alex groused.

"Your idea of using the life rune on Sorsha will give us more time. We mustn't lose hope."

Alex chuckled darkly at that.

"What we need is for you to be able to write multiple runes at a time."

Now it was Iggy's turn to chuckle.

"The only person who made that work was that Maple fellow," he said, referring to the Happy Jack rune company that used mind-controlled slaves to mimic the movements of skilled runewrights.

"We could do that," Alex said out of nowhere.

"I hope you're not serious," Iggy admonished him. "In order to do that, we would have to mind-control other runewrights, make them slaves. Yes, we know how to do it, but that doesn't give us the right."

Alex shook his head as an idea bloomed, fully formed into his mind.

"What if we got runewright volunteers," he said, leaning across the table. "We could set up a shop and have them mimic your movements, just until Sorsha is free of the Gordian rune."

Hostile Takeover

"First," Iggy said, giving him a serious look, "I doubt you'll find anyone willing to sacrifice their free will to write runes for someone else. Secondly, I don't know about you, but personally, I don't want that kind of power over someone else. I shudder to think about the temptations associated with such a scheme."

Alex understood Iggy's objections, but he wasn't ready to throw in the towel yet.

"What if we did the copying inside a vault?" he posed. "We use the mind rune on the volunteers inside, they do the work, then when they leave the vault, we close it and the connection is broken."

"The mind rune takes multiple exposures over an extended period to take hold," Iggy pointed out. "You'd have to modify it to work instantaneously. That might be difficult as well as dangerous."

"But we could figure it out."

Iggy opened his mouth to reply, then hesitated.

"No, lad," he said at last. "Even if we could figure it out, and even if we got volunteers to help us, what are the odds we could keep this secret? Think what could happen if anyone ever found out that we could make completely obedient slaves with a rune? I'd barely trust you and me with that kind of power, imagine if Hitler or Mussolini got hold of it."

Alex wanted to argue, but he had no rebuttal. Iggy was right: of all the runes they knew, the ability to magically rip away someone's free will was terrifying. He'd trust Iggy with that power and even himself, but if anyone else ever got hold of it, the results could be catastrophic.

He slammed his fist down on the kitchen table and instantly regretted it. The heavy oak table didn't give at all, and his hand stung.

"I know, lad," Iggy said in a quiet voice. "It seems like there's nothing we can do, but you need to remember that we are doing what we can. It only takes time."

When Alex didn't respond, Iggy stood up and began fixing another plate. When he was done, he went to the china cabinet and got a cover, placing it over the plate before he put the whole thing in front of Alex.

"Here," he said. "I'll clean up tonight. You take this to Sorsha and let her know what we're planning." He patted Alex's arm, then turned and began gathering the dishes.

"All right," Alex said, standing. "I'm sure she could use some company."

He picked up the plate but left the rune book for Iggy, then went upstairs to his room.

One short trip through his vault later, he stood in the cavernous foyer of Sorsha's flying home.

"Did we have an appointment?" Sorsha's voice floated down to him from the upstairs balcony.

He looked up to see her smiling down at him over the banister. She wore a shimmering silver pajama set with a white robe as if she'd been ready for bed, but her hair and makeup were perfect.

"No," he answered, holding up the covered plate. "Iggy thought you'd like a decent meal."

She held his gaze and raised an eyebrow.

"And I wanted to check up on you, too," he said.

"Better," she said, her smile returning. "Why don't you meet me in the dining room."

Alex crossed the foyer to a large set of polished maple doors. Beyond them was Sorsha's dining hall. It was as wide as Alex's waiting room and at least one hundred feet long. Three massive sideboards occupied the left-hand wall with an impressive liquor cabinet and china hutch on the right. In the center was a cherrywood dining table that could seat at least thirty people. Elegant chandeliers hung over it, illuminating the table's mirror-like surface. The table had a slight oval shape to it, making it wider in the middle than at the ends, and, at the head of the table stood a truly impressive captain's chair.

Alex snickered at the thought of Sorsha in the massive chair. With her height and slight build, the chair would make her appear small, the opposite of its intended effect.

Given the finish on the table, Alex set the covered plate on the nearest sideboard and began looking for a placemat.

"Bottom drawer," Sorsha's voice directed him as he searched in one of the china hutches.

Shifting his focus, he found a linen mat and placed it in front of the big chair as Sorsha sat down.

"What is it?" she asked as Alex set the plate in front of her. Up close, Sorsha looked tired, and even with her makeup in place, Alex could see the dark circles under her eyes.

"Stew with rice," he said, fixing an encouraging smile on his face as he lifted the cover off the plate. It wasn't until that moment that he wondered if the sorceress was up to such a heavy meal. He needn't have worried. Iggy had filled a bowl with what appeared to be mostly the broth from the stew with a small pile of rice and a slice of bread on the side.

"Oh, thank God," Sorsha said, tearing off a bit of the bread and sopping it in the gravy. Without any pretense of delicacy or feminine mystique, she popped the bread into her mouth and chewed. After a moment, she let out a contented sigh.

"Things can't be that bad around here," Alex observed.

"I haven't been to a decent restaurant in over a week," she said, tearing off another bit of bread. "My girl, Hanna, does her best, but she's a ladies' maid, not a cook."

"Why not hire a cook?"

Her smile of pleasure evaporated and she looked down.

"You know why," she said in a low voice. "The more people I have regular contact with, the more chance word of my condition will get out. Even if I had meals brought in, someone would notice and wonder why."

Alex reached out and took her hand.

"Iggy and I are working as fast as we can," he said.

She looked up at him, catching his eyes and holding them.

"I know you are," she said. "I didn't mean to imply anything else."

Alex squeezed her hand.

"Well, until we get you fixed up, you'll have to start having dinner with us," he said.

"What will Dr. Bell say to that?" Sorsha said with a small grin that vanished almost as quickly as it came. "I don't want to be a burden."

"Iggy loves to cook, and he likes you more than he does me."

Sorsha regarded Alex with a raised eyebrow and a skeptical look that made him chuckle.

"I'll even tell him to fancy up his fare," he said.

She gave him a sly smile and squeezed his hand as she continued eating. As she ate, Alex told her about their plan to use the life transference rune on her in a few days.

"How many times can you do that?" she asked.

"Well, it takes three days to write the runes that make up the construct," Alex said. "We don't want to do it too often, though." He explained about Iggy's initial experiments with the mayfly.

When he finished, her shy smile was back.

"Thank you, Alex. I know how hard you and Dr. Bell have been working and I'm grateful."

"Well," Alex said, stretching the word out.

That elicited a genuine laugh from Sorsha and she reached out to put a finger on Alex's lips.

"Keep whatever inappropriate thing you were about to say to yourself," she said.

"How do you know it was inappropriate?"

"Because," she said, looking him right in the eye with a sardonic stare, "you are incorrigible."

"Then maybe you should give me more incorrig-ment," he replied, deliberately mispronouncing the word.

Sorsha's amused smile turned playful, something Alex rarely saw.

"I guess you'll just have to break this rune," she said. "Then I'll have lots of time and energy to lead you on." Her smile stayed in place, and she pushed her half-eaten plate of food away. "Now I'm feeling tired. Come kiss me before I go to bed."

Alex helped her out of her chair and did as he was told.

7

THE HUSBAND

Alex had managed to get to bed early after his impromptu dinner with Sorsha. The fact that Iggy was studying the Gordian rune book helped ease his mind. Despite getting a good night's sleep, however, he found himself dozing as the cab rumbled along the rural roads of Westhampton.

"This is the place, Mr. Lockerby," an unfamiliar voice roused him.

He opened an eye and found the cab moving up a long drive toward a truly impressive mansion. It was built primarily of brick but gave the impression that, if it had been built in England, it would have been a castle.

"Just like I said," the cabbie went on. "Do you want me to wait for you?"

Alex considered it, then shook his head.

"Only until I get inside," he said, handing the cabbie a dollar-ten for the ride.

Alex had wanted to spend the bulk of the day running down Ethel and Lucius Briggs' mysteriously pushy home buyer, but he needed to get the Waverly case out of his way first. A quick trip to the brownstone's library that morning had yielded the fact that the Waverlys lived on Long Island. According to Iggy's copy of *Who's Who*, Thomas

Waverly lived with his widowed father, Marshall, the founder of Waverly Radio.

Three hours, one train trip, and a taxi ride later, and he was standing in Tommy's driveway.

Alex tipped the cabbie, then turned and mounted the stairs to the enormous porch. Before he could ring the bell, however, the door opened and Alex found himself staring at an attractive young woman. She looked to be in her mid-twenties with dirty blonde hair, brown eyes, and prominent cheekbones. With a slim nose and a dimple on her left cheek, she was strikingly pretty.

"Can I help you?" she said, seeming startled by his appearance.

The woman's clothes weren't those of a domestic servant; she wore an expensive white blouse with a black skirt that had been tailored to hug her considerable curves. Her makeup was tasteful and understated with a muted red lipstick that matched her wide leather belt.

Alex recovered himself and fished in his pocket for a business card.

"I'm Alex Lockerby," he said, handing one over. "Mr. Waverly's insurance company asked me to follow up about the death of Fredrick Chance."

The woman looked confused as she read the card, but she rallied and asked Alex to come in.

"Wait here," she said, giving him a wide smile. In addition to having curves in all the right places, the girl's dimple made her smile adorable. "I'll go inform Tommy that you're here."

She turned and walked away, and Alex watched her do it until she disappeared around a corner. Based on her appearance and the fact that she called Mr. Waverly, "Tommy," Alex assumed this was the nurse. Her familiarity wasn't proof of an affair, but it was suspicious. Alex wondered why Lillian had ever allowed a girl that good-looking into her house.

Unless she wanted her husband out of the way, he thought. Putting such an attractive nurse in her husband's life seemed like a deliberate invitation for him to cheat.

Assuming he's actually having an affair, Alex reminded himself. Just because the girl who answered the door was a knockout, that didn't mean Waverly was sleeping with her. She might be a relative for all Alex knew.

"Mr. Lockerby?" the woman said, appearing at the corner. "This way."

She waited for Alex to join her, then turned and led him along a wide, tiled hallway. Burnished doors of dark wood with gleaming brass hardware passed on each side of the hall, until finally the shapely young woman turned at a large set of double doors. A large wooden molding surmounted the door, bearing a metal shield with the family coat of arms painted on it. Without a pause to admire the opulence of the doors or the crest, the buxom woman turned the handle of the right-hand door, pushing it open to reveal a large library. Shelves full of books lined the walls, illuminated by a glass ceiling. Couches and chairs were arranged around the room so that occupants could sit in groups to talk, or alone to read. A gigantic marble hearth dominated the back wall with a gleaming brass screen in front of it, and photos and mementos on the mantle above.

In the center of this opulent room sat a man in a wheelchair. To Alex he didn't look sick, but polio was a strange disease that could attack one part of the body while leaving the rest more or less alone. The man, who could only be Thomas Waverly, was dressed in a loose-fitting shirt with a vest and had a blanket covering his legs. His face was handsome with a strong chin and deep blue eyes under a mop of blond hair. An open book sat in his lap, and he wore a pair of spectacles low on his nose; he looked over the top of them as Alex entered.

"Mr. Waverly?" Alex asked, approaching the wheelchair.

"Call me Tommy," he said, closing his book and removing the spectacles. "Do I understand correctly that an insurance company sent you?"

"That's correct, and you can call me Alex. I'm here looking into your insurance policy."

"I'm sure my father has quite a few policies on this house and the grounds," Tommy said, "so I'm not sure what policy you're referring to."

That surprised Alex. Arthur Wilks had telephoned Lillian to warn her that someone would be investigating Mr. Chance's death.

"The key-man policy that your company had on your runewright, Fredrick Chance," he supplied.

"Oh," Tommy sighed, setting his book on a side table and adding his spectacles on top. "I'm afraid you've wasted your time, Alex. I wouldn't know anything about what happened to Fredrick, or any key-man policy Lillian might have taken out on him. I haven't had anything to do with Waverly Radio for almost a decade." He indicated his wheelchair as if Alex might have somehow missed it.

"But you are still an owner, aren't you?"

Tommy laughed at that, a sound somewhere between amusement and bitterness.

"Is my name on the building? Yes," he said. "But after I made her what she is today, that bitch I married cut me out."

"Out of the business?"

"Out of everything," Tommy said. "I don't even have access to the family bank account any more. Lillian took all of it."

That sounds like motive, Alex thought.

"It sounds like you don't think very highly of your wife," Alex said, eliciting a genuine laugh from Tommy. "Do you think she could have killed Mr. Chance?"

That surprised Tommy, and he sat back in his wheelchair for a moment before he spoke.

"Could she have killed Fredrick?" he postulated. "Easily. That woman has ice water in her veins. If she thought Fredrick posed a threat to her, you bet she would have killed him. The problem with that is that Fredrick wasn't a threat. In fact, she won't be able to run the business without him."

"How do you mean?" Alex asked, pulling out his notebook.

"That's a bit of a story," Tommy said, indicating an overstuffed chair for Alex to occupy. "When I took over the company from my old man, Waverly was just another radio company. I took a chance on the Bakelite process and that gave us the tiniest bit of an edge, but most people don't buy radios for how they look."

"What happened?"

"This kid walked into my office one morning and told me he could make Waverly the biggest radio manufacturer in the country. He had this vacuum tube in his pocket and he asked me to bring up one of our radios." Tommy sighed and looked a bit wistful. "When I put Fredrick's tube in one of our radios, the difference was like night and day. I offered him a job on the spot."

"So it was you who hired Fredrick," Alex said, scribbling in his notebook.

"No," Tommy admitted. "Fredrick had some special rune that made the receiver tube work so well and he didn't want to sell that, he wanted us to hire him to make them. As you can imagine, working out the legalities of that took some time. Unfortunately, it was time I didn't have." He tapped the armrest of his wheelchair.

"Is that when Lillian started running the company?" Alex asked.

Tommy Waverly chuckled and shook his head.

"Yes," he admitted. "And I'm the idiot that gave it to her."

When Alex didn't say anything, Tommy went on.

"When I started having trouble getting around, I conceived a plan. I'd make Lillian the president of the company. I'd teach her how to act in meetings and work with vendors and the employees. At the end of the day, she would go over everything and I'd tell her what to do the next day."

That actually sounded like a decent plan. Tommy would maintain his position in the company with his wife acting as proxy.

"What went wrong?" Alex asked.

"She was actually good at it." Tommy shook his head as if he still couldn't believe it. "I walked her through most of the legal stuff with Fredrick but by the time he started working there, making the runes that put Waverly on the map, Lillian was running things by herself."

"But you were still on the board, right?"

Tommy nodded at that.

"I didn't like Lillian going behind my back and making decisions, so I tried to put pressure on her through the board of directors. Come to find out, she'd told them that the polio had affected my mind, made me paranoid."

Alex could see where this was going. If the board believed that Tommy wasn't in his right mind, they'd do the reasonable thing and transfer his position to his nearest relative…in this case, Lillian.

"Where were you Wednesday evening?" he asked.

Tommy looked down at his wheelchair, then back up at Alex.

"Really?" he asked with an amused smile.

Alex simply returned his smile.

"You seem to be an intelligent and, if I may say, well-motivated man. I imagine a little thing like that chair wouldn't stop you."

"I admit, I hate Lillian with an unholy passion," Tommy said, "but I'd never do anything to hurt my father's company."

"Humor me," Alex said.

Tommy took a deep breath and let it out slowly.

"On Wednesday I was here," he said. "Alone. I read for a while, here in the library, then I had a drink and went to bed."

"Can anyone confirm that? Your father, perhaps?"

"My father had a stroke six months ago. He's been bedridden in a sanatorium upstate since then."

"My condolences," Alex said.

"I'd appreciate it if you'd keep that information to yourself," Tommy said. "I don't want my father's illness to become fodder for the tabloids."

"I don't see any reason for me to pass that fact on," he said. "I do need an alibi from you though. I was told you had a nurse; was that the young woman who showed me in?"

Tommy smirked at that.

"Oh, you were told about Irene, were you?" he scoffed. "I can guess who told you about her, and what they implied."

"Your wife thinks you're having an affair with her," Alex said, being careful to keep any emotion out of his voice. He knew from experience that getting in the middle between feuding spouses was dangerous, so he resolved not to take sides.

Tommy Waverly sat, staring at Alex with a predatory smile. It was obvious from the look on his face that what Lillian suspected was true. He was sleeping with the young and beautiful Irene.

That changed the math considerably. Maybe Tommy was being honest about not doing anything to hurt his father's company, but what about Irene? And if Lillian had proof of her husband's affair, what would she do? She seemed cold and dispassionate, but what if that was an act? What would a smart, capable, scorned woman do to take revenge?

"You said you were here alone on Wednesday evening," Alex said, pressing on. "Where was Irene?"

"Wednesday is her day off," Tommy said, a ghost of his predatory grin lingering on his lips. "As I understand it, she took the train into the city, then went across the river to visit her mother in Hoboken. She was there all day and didn't come back till the following morning."

Alex would have to check with the parents to see if Irene had actually been there, not that they'd be the most reliable of witnesses. Still, there was probably a neighbor who saw her coming or going.

"Irene didn't have anything to do with Fredrick's death," Tommy suddenly insisted.

Clearly his relationship with his nurse meant more to him than a passing fling.

"We're not even sure Mr. Chance was murdered," Alex admitted. "It's possible his death was an accident."

"Let me tell you something, Alex," Tommy said, his voice earnest. "If Fredrick was murdered, it was Lillian who did it. There's nothing that woman wouldn't do out of pure spite."

Alex nodded noncommittally, and tucked his notebook back into his shirt pocket.

"You don't understand," Tommy said, reaching out and grabbing Alex's arm. "Lillian will do anything to keep me from returning to my company."

"Including burning it down?" Alex asked, somewhat incredulously.

Tommy looked frustrated, then he pointed to his wheelchair.

"You know there's a cure," he said, "for polio."

"I've heard that," Alex hedged.

"Well, when I told Lillian about it, she tried to have me committed. By the time I proved to the doctors at the state hospital that I was sane, that bitch had moved all the money out of the family accounts into one she controls. Since she was the president of Waverly Radio, the bank didn't even question why she was doing it."

"So your wife is keeping you from getting a cure for polio because she doesn't want you coming back to the company?"

"Exactly," Tommy said.

Alex hesitated for a moment before speaking. Clearly Tommy believed what he was saying, but it sounded a bit insane.

"Well, thank you for your insights and your time, Tommy," he said, offering the man his hand. "If anything untoward happened to Fredrick Chance, I'll find out."

Tommy gripped his hand and held it.

"Do that, Alex," he said, then he let go.

Alex stood and headed back out the way he'd come. If everything Tommy told him was true, Lillian was a monster. Of course, a lot of what Tommy claimed sounded plain crazy. With the two clearly hating each other, the truth was probably somewhere in between.

When he reached the front door, he found what he'd hoped to see. Irene the nurse was sitting on a bench by the front door. She'd been going out when Alex arrived, and he'd figured she wouldn't leave her lover alone in the house with someone he didn't know.

"Are you finished with your questions, Mr. Lockerby?" she asked with a smile that could stop traffic.

"Yes, Miss…"

"Irene Masterson," she said, offering him her hand.

"You're headed out," Alex said, indicating her handbag on the bench beside her. "Your day off?"

"No, that's Wednesday. I'm going into town to run a few errands for Tommy."

"Would you like to share a cab?" he offered.

"No thank you," she said with an amused smile. "But I have a car, so maybe I can drop you somewhere."

"The train station would be great," he said, offering her his arm.

She rose and took it before allowing Alex to lead her out the front door and down to her car.

Alex opened the door between his vault and his office only a few short minutes after Irene dropped him off at the Westhampton train station.

Once he was sure she'd left to pursue her errands, he'd chalked a door on the wall of a deserted storeroom and opened his vault.

During the car ride from the Waverly estate, he had managed to get Irene's alibi. She told the same story Tommy had about visiting her parents in Hoboken. He'd still have to confirm it, but since Tommy and Irene didn't have time to coordinate their stories, he was relatively sure she was out of town when Fredrick Chance died. All of that meant he was back to square one. If Fredrick was murdered, the ones with motive didn't have the opportunity, and the one with opportunity didn't have a motive.

Alex resolved to go over the details with Iggy since he was missing something, probably something painfully obvious.

Shutting the door behind him, he crossed the hall to his office. As he expected, there was a blue folder in the center of his desk. Those would be Sherry's notes on the vote-changing historical commission members.

Moving to his desk, Alex sat and opened the file. He was tempted to call Arthur Wilks and tell him that Mr. Chance's death was looking like an accident, but something stopped him. He had a feeling there was more to this case and he had five more days to figure it out. If he was still without a viable suspect then, he'd call Wilks and give him the bad news.

In the meantime, Alex pulled the blue folder closer and began paging through the notes Sherry had prepared for him.

8

WINDFALLS

Alex poured himself a Scotch and closed the blue folder that Sherry had left him. Of the three people who had changed their vote on Hathaway House, all of them had come from different careers before being appointed to the Historical Commission. The first was Leslie Barrett, a woman who had worked as a guide at several of New York's museums. Next came Phillip Laslow, a real estate appraiser with expertise in old buildings. Last of all was Milton Brinkmore, a builder who specialized in historical restorations.

The other two members had similar qualifications for their appointments, but even a cursory examination of their backgrounds revealed a striking difference. Annie Cunningham had been a debutante, donating millions of her husband's money to museums and art galleries. Then there was Benjamin Goldberg, who had been an antiquities dealer to the rich and famous, filling their houses with historical knick-knacks from all over the globe. To Alex it was obvious why they hadn't been targeted to have their votes changed – they were both too rich for simple bribery to work.

That little detail told Alex volumes. If the three vote changes were bribed, there would be money somewhere, in their bank accounts, their safety deposit boxes, under their mattresses, or even buried in a coffee can in their back yards. If they put it in the bank, Alex could bring in Danny, who could get a court order for bank records.

To do that, of course, he would need some actual evidence so he could get a warrant, but that shouldn't be too hard. People who suddenly got a big pile of free money tended to go on spending sprees, and that would be easy to document.

Pulling out his watch, Alex thumbed the crown to open the lid, revealing the time to be three-forty. If he moved quickly, he might have a chance to go by the houses of Leslie, Phillip, and Milton before it got too late.

"Sherry," he said, pressing the key on his intercom. "Is there anything that needs my attention right now?"

"I've got a few cases for Mike," she replied, her voice sounding tinny through the little speaker, "but everything else can wait."

"Good. I'm going out," he said. "I'll probably be gone for the rest of the day."

"I'll hold down the fort, boss," she said, then the speaker switched off.

"Right here will do," Alex said, handing his cabby fifty cents for his ride. He got out, handing a tip back through the open window, then waited for the cab to drive off before turning toward the modest, mid-ring home a few houses down. It was a modern brick structure with white shutters and a porch that ran the entire length of the house. The lawn was neat and clean with flower beds around the perimeter that looked freshly planted. It was still early March, so nothing was growing yet, but Alex could see how it would be beautiful by April.

A low brick wall encircled the lawn with a wrought iron gate leading to the walk. Alex didn't see a dog, not that the low wall would contain a dog of any size, so he opened the gate and passed through to the stone walk.

This house belonged to Phillip Laslow, the real estate appraiser. Alex decided to come here first because he could claim to be looking for an appraiser as an easy way to strike up a conversation.

As he approached the porch, Alex could see that the paper had been taken in and the empty milk bottles put out, so someone was definitely home. He mounted the steps to the porch with a spring in his step and rapped on the door. A moment later a young woman answered. Alex knew from his research that the Laslows didn't have any children and this girl was much too young to be Phillip's wife.

"Yes?" the girl said.

The girl was pretty in a fresh-faced kind of way, with very little makeup and dark, loose hair cascading over her shoulders. She wore a simple blue dress with a wide belt and her feet were bare. Clearly she was at home here.

"I'm looking for Philip Laslow," Alex said, taking off his hat. "Is he home?"

The girl smiled but shook her head.

"Sorry, but they're out of town," she explained. "I'm here looking after their dog."

Alex resisted the urge to grin. This was perfect; he could pry into Phillip's business without sounding like a busybody.

"Do you know when they'll be back?"

"Not for a few weeks," she said. "They're on vacation."

"Oh," Alex said, feigning disappointment. "I guess I'll come back later, then. Where did they go?"

"Aruba," the girl said with a sigh and a far-away look. "Isn't that romantic?"

"Very," Alex agreed.

And very expensive, he added to himself.

He bid the young lady farewell and headed back to the sidewalk. The next house, the one belonging to Leslie Barrett, was several miles away, so he'd have to walk to the nearest crawler station before he could head that way.

"You need to get a car," he told himself, then turned up the sidewalk and started walking.

Alex opened his watch to release the cover door that separated his vault from his bedroom in the brownstone. As he did, he noted that it was after five — closer to six. It had taken almost three hours to make his way around the city to the homes of the vote changers on the New York Historical Commission and he was tired and a bit discouraged.

Worse, he had the nagging feeling that he was forgetting something.

Taking off his suit coat, he tossed it on his bed, then headed downstairs. The moment he hit the landing, he could smell the aroma of rich food. If his nose was any judge, Iggy had outdone himself.

"There you are," Iggy said when Alex appeared in the kitchen. He wore his customary apron and had three pots on the stove as well as something in the oven by the smell of it.

"I'm only a bit late," Alex protested, though as tired as he was, he didn't put much energy into the protest. He was about to start setting the table when the phone on the wall rang.

"I'll get it," he said.

"You might as well," Iggy chuckled as Alex turned toward the phone. "It's for you."

As Alex picked up the receiver, his tired synapses finally started firing and he cringed.

"Sorceress," he said before she could speak. "I was just on my way to get you."

"I'm certain of it," she said. The tone of her voice, however, indicated that she didn't believe that in the slightest. "I was told that dinner was at five-thirty," she went on, "and that you'd be here to get me right after five."

"Things ran a bit late at the office," he lied. "I'll be there in half a minute."

"I shall await your arrival with bated breath," she replied, her tone still edged and sarcastic.

"I need to run upstairs for a minute," Alex said to Iggy once he'd hung up the phone.

"I imagine so," he chuckled. "That's the third time she's called."

That wasn't good. It meant that Sorsha was really looking forward to this evening and Alex's preoccupation with work might have already ruined it.

He hurried upstairs, grabbing his suit coat off his bed as he flipped open his pocket watch. The door to Sorsha's castle was to the left as he exited the hall that held his kitchen and vault bedroom. He passed his storage area and work table with quick steps. The telephones Sorsha had rigged up to work in her flying castle were in her bedroom, her office, and her kitchen, so if he hurried, he'd have the cover door to his vault open before Sorsha reached it.

When he opened the door, he found the sorceress newly arrived. She wore a turquoise blouse with a black pencil skirt and dark navy-blue lipstick that split the difference between the two colors. Alex knew she was having trouble sleeping, but her makeup completely covered the dark circles under her eyes. She looked radiant, and Alex said so.

"Liar," she chided as she took his arm, "but thank you."

He escorted her through his vault to the bedroom in the brownstone. When they reached it, Sorsha paused, looking around.

"So this is where you've been living?" she said. "It's very...neat."

Alex remembered the time he'd seen her bedroom, right before a deranged Nazi spy had tried to drop her flying castle on Empire Tower. Sorsha's bedroom had been strewn with discarded clothes and open makeup pots on her dressing table. He was certain his room seemed orderly by contrast, but really, Alex had never had very many possessions, so keeping his room neat was easy. That and the fact that all his important stuff was in his vault.

"I grew up at a Catholic mission," he explained. "Father Harry was very opinionated about the way to make a bed and keep a room."

Sorsha gave him a warm smile and leaned more heavily on his arm.

"I have no doubt."

They moved on, Alex holding her arm while she gripped the banister in her other hand as they descended the stairs.

"Ah, Miss Kincaid," Iggy said as Alex led her down the short hall from the library to the kitchen. In Alex's absence, he'd set the table and changed his cooking apron for his smoking jacket.

"Dr. Bell," Sorsha said as Iggy pulled out a chair for her. "Alex tells me you've been making a life restoration construct for me."

"Yes indeed," Iggy said as he and Alex sat. "I'll be finished tomorrow, so it will be ready when the slaughterhouse receives its new shipment of swine on Monday."

"Is...is this really the best way to help with my...my condition?" she asked, suddenly looking at her plate.

"Come, come, my dear," Iggy said as Alex put his hand on her shoulder. "This is perfectly safe. How else did you think we kept Alex alive all this time?"

Sorsha took a deep breath, then let it out suddenly.

"I'm just a bit nervous," she confessed. "Every day I can feel myself getting weaker, and if this doesn't work..."

"It will," Alex assured her.

"What if I'm too far gone?" she asked, looking up at him with desperation in her eyes.

Alex laughed at that and shook his head.

"You don't remember how far gone I was," he said. "By the end, I could barely stand."

"I'm getting there pretty fast, myself," she said with a shiver.

"Trust us, Sorsha," Iggy said in a gentle voice. "All this can do is help."

"And give us more time to figure out what those Legion bastards did to you," Alex growled.

Sorsha smiled up at him shyly and he could tell she was still worried.

"Trust me," he said. "You'll be fine. Iggy has done this twice already."

Something about that made Sorsha snicker and she quickly covered her mouth.

"What?" Iggy asked, somewhat indignantly.

"I knew you looked younger," she said, still smiling behind her hand.

Iggy and Alex both laughed at that. She was right, of course; Iggy had been looking and acting younger after each use of the life transference rune.

"That isn't going to happen to Sorsha, is it?" Alex asked his mentor doing his best not to smirk. "I mean if it did, she'd look like a teenager, and no one would take her seriously."

Iggy snorted, then blushed at his inability to stifle his mirth.

"Neither of you is funny," Sorsha said. Her voice was frosty, but she was grinning openly.

That broke the ice for the rest of the evening, and they carried on a lively conversation as they ate. Sorsha seemed to be much more like her old self and, for a few moments at least, Alex stopped worrying about her.

"So," she asked once Iggy had finished telling a funny story of his time in the navy, "what are you working on these days, Alex?"

Alex suppressed a sigh. He should have expected this question and had a more interesting answer than his two current cases. He set his fork down and launched into the case of the possible insurance murder.

"So," Iggy said once Alex brushed over the details of the death of Fredrick Chance, "do you think the wife did it to destroy her soon-to-be ex-husband's company?"

"Or was it the husband," Sorsha cut in, "trying to pry his wife loose from the family business?"

Alex shrugged.

"The wife has an alibi, but that doesn't mean she couldn't have had someone tamper with the flue in Mr. Chance's office for her," he said. "Same goes for the husband. His nurse was in Hoboken that night and he's in a wheelchair, but a determined man could have managed in spite of all that."

"Not to mention anyone in the company who might have had a quarrel with Chance," Iggy said. "You said Katrina was certain he wasn't having an affair with the only other woman in the office, but all the men who work there have wives. He might have gone further afield for a paramour."

Alex hadn't considered that.

I must be slipping, he chided himself. To be fair, it had been quite a while since he'd trailed a cheating husband. He made a mental note to find out if there had been a company picnic or maybe a Christmas party where Fredrick could have met the spouse of someone at the factory.

"So if you talked with that Waverly fellow this morning," Sorsha said, "why were you so late picking me up for dinner?"

"Well, that's my other case," Alex said. He reiterated the story of Lucius and Ethel Briggs and their insistent buyer.

"The facts suggest that the buyer wants it for sentimental reasons," Iggy said once Alex finished, "but since the Hathaway House has been in Lucius' family from the beginning, that can't be right."

"Is it on land some developer wants to put a skyscraper on?" Sorsha posited.

"Not that I know of," Alex said, though he hadn't yet gone down to the office of the city planner to make sure. "As far as I can tell, the only thing unique about the Hathaway House is its history, and someone paid a lot of money to keep it from getting a historical building designation."

"Could be they want to demolish the building," Iggy said. "Once a property is designated historical, it becomes almost impossible to tear it down."

"Are you sure the three turncoat committee members were bribed?" Sorsha asked.

Alex nodded.

"The first one I visited went out of town, to Aruba no less."

"I hear Aruba's lovely this time of year," Sorsha said with a smirk.

"What about the others?" Iggy added.

"Milton Brinkmore, the builder, was out of town as well, but he's only visiting his mother in Moorhead City."

"That doesn't sound extravagant," Sorsha said.

"I learned about Mr. Brinkmore's whereabouts from his company foreman," Alex explained. "While he and his wife were down south, his company is doing a little work on his house."

"How little?" Iggy asked.

"A new library and master suite for the house and a glassed-in greenhouse in the back yard."

Iggy whistled.

"He must have come into some money recently."

"That's what I thought," Alex said, returning Iggy's knowing look.

"What about the last one?" Sorsha asked.

"Leslie Barrett," Alex supplied. "She and her husband were home when I called, but wouldn't speak to me once I mentioned the Historical Commission. Leslie looked like she might faint."

Sorsha looked at Alex with an appraising eye.

"You didn't just leave it at that, did you?" she asked. Her tone implied that she'd be severely disappointed if he did.

"No," he said with a chuckle. "Bribing a government official is a crime, so I figure I'll borrow Danny for a half hour tomorrow and have him flash his badge at her. That ought to loosen her tongue."

"I'm still curious as to why this mysterious buyer wants Hathaway House so badly," Iggy said. "I think you'd better figure that out if you want to really understand what's going on here."

"Mmmm," Sorsha made an agreeing sort of noise. She was leaning on her arm and seemed on the verge of drifting off. "Why would anyone care about an old house?" Her voice had a delirious, sing-song-y quality to it.

"I think it's time I got you home," Alex said, rising.

"I am a bit tired," she said with a little sigh.

"Thank you for joining us, Sorsha," Iggy said, giving her a big smile. "We'll see you again tomorrow."

Alex took her by the arm, and she rose out of her chair. She had been fully engaged, asking good questions about his cases a moment ago, and now she was having trouble walking a straight line. As he escorted her up the stairs, he made a mental note to check with Iggy that everything was ready for the life transference rune. He didn't know how much time Sorsha had left, but it seemed to be dwindling rapidly right in front of his eyes.

Fifteen minutes later, Alex was back in his vault, having escorted Sorsha up the stairs from her foyer and into her bedroom. Miss Potter, Sorsha's ladies' maid, had taken her from there, promising to get her directly into bed.

Hostile Takeover

As Alex passed through his vault and into the brownstone door, he caught sight of the Gordian rune book, sitting on the side table next to his bed. Iggy must have put it there when he was done. Alex wanted to talk to Iggy about it, but he had work to do on the life transference rune. What Alex needed was to do something useful.

The problem was that he'd been through the little blue book four times and hadn't found a single helpful thing in it. He had learned how to make a Gordian rune, but the whole purpose of that was to make a construct that defied being unmade.

He needed to find something, a way to crack the unintelligible thing.

Alex stopped cold, looking at the little book. There might be a way to coax more information out of it, after all. With a self-satisfied grin, he rolled up his sleeves and headed back into his vault to get what he would need.

9

TAKING STOCK

Alex woke up slowly, consciousness drifting back to him. He'd left the lights on in his room, and he blinked against their brightness as he tried to get his arms and legs working. There was a taste in his mouth like copper, and his shoulders, hips, and neck were killing him.

"Mhuuug," he managed as he tried to lift himself up. His bed was harder than it should be, and he decided to focus his efforts on getting his eyes working.

Gradually, his vision returned, and he found himself looking at his reading chair, the one in front of his fake hearth in his vault. The scene was tilted at a bizarre angle and it took him a minute to realize that he was lying on the stone floor in the main vault room.

"Whaa?" he grunted, finally managing to get his arms to push his body up into a sitting position. He tried to remember how he could have ended up sleeping on the floor in his vault, instead of in any of the three comfortable beds that were in easy walking distance.

Had he lost his pocketwatch and been stuck in his vault?

No, he had a bedroom inside the vault, no pocketwatch required.

There was also a bathroom in the vault and the sudden need that realization brought Alex compelled him to his feet. He staggered past the library area into the hall that led to the brownstone door. Just past the vault bedroom, he reached the bathroom and gratefully relieved himself.

"What happened?" he groaned as he inspected himself in the mirror. The left side of his face had a red mark on it where his face had been touching the stone floor and his eyes were bloodshot.

Little by little the events of the previous evening began to return to his mind. After dropping Sorsha off, he'd resolved to study the Gordian rune book again. At some point he may, or may not, have downed a full bottle of Scotch and chased it with some cheap bourbon he still had around.

"May," he decided as his head began throbbing from the simple act of thinking.

Alex pulled open the medicine cabinet behind his bathroom mirror and found his aspirin bottle. Taking a small handful, he crossed the hall to the kitchen and filled a glass with water from the tap.

"Bottoms up," he slurred, then washed the aspirin down.

He waited, leaning on the sink in the little kitchen for a while, then sighed and straightened. It had been a long time since he'd been on a bender, and now he remembered why.

Moving slowly, he made his way back into the main room. On the floor, next to the spot where he'd been sleeping, was an empty bourbon bottle and he leaned down to grab it.

"Nope," he said as pain exploded through his brain.

Easing back up to a standing position, Alex walked carefully over to his drafting table. An empty Scotch bottle sat on the rollaway cabinet, along with his shot glass, and the blue book on Gordian runes. His drafting table was strewn with drawings he'd made, all depicting various kinds of Gordian runes, but they were just as unintelligible as the one on Sorsha.

To the left of his workspace was a long-legged side table whose top was roughly equal in height to the bottom of the drafting table. On top of the little table was a typewriter, like the one he had in his office. Alex used it for typing up notes for his official case files when he was working in the vault. In the typewriter was a piece of paper with several notes on it. Due to his state of inebriation, they were a bit scattered and there were several incomplete thoughts, but mostly it was understandable.

Alex pulled the paper from the machine's roller and held it up to get a better look. After half a minute of trying to get his eyes to focus on the neatly printed lines of text, he found the sweet spot and began reading.

A moment later, he almost dropped the paper.

"Iggy!" he shouted, ignoring the pain in his head as he did so. Alex looked around, wondering where his mentor had gone, then he realized he was still in his vault and set off at a quick stagger in the direction of the brownstone door.

"You look terrible," Iggy remarked once Alex had managed to carefully pick his way down the stairs to the first floor of the brownstone. "Were you up working all night? You know that's not good for your faculties."

"I slept," Alex said, speaking the absolute truth.

"In your clothes, I see," his mentor countered. "Well, at least you're dressed; we need to leave in a few minutes if we want to be at Mass on time."

Alex had completely forgotten that it was Sunday, and he pushed that thought back out of his mind.

"Never mind that," he said, holding out his typewritten page, "have a look at this."

Iggy took the page and squinted at it, scanning down the several lines of text.

"This is poorly written, lad," he admonished.

"I may have been a little drunk," Alex said.

"Well," Iggy said with a raised eyebrow, "that explains the sleeping in your clothes. Now, let's see about this."

He refocused on the paper and read it through, then he read it through again.

"This is an interesting idea," he said, reading it through again. "I can honestly say I have no idea if it would work."

"But it's not insane, right?" Alex pressed.

"No," Iggy admitted, "but that doesn't mean it will work. We'll have to test this when we get back, but if you're right, we might just have a shot at unraveling Miss Kincaid's Gordian rune."

Alex was so excited, he didn't even worry about turning up to church unshaven and in rumpled clothes.

Alex woke up the following morning to the alarm clock in his bedroom in the brownstone. He had no trace of a hangover, but the cheery sound of the ringing bell bothered him all the same. Switching it off, he rose, showered and shaved, then dressed in a neatly pressed suit.

Despite his calm exterior, he was roiling on the inside. He and Iggy had worked most of the day yesterday on his idea of temporal ghostlight and had come up with nothing to show for it.

Bupkis.

Zilch.

He ground his teeth, which made them hard to brush. It was such a good idea: expose the Gordian rune to amberlight and that would make the individual symbols of the construct separate, their ghostly images trying to flow back to where they were originally written. All he needed to do then was shine ghostlight on the streaks to light up the individual symbols. He and Iggy would be able to reassemble the entire rune that way, bit by intelligible bit. Once they had the pieces, they could figure out each construct and the order in which they appeared. That would tell them exactly what the rune did, and hopefully how to unravel it.

"Except it doesn't work," he almost yelled at his reflection.

Unsurprisingly his reflection had no thoughts on the matter, so Alex straightened his tie, put on his suit coat, and headed downstairs to breakfast.

"Don't let it get to you, lad," Iggy said, as Alex sat down at the kitchen table. He slid a fried egg onto a plate for him, then added a slab of ham. "I think your idea is sound, but we need to find another approach."

Alex resisted the urge to clench his fists. Iggy was right and he knew it. Of course, being right didn't solve the problem of Sorsha slowly 'bleeding to death' by the Legion and their cursed rune.

He put his plate down on the table and took a deep breath. It was exactly like when his own life had been running down to the end. He had to forget the ticking clock and focus on the work. Playing 'what if' games would drive him crazy.

"You're right," he said as Iggy sat down. "Any ideas?"

"A few," his mentor said. "Nothing I'd be willing to speculate on at this point, but I'll make a few calls today. Now eat your eggs and read the paper. That should take your mind off things."

Alex didn't want to distract himself. If he lost Sorsha, well, he didn't know what he would do.

Pushing those thoughts from his mind, he did as Iggy instructed and picked up the morning paper. The headlines were all about the goings on in Europe. Hitler had been making speeches for months about reuniting Germany. According to him, Austria was a part of the Fatherland and he wanted the two nations to reunite. Austria, it seemed, wasn't too keen on the idea and many were worried it would come to open conflict.

Having read the same story about all this for weeks, Alex paged past the headlines and the lesser news, stopping a few pages in. He found himself on the financial page and was about to move on when a headline caught his eye.

'Waverly Radio Stock Takes Near Fatal Dive, Time Could be Up for Former Market Leader.'

The story was about the effect the death of Fredrick Chance was having on the radio company. Already their stock value had crashed, and the company was in danger of becoming insolvent.

Alex read the short article again, but it still didn't make a lot of sense. He'd been to the Waverly factory a few days ago and they still had plenty of product. They even had a stock of Fredrick Chance's runes on hand. So why was everyone panicking?

"Iggy," he said, setting the paper aside and taking a bite of his egg, "do you have any money in the stock market?"

"Trying to find out if you're in my will?" he joked.

"Seriously, I've got a question about how the market works."

Iggy stroked his mustache for a moment, then nodded.

"I have some of my money in the market," he said, "but I have a man that takes care of how it's distributed."

"I'd like to talk to him," Alex said.

"Well, his name is Beauregard Mayweather and he runs an agency in the core."

"Beauregard Mayweather?" Alex repeated. "Really?"

"I'm told it's a southern name with a rich and storied history," Iggy said with no trace of a smile.

"Where do I find Mr. Mayweather?"

"As I said, he has his own agency, the Mayweather Brokerage," Iggy explained. "I doubt you'll have trouble finding it, or seeing Beau, he's Andrew Barton's broker as well. Beau's office is in Empire Tower."

"You're kidding?" Alex said, then shook his head when he realized his mentor most definitely was not. "Well, I guess it won't take long for me to swing by."

"That's the spirit," Iggy said, taking away Alex's now-empty plate. "Now get to work, but don't forget that we're taking Sorsha over to the slaughterhouse at seven."

Alex laughed and Iggy gave him a reproachful look.

"Just imagine if someone else had heard that," Alex explained.

After a moment, Iggy chuckled and shrugged.

"It's a charmed life we lead," he said. "Charmed and strange."

Alex had no rebuttal.

As it turned out, Mayweather Brokerage was one floor down from his own offices, on the eleventh floor of Empire Tower. Their waiting area had a stock ticker prominently displayed on the other side of a glass booth. Inside the booth stood a man with his sleeves rolled up and held in place with arm garters; he was busy reading the tape that emerged from the ticker.

"Can I help you?" an attractive woman said, coming to stand beside him. She was dressed fashionably in a form-fitting yellow dress with matching flats, and her hair was put up in a decorative style. Her face had a pleasant roundness to it, framing her brown eyes and pert nose.

"I'm Alex Lockerby," he said, handing her a business card. "I wonder if I might have ten minutes of Mr. Mayweather's time?"

The woman's smile became a bit pained, but then something made her hesitate as she read the card.

"Are you the Alex Lockerby who has an office one floor up?" she asked.

Alex had no idea how she came to know that, but he nodded.

"Wait a moment," the woman said, withdrawing through a door in the sidewall. Three minutes later the woman was back with the strangest looking man Alex had ever seen. He was short, maybe five foot five, and heavyset without being fat. He looked more like a fireplug than anything else, with an expensive silk suit and shoes made of alligator leather. His hair was a sandy blond color, combed in a loose style, and he had a mustache and goatee that made him look like Buffalo Bill Cody.

"Well, as I live and breathe, Alex Lockerby," he said in a bold southern drawl. He held out his hand for Alex to shake. "I can't tell you how good it is to finally meet you."

"It is?" Alex asked, taking the man's hand.

"I couldn't be happier if I was twins," he said. "I'm Beauregard Mayweather, but you already know that, and you can call me Beau."

"It's, ah," Alex hesitated. "It's good to meet you, Beau, but I'm a little confused as to how you know me."

"Why, Andrew, of course," Beau said, putting his hand up on Alex's shoulder and steering him toward the door in the side wall. "He said you'd be by sooner or later, looking for somewhere to put your money."

That actually sounded like Andrew Barton. The sorcerer had made no secret of the fact that he had plans for Alex's future.

Beau led Alex to an office with a nice view of the city and directed him to a chair in front of a relatively plain desk. In fact, as Alex looked around, he found Beau's office to be reserved and tasteful, with a minimal amount of furniture and only a few paintings and certificates on the walls.

"I have to tell you, Beau," Alex said as the stockbroker took his seat behind his desk. "I'm only here today because I have a few questions about the market. It's for a case I'm working."

"Oh," Beau said, looking disappointed for the briefest of moments before he rallied. "Well, that's all right. If Andrew says you'll come by sooner or later, I've learned not to bet against him."

"I know what you mean," Alex chuckled.

"So," Beau said, folding his hands on the desk in front of him. "What is it you want to know?"

Alex explained about the murder of Fredrick Chance and the plummeting fortunes of Waverly Radio.

"I guess I was wondering why all this is happening when their business hasn't even been affected yet," Alex concluded.

Beau thought for a moment, and Alex could tell he was wrestling with how best to explain.

"Well, Alex," he began, "you have to understand that there are two primary forces that drive the markets: greed, and fear."

"Fear?" Alex said, a bit surprised.

"Certainly," Beau said. "Some people invest because they're afraid of missing out on a good thing. Others pull money out because they're afraid of losing it."

"So a bunch of people read that Waverly's key man was killed and they're afraid," Alex said. "They're afraid Waverly will go broke in the future."

Beau nodded.

"The problem is that by pulling their money out now, they're driving Waverly to exactly the same kind of insolvency they were afraid of in the first place."

"So Waverly Radio is just...doomed?"

"No," Beau shook his head. "If Waverly somehow finds another runewright to make their fancy receivers, then the stock will come roaring back."

That made sense; if Waverly were headed back to the top of the radio business, a lot of people would want to be on board for the ride.

"In fact," Beau went on, "I'd bet the stock has already recovered a bit."

That didn't make sense.

"But you said that Waverly would have to find another runewright for that to happen," he said.

"No, no," Beau laughed. "If Waverly does that, their stocks will shoot up higher than they were before. What's happening now is the bargain hunters, people who look for stocks they think are artificially low. When they find stocks like that, they buy up a few shares just in case. Remember the other thing that moves the market, greed."

"But if Waverly does go out of business, won't they lose their investment?"

"They will," Beau said. "Think of it as a form of gambling. Bargain hunters see a low stock and, if they think it can recover, they buy in. If they're right, they can make a lot of money when the stock goes up."

Now that sounded like motive.

"How much money?" Alex asked.

"Most of these stocks are fairly cheap," he said. "That means that an investor who bets right can increase their money ten times, twenty times, even a hundred times if they're lucky."

"So if someone knew that Waverly Radio was going to bounce back," Alex said, "then they'd want to buy up as many shares as they could while it was cheap."

Beau nodded.

"That's exactly what they'd do," he said. "But if someone knew the Waverly stock was going to come back, they'd probably try a hostile takeover."

Alex had heard that term bandied about in the papers, but Beau might as well have been speaking French for all Alex understood.

"What's a hostile takeover?" he asked.

"It's when you take over a company by purchasing more than fifty percent of their stock."

"But if someone else owns the company, how does buying stock make someone else able to take control?"

"When a company offers stock, everyone who buys a share is a part owner in the company," Beau explained. "It doesn't matter who built the company; if you've got enough shares, your word is law."

"So," Alex said, trying to process what the stockbroker said, "if someone wants to take over Waverly Radio, they would want the stock price to be low so they could buy more shares."

"You've got it," Beau said.

"And no one else would buy up massive amounts of shares because they'd believe that the company was doomed."

Beau shrugged at that.

"The bargain hunters will buy some, but most people will stay away. Only the vultures will be really interested."

"Vultures?"

"If Waverly goes bankrupt, the shareholders will get first crack at their inventory, machinery, supplies, and anything else that's valuable. Sometimes a company's competitors will buy up stock so they can loot it once it's out of business."

Alex nodded, running through what Beau told him. It was a lot to take in, and it gave him new motives and new suspects in the death of Fredrick Chance.

Alex stood up and offered his hand to the stockbroker.

"Thank you, Beau," he said. "I think you've given me exactly what I need."

10

THE AGENT

Since his office was only one floor up from Mayweather Brokerage, Alex skipped the elevator and took the stairs.

"That was fast," Sherry said as he entered. "I thought you were going to see someone over on Wall Street."

"He is a stockbroker, but his office is here in the building," Alex explained. He crossed to her desk and offered Sherry a cigarette. She selected one from his silver case, then Alex lit it for her with the touch tip lighter on the desk.

"So, what do you want me to do?" Sherry asked as Alex lit a cigarette of his own.

"Who says I want you to do anything?"

Sherry smirked at him for a long moment.

"You offer me a cigarette every now and again," she explained. "But if you offer one while sitting on the corner of my desk, it's because you're going to give me a list of things to do."

Alex hadn't realized he was sitting on her desk, and he chuckled. He'd gotten in the habit of sitting there when Leslie Tompkins had been his secretary.

"You're getting very observant," he said. "Maybe I should start sending you out with Mike and get someone else to cover the desk."

"Not just yet," she said, giving him a sly look. "The time isn't right."

"Are you saying that it isn't in the cards?" he asked.

"Something like that."

Alex knew better than to argue with Sherry when she read cards; her abilities as an augur were never wrong.

When they work, he reminded himself.

"So," Sherry said, pulling his wandering attention back to the task at hand, "what have you got for me today?"

She picked up her notepad as Alex tapped his cigarette over her ashtray.

"When the Briggs' came to see me, Ethel mentioned that she received a letter with a bid for Hathaway House," he began, "so call her and see if she managed to find it. If she did, get the phone number that came with the offer. Call it and, if anyone answers, find out who they are. If they're talkative, ask if they have an office."

Sherry finished scribbling on the pad and looked up.

"Anything else?"

"That's it for now. I've got to call Lillian Waverly and ask her about her competitors." He stood up and picked up his hat from the desk. "Let me know as soon as you get a name to go with that offer, though."

Sherry promised she would, and Alex headed for his office.

There were a few file folders waiting on his desk, cases that Sherry wanted him to review, and he pushed them to one side. He retrieved a note pad and a pencil from his center desk drawer, then picked up the phone and dialed the number of Waverly Radio. After a brief conversation with their receptionist, his call was forwarded.

"Lillian Waverly," the voice on the other end of the line said.

"This is Alex Lockerby. I think I may have an idea why Fredrick Chance was murdered."

"You mean 'if' he was murdered in the first place," Lillian corrected him.

Alex let that go and pressed on.

"This may be part of a scheme to take control of your business, Mrs. Waverly," he said, "or gain access to your inventory at pennies on the dollar."

"So you think it's a hostile takeover or an act of corporate piracy,"

Lillian said, a thoughtful tone in her voice. "I suppose that's possible, but I thought you'd be more interested in my husband at this point. I heard you met with him."

"I did," Alex admitted.

"And...?" Lillian asked, letting the sound stretch out for a moment.

"And I'm looking into what he told me."

"Oh, come on," she laughed, "you can't possibly believe his 'poor me, I'm a victim' story. Please tell me you're smarter than that."

"There were parts of his story that seemed a bit far-fetched," Alex admitted, "but there were parts that seemed perfectly rational."

"Would that be the part where I'm a horrid bitch who's ruining his life?" Lillian said with an amused laugh. When Alex hesitated, she went on, "Oh, don't worry about sparing my feelings, Alex. I know what my husband thinks of me."

"And that doesn't bother you?"

"Not in the slightest," she declared. "He started hating me when I learned how to run this business without his help. I was young then, and fool that I was, I thought he'd be proud of me. I thought he'd love me even more for stepping up to save his company...but I was naive. As it turned out, Tommy wasn't the gallant gentleman I thought I'd married, he was a jealous little twerp."

"What did you do when you figured that out?" Alex asked. If Lillian had taken a lover during that time, then he might be a suspect in Fredrick Chance's death.

Assuming he believed that the thing keeping them apart was Waverly Radio, Alex thought.

Lillian sighed.

"I stuck with him for a few years," she said. "I figured he'd grow up at some point and realize what great work I was doing," she paused and sighed, "but he didn't." There was a wistful tone in her voice that made Alex wonder if she regretted those bygone years.

"And you think he's finally trying to get back at you by killing Mr. Chance?" he pressed on.

"Jealousy is a poison, Alex," she said. "The longer it festers the worse it gets. At this point, I think Tommy is capable of anything if he thought his actions would hurt me. Even murder."

Alex took a moment to process that. Tommy Waverly hadn't bothered to conceal his hatred of his wife, and Alex was sure that it wasn't an act. That said, if Tommy had killed Fredrick Chance, he probably would have done a better job of hiding such an obvious motive.

"I appreciate your candor," he said, "and I'm still following all possible lines of investigation. Which brings me back to the topic at hand: do you know if any of your rivals have been sniffing around since Mr. Chance's death? Or before?" he added.

Lillian snickered at that.

"If there were, they'd be sure to hide it from me," she said. "As far as I know, no one had expressed an interest in Waverly Radio. We didn't have any buyout offers on the table before Fredrick's death, and nothing has come in since."

"Could be they don't want to show their hand until you're on the verge of bankruptcy," Alex said.

"That's possible," Lillian said, "but isn't that just speculation, if Fredrick's death was an accident?"

She had a point. So far, Alex hadn't found any direct evidence that Fredrick Chance's death was murder.

"I think I'd better take a closer look at your competition all the same," Alex said. "Who, would you say, is your nearest competitor?"

Alex could hear Lillian sigh on the other end of the phone.

"All right, Alex, I'll play your game," she said, "but, I want something from you in return."

"Like what?" he asked.

"Can you meet me here, in my office, tomorrow?"

"I can probably fit it in," Alex hedged, running through his cases quickly in his head.

"How about you join me for lunch," she said. "I was planning on having something brought in anyway."

"All right, Mrs. Waverly," he said after taking a moment to think about it. "But I need that list of your competition today."

"Very well," she said, "do you have a pencil?"

"I found the mystery buyer for Hathaway House," Sherry's voice interrupted Alex's thoughts from the open door to his office. She grinned and held up a notepad "It's a realtor in the west side mid-ring called Manhattan Land and Building." She sauntered over to his desk and tore the top page from her notepad, dropping it on the top of Alex's fancy desk. "That's their address."

Alex picked up the paper and checked the address. It wasn't very far from the Philosopher's Stone, Charles Grier's alchemy shop.

"I didn't mention Hathaway House when I called," Sherry said as Alex copied the address into his flip notebook, "so they won't see you coming."

"Thanks, doll," Alex said, putting away his notebook and tearing the top page from the pad on which he'd been working. "Can you knock off for a couple hours?" he asked. "I've got some research I need you to do."

Sherry shrugged and nodded.

"It's been dead all morning," she admitted. "What do you need?"

He handed her the list as he stood.

"These are Waverly Radio's major competitors. I need to know if any of them are having financial trouble or if any of them had an unexpected windfall recently. Also, find out who runs each company."

Sherry made a few notes of her own on the paper, then grinned.

"Can I get lunch while I'm out?" she asked, putting on her most winsome smile.

"Sure," Alex said. "Grab a couple of bucks from the cashbox and go somewhere decent."

She promised that she would, then turned and left his office. Alex followed closely, only hesitating long enough to enter his vault and strap on his 1911. He didn't know exactly who he'd be dealing with at Manhattan Land and Building, so he wanted to be prepared.

Alex took a cab to the west side, eventually ending up in front of a run-down office building. Since Barton's new generators were so much more effective now, the old power rings didn't matter as much. That said, people still used them to reference the quality of the neighborhoods they covered.

When Sherry had said Manhattan Land and Building had a mid-ring address, Alex hadn't been surprised. When he stepped out of his taxi, however, he was a bit taken aback. The building was an old one, with crumbling brickwork and sagging eaves. Only the awning out front looked relatively new. In previous years, this building would have been right on the border between the middle and outer rings. Sometimes a business could find a good building with reasonably priced offices in such locations. Alex had been in one for almost ten years. This building, however, was not one of those fortunate few, and Alex wondered why a company that had frequent interactions with the public would occupy such a place.

Even stranger, when Alex entered the lobby, he found the offices of Manhattan Land and Building on the first floor. The building had five stories and usually companies that wanted more prestige sought higher floors, leaving the ground floor for shops that depended on walk-in business.

Pushing such thoughts from his mind, Alex moved along the hallway behind the lobby until he found a sturdy door with a brass plaque that read Manhattan Land and Building. He twisted the doorknob and went in without knocking.

Beyond the door, he found himself in a small reception area with a single couch and a thickly painted desk with a middle-aged receptionist behind it. She looked up eagerly when Alex came in, a wide, genuine smile spreading across her face.

"Can I help you?" she asked in a smooth, pleasant voice. Her face was round with large eyes and a thin nose that gave her a pleasant, trustworthy appearance. She wore a simple floral dress, but it was clean and well-pressed.

"This agency made an offer on a property recently," Alex said, easily rehearsing the story he'd cooked up to explain his presence. "I represent the owners and I wanted to discuss your offer."

The woman's smile never wavered as she took out a notepad.

"What is the address of the property?" she asked.

Alex took out his notebook and tore out the top page, dropping it on the pleasant receptionist's desk. He'd prepared that in advance too, with the address for Hathaway House.

"Just a moment," she said, picking up the paper. She opened the top drawer of her desk and pulled out a large book. Like Alex's rune book, it had brass screws holding it together so the pages inside could be changed whenever needed.

Opening the book, the secretary compared the address to a map of Manhattan on the front page. The island had been divided into sections, each bearing its own number. The receptionist checked the address, then moved her finger along the map until she was certain which zone it was in, then she took hold of a tab with the same number and opened to it.

Behind the tab were individual pages for properties in that zone. Presumably they were the ones Manhattan Land and Building was buying or selling.

"Here it is," she said after turning a half dozen pages. "Mr. Buckthorn is responsible for that property." She shut the book, returning it to her desk, then stood. "Who may I say is calling?"

"Alex Lockerby."

"Wait here a moment, Mr. Lockerby. I'll be right back."

Alex nodded and the receptionist left through a door in the back wall. He could hear the creaking of the floor as she went, marveling again at the run-down nature of the building.

A series of heavier creaks announced the receptionist's return with the agent, Buckthorn. He turned out to be a pleasant-looking man in his thirties with wire rimmed spectacles and a lean, narrow frame. His hair was slicked back from his long, narrow face and he wore a smile of perfect geniality.

"Mr. Lockerby," the receptionist said, "this is Mr. Buckthorn."

Buckthorn stuck out his hand and Alex shook it.

"I understand the owners of Hathaway House sent you?" he said. When Alex nodded, his smile got wider. "Let's go back to my office."

He led Alex back through the door and along the creaky hallway to an office at the far end. As they went, Alex noticed a half dozen other offices, most with agents inside either on the phone or going through paperwork. One of the agents looked up as he passed, his face screwing up into a scowl when he saw Alex and Buckthorn.

Must be a very competitive office, Alex thought.

Buckthorn's office was plain and simple, with two wooden chairs facing a cheap but functional desk. A single file cabinet stood in the corner and there was a phone on the desk, but otherwise the room was bare.

"Have a seat, Mr. Lockerby," Buckthorn said as he stepped around the desk to his chair.

Alex took the chair on the right and sat, taking out his silver cigarette case.

"Call me Alex."

"And you can call me Ruben," Buckthorn said. "Now that that's out of the way, why don't you tell me what kind of deal your clients are interested in?"

Alex crossed his legs and lit a cigarette.

"They're not interested in any kind of deal, Ruben," he said. "Over the last few weeks, my clients, Lucius and Ethel Briggs, have been subjected to rude and abusive men offering to buy Hathaway House. They're quite insistent, to the point of being threatening. I came here to tell you, in no uncertain terms, that the Briggs have no intention to sell Hathaway House and to ask you to stop your attempts to acquire it."

Alex had rehearsed that speech several times to make sure it was both polite and direct. He'd heard of such tactics being used in the past, of course. They were especially common when a builder was attempting to put up a new skyscraper and needed the land, but the houses around Hathaway House were still privately owned, so that possibility seemed unlikely.

As he sat in the aftermath of his declaration, Alex watched Ruben Buckthorn's reaction. For a solid half minute he seemed to be at a loss for words.

"I'm sorry if the Briggs have been subjected to threats," he said, in a sincere voice, "but they're not coming from us. I'm the only agent working this property and my only communication was a letter with an offer."

"A very generous offer," Alex said. "Is that how you acquire all your properties? How do you stay in business?"

Buckthorn blushed slightly at that, but rallied quickly.

"In this case, we were making the offer on behalf of a client," he said. "It was their offer."

"They must really want that building. Why would anyone be interested in paying top dollar for a run-down hotel?"

"That's easy," Buckthorn said, "there's a booming business in historical buildings, Alex. People want them for the prestige, or to turn them into museums, or even to refurbish them and trade on their historical mystique."

"What's so important about Hathaway House, then?"

Buckthorn shrugged at that.

"We don't deal in motives, Alex," he said. "We negotiate the sale and take care of the legal paperwork, transfer of title, taxes, that sort of thing."

Alex sat for a long moment, puffing on his cigarette. Buckthorn seemed to be exactly what he appeared, a middle-man with no knowledge of his client's motivations.

"I guess I'd better speak to your client, then," Alex said. "I don't know why he's so keen to buy the Briggs' building, but the bullying tactics have got to stop."

Buckthorn blanched at that and raised his hands in a gesture of helplessness.

"I'm afraid the identity of my client is confidential information," he said. "I can't imagine why someone would go to the lengths you describe, but if I had to guess, whoever is doing this must have some personal connection to the property."

That was one possibility, of course, but Alex suspected that it wasn't anywhere near that simple. Someone with a personal connection would have led with that when they approached the Briggs.

No, this is something bigger, he thought. *Something to do with money, probably a lot of it.*

Alex stood and thanked Buckthorn, asking him to pass the Briggs disinterest in selling along to his client, then turned and left the office.

11

LUNCH WITH A SIDE OF BACON

Since he wasn't getting anywhere with Manhattan Land and Building, Alex caught a cab downtown to the Central Office of Police. Five minutes later he was outside the glass window of Danny Pak's office. Inside, his longtime friend sat behind a heavy desk littered with papers and files, furiously scribbling notes on the top page of an open folder.

Alex stepped around the door and knocked on the glass of the window.

"What are you doing here?" Danny demanded once he recognized his friend.

Alex noted that it took a few seconds for his brain to make the connection.

"You look like hell," he said with a chuckle.

"I used to think Callahan had an easy job," Danny replied, scrawling his signature below the notes he'd made and shutting the folder. "Being a lieutenant is going to grind me down to nothing."

"Don't let Detweiler hear you say that," Alex said, stepping inside the office.

"Maybe if he does, he'll show me the secret to all this," Danny said, setting the file folder on top a stack to his left.

"Don't worry too much," Alex chided him. "You'll get a handle on it soon enough. In the meantime, you look like a man who could use a break."

Danny nodded at that but a moment later, his face clouded over with suspicion.

"What do you want?" he said in a guarded voice.

Alex touched his chest with the tips of his fingers in a gesture of wounded pride.

"Why, Lieutenant Pak," he said with all the maudlin insincerity he could muster, "if I'd known you were going to impugn my honor in such a grotesque fashion, I never would have come."

"What do you want?" Danny repeated, his voice still low and suspicious.

"Just to take you to lunch."

"And?"

Alex placed the back of his hand against his forehead and affected a Southern accent.

"I don't know what this world has come to," he said. "When the very act of a man inviting his bosom companion to share a meal is grounds for such suspicion, what has happened to society? I ask you sir, what has happened to society?"

"And?" Danny said, his voice hardening.

"And go with me to the house of Leslie and Mark Barrett," Alex admitted. "Maybe flash your badge around and ask them a few questions about who bribed them to keep my client's building off the historical buildings registry."

Danny gave Alex an irritated look, but then looked down at the mountain of paperwork in front of him.

"Just a few questions?"

Alex nodded emphatically.

"Maybe suggest that taking a bribe like that could land them in prison," he added.

"The New York Historical Commission is a state government position," Danny said. "If they took a bribe, that *is* a serious crime. They could very well end up in prison."

"So much the better," Alex said. "Now grab your coat."

"Lunch better be somewhere good," Danny growled as he stood.

"How about that place where all the Broadway starlets eat?" Alex suggested. "Sardi's."

"Is their food any good?"

That was a strange question and it shocked Alex's mind back into more serious trains of thought. Danny never passed up a chance to flirt with pretty girls, and Broadway had some of the prettiest in the city.

"I hear it's excellent," Alex replied.

As Danny put on his suit coat, Alex looked for obvious signs of injury or illness but found neither.

He must really need to get out of the office, he thought. Whether that was true or not, it did make Alex feel better about dragging his friend out to help him with a case.

The snug, middle ring home of Leslie Barrett was almost exactly as Alex remembered it. It was a single-story home, surrounded by rosebushes and well-manicured grass. The shutters were whitewashed with no sign of fading and the little brick walkway that ran up from the street had been swept. The only difference was that this time there was a large For Sale sign stuck into the grass by the sidewalk.

"Uh-oh," he said as he climbed out of Danny's green twenty-seven Ford coupe.

Danny looked up sharply at that, but since nothing seemed amiss, he gave Alex a questioning look.

"It wasn't for sale when I was here before," Alex said, nodding toward the sign.

"You said they were spooked when you were here on Saturday," Danny said, coming around the car. Alex had explained the Hathaway House case to him on the ride over. "Maybe they were more scared than they let on."

Alex sighed.

"One way to find out."

They both stepped off the sidewalk onto the bricks that led to the Barretts' front door. When they reached it, Alex raised his hand to knock, but Danny put a restraining hand on his arm. Raising his index finger in front of his lips, he took off his hat and put his ear to the door.

"It's very quiet inside," he said after a moment.

Alex rapped smartly on the door and waited. Danny pushed his ear to the door again, then shook his head.

"You think they went on the lam?" Alex asked.

"Not in so many words," Danny said, putting his hat back on. "Whatever you said to them spooked them enough to move, though."

"All I need is to find out who paid them. Do you think you could get a warrant to look at their bank records?"

"Not without lying to a judge," Danny said. "We don't have probable cause, just some thin guesswork from you. And before you ask, I need to maintain good relations with the judiciary in case I need a warrant for actual police work."

Alex sighed.

"Well, it was worth a try, I guess."

"And we have lots of time for lunch," Danny said, a broad grin spreading across his face.

"Lunch it is," Alex declared, then they piled back into Danny's car and headed for the theater district.

Lunch with Danny took an hour, which was longer than Alex wanted to spend, but his friend was in a much better mood when they parted company, so Alex considered it time well spent.

Once Danny was on his way back to the Central Office, Alex caught a cab south to the Hall of Records. With the three bribed members of the New York Historical Commission safely out of his reach, he needed to find another avenue to get the information he needed to help the Briggs. Perhaps if he could find out who owned Manhattan Land and Building it would give him some leverage.

It was thin, but it was all he had.

Alex had been to the Hall of Records many times to look up everything from land titles to business records. It was safe to say that he knew the building inside and out. That turned out to be a good thing, because every time he entered the building's massive open foyer, he glanced at the information desk sitting right in the center. That was where he'd last seen Edmond.

When Alex came looking for land records, he'd met the helpful elderly man calling himself Edmond Dante. It was only later that Alex discovered he was really Duane King, a man enacting an elaborate revenge on the men and women who had cheated him out of a fortune and therefore sealed the fate of his wife, Beatrice.

King was a killer, plain and simple, but when Alex saw the information desk in the lobby, he couldn't help but remember the kindly man he'd met. He preferred remembering King as Edmond, mostly because as bloody as his revenge had been, Alex understood King's motive. Those he went after had taken everything from him. In the dark recesses of his heart, Alex wondered what he would do if that happened to him. The part that frightened him was that even though he'd like to think he'd never do something like that, some part of him was still unsure.

What would he do if someone took Iggy from him, or Danny, or Sorsha?

He had no good answers to those questions, and he felt his hands clenching into fists. Forcing himself to turn away from the information desk, Alex turned right and went to the bottom of the long stair that ran up the right-side wall all the way to the third floor.

The clerks in the Office of Business Records knew their business and soon Alex was looking at the articles of incorporation for Manhattan Land and Building. Within five minutes, he knew this was a wild goose chase. Manhattan Land and Building was owned by two other companies that had come together to form it. Alex had seen this kind of thing before. Usually it was done when the owner of a business didn't want to be associated with the business itself.

"Mobsters do this all the time," he growled to himself.

It was a shell game where the companies involved never had real owners, only companies attached to them. If you went down the rabbit hole long enough, you'd come back to the top again. It was like the

Gordian rune, designed to be impenetrable so it could protect whatever crook was behind it.

Of course, knowing that Manhattan Land and Building was a shell company was a clue in-and-of itself. It told Alex that someone there had secrets they wanted to stay secret. He could work with that.

Closing the file, Alex handed it back to the record clerk and took the elevator down to the basement. Heading to a janitorial closet he'd used before, Alex opened his vault and stepped inside. The thought of the Gordian rune reminded him that they were taking Sorsha to the slaughterhouse at six. It wasn't the most exotic date he'd taken her on, though it wasn't the worst either, but he did want to be early to pick her up.

Crossing his vault, he headed for the bedroom opposite his kitchen. He'd recently made the bedroom bigger, adding a walk-in closet and an attached bathroom with a large copper tub. The tub was a gift from one of his clients, and Alex had to double the size of his water cistern as a result. Above the tub, a heavy box had been mounted to the wall that held three boiler stones. Alex didn't have hot running water in his new bathroom, but he could heat the tub in less than ten minutes, so it didn't much matter.

Stripping out of his suit, Alex hung it up neatly in his vast closet. He removed his button-up shirt as well, tossing it into a laundry hamper by the entrance. Down at the end of the hanging garments, Alex had built a dresser cabinet into the wall, then installed actual wooden drawers in it. From the top drawer, Alex removed a lightweight cotton pull-over shirt, then retrieved a pair of dungarees from the next drawer down. Putting them on, Alex picked out a thick work sweater from the hanging row, putting that on as well. A heavy set of work shoes completed the ensemble, and now Alex looked like any common laborer.

Satisfied that he was ready for the work that needed to be done in the slaughterhouse, Alex put his rune book and pocketwatch into his kit bag and headed for the door to his Empire Tower apartment. The slaughterhouse was on the west side by the rail yards, so Empire Tower gave him the shortest travel time.

Iggy was already at the slaughterhouse when Alex arrived. It was a run-down wooden building that had been there for going on twenty years. A faded sign above the large carriage doors in front read, *Carlin Meat Processing*, complete with the image of a smiling cartoon pig.

Alex entered on the main floor where rows of pig pens all fed down to the end where the giant chain wheel stood. As he moved along the pens, workers at the end looped a chain around the hind leg of one of the pigs and, as the wheel turned, it jerked the pig up into the air. The moment the pig felt the pull, it began squealing. It was more of a scream, really, and it gave Alex chills to hear it. Somehow the pig knew what was coming and shrieked in mortal terror.

"Mr. Lockerby," a voice pulled his attention away from the drama at the back of the room.

Alex turned to find J.D. Carlin standing behind him. J.D. was a short, heavy-set man with a balding head, a flat nose, and deep-set eyes. He bore a striking resemblance to the swine in which he dealt and it was all Alex could do not to chuckle every time he saw him.

"J.D." Alex said, giving the proprietor a friendly nod.

"Dr. Bell is upstairs in the loft," he said. "He said to send you up once you arrived."

Alex thanked J.D. and made for the long stairway that ran along the back wall. As he passed the pen in the middle of the room, Alex could see the rune papers Iggy had attached to poles around the pen. Originally, he had simply stuck the papers to the posts of the pen, but that made calibrating the distances more difficult. The metal rods could simply be driven into the ground wherever they were needed.

"You're here early," Iggy said as Alex reached the top of the stairs. He had a chalk line laid out on the floor from a spot above one of the runes below. He wore a pair of overalls with a heavy work shirt and muck boots.

"Those people that got bribed picked up and left," Alex said with a shrug. "They even put their house up for sale."

Iggy raised an eyebrow at that, then turned back to his measuring.

"Sounds like you're on to something," he said. "Now hold the end of this line while I make a few more measurements."

Alex took the line and Iggy measured again before snapping it and leaving a straight chalk mark on the floor. The life transference rune required precise placement of the rune papers, both in their distance from each other and the position of the chair.

With Alex there to help, the work went quickly, and soon they had everything arranged.

"All right," Alex said, standing back to survey their work. "Should I go get Sorsha?"

Iggy pulled out his pocketwatch and flipped open the cover.

"It's only five," he said. "Let's wait an hour for the workers to clear out. Also, I want to get out of these clothes and into something more appropriate before I see the Sorceress."

Alex nodded in agreement, then chalked a door on the wall and opened his vault. Iggy was right about changing clothes, and Alex suspected he need a shower before he donned his suit again. The good part was that he and Iggy could get to the brownstone through the vault, and Alex could pick up Sorsha the same way. If he left the door in the slaughterhouse open, they could all return that way as well, so Alex closed his security cage door behind him and followed Iggy to the brownstone.

Two hours later, Alex escorted Sorsha through his vault to the slaughterhouse. Iggy was waiting there in one of his best suits, smoking a cigar to ward off the aroma of the pig pens below. When the aroma reached the sorceress, she looked startled, then made a hand waving gesture and spoke in her magic voice.

"You certainly take me to the most exotic places," she said, leaning heavily on him.

"Only the best for you."

"Now, are you going to explain this process to me," she asked, "or do you just expect me to trust you?"

"Right this way, my dear," Iggy said, indicating the chair he'd put in the center of the open floor. "We've already placed runes around the hogs below. With you in the chair, we'll activate the construct, and it will transfer a portion of the lives of the swine into you."

"That'll give us more time to find out how to break the Gordian rune," Alex supplied.

"Is this safe?" she asked as Alex helped her into the chair.

"Nothing at all to it," Iggy assured her. "Both Alex and I have undergone this process."

He left off the part about its being intense the first time you used it, but Alex saw no reason to worry the sorceress by explaining that.

"Now," Iggy said once Sorsha had composed herself on the chair, "sit still and I'll get the process started." He turned and went to where he'd set his doctor's bag on the wooden floor of the loft.

Alex reached into his pocket and pulled out two folded pieces of flash paper, then followed his mentor.

"Here," he said, handing one of the runes to Iggy.

"One of your climate runes?" he said after opening it. "What's this for?"

"Remember how intense the transfer can be? Especially the first time?"

Iggy thought about that, then nodded emphatically.

"I see," he said, sticking the paper to his suit coat. "Good thinking."

He lit the paper with his cigar, then touched the tip to the paper Alex had stuck to his vest.

"All right, Sorsha," Iggy said, picking up the master rune paper. "The magic will take a few moments to get going, so I want you to sit there and try to relax."

Sorsha gave him a weak smile and nodded.

"Ready?" Iggy asked, placing the rune paper onto a chalk 'X' he'd marked on the floor. "Here we go."

12

FINAL OFFER

Alex paced back and forth in his vault's little bedroom until Iggy demanded that he stop. He sat in one of the simple wooden chairs from the kitchen across the hall, attempting to read a book in spite of Alex's nervous energy.

"She should be awake by now," the younger man growled.

Between them, in Alex's bed, lay Sorsha, covered by a blanket. The rune had gone off normally and at first it seemed everything had worked fine. Sorsha experienced the initial rush of energy that Alex remembered so clearly. In his case, he'd been tied to a wooden chair that he'd shattered by simply standing up. Sorsha hadn't been tied down and when the rush of energy hit her, she screamed and froze the attic of the slaughterhouse solid in an inch-thick layer of ice. Only the forethought of Alex's climate rune kept Iggy and himself from being killed instantly.

After Alex had torn the chair apart, he'd collapsed on the floor, unable to lift himself for almost a quarter of an hour. Sorsha had collapsed, but she'd been unconscious. When she didn't wake after five minutes, Alex picked her up and carried her to his vault's bedroom.

That had been almost an hour ago.

"Something's wrong," he said, clenching his fists in frustration.

"Obviously," Iggy said, turning a page in the book he was reading. "But pacing about like a tiger in a cage isn't helping. I suspect that Sorsha's body has been severely weakened by the Gordian rune that's sapping her life. The transference rune probably put a great deal of strain on her."

"Which likely means we won't be able to use it again."

Iggy thought about that for a moment, then nodded.

"It's likely," he said in a low voice.

"Meaning that whatever life energy we managed to give her…"

"Is going to be all we can give her," Iggy finished.

Iggy reached in his pocket and pulled out a pocket watch. It resembled the one Alex carried in his vest, but this one was smaller in diameter, lacked the flip-open cover, and was made of silver. Ladies often used these kinds of watches, pinning the fob to their shoulder and letting the watch hang down into the breast pocket of a jacket or dress.

"What' that?" Alex asked.

"Yesterday, I realized that when I wrote the rune that made the life meter in your watch, I didn't make just one," Iggy said, handing Alex the little silver watch. "I kept a copy in my files in case of emergency. When I remembered that, I figured we'd better make one for Sorsha."

Alex turned the little watch over. Like his, the back cover had been inscribed with half a dozen runes that would create a magical third hand in the watch. The magic hand would reveal how much life energy Sorsha had remaining. Or, it would, if Sorsha were awake to bond with the construct.

As Alex stared at it, the little watch flatly refused to tell him anything.

"Put it in your pocket," Iggy said without looking up from his book. "You can give it to Sorsha when she wakes up."

"You mean if—," Alex began but Iggy waved him silent.

"Why don't you go put the kettle on," he said. "I'm sure Sorsha will want a nice cup of tea to fortify her when she wakes up, and I could use one myself."

Alex clenched his teeth, but realized the common sense of Iggy's words. He dropped the silver watch into his pocket and crossed the hall to his little kitchen.

The stove he'd installed was a new, electric one with a built-in link to Empire Tower. Alex turned the knob and the metal coil on the top began to heat up. He filled the kettle with water from the sink, then set it on the stove to boil.

He wanted to go back across the hall, but the only thing he was accomplishing by pacing back and forth in his bedroom was to wear out the rug on the floor. With a sigh of frustration, he sat down at his kitchen table and pulled out his notebook. To keep his mind off Sorsha, he flipped through his two active cases.

He still wasn't convinced that the death of Fredrick Chance had been an accident. There were plenty of people who would have benefited by killing him, but all of them had alibis.

If you eliminate the impossible, and nothing remains, Iggy's voice echoed inside his head, *then some part of the impossible must be possible.*

Tommy Waverly's alibi was that his being in a wheelchair made it impossible for him to journey from his house to the factory unobserved. That certainly seemed like an ironclad alibi. There was a cure for polio, though, and if Tommy had been taking it long enough, he might be able to walk.

Of course, Tommy claimed that money was the source of his dispute with his wife, or rather her withholding the money for his treatment. Alex needed to find out if he was really cut off. If he was, then there was no chance he was getting alchemical treatments for polio.

Then there was Lillian. She was at an opera the night Fredrick died, but she had a private box. Alex had been in a private box, and he knew they were both dark and high above the floor seats. She might have sent someone to pretend to be her, or she might have snuck out during the performance. The theater wasn't too far from her office, so she could have been out and back before the final curtain.

I'll have to interview anyone who saw her, he thought, not looking forward to the task of tracking them down.

And on top of all of that, there were the other companies who may or may not want to scoop up Waverly Radio in her time of need.

Deciding not to worry about that, Alex flipped a few pages to his notes on the Briggs and their troubles with Hathaway House.

"There's definitely something funny about that real estate company," he said.

Before he could go on, however, the kettle began to whistle.

He rose and lifted the kettle off the burner, switching it off as he went. Taking out a plain serving tray, he set out two china cups and filled them with the hot water, adding tea bags to each cup. Satisfied both cups were steeping properly, Alex picked up the tray and headed across the hall.

When he arrived, he found Sorsha sitting up in bed while Iggy listened to her breathing with a stethoscope. Alex knew he was concerned, but he wasn't prepared for the sudden wave of weakness that threatened to make him drop the tray.

"Oh thank God," Sorsha gasped when she saw Alex. Her voice was raspy and rough. "My mouth feels like the Sahara."

Alex steadied himself and bent down so the sorceress could take one of the cups.

"Everything sounds normal," Iggy said, removing his stethoscope and dropping it into his bag. He reached out and took the second cup from the tray, blowing on it before sipping.

"Needs more time to steep," he said, wrinkling his nose.

If Sorsha thought so, it didn't affect her. She drank the weak liquid down in one gulp.

"Much better," she said. "Since I'm not dead, I take it your life transference rune worked."

"Indeed it did," Iggy said.

Alex set the empty tray on the bed and dug the silver watch out of his pocket.

"Ah, excellent timing lad," Iggy said, as Alex held the watch out to Sorsha. "This will help us determine how well the rune worked. Take the watch and hold it between your hands."

Sorsha hesitated with her hand above the watch, then she took a breath and picked it up.

"Nothing to worry about, my dear," Iggy said, reaching out to touch the watch fob that dangled between the sorceress' hands. As he did, Alex felt a rune activate and a red glow began to emanate from the front of the watch.

"What did you do?"

"The watch has a construct on it," Alex explained. "Look at the face."

Sorsha opened her hands and did a double take when she saw the tiny magic hand among the normal black ones.

"What does this one mean?" she said, pointing to the face. "It's pointing at eleven."

Iggy craned his neck to see the watch, then looked up at Alex.

The hand was red.

When Iggy first used his runic construct on Alex, the hand had turned blue, which meant he had more than one year of life. A red hand meant that despite their best efforts, Sorsha only had 11 months left.

Probably less than that, Alex thought. After all, the Gordian rune was stealing her energy away at an ever-accelerating rate.

When Alex's wandering thoughts returned to the moment, Iggy was explaining the magical hand to Sorsha.

"Keep watch on it over the next few days and we'll see how it's going."

Sorsha nodded, and slipped the watch into her pocket.

"At least we've got more time to figure out how those Legion bastards are killing me."

Alex nodded, giving her a smile he didn't feel.

"Well," she said, sliding her legs off the side of the bed. "I'm hungry, what do you gentlemen say to dinner?"

"That's an excellent idea," Iggy said, his mustache fluffing up as he smiled.

Alex woke early the following morning. He hadn't planned on being up before seven, but almost everything had gone perfectly with Sorsha the night before. She'd taken longer than he or Iggy expected to recover from the initial transfer, but after that she'd been hungry, which was a good sign. After a leisurely dinner at the Lunch Box, Sorsha was tired again, so Alex walked her home. He wasn't happy about her only having eleven months of life energy, but with luck that would be enough time to figure out the Gordian rune.

Throwing his legs over the side of his bed, Alex pushed the Gordian rune from his mind. He needed to finish up the Waverly Radio case and then track down whoever really owned Manhattan Land and Building.

He hurried through his morning routine, stopping only long enough to slap some of Iggy's scrambled eggs and bacon between two pieces of bread before heading to his office.

Sherry had put a folder on his desk, outlining all the research she'd done into Waverly Radio's rival companies. Alex reviewed the notes as he finished his sandwich and by the time he was done, his pool of potential suspects had dwindled significantly.

There were a couple of small companies like Waverly in the radio business, Addison and Emerson, that had offices in New York. The problem with them was that they *were* small, with narrow profit margins. According to the research Sherry had done, none of them had the ready money to buy out Waverly. They might sell off property, but Sherry's notes said they both owed on their production facilities, meaning they couldn't borrow any substantial amount of money against them.

Other small companies like Motorola, Stewart-Warner, and Zenith were out of state, with no offices in the city. That didn't mean they couldn't have arranged the death of Fredrick Chance, but if his death was murder, it betrayed a certain familiarity with the man and his habits. Alex doubted an out of state company could have pulled off a murder that sophisticated at a distance.

The big players in the radio business were Philco and RCA. They certainly had enough ready money to make a bid for Waverly in her current, diminished condition, but as far as he could tell neither had. Of the big two, only RCA was located in New York. According to Sherry, their manufacturing plant was on Long Island, but their corporate offices and broadcast studios were in the imaginatively named RCA Building, which was part of Rockefeller Center.

Of all the names on his list, RCA was the eight hundred pound gorilla. They did radio, television, and had a studio in Hollywood. If they wanted to buy out a small fish like Waverly, all they had to do was make them an offer they couldn't refuse.

Unless they did refuse it, he thought. Waverly was a family company, and maybe the family wouldn't give her up for any amount of money.

With a sigh, Alex closed the folder on RCA and sat staring at it for a minute. It was highly unlikely that such a big company would resort to murder to take out Waverly, especially since they hadn't made any public move on her devalued stock.

Maybe they think it will go lower still, he thought.

He shook his head and stood, picking up his suit coat from the back of his chair. It didn't matter what he guessed at this point. The only thing to do was to go over to Rockefeller Center and find out.

It only took Alex ten minutes to get to Rockefeller Center by sky bug, but he spent considerably longer trying to locate the office of RCA's radio manufacturing division. Everyone assumed he wanted the head of broadcast radio and he had to explain himself over and over. Eventually, a helpful secretary pointed him to a corner office on one of the lower floors. It had a polished door with a brass nameplate that read, *Jared McNamara*.

Alex knocked and, when there was no answer, he tentatively opened the door. Mr. McNamara's office was large and tastefully done, with white shelves lining the walls full of impressive-looking knick-knacks. A large desk made of warm-colored maple stood by a large window so that sunlight illuminated its marble top. A white leather couch was against the wall opposite the shelves and three comfortable looking chairs stood on the near side of the desk. To the left side of the desk, there was a narrow doorway with a handle but no lock.

As Alex surveyed the room, he noted how everything in the room was clean and orderly. Even the papers on McNamara's desk were neatly stacked and perpendicular to the edge. The only thing that looked out of place in this bastion of organization was a table behind the door with an overlarge brass and wood contraption on it. It had a large disk in the middle with some kind of picture printed on it and a thick glass lens to one side. The rear of the device was contained in a wooden box with vents cut in the sides. Alex stooped down to squint inside, but he couldn't see anything.

"Don't touch that," a new voice interrupted his examination.

Alex straightened up and found a short, energetic-looking man emerging from the narrow door on the opposite side of the room. He had chestnut brown hair that he parted in the middle, with brown eyes, a short nose, and a smile full of perfectly straight teeth. He had on a white shirt with suspenders holding up his trousers and a blue tie that matched the suspenders.

"That's an original Zoopraxiscope," he said, a wide grin spreading across his face. "She's a beauty, isn't she?"

"Uh," Alex said, caught off guard by the man's appearance. "Two questions: Are you Mr. McNamara? And what's a Zoopraxiscope?"

The man chuckled and held out his hand.

"That's me," he said. "Call me Jared."

"Alex Lockerby," Alex said, taking the man's offered hand.

"And this here is a Zoopraxiscope," Jared said, jerking his thumb at the machine. "It's the original movie projector. Built by a man named Eadweard Muybridge; he's the photographer who took the pictures of the galloping horse."

Alex didn't know who Muybridge was or what pictures Jared was talking about, so he put on a wise face and nodded sagely.

"I'd show you how it works," Jared said, crossing his arms over his chest, "but I just got this, and I haven't had a chance to make sure it's in working order." He turned as if he suddenly remembered something and took what looked like a small lamp with a black shade off a shelf. "This will give you an idea."

He placed the lamp on his immaculate desk and Alex could see that the shade had slits running regularly around the rim. Jared put his fingers on the rim of the shade and then spun it. The top and bottom were apparently connected by a bearing that let the top turn.

"Look down inside here," Jared instructed.

Alex stepped over and glanced into the shade. On the inside of the round part was a white paper, mounted to the inside, near the bottom.

DAN WILLIS

To Alex it looked like a smear of ink, but he could tell it was supposed to be an image of some kind.

"Not like that," Jared chuckled. "You have to look through the slats on the top."

Alex crouched down so he could do what Jared said and suddenly the smear of dark ink transformed into the crude likeness of a galloping horse.

"Neat, huh?" Jared said, sitting down behind his desk. "Now, what can I do for you, Alex?"

"Are you in charge of radio production for RCA?"

Jared's smile didn't waver, and he nodded.

"So, why do you have an early projector?" Alex couldn't help but ask.

"Moving pictures are the future," Jared replied. "Our television division is going to be producing more programming than ever before next year."

"Not a very positive attitude for the head of radio production," Alex chuckled, "unless that projector is a gift for whoever is in charge of all that new television production."

Jared looked shocked for a moment, then he grinned and shrugged.

"Are you an ad buyer?" he asked.

"I'm a private detective," Alex explained. "I assume you know about the troubles Waverly Radio has been having?"

Jared shrugged.

"Only what I read in the paper," he said. "Waverly had a good thing going with that magically-enhanced tuner of theirs. It's too bad their runewright died."

"The death of their runewright has dropped their stock quite a bit," Alex said. "Seems ripe for some bigger fish to come along and swallow them up."

Alex was worried Jared might take offense at his obvious inference, but instead, the man laughed.

"Why would anyone want to buy out Waverly?" he said. "The only thing they had going for them was their magic receivers, and the guy who made them is dead. Everybody knows that was his proprietary technology, so with him dead, Waverly is only a little company with a little factory and nothing special about them."

"What about RCA?" Alex asked. "Wouldn't you want more manufacturing space?"

Jared laughed again.

"You obviously haven't been over to our factory. We're got more than enough space. I don't know where you're going with all this, Alex, but there's really nothing worthwhile at Waverly. Without their magic receiver, they're pretty much worthless."

Alex didn't know if he believed Jared, but he was pretty sure Beauregard Mayweather would be able to shed more light on it.

"Between you and me, Alex," Jared went on, "Waverly wasn't going to be around much longer anyway. New radio towers are going up all over America and pretty soon, you won't need a fancy receiver to get all the stations you want."

Alex could tell that whatever the truth really was, Jared McNamara believed what he was saying. Rising, he shook the radio man's hand again, thanked him for his time, and headed for the elevators.

13

THE AGENT

When Alex reached the lobby of the RCA building, he made for the bank of phone booths along the side wall. His meeting with Jared McNamara hadn't gone the way he expected, but it had been profitable. RCA had clearly looked at acquiring Waverly, but in their opinion Fredrick Chase's death made the company virtually worthless as an acquisition. If RCA thought this way, it was a good bet that every other company thought the same.

It did give more motive to the smaller local companies, though. The real question would be if any of those companies would be willing to kill to destroy Waverly? As far as Sherry's research indicated, there wasn't a clear heir apparent among the other small companies. If that was right, Waverly's loss of their competitive advantage wouldn't change much for any individual company.

"So why kill Fredrick Chance?" he growled as he fished in his pocket for a nickel. The more he thought about it, the more likely it seemed that Fredrick's death was what it appeared to be, an accident.

Except he simply didn't believe that.

"Lockerby Investigations," Sherry's voice greeted him, pulling his mind out of his musings.

"It's me," he said. "I just got finished at RCA and I'm pretty sure it's a dead end. Do you have anything for me?"

There was a pause on the line that aroused his suspicion.

"I don't have anything definite," she hedged, "but I think you need to come back to the office. The sooner the better."

Alex suppressed the chill that threatened to race up his spine. Sherry was an augur, one of the incredibly rare practitioners of foretelling magic. Her magic was finicky, but when it made an appearance, Alex made a point to listen. The way she spoke, in vague terms with a hesitant voice, told him that her entreaty wasn't a suggestion.

"Any special reason?" he asked, not sure he wanted an answer.

"Something bad is coming?" she said, but her voice was tentative.

"I'll be right over," he said, then hung up. This close to the core, it wan't worth a vault rune, so Alex put on his hat and headed for the sky crawler station.

Eleven minutes later, Alex stepped off the elevator and turned left toward his office. His door looked exactly like it had every day since he'd first moved into the building, but with every step he took, he could feel a weight pressing down on him.

"Shake it off," he muttered as he grabbed the doorknob. "Sherry's got you spooked."

He took a breath and pulled the door open. Sherry sat behind her desk, looking up sharply as he came in. Other than her, the room was empty.

"I'm here."

"You're early."

The words were barely out of her mouth when Alex heard the elevator chime out in the hall. He turned and reached for the door.

"Wait," Sherry said. "Come over by my desk."

Alex had been trusting her hunches from the beginning and he wasn't about to stop now, so he strode across the room and sat on the edge of the desk as he'd done hundreds of times before.

A moment later the door opened, and Ethel Briggs came in. Of all

DAN WILLIS

the things Alex was expecting, Ethel wasn't it. She was dressed in a dark dress with a white vest and matching cuffs on the end of her sleeves. As she came in, she quickly turned and shut the door behind her.

"Mrs. Briggs," Alex said, rising.

"I'm sorry to bother you, Mr. Lockerby," she said, turning to face him. Her face was drawn, and her eyes were unfocused.

"Are you all right?" he asked.

"I need to settle my bill," she said, opening her handbag.

"I'm still working on finding out who's been harassing you," he said. "That real estate company you heard from is a shell company, so I'm headed out to the hall of records to figure out who really owns it."

"Mr. — Alex," Ethel said. "I don't need your services anymore. I'm sorry."

"What about your husband?"

"He's dead."

It actually took Alex a moment to process what Ethel said.

"How?" he finally demanded.

"He's been worried about the house," she said, her voice small and detached, "staying up to watch it at night. Last night he went down to the store at the end of the block for cigarettes. He didn't come back."

She clutched her hands to her chest and the dam holding her emotions back cracked.

"Someone found his body this morning," she sobbed. "The police said he'd been mugged."

Alex didn't believe that for a second. Whoever wanted Hathaway House stepped up their efforts to get it.

They stepped up because you started pushing, he told himself. *You went to Manhattan Land and Building and two days later Lucius Briggs is dead.*

This is your fault.

Alex crossed to the door and put his arm around Ethel's shoulders as she sobbed quietly.

"I'm sorry," he said. "I'll go to the police. I have friends there. I'll find out who did this, and I will make sure they pay."

"It doesn't matter," Ethel said, leaning against him. "My family lives in Baltimore. I'm going to stay with them. I can't afford to lose any more."

"No," Sherry said, coming around to stand in front of Ethel. "You deserve something back. We can't bring Lucius back, but we can stop the people who took him from you."

"I can't pay you. Lucius handled our money, and it will take me weeks to figure everything out."

"Your money's no good here," Alex said, trying to keep the anger out of his voice. "Go to your family, but leave their number with Sherry. I'll handle things here."

Ethel shuddered, then pushed away from him, wiping her eyes with a handkerchief from her handbag. She hesitated a minute, then finally looked back at him and nodded.

"Leave the key to Hathaway House," Alex said. "Whatever these people want, I'll make sure they don't get it." He looked to Sherry and she nodded back, indicating that she could take care of things here. "I'm going to the Central Office. Make sure Mrs. Briggs gets on the train safely."

Sherry nodded and Alex turned and left.

If the police believed that Lucius Briggs had been killed in a mugging, then his body was already in the morgue and whatever detective caught the case would be typing up the paperwork. Muggings were crimes of convenience, their only motive was whatever cash or valuables the mark had on them. Unless there was an eyewitness, the police would consider the murder of Lucius Briggs a cold case and file it away. They might make an effort to track down his watch or his wedding ring, assuming they were suitably unique, but that was all.

Alex clenched his fists as he rode the elevator up to the Central Office's fifth floor. He reminded himself that the police weren't being negligent or callous; cases without clues or a solid motive were often impossible to solve. Normally, Alex would try to convince the detective in charge to reopen the case, or at least let him work it for a few days.

Not this time, he thought.

With the mugging relegated to the cold case file, Alex could get the detective to give him the file. It was likely the man would be happy to be rid of it. That would give Alex all the information on the mugging with no authority figures looking over his shoulder while he tracked down Lucius' killer.

That suited Alex just fine.

The chime on the elevator rang and the automatic door opened, revealing a narrow hallway along the right side of the building. At the far end, the hallway turned to run along the back of the Central Office; that was where the offices were for the lieutenants who ran the various divisions. About halfway down the hall on the left was a set of swinging double doors that would lead Alex into the bullpen where the detectives had their desks. That was where he would end up, since one of those detectives had Lucius Briggs' case file, but he wouldn't know which one until he made another stop first, so Alex passed the double doors and headed for Danny's office.

When he reached it, he looked through the long window that made up the front wall. Danny was sitting behind his desk in his shirtsleeves with his suit coat thrown over the back of his chair. Several folders sat open in front of him, and he quickly signed something in one of them, then dropped it in the out box. He looked up as Alex came around the door frame.

"I don't care where you want to go to lunch," he said, "I'm too busy."

Alex chuckled at that despite his mood. He'd gotten in the habit of only seeing Danny when he needed something and that had to change. He simply didn't have time to think about that now.

"I just need you to look up a case for me," he said. "A guy got murdered over on the lower east side late last night, name of Lucius Briggs. The detective in charge called it a mugging."

Danny looked up from his work and ran an appraising eye over Alex. After a moment, he raised his eyes to meet Alex's gaze.

"I'm going to assume you think it wasn't a mugging," he said.

Alex nodded.

"Lucius was a client," he admitted. "Someone had been strong-arming him, trying to get him to sell a house he'd inherited. Saturday I went by a real estate company that made an offer on the property. They claimed not to know anything about the high-pressure tactics, but two days after I visit them, my client is a guest in your morgue." He gave Danny a direct look and raised his left eyebrow.

"Okay," Danny said after a moment. "It's very coincidental, I'll give you that."

"And we both know that there are no coincidences where murder is concerned."

That wasn't technically true, of course. Coincidences happened all the time, murder or no. For a detective, however, it was always a good idea to assume there were no coincidences in your case, at least until they could be confirmed.

"You got anything else?" Danny asked.

"No, but someone's got the file and Lucius' body is in the morgue. All I need is a little access and I'll know if there's anything nefarious to my client's death."

Danny wavered for a minute, then picked up his desk phone and pushed one of the numbered buttons that ran along the bottom of the base.

"There was a mugging death on the east side last night," he said. "Find out who caught the case, will you." There was a pause while Danny listened, then he looked up at Alex. "What was the victim's name?"

"Lucius Briggs," he said.

Danny repeated what Alex told him, then hung up.

"You might as well sit," he said, indicating one of the wooden chairs in front of his desk. "It'll take a few minutes to track it down."

Alex growled to himself, but sat down.

"It's not your fault," his friend said, going back to his paperwork.

"Says you," Alex snapped.

Danny looked up with a look that managed to be both sad and amused.

"You private dicks don't go through this very often," he began, "but every homicide detective out there has to face this all the time." Danny nodded in the direction of the bullpen. "It's an occupational

DAN WILLIS

hazard. You start investigating a case and suddenly one of your witnesses is killed. It leaves you wondering if you missed something, if something you did got that person killed because you weren't smart enough to stop it." He put his pen down and sat up, staring off into the space above Alex's head. "If you let it get to you, it'll drive you mad, or at the very least make you second guess everything you do, everything you think." He dropped his eyes back to Alex's. "It's poison."

Danny was making sense and it irritated Alex. In his years of being a private detective, he'd never lost a client who had come to him for protection. He had to face the fact that his friend was right.

"How do you let something like that go?" he said with a frustrated sigh.

"You need to remember that it wasn't you who killed Mr. Briggs," Danny explained in a matter-of-fact voice. "Someone else did that. Maybe they acted sooner because you were on the case, but if they were willing to kill him now, they'd be willing to kill him later."

Alex nodded. Danny made a lot of sense. Whoever killed Lucius Briggs might not have known he'd hired a private detective. They might have simply grown impatient and decided to move their plot along the hard way.

"Lieutenant," a familiar voice said from the open door. "I found out who caught that mugging you wanted."

Alex turned to see the round face and unkempt hair of Detective Derek Nicholson.

"Oh, hiya Alex," he said, his face splitting into a wide grin. "This something you're looking into?"

Alex shrugged and tried to appear disinterested.

"He was a part of a case. I just want to make sure this mugging is unrelated."

He could tell Danny his real motives for wanting the police file, but it wouldn't do to have his name attached to a case the police considered closed. If he proved that Lucius had been murdered, some detective would have egg on his face. Some detectives took things like that personally and Alex already had enough enemies in the department.

"Well, the case went to Detective Lowe," Nicholson said. "He's one of Lieutenant Scott's boys."

Alex felt relieved at the news, but Danny's face clouded over for a moment.

"Thanks, Derek," he said.

Alex waited until Nicholson was gone, then gave Danny a questioning look.

"What?" he said.

"Remember a year ago, when someone in the department was trying to spike my wheel?"

Alex had never gotten the details, but then Lieutenant Callahan had said that someone had it out for Danny.

"Turns out it was Lieutenant Scott," Danny explained.

A lot of people didn't like Asians, and this might just be simple bigotry, but Alex decided not to lead with that.

"He got some kind of beef with you?"

Danny shrugged.

"Not that I know of, but he might have been trying to make Callahan look bad for having me on his team."

"That was right before he became Captain," Alex said. "You think maybe Scott was on the short list?"

Danny shrugged again.

"I don't know, but what I do know is that he doesn't like me much. He keeps a civil tongue when we talk, but he makes Sorsha look warm and fuzzy."

The mention of Sorsha made Alex grimace involuntarily, but he recovered quickly. He'd escorted her to work that morning, through his vault, and she'd seemed fine.

"I won't have to bother the lieutenant," Alex said, pushing thoughts of the Ice Queen from his mind. "I met Detective Lowe before, when I was investigating the death of Hugo Aires. That was a closed case and he practically shoved the folder into my hands."

Danny looked dubious, then shook his head.

"Don't mention my name," he said, going back to his paperwork.

Alex promised to restrain himself, then headed for the bullpen.

The elevator chimed as it lurched to a halt and Alex waited for the slow automatic door to open. Stepping out into the dimly lit, tile hallway, he turned right and headed down to the second door on the left.

"You," the snide voice of the county coroner assaulted him. "What frivolous task have you brought to waste my time today?"

Dr. Daniel Wagner had replaced the previous coroner, Dr. Anderson, a few years ago and ever since, he'd made Alex's life difficult. Wagner was a lean, handsome man in his thirties with an imperious look and a roving eye.

"Actually," Alex said, dropping the official police file on the Lucius Briggs mugging onto Wagner's desk, "I came to make your job easier."

"What's this?" Wagner asked, not bothering to pick it up.

"Detective Lowe wanted me to take a look at his mugging victim," Alex lied. He expected Wagner to protest, but instead the man's haughty expression faltered.

"You mean that milquetoast idiot actually paid attention for once?" he said.

Alex had no idea what the coroner was talking about, but it seemed positive, so he smiled and nodded.

"Well," Wagner said with a raised eyebrow. "I can't speak for the man's taste in consultants, but at least he's listening to his betters. I'll have to raise my opinion of him."

Wagner stood and headed for the door, leaving Alex to scoop up the folder and hurry after him.

"The body of Mr. Briggs is in operating theater two," he said, leading the way down past the elevator to the far end of the corridor. "Use whatever you've got in your charlatan's bag of tricks, then come get me." He unlocked the door with a key, then pushed it open for Alex. "Let's see if you can figure out why I think this man wasn't killed by accident."

With that, Wagner turned and stalked back to his office. Alex watched him go until he was out of sight. Apparently, the coroner didn't enjoy having his opinions ignored by little people like police detectives. Alex filed that particular bit of information away for a rainy day, then took a deep breath and turned to face the body of his former client.

14

MURPHY

Alex set down his kit bag, then pulled the white sheet off Lucius Briggs' body. With the exception of being completely naked, he appeared as Alex had seen him in life. He even seemed to retain that look of boundless enthusiasm he'd had when telling Alex about his plans for Hathaway House.

Sighing, Alex wadded up the cloth and tossed it on the equipment table by his kit. He would check for magical residue, of course, but first came the examination of the body itself. It was possible to destroy physical evidence when using the oculus simply by moving the body to get a better look at something. Since magical residue was fairly durable, Iggy had impressed on Alex the need for the physical examination first.

Following his mentor's methods, Alex circled the body, looking for anything that was out of place. As far as he could see, there were no wounds or abrasions. Moving to Lucius' hands, Alex turned each one palm up and inspected each finger. There weren't any marks to be seen there, or on the backs, so he put down the hand he was examining.

"I hate to admit it," he said to Lucius' corpse, "but Dr. Wagner was right. You never saw the man who did this to you."

Confident in what he would find, Alex pulled the body toward him, then rolled it over onto the cold, metal gurney. The blow that had killed Lucius was plainly evident now, a long, round depression in the back of the man's skull.

"Pipe," Alex guessed, and he gently probed the wound with his fingers. It was deeper on one side and angled upward to the opposite edge of the wound. As he moved, his fingers found a smaller, more shallow depression higher up on the head.

Alex sighed and took a step back. He didn't need to examine the body further; he knew what had happened. Still, Iggy would chastise him if he left the job half done.

"All right," he said out loud. "Let's get this over with."

"Took you long enough," Dr. Wagner sneered when Alex finally opened his office door.

"Some of us like to be thorough," Alex snapped back.

Wagner gave him a long-suffering look and sat back in his chair, crossing his legs as he did so.

"Well Mr. Thorough, what did you find?"

"This was no mugging," Alex said. "Lucius Briggs was murdered."

Wagner raised an eyebrow as he fished a cigarette pack out of his shirt pocket.

"And how do you know that?" he said, flicking a gold lighter to life and touching it to the end of his cigarette.

"A mugger would have brandished a weapon and demanded money or valuables," Alex explained. "He would only have attacked if Mr. Briggs had refused him."

"Maybe he did."

Alex shook his head at that.

"First," he explained, "if someone in front of Lucius had attacked him, there would be defensive wounds on his hands…and there aren't any. Second, there are only two wounds on the body, both made by a pipe or a metal rod. One is shallow and high on the back of the head; that was the first wound."

"How do you know that?" Wagner interrupted, blowing smoke at Alex.

"Because the second wound is deep on one end and gets shallow as it goes," Alex said. "That's because Lucius was on the ground when his assailant did that. That's why the wound track slopes up."

"Very good," Wagner said, sarcasm in his voice. "The only reason for the assailant to hit Mr. Briggs while he was face down and stunned from the first blow, is if whoever did it intended to kill him all along. A cold-blooded murder."

"No doubt about it," Alex said, managing not to growl out the words. He really needed to find out who did this and make them pay. Lucius had been a decent sort with big dreams and goals to make his little corner of the city a better place.

And someone murdered him for it, Alex thought.

"I have to admit, scribbler," Wagner went on, oblivious to Alex's internal struggle, "I'll have to raise my opinion of you. Not much, of course, but you did pretty good today. Now run along and tell Detective Lowe to pay attention the next time he feels inclined to dismiss my professional judgement."

"I'll be sure to let him know," Alex said, giving Wagner the most insincere smile he could muster. Then he picked up his kit and headed for the elevator.

The sky bug ride from the morgue to Empire Tower only took a few minutes, but Alex used the time to go over what he knew. As the crawler arrived at Empire Station, he had to admit, it wasn't much.

Someone wanted Hathaway House, and they wanted it badly enough to kill for it. The real estate company swore they weren't involved, but they were hiding their true ownership behind a mountain of bureaucratic filings. And then there was the real kicker: Lucius had been murdered two days after Alex started asking questions, and one day after Leslie Barrett and her husband put their house up for sale and disappeared.

"I wonder what real estate agent the Barretts are using to sell their house?" Alex muttered as he made his way across the station toward the coffee counter. "No," he admitted, "it couldn't be that easy."

"What's that, Mr. Lockerby," the fresh-faced, young man behind the counter said.

Alex shook his head as he reached for his change purse.

"Nothing," he said. "Just working on a case."

The young man, whose name was Hans if Alex remembered correctly, filled a ceramic cup with coffee, added cream and two sugars, then handed it over. Alex paid him, then wished him a good day before heading to the elevator.

Sipping from his cup, Alex rode the elevator up to the twelfth floor, then turned left toward his office door. A few moments later, he was inside, where Sherry gave him a muted smile.

"Did you get Ethel on the train?" he asked, coming over and sitting on the corner of her desk. He didn't have to ask if she'd gone out, because there was a ceramic cup like the one he was holding, sitting on her desk. Somewhere under the desk, there was a bag with several of the ceramic cups in it, waiting to be returned.

Sherry nodded solemnly.

"We went by Hathaway House to get some of her things, then we went straight to the station." She looked like she wanted to say more, but hesitated.

"Anything else?" Alex prodded.

"I got the feeling we were being watched," she said.

"At Hathaway House?"

Sherry shook her head.

"From the moment we caught a cab downstairs."

Alex stood and went to the window, looking down at the street far below. From this vantage, he had no chance of spotting anyone suspicious, but he felt better for having done it.

"I want you to go over to the courthouse," he said, coming back to stand beside the desk. "Talk to the clerks in the civil division."

"What am I looking for?" she asked, picking up one of her notebooks and a pencil.

"I want to know if there have been any lawsuits filed by Tommy or Lillian Waverly, or if either of them are suing for divorce."

Sherry gave him a sardonic look.

"That sounds like private information," she said. "You think anyone will actually tell me?"

"Court filings are public information," Alex corrected her, "and being a courthouse clerk isn't exactly a glamorous job. If any of them give you trouble, pop another button on your blouse and give them your biggest smile."

Sherry smirked.

"Oh," she cooed, lowering her head and looking up at him with heavily lidded eyes and a pouty expression, "it's one of those jobs."

Alex chuckled.

"You'll do fine."

Sherry blew him a kiss and started to gather her things.

"When you're done with that," Alex went on, "I want you to go home."

Her flirty, playful mood melted away to be replaced by one of anger.

"I want you somewhere safer than your apartment," he said before she could object. "Tell your landlady that you'll be staying with friends for a few days, then pack a bag and head back here. You can use my suite upstairs until this case is over."

He expected her to argue. Sherry was a very independent woman, and she wouldn't like the idea that Alex thought she needed protecting. Instead, her face shifted to a look of mock outrage.

"Mr. Lockerby," she said in a shocked voice. "I'm a single woman, I can't sleep at your apartment. What will people say?"

Alex gave her an unamused look.

"Since you'll be using my vault to get up to my apartment from here, no one will say anything because they won't know you're there," he said. "And you know very well that I sleep at the brownstone."

"Do you have any food in that place?" she asked, picking up her handbag.

"When you get back, call and have some sent up."

"Will do, boss," she said as she headed for the door. "Are you going to be here while I'm out?"

Alex nodded.

"I've got to figure out what to do next to find Lucius' killer, then I need to make a few more calls in the Waverly Radio case."

Sherry wished him luck, then disappeared into the hall.

Alex waited until he heard the elevator chime out in the hall, then he went to his office to retrieve the folder on Hathaway House and Sherry's research on Waverly's competitors.

He spent the next hour at Sherry's desk, going through the Hathaway House file. As far as he could tell, there was no indication that the people who wanted the historic building would resort to murder. Up to this point, all they'd done was make a few heavy-handed offers on the house, most of them more than the house was worth. Murder was a serious escalation.

I'd expect to see some sort of minor violence first, Alex thought. *Maybe somebody brandishing a weapon.*

He had to face the fact — the only thing that had changed was him going to Manhattan Land and Building. As far as he could tell, that was the catalyst that prompted the escalation.

Unless it's something you don't know about, he reminded himself.

Alex set the folder down and rubbed his eyes. The one thing that was clear in this case was that he simply didn't have enough information.

"But I know where to get it," he growled to the empty room.

Reaching into his suit coat pocket, he pulled out his rune book and flipped to a spot near the back. This was where he carried useful runes that he didn't use very often. Some were highly specific and others were just expensive, but they were handy to have if you turned out to need them.

He stopped briefly on a triangular rune with a symbol in the middle that looked like a melting duck, then he paged to the very back. Here were three of the same rune, all done in pencil, with two interlocking triangles forming a star. Each point formed a small triangle of its own and those all had tiny lines of text in them. In the center was a runic symbol that looked uncomfortably like a pistol trying to be intimate with a mailbox.

Alex smiled and tore out the unlocking rune and then one of the cleaning runes. He'd need two more runes for what he planned, but it was early afternoon. There would be plenty of time to write them before midnight. After that, he'd go back to the offices of Manhattan Land and Building and find out for himself what they were hiding.

Three hours later, Alex sat at his drafting table. He'd already made the activation rune and the several linking runes he'd need for the evening's festivities, but he wanted to add one more thing to his arsenal.

About six months ago, he'd used an escape rune to dump the murderous blood mage, Paschal Randolph, into the north Atlantic. Since then, he'd worked on a new escape rune, but they were exacting and time consuming and he simply hadn't put in the time to finish it.

Now, as he sat at his desk carefully drawing a line with a straight edge, he could feel the rune coming together. The line that trailed behind his pen was a deep purple color, the ink having been infused with powdered amethyst and an alchemical binding agent.

As the pen connected the trailing purple line with a sparkling diamond-infused line, Alex felt a rush of blood, like he'd stood up too quickly after sitting for hours. Being careful to lay the pen aside in its tray, he held on to the edge of his drafting table with his left hand until the dizziness passed.

When he finally looked up, his new escape rune glittered like a cathedral's rose window. Running his fingers along the top edge of the paper, Alex could feel the power contained in the construct radiating outward. It wasn't just the magic he'd put into it, but all the energy he'd granted the rune as he'd drawn it. It had taken weeks and the lines almost glowed with their caged power.

"You'll do," he said with a grin. "Now for the new bit."

Alex rose and picked up the escape rune. Unlike the first one he'd ever made, this one did not have to be painstakingly tattooed on his arm. Thanks to his ever-expanding knowledge of how linking runes worked, he could connect this rune directly to his arm and leave the rune itself safely tucked away here in his vault.

The last time he'd tried this, he drew his rune on regular paper.

That turned out to be a mistake that almost killed him. Normal paper takes a lot longer to burn than flash paper and his escape rune hadn't activated as quickly as Alex would have liked. This time he corrected that mistake, drawing the extensive construct on a slightly thicker piece of flash paper. The problem with that was that flash paper was relatively fragile, making the work of drawing the complex rune more exacting.

Alex crossed to one of the workbenches along the right-side wall of his vault. On the top of the workbench was a silver frame for a picture with the glass and the backing removed. Alex set the rune down and examined the balsa wood backing, making sure there were no rough spots that might tear the delicate paper.

Taking extreme care, he placed the rune paper on the backing and squared it up with a line he'd drawn in pencil. Satisfied that the rune was correctly positioned, Alex picked up the glass and laid it gently atop the backing.

"Now comes the tricky part," he said, pulling a folded linking rune from his shirt pocket. In order to get the link to attach to the escape rune, the linking rune would need to be activated close by. The first time he'd done it, the escape rune had been written on regular paper, so there was no fear it would combust when the flash paper went off. Flash paper burned too fast for regular paper. Now, however, he couldn't let the linking rune get anywhere near the escape rune.

The idea of using the glass from the picture frame felt like a genius idea, but Alex couldn't be sure that the glass would allow the link to form. He'd just have to try it and find out.

Dropping the linking rune on the glass, he took out his lighter and squeezed it to life. He held his breath as he touched the flame to the paper. It vanished instantly, as he expected, and it left a gold version of itself hanging in the air for a moment. As Alex watched, the rune simply faded away as if it had been a trick of the light.

That was a good sign; it meant that the link had been successful.

Lifting the glass and backing together, Alex carefully slid them down into the silver frame. A small metal tab had been attached to the back of the frame, and Alex bent it in place to keep the glass and backing from sliding out.

Alex held the frame up in front of him and let out a pent-up breath.

"Halfway there," he said.

Rising, he crossed to the back wall and hung the picture on a hook he'd prepared for it. With the rune finished and linked, all Alex needed to do now was to create the other end of the runic link on his own arm. Once he did that, the rune would be connected to him, letting him activate it whenever he wanted. He didn't expect to need an escape rune tonight, but he didn't like leaving things to chance.

As Iggy was fond of saying, *It never pays to dance with Murphy*.

The Murphy to which he referred was the one from Murphy's Law, the idea that anything that can go wrong, will go wrong, and always at the most inopportune time. Iggy's reasoning was that if you gave Murphy an opening, he would nail you, so the best way to avoid that was to be as prepared for contingencies as possible.

Alex unbuttoned his left shirt sleeve and rolled it up to his elbow. Taking another linking rune from his shirt pocket, he checked the bottom edge where he'd written the words, *Escape rune link*. Since linking runes were created in pairs, he needed to make sure this was the correct one. He needn't have worried, since the two links he needed were the only runes he'd put in his pocket, but it didn't pay to dance with Murphy, so he checked anyway.

Touching the top corner of the rune paper to his tongue, Alex stuck it to his forearm, then fished his lighter out of his trouser pocket. He quickly lit the paper and watched as the golden rune appeared, hovering over his arm. Instead of fading away, however, the glowing construct seemed to waver in the air, as if it were trembling.

Alex knew something was wrong, but before he could do anything about it, the rune exploded with an ear-shattering bang. Hot, searing pain erupted in Alex's forearm and he cried out, pulling back from his desk so quickly that his chair tipped backward. He hit the stone floor with the back of his head and all the lights went out.

15

DATE NIGHT

Alex groaned as someone pulled his head off the floor of his vault. This was the second time in a week he'd awakened on the hard stone, and he definitely didn't want that becoming a habit.

He tried to open his eyes, but they didn't seem to work at the moment.

"Where do you want him?" a familiar voice said from somewhere.

"He's got a medical room over here," Iggy responded.

That explained a lot. Iggy was the only other person who could disable the wards that kept his cover doors closed. All of them had wards to keep them shut, even the one that went to Sorsha's castle. He was relatively certain that door was secure, but it never paid to take chances.

"Carpet," he rasped even before he'd managed to get his eyes open.

"He said something," a third voice said. This one was definitely a woman.

"Need to put down a carpet in here," he mumbled.

"I daresay you do," Iggy agreed. "Especially if you intend to keep landing on your head when you fall."

"This arm is burned," the first voice said. "Do you think he was attacked?"

"In here?" Iggy scoffed, but then he paused. "I suppose Moriarty could have managed it, though I don't know how. He got into Alex's vault once before."

"I thought you said he was a friend?" the first voice said again. Alex belatedly recognized her as Sorsha, which would make the other voice Sherry's.

"No," Iggy corrected Sorsha. "I said it wasn't likely he was an enemy, but that's a long way from being a friend. Put him down on the table."

"No need," Alex said, slurring his words. "I'm awake."

He tried to sit up, but Iggy put a hand on his shoulder and pushed him back down on the examination table.

"I can see that," Iggy observed, "but despite that fact, you might have a concussion. Now lay there like I told you or I'll have Sorsha immobilize you."

Alex was in a mood to be obstinate, but the thought of Sorsha's paralyzing power made him shake involuntarily. Discretion, he reasoned, was the better part of valor, and he lay back down as he'd been instructed. His vision was starting to come back, though it was just a small circle in the middle of a vast blackness. From his position on the table, all he could see was the gray ceiling of his little medical room.

Gray is a dull color, he thought. *I should probably paint the ceiling.*

"He's going to be okay, isn't he?" Sherry asked. Her voice sounded worried.

"Don't you already know?" Sorsha said, with a slight edge in her voice. As far as Alex knew, the sorceress and his secretary didn't have any bad blood between them, so he was surprised to hear her tone.

"You know it doesn't work that way," Sherry said. Her voice held nothing but worry in it, so Alex was forced to surmise that whatever was going on was only on Sorsha's part.

That means it's something you did, he thought.

"What's that?" Sorsha asked as Iggy's face appeared in Alex's vision. He wore an oculus over his right eye, but it was unlike any Alex had ever seen. This was shorter than even Alex's new model, and looked like a brass ring with a bit of prismatic glass in it.

"New toy," Iggy answered Sorsha, his voice both mirthful and enigmatic.

Alex had seen that glass before.

"How did you get Dr. Kellin's Lens of Seeing?" he asked, trying to force his slowly expanding field of vision to go faster.

Iggy chuckled at that.

"Don't be absurd," he said. "Andrea made that lens for herself, so it would never work for anyone else." He looked up suddenly, stroking the ends of his mustache with his forefinger and thumb. "Well, it might work for Linda," he continued absently. "I'll have to talk with her about it. Now, getting back to you," he said, leaning over to peer through the oculus at Alex.

"So what is that?"

Iggy puffed out an exasperated breath, making the hairs of his bottlebrush mustache ripple.

"It is a lens of seeing," he admitted. "I bought Andrea's recipe from Linda, and Charles Grier has been working to make it ever since."

Alex remembered Dr. Kellin telling him it took her two years to get the growth medium right to make the lens.

"Charles must be a better alchemist than I figured," he said. Grier was a great alchemist, but Dr. Kellin's skills were well beyond him.

"Andrea's notes made the process much easier than it would have otherwise been," Iggy said. "Well, I don't think you're concussed," he added, stepping back from the exam table.

Alex started to get up, but Iggy waved him back as he dug around in his doctor's bag. While he waited, Alex turned to Sorsha.

"How'd they drag you into this?" he asked.

"I called her," Sherry said before Sorsha could speak. "When you weren't in the office when I got back, I figured you were in here, so I knocked on the door. When I didn't get a response, I figured you might have gone to check on Sorsha—"

"So you called her," Alex finished. "She told you to call Iggy, in case I'd gone home, and he let you into the vault so you could get to my apartment."

Hostile Takeover

"Yes," Sorsha said in a voice so frosty Alex was sure some of the potions on his medical shelf froze over, "about that."

So that's it, Alex thought.

He took a deep breath and gave her the most dismissive look he could muster.

"That's what you're all worked up about?" he said, rising up on his elbow to see her better. "Me letting Sherry use my place to keep her safe?"

"You're letting her use your apartment," Sorsha said, as if that explained everything.

"But I'm not in it," he protested. "You know very well that I sleep at the brownstone."

"And where does your vault door come out in the apartment you're loaning to Miss Knox?"

Alex opened his mouth and then shut it again. The door from his vault to the apartment in Empire Tower exited directly into the master bedroom.

"That's what I thought," Sorsha said, reading his expression.

"I'll tell you what," he said as Iggy turned back to the table. "I'll put a bolt on the inside so Sherry can lock herself in; will that be all right?"

She gave him a hard look, then sighed.

"I suppose it will."

"Lie back down," Iggy said, pushing Alex onto his back. His mentor lit his multi-lamp and a pale greenish light began to shine out of it. Taking hold of the brass ring that kept the lens of truth in place, Iggy rotated it. As he did, Alex could see a second piece of glass moving behind the lens. After a second, it shimmered and began to softly glow green.

"Why did you put a ghostlight lens in there?" he asked, as Iggy began to examine him again. "Doesn't the lens of seeing distort what you view?"

"It does indeed," Iggy said with a sly grin. "The lens lets you see the flow of energy inside the body. By adding the ghostlight lens, I can now see the flow of magic inside you."

He reached down and picked up Alex's left arm, turning it over so he could examine the burn mark.

"When did you do all this?" Sorsha asked, leaning around to get a better look at the medical oculus.

Iggy chuckled and opened his left eye to better see the burn mark.

"You didn't think I just read books, tend my orchids, and cook all day, did you?"

"I suppose not," she said, crossing her arms.

"How did you get this burn?" Iggy asked, turning back to Alex. "The mark looks like a linking rune."

"That's what it was supposed to be," he responded. Alex told him the story of his new escape rune and how the final link had exploded.

"Let me see your book," Iggy said, holding out his hand.

"It's on my drafting table."

"I'll get it," Sherry said, then turned and left the little room. In a moment she was back with his red book.

Iggy accepted and paged through to the back. After turning a few pages, he closed it and handed it to Alex.

"What were you looking for?" he asked.

"I was checking to see if any of your other linking runes were written poorly or unpaired," Iggy said. "Everything in there is fine, so that's not the problem."

"Well then, what is?" Alex said, probing the burn with his fingers. It stung at the barest touch and looked an awful lot like he'd been branded.

"Here," Iggy said, handing him a small, round glass container. "Rub this ointment on the burn while I get a bandage ready."

Alex sat up and did as he was told, wincing as he went.

"How many escape runes have you used to date?" Iggy asked as he slathered a cotton bandage with a viscous yellow liquid.

"Uh," Alex managed, unprepared for the question. "Three," he said after a moment to think. "The one with Sor...I mean the Nazi saboteur." Sorsha was still angry about the fact that her castle had been destroyed in that incident. It wasn't really Alex's fault, but he was the only one still around for her to take her irritation out on. "Then there was that time with the Brothers Boom," he said. "And lastly that incident with Paschal Randolph."

Iggy stroked his mustache again, then blew out the burner in his multi-lamp. He took off his medical oculus and stowed it and the lamp in his medical bag.

"There's a section in the monograph," he began. "It's in the revealed section."

The revealed section was what Iggy and Alex called the part of the Archimedean Monograph that could only be read by ghostlight. It stood to reason that those parts were written much later than the book proper.

"What does it say?" Alex asked, absolutely certain he didn't want the answer.

"It talks about the artificial transfer of both life and magical energy," his mentor explained. "As I recall, it mentions that such transfers can leave residual, unbound magic behind. Over time the body absorbs these fragments, but if they build up you can get what the monograph called transfer toxicity."

"Transfer…?" Alex tried to wrap his head around that. "What's that?"

Iggy moved back to the table and picked up Alex's arm.

"Unless I miss my guess, it's like a severe allergic reaction," he said.

Alex shook his head to clear it, certain that he wasn't understanding correctly. Iggy began.

"The first time you used your escape rune," Iggy began, wrapping the bandage he'd prepared around Alex's forearm, "you moved almost your entire stock of life through it. Then Moriarty put a year of your life back and then we put even more. After that you probably spent, what? Another year of life energy with those last two escape runes? That's a lot of energy you've been moving through your body in a relatively short space of time."

As Iggy spoke, Alex felt a chill run up his back. The term 'artificial transfer' definitely applied to escape runes and life transfer runes, but what about his regular, everyday runes? Didn't they transfer magic from him when he made them?

"So," Alex said, "because I've transferred a lot of life energy, my body is allergic to it now?"

"Something like that," Iggy said. "This reaction," he held up Alex's arm, "seems to be your body rejecting the link you tried to establish to the escape rune."

"But I didn't use the escape rune," he protested.

"Remember that we use our power when we make the runes. Undoubtedly, your body knew what the rune was for when you tried to link with it."

"So I can still use runes," Alex said, "just not transfer my life energy around."

"That's the way I see it," Iggy said. "If this affected your ability to use magic, it would have happened when you wrote the rune in the first place."

Alex sighed with relief at that, at least until he realized what it really meant.

"What about my life energy?" he hissed, grabbing Iggy's wrist with his good arm. "It's a good bet if I can't move life energy out, I won't be able to put any in. What happens if I need to top up the tank?"

Iggy thought about that for a long minute and Alex could feel panic rising in his mind for every second that passed.

"Easy, lad," his mentor said, putting a calming hand on his shoulder. "The monograph wasn't specific about dealing with transfer toxicity, but I suspect it's like any toxin. Over time, your body should absorb the magical fragments that are causing it and you'll be right as rain."

Iggy sounded very sure of himself, but Alex wondered if he really believed that, or was putting on a brave face for his benefit.

"So we give it time," Alex repeated.

Iggy nodded sagely.

"We'll cross that bridge if and when we come to it," he said. "Now, I think you'll be fine from here on out, and I have a roast in the oven that I don't want to burn, so if you'll excuse me..."

"Thanks for patching me up," Alex said.

Iggy gave him a grin, then picked up his bag.

"Think nothing of it, lad," he said as Sorsha and Sherry stepped back, allowing him to pass out of the narrow room. Before the sorceress could step back up to the examination table, Sherry crossed the gap and enclosed him in a fierce hug.

"I'm glad you're okay, boss," she said.

Alex patted her on the shoulder until she let him go. Iggy and Sorsha were used to the trouble he got into, but Sherry was still relatively new to it, and she'd been really worried for him.

Sorsha was giving him a look that was half amusement, half irritation.

"Let's get you situated," he said, hopping off the table. He led the way out of the medical room, then turned left where the apartment door stood at the end of the hall.

Taking out his pocket watch, he flipped it open to release the door, intending to open it for her. He would have, too, if his left arm didn't burn when he tried to move it.

"I think you'd better get the door," he said through clenched teeth.

Sherry opened the door and gasped.

"This is your bedroom?"

Alex could almost feel the air behind him getting cold as Sorsha followed them down the hall.

"I've only slept in here once or twice," he said quickly. "And everything's been changed since then."

"I'm not worried about that," Sherry said, stepping into the room. "You wouldn't believe where a person had to sleep back in the day."

Alex knew that meant back almost three thousand years.

"I mean this room is bigger than my entire apartment." She literally spread her arms and twirled in place. "Can I live here forever? I mean, you don't use it."

"No," Sorsha said stepping in behind him. She looked around the room with a critical eye and Sherry stuck her tongue out at her when her back was turned.

"Andrew always did overdo things," she said, shaking her head.

Alex wasn't sure what she meant. He hadn't really decorated this place, but the bedroom seemed simple enough, though the furniture and the architecture was top notch.

"Thanks for letting me stay here, boss," Sherry said, looking somewhat longingly at the door leading to the bathroom.

If she liked the bedroom, the bathroom might send her into hysterics.

"I left my suitcase by the door to the office," she said, heading back into the vault. "Be right back."

Alex turned to face Sorsha. With Sherry gone, she would be feeling free to express her opinion, and if Alex knew her like the thought he did, she wouldn't be able to resist.

"So," she said, right on cue. "You intended to set up a new escape rune."

Alex was prepared for her to give him a hard time about putting Sherry up in his vacant apartment, but this caught him flat-footed.

"Well..." he managed. "I try to have one on hand. I had one when we first met."

"True," she said stepping close to him and sliding her hands up the front of his vest. She took hold of his tie and straightened it, smoothing out the knot. "You had one prepared then, but in more recent times you seem to only worry about them when you have plans."

Alex opened his mouth to reply but she cut him off.

"And by 'plans,' I mean that you're about to do something stupid or dangerous." She raised an eyebrow and looked him over for a moment. "In your case, probably both."

Alex wanted to smile, but the reasons for his upcoming outing wouldn't allow it.

"A client of mine was being bullied into selling his house," he explained. "The people behind it used a real estate company to cover their actions and when my client didn't sell, he wound up dead."

"Did they kill him?"

Alex shrugged.

"The real estate company won't divulge the name of their client," he explained. "I'm going to break into their offices tonight and get that name."

"And then?"

"Then, in the morning, I'll go ask them why they wanted my client's house so badly."

She looked at him with a level gaze.

"All this for a client who's dead?"

He nodded.

"And being dead, he can't pay you," she said.

"That doesn't matter," he said with a slow shake of his head.

Sorsha regarded him for a long moment. Her hands were still on his lapels as she looked up at him. After a moment, a slow smile spread across her face, eventually turning into a smirk.

"You really are one of the good ones," she said, cocking her head to the side. "Aren't you?"

Alex chuckled and returned her smirk.

"You're buttering me up because you want to come with me," he said. It wasn't a question but a statement of fact.

Sorsha actually laughed, sliding her hands up to his neck.

"You know me so well," she said, a wicked gleam in her eye. "And you always take me on the most interesting outings."

By the time Sherry returned, she'd pulled his head down and was kissing him.

16

WHAT'S IN A NAME?

"How much longer is this going to take?" Sorsha asked from behind Alex.

Her voice was stern, but Alex knew if he turned to look at her, she'd be wearing the biggest smirk she could manage. He took a breath to focus and returned to picking the front door lock of Manhattan Land and Building.

Despite the office's ground floor location, the lock was new and top of the line. Alex lightened his touch on the pick, scraping it forward searching for the last pin. He'd already managed to find and trap four others, but the lock hadn't yielded, so there must be at least one more.

"Do you want me to open it," she went on, not bothering to disguise the mirth in her voice.

"No," Alex growled. "I don't want you to use any magic at all while we're here. You sorcerers leave a lot of magical residue behind when you throw around your flashy powers."

"You're just jealous."

Alex suppressed the urge to sigh and kept working.

"How did I let you talk me into coming along on this errand?" he growled, more to himself than to Sorsha.

"That's an easy one," Sorsha chuckled. "I stole away your will by pressing my lips to yours. Besides, someone with sense had to come along to keep you out of trouble."

Alex gave her a quick look of irritation over his shoulder, but she ignored him. He almost lingered on her appearance, but he needed to focus on the lock. Sorsha wore a dark pair of slacks with a dark blue shirt and a black vest. Apparently this was her idea of keeping a low profile. A black cloche hat covered her platinum hair, which did manage to reduce her visibility. Not that it would help, since her expensive wardrobe stood out in this neighborhood like a Duesenberg at the dockyards.

He was about to comment on her appearance but caught sight of the silver necklace hanging down over her shirt. It was a delicate thing with a tiny chain that held up a round ornament shaped like a rose. Alex had given it to her before they left his office. It wasn't really her style, but it did have a linking rune on the back that connected to a steel plate in Alex's vault that contained a shield rune. He hadn't had time to test it, but he figured etching the rune in steel should give it more than the five uses he got out of his suit coat. Sorsha could protect herself from regular bullets, of course, but if Alex was right and the Legion was involved in all this, he wouldn't put it past them to be armed with spellbreakers. As far as Alex knew, spellbreakers didn't affect shield runes.

"Why are you trying to pick that lock?" she demanded impatiently. "Use another unlocking rune like you did on the front door!"

"I'm picking the lock," he said through clenched teeth, "because a good unlocking rune costs around two hundred and fifty dollars and five days to make. I could make a cheap one for about thirty, but they aren't reliable, and they don't work on these new pin and tumbler locks."

Alex felt the probe catch the last pin and he held his breath. Moving slowly, he centered the probe, then pushed down on the handle end of the probe, forcing the pin upward. He had to be careful here; his other hand held the 'L' shaped tension tool that was applying torque to the cylinder. If he loosened his grip, the pins he'd already opened would fall back into place and he'd have to start again, but if he put too much torque on it, the last pin wouldn't be able to move up.

Pushing with just the right amount of pressure and torque, Alex coaxed the pin upward until it cleared the cylinder. At that moment, the lock broke free and he turned it with the tension tool. The deadbolt in the door slid back and Alex pushed it open.

Alex sat back on his haunches and looked up at Sorsha.

"As they say in French, viola."

Sorsha snorted with laughter and quickly covered her nose and mouth.

"That's pronounced, 'voilà'," she giggled. "A viola is a big…"

She stopped when she saw Alex's matching smirk as he stood.

"You did that on purpose," she accused him, crossing her arms and giving him a hard look. "Why do you encourage people to think you're an idiot?"

Alex's smile got even wider, and he stood.

"People who think I'm an idiot don't watch themselves around me," he answered. He stepped forward and pulled the sorceress into an embrace. "They let their guard down and I find out things they don't really want me to know."

Sorsha looked up into his eyes and her irritation vanished.

"I see," she said, a slight huskiness to her voice.

Alex leaned down to kiss her, but the sorceress put a finger on his lips before he could.

"Since we're standing in an open hallway in front of a door you illegally unlocked," she said, her smirk returning. "I suggest we get busy finding whatever you came for."

Alex sighed and let her go. Sorsha could be a real tease when she wanted to be.

"All right," he said, pulling a pair of thin rubber gloves from his pocket.

"Where did you get those?" she asked, accepting the gloves.

"Dr. Wagner's office," he said, pulling out a similar pair for himself.

"So you stole them," Sorsha admonished.

"No," he laughed, pulling on the gloves. "I got a few boxes of those when I stocked the medical room in my vault."

The gloves were snug without being tight and stretched to fit his hands as he pulled them on. The best thing about them was that they were thin enough to allow Alex to feel the things he was touching without leaving any fingerprints.

"All right," he said, stepping inside the front office of Manhattan Land and Building. "Let's go."

He stood aside so Sorsha could enter, then shut and locked the door behind her.

"What are we looking for?" she asked, squinting in the near total darkness of the reception area.

"Files on who hired them to acquire Hathaway House," Alex explained, pulling a small brass ball from his coat pocket. The ball was about the diameter of a silver dollar and consisted of two halves, joined together by a spring-loaded hinge. On one side of the hinge, the ball had a flat cut-out where a person could grip it. When you squeezed the two flat spots, the front edge of the ball would split open a crack. The more pressure you applied, the wider the crack got. If you placed an alchemical glow-stone inside, you had a flashlight that would last for days of use.

Squeezing the ball gently, Alex released a beam of light. He played it around the room, making sure it was as he remembered it. The receptionist's little desk stood by the door to the rear area with the rest of the room being mostly bare.

"It's not the kind of place I'd expect to deal in land," Sorsha observed.

Alex had the same thought when he'd been here earlier.

"The agent who made the offer on Hathaway House is named Ruben Buckthorn," Alex said, opening the door behind the reception desk. "His office is near the back."

"Aren't his files going to be locked up?" Sorsha asked, following Alex through the dark opening.

"That's why I brought the lock picks," he said. "Now stay close, and with any luck we'll be out of here in an hour."

Alex sat at Ruben Blackthorn's desk holding the umpteenth file under the glow of a desk lamp. Like all the previous folders, this one held no useful information on who was after Hathaway House.

"How is this possible?" he snarled, slamming the paper cover of the folder closed. He shoved it over to the side of the desk, away from the light. "There's nothing here."

Sorsha reached out and stopped the folder before it could fall on the floor.

"You found the name of the Hathaway House buyer two hours ago," she said, replacing the folder into the open file cabinet.

"Inge Naido?" Alex said, giving her a steady look.

"Is that someone already associated with the case?" she asked.

Alex sighed and rubbed the bridge of his nose.

"Inge Naido is the word Incognito split in half and made into a name," he explained. "It's obviously a pseudonym."

"Oh," Sorsha said, going a bit pink. Clearly she hadn't made the connection.

"Sorry," Alex offered her an olive branch. "I should have pointed that out right away."

"If this is a dead end," Sorsha asked wearily, "then what are we still doing here?"

Alex picked up the folder for Hathaway House.

"Since I can't look up a pseudonym, I was hoping Miss Inge Naido bought some other properties. Then I could go by those properties and see who was living in them, maybe run into Miss Naido herself. The problem is," he said picking up the few folders remaining on the desk, "none of these houses were sold to someone using that pseudonym."

Alex rubbed his eyes and took a deep breath to steady his fraying nerves.

"Here," Sorsha said, reaching into the air and pulling out two tumbler glasses. She put them down on the desk, then pulled a thin bottle of bourbon as well.

"Thanks," Alex said, taking the bottle and pouring two fingers' worth in each glass. He raised his glass and Sorsha clinked hers to his before he drank. Alex hadn't bought much bourbon since his finances allowed him to move up to Scotch. That said, the sorceress' bourbon was some of the fanciest liquor he'd ever had. He could swear it had a hint of sweet fruit and cinnamon, or maybe nutmeg.

Alex set the glass back on the table and sighed, leaning back in the desk chair.

"Have another," Sorsha said, but she vanished her own glass back into thin air. As Alex reached for the bottle, she turned back to the file cabinet and began going through the folders.

Alex poured another bourbon but instead of drinking it, he sat, staring at it. He had no idea what time it was, but he'd probably been awake for almost a full day.

"—lex," Sorsha's voice came from somewhere far away. He hadn't been aware of falling asleep, but he must have, because his eyes were hard to open and there was a crick in his back.

"Alex," Sorsha said again.

"Sorry," he said. "I must have dozed off."

When he got his eyes open, Sorsha pushed the glass of bourbon into his hand.

"Drink."

Alex did as he was told and could almost feel his synapses starting to fire as the liquor began to warm him. When he finally focused on the desk, he found that Sorsha had laid out five folders in front of him, in addition to the one on Hathaway House.

"What's this?" he asked.

"You looked like you needed a rest," she said. "So, while you had a little nap, I went back through the folders, and," she reached down and began opening them, "I found these."

Alex looked over the folders, recognizing them from his earlier investigation.

"Okay," he said, still tired. "What am I looking at?"

Sorsha reached down and indicated the client name on the first document.

"I didn't find any more plays on the idea of being anonymous, but take a look at this," she pointed at the line on the form.

"Adam...Zapel," Alex read, struggling to focus. "Okay, so what?"

"Read it faster."

"Adam Zapel," Alex said. "Wait, Adam's Apple?"

Sorsha grinned and moved her finger to the next file.

"And this one is Luc Wharm." She moved to the next one. "And Orson Carte, and Rhea Curren, and this last one is Brighton R. Lee."

Alex picked up each of the files and scrutinized them.

"How could I have missed this?" he whispered, his mind fully awake now.

"You were looking for obvious aliases," she said. "Some of these are actually quite clever."

Alex took out his notebook and began scribbling down the address of the houses and the fake names of the buyers.

"You really came through on this, doll," he said absently as he scribbled.

"Don't call me doll," she said.

Alex looked up to find her smirking.

"I suppose this was a pretty fun date, though," she continued. "We should do this more often."

As Alex looked up at Sorsha in her dark, tight-fitting pants and cloche hat, he suddenly became aware that the room was much lighter than he remembered.

"What time is it?"

Sorsha pulled out the watch Iggy had given her to track her life energy and she gasped.

"It's ten minutes to seven."

Alex stood up quickly and began closing the folders. He was surprised that someone hadn't come in already, but he was certain they would in the next few minutes.

"Here," he whispered, handing the folders to Sorsha. "Put these away and shut the file cabinet."

"But it's still unlocked," Sorsha hissed back at him.

"Don't worry about that," Alex said, chalking a door on Ruben Buckthorn's wall. "He'll think he left it unlocked."

Working quickly, Alex returned his chalk to his pocket and took out his rune book. There were two folded runes inside the front cover ready for use and Alex stuck one of them inside his chalk outline and the other outside it.

"What's that one?" Sorsha asked, switching off the desk light.

"It's a cleaning rune," Alex said, pulling out his lighter and igniting the vault rune. The heavy steel door melted out of the wall just as Alex heard the front door of the outer office open. He slipped his key into the door and pushed it open wide enough to admit Sorsha and himself.

He beckoned the sorceress through, then ducked inside himself. As he pushed the door closed, he could hear heavy footsteps coming down the hall. When the door closed completely, Alex locked it, removing the steel door from the Buckthorn's office wall, then he pulled a rune paper from his shirt pocket and ignited it with his lighter.

"This is linked to the cleaning rune," he answered Sorsha's unasked question. "Right now the chalk outline is being removed from the wall. No one will ever know that we were there."

He looked back at the wall, as if he could somehow see through back to the office to make sure his cleaning rune worked. Realizing that was stupid, he chuckled and shook his head. It had been a long day followed by a long night and he was feeling loopy.

When he turned back, he found Sorsha laughing at him with her hand over her mouth.

"May I escort you home?" he asked, offering his arm to her.

Her smile widened, but she took his arm and turned toward the back wall of the vault.

"This really was fun," she said, leaning against him. "We haven't been able to do this for months thanks to that curse."

"We didn't do this even before that," Alex said.

"We were always too busy," she said. "Let's not make that mistake again."

"Is that an invitation?" he smirked down at her as they reached the door to the castle.

"Certainly not," she said. "You've got five houses to investigate today, and you'll need at least six hours of sleep before you start."

She leaned up on tiptoes and gave him a sincere kiss on the lips, then nestled her head on his shoulder for a long moment.

"Good night, Alex," she said when she finally stepped away.

"How much life energy do you have left?" he asked, seemingly out of the blue.

She started to reach for her watch, but halted with her hand in mid-air.

"I'll look after I've had some sleep," she said. "I don't want to think about that right now."

Alex kept the scowl off his face, but only barely. Her answer told him what he needed to know. Instead of insisting he show her, he opened his own watch and released the seals on the door to her flying home.

"Good night, beautiful," he said as he held the door open for her.

"Much better than 'doll'," she said, then stepped across the threshold.

Alex watched her go for a moment, then shut the door. He stood there, looking at it for a long moment before he turned away.

His bed was calling him; he could feel the pull of his desire for sleep as if it were a physical thing. Turning away from the hall to the brownstone, he looked at his drafting table.

Closing his eyes, Alex called up the memory of Sorsha checking her watch. When Iggy had given it to her, the red hand inside had been pointing to eleven. Now Alex could see it clearly in his mind's eye. When Sorsha had checked the time, the red hand had been pointing to the eight. She'd lost the equivalent of three months of life in just over a day and a half.

The loss is still accelerating, he thought.

He needed to do something, but he was too tired to make any meaningful attempt. If he set to work now, he'd have to redo any work he did tonight anyway. Clenching his fists in impotent anger, Alex turned away from his desk and headed for the brownstone. Time was running out for Sorsha, and if he didn't do something soon, she was as good as dead.

17

CONNECTIONS

Alex started up into a sitting position. Adrenalin burned in his veins and he was breathing like he'd run a mile. Immediately his fists came up into a guard position and he scanned the room for an opponent he was certain would be there.

When he finally realized what he was seeing, however, he forced himself to take a long, shuddering breath and relaxed.

"Just a nightmare," he muttered, reaching for his alarm clock on the bedside table.

Normally, Alex would have to turn on the lamp sitting beside the clock in order to read the time, but the light shining through his bedroom windows was already bright enough. That meant that it wasn't the middle of the night.

"Five fifty-six," he read aloud. The alarm was set to wake him at six fifteen, so there was no sense in going back to bed. Alex turned the clock over and wound it. Once the spring was tight, he pulled on the post that set the alarm time. It pulled outward about a quarter of an inch, which disengaged it from the alarm mechanism.

Returning the clock to the side table, Alex threw back his covers and swung his feet out, onto the cold floor. The shock of his warm, bare feet on the cold boards of the wood floor prodded Alex's drifting mind into focus. He'd been dreaming about something, something that left him with a warm, positive feeling as his mind skipped over the actual details.

Then something went wrong, he thought, trying to force his mind to recall the information. No details emerged but he did recall a scent, something floral with a hint of spice.

"Stardust," he said. It was the name of the perfume Alex had given Sorsha almost a year ago.

The sorceress' face flashed into his mind's eye and triggered a long sequence of images. Alex saw her at the slaughterhouse when they refilled her life energy, then the image of her watch with the red hand pointing at seven. Finally he saw her back at the slaughterhouse, only this time Iggy wasn't there. Alex used a life transference construct but something went wrong and the energy was too much. Sorsha wrapped her arms around her middle and dropped to her knees, then looked up at Alex and exploded.

The memory of the image startled Alex even though he was now awake. He understood completely why he'd almost leapt out of bed.

"It was only a dream," he told himself.

He wasn't prone to having nightmares, but he didn't often remember his dreams, so the few bad ones tended to stick out. With a sigh, he got out of bed, pulled the covers up neatly, then headed for his tiny bathroom to take a shower. The urgency to work on Sorsha's curse was still there in the back of his mind, prodding him, but he didn't really know what to do about it. Hopefully a shower would shake things loose in his brain.

He did some of his best thinking in the shower.

"You also do good thinking down in the library with a cigar and a good bottle of Scotch," he growled as he stripped out of his pajamas.

Despite his earlier confidence, Alex hadn't gained any insight while he cleaned himself and now he stood facing the mirror, dutifully removing the traces of beard that appeared on his face overnight. Unbidden, the image of Sorsha exploding appeared again in his mind's eye and he almost cut his ear as he jerked the straight razor away from his face.

"Yuck," he said, trying to force the gruesome image from his consciousness. It was far more vivid and visceral than it had any right to be, and Alex shivered. He remembered watching the little mayfly in the bell jar explode when Iggy was first designing the life transference construct, but thankfully Alex had never seen anything like that outside of the test.

He raised the razor to his face to continue shaving and froze. Standing there with his reflection blinking back at him, Alex's mind ran at full speed.

"Bradley Elder," he gasped as he realized what his subconscious had been trying to tell him.

Setting the razor aside, Alex ran out of the bathroom with half his face still covered in lather and a towel tied around his waist. He pulled open the door to the hall and pelted down the stairs as fast as his bare feet would stand.

"Iggy," he shouted as he rounded the corner in the foyer and passed through the library on his way to the kitchen.

"In here," Iggy called back from the kitchen. "Is there something... I suppose there must be," he said when he caught sight of Alex in his towel.

"I think I know how to save Sorsha," he blurted out, "or at least give her more time."

"Why don't you wipe the shaving cream off your face," Iggy said, handing him a kitchen towel, "then sit down and tell me."

Iggy took the seat at the foot of the table and Alex joined him a moment later. He told his mentor about Sorsha's loss of four months of life in just two days.

"That isn't good," Iggy said. "It takes three days to write the life transference rune. If you're right about how quickly she's losing life energy, there may not be time to make another construct for her."

"We may not have to," Alex said. "Remember Bradley Elder?"

"From the Limelight incident," Iggy said. "He worked with Barton before you did."

"Remember that construct he made?"

Iggy gave him a dubious look.

"I remember you used some of that despicable drug to figure it out."

"Well, the whole point of that rune was to convert electrical energy from Barton's towers into magical energy and feed it to Bradly," Alex said. "What if we do the same thing, but instead of converting electricity to magic, we convert magic to life energy."

Iggy stroked his mustache.

"Well," he said at last. "We know the rune for life energy, and I have a fantastic conversion rune."

"All we need is the rune for magical energy," Alex said, then he frowned. "It would be part of Bradly's construct, but I have to admit, I didn't take very good notes about that."

"I did," Iggy said. "While you and the two sorcerers were out dealing with the ambitious Mr. Elder, I copied down everything you figured out."

"So you have the rune, and we have all the other parts; can we remake Bradly's rune to channel magic energy into Sorsha?"

Iggy frowned.

"That's a dangerous idea, Alex," he said. "She's being drained of her energy and we've already put some back. She could be at risk for the very toxicity that's keeping you from using a new escape rune."

"That's a risk we're going to have to take," Alex pushed back. "If we do nothing, she'll be dead before the week is out."

"There's something else you've overlooked," Iggy said. "We're going to need a source of magical energy, and Sorsha's not up to that at the moment."

Alex gave his mentor a sly grin.

"I haven't overlooked anything," he said. "Barton's power grid works by converting raw magic from a spell he's cast at Empire Tower, into electrical energy wherever his generators are. As soon as I'm dressed, I'll go see him and get him to create a smaller version of the spell just for Sorsha."

Iggy nodded but didn't look convinced.

"You realize you're going to have to tell him some things you might prefer to keep secret," he said. "Barton's going to want to know what's happening to Sorsha and that means you'll have to explain about the Legion and the Gordian rune."

"He already knows about the Legion," Alex said. "But if I don't…"

"If you don't, then Sorsha dies," Iggy sighed. "Go finish shaving and get dressed," he said, standing up. "I'll make you an omelet sandwich to take with you."

Alex intended to pass through his vault to his apartment in Empire Tower. He'd still have to ride the residence elevator down to Empire Station to get the elevator up to the offices of Barton Electric, but at least he'd already be inside the security area. He'd gotten halfway through his vault when he remembered that Sherry was using his apartment. He continued to the cover door and knocked, but there was no answer.

Since she was on his approved person list, she could simply use the elevator to go down to Empire Station and then back up to the office. Alex was tempted to go in, since Sherry was most likely gone.

"Or she's in the shower," he said.

That was all he needed, to walk in on Sherry in a compromising position. If he managed to save Sorsha's life, she'd kill him.

With a sigh, Alex turned and headed for the door to his office. Unsurprisingly, when he reached his office and moved along the little hallway to the waiting area, Sherry was already there. She sat at her desk with three notepads laid out in a semi-circle and another pad right in front of her. As Alex entered, she was copying something from one of the peripheral notepads to the one in front of her. Her hair was tied into a braid that went over her left shoulder, trailing down the front of her blue blouse, and her nails had been freshly painted.

"Someone had a good night," he said.

She looked up and sighed, putting her elbow on her desk and her chin in her palm.

"How do you not live in that place?" she asked, a dreamy look crossing her features. "I didn't want to leave this morning."

"Stay as long as you want," Alex said, then nodded at her desk. "Do you have something for me?"

"Just putting together my notes from the courthouse," she said. "Go talk to Barton and I should be done when you get back."

Alex chuckled and headed for the door. He didn't have to ask how Sherry knew where he was going and since she didn't add anything to that statement, he headed across to the door and out into the hall. He rode the elevator down to the terminal and headed immediately for the security station. As he passed Marnie's coffee bar, the smell enticed him to linger, but he'd already wasted too much time with Sherry. Alex needed to talk to Andrew as soon as possible.

The express elevator up to the Barton Electric Lobby moved much faster than a standard elevator, but it still took almost a minute to ascend the skyscraper. When the door opened on the cavernous lobby, Alex was a bit surprised. He was up here at least once a week, checking on the runes that connected Andrew's massive power spell to the generators that, in turn, converted the power into electricity. Usually, he found a crowd of people in the lobby waiting to meet with New York's preeminent sorcerer. Today the lobby was empty save for the pudgy, tuxedo-clad form of Andrew's valet, Gary Bickman, who stood at a podium near the back wall.

"Good morning, Alex," the valet said as he approached. "This isn't your usual day to check the runes, so what brings you out?"

"I need to speak to Andrew. It's urgent."

Bickman's face fell and he leaned in close.

"I'm afraid Mr. Barton is out of town today," he said, keeping his voice low.

"You and I both know that's not actually a deterrent for a sorcerer," he said. "I really need to talk to him as soon as possible, so give him a call wherever he is."

"I would, Alex," Bickman said in his formal British accent. "You know I'd do anything in my power to help you out, but in this case I can't."

That took Alex by surprise. He knew Gary Bickman well enough to know that he wasn't lying, but the idea that Andrew Barton was somewhere he couldn't be reached seemed incredible.

"How is that possible?" Alex asked, not willing to give up yet.

"Mr. Barton likes to seclude a day or two for himself every few months," Bickman explained. "He says not having a telephone around gives him time to think."

Alex sighed in frustration.

"When is he due back from this thinking excursion?"

"Well, he'll have to be back by tomorrow at ten," Bickman said. "He has a meeting with the Mayor of Jersey City to pick a site for the new tower."

Alex knew Andrew wouldn't miss a meeting about a new power tower, so he'd just have to corner the man before the meeting.

"All right," he said. "I'll come back tomorrow at 9 and see if I can catch him. Let him know I'm looking for him when you see him, and it's urgent."

"Absolutely," Bickman said, standing straight again. "You may rely on me."

Alex trudged into his office fifteen minutes later, clutching two cups of Marnie's coffee.

"Aw," Sherry said when she saw him, "you do care."

Alex crossed to her desk and set one of the cups down.

"Please tell me you have something for me," Alex said as she picked up the cup and sipped.

"No luck?" she said, setting down the cup and opening the middle drawer of her desk.

"Long story," Alex said, not wanting to explain everything with Sorsha. Sherry knew some of the story, of course, but Sorsha's current crisis was something he wanted to keep private. "Let's just say I need something to keep me busy."

Sherry took out a cigarette and lit it as Alex talked. When he finished, she picked up the notepad that was still in front of her.

"Here's everything I learned at the clerk's office."

Alex took the notepad and skimmed through it while Sherry went back to her coffee. It was all pretty much what she'd told him yesterday. He was about to set it aside when something caught his eye.

"Is this right?" he asked, pointing to the page.

Sherry leaned over so she could see the page, then nodded.

"I told you about that," she said. "There was no official divorce decree, just an information request."

"About the Waverly family trust?"

Sherry nodded as she puffed her cigarette.

"That means that the Waverlys *have* a trust," Alex said.

"Is that important?" she asked.

Alex nodded.

"Tommy Waverly told me that his wife kept him from accessing their money," Alex said, "but if there's a family trust, there's no way Lillian controls that. It's likely that she's not even a member."

"Let me guess," Sherry said, giving him a sly look. "You want me to go over to the hall of records and find out who's in the Waverly family trust."

"And find out who the trustee is while you're at it," Alex added.

Sherry tapped out her cigarette and finished her coffee before standing.

"You going to be okay here without me?" she asked, opening a drawer and withdrawing her handbag.

Alex put the notepad down and nodded.

"I've got a list of houses I need to go look at," he said. "I want to wait till mid-day for that, but until then I need to look into the current Waverly Radio stock for sale."

"Do you want me to call you when I get the information?" Sherry asked, headed for the door.

Alex considered that for a moment, then shook his head.

"I've still got three days before I have to give Wilks my report," he said. "Besides, it's likely I'll be out most of the day."

"All right," Sherry said, opening the door to the hall. "I'll see you back here this evening and I'll tell you what I found."

Alex nodded, then Sherry shut the door behind her. He pulled out his notepad and transferred the notes Sherry left him onto a blank page. Once he finished, he stepped out into the hall himself, locking the door behind him. He made his way to the elevators, then waited for one to arrive. When it did, he punched the button for the eleventh floor and headed down to the offices of Mayweather Brokerage.

18

ON THE ROAD

"Alex," Beauregard Mayweather's voice boomed as soon as Alex opened the door. He was standing beside the receptionist desk with a folder in his hand. "I was hoping you'd be back."

"Got someone that needs to be investigated?" Alex asked.

Beauregard looked confused for a moment, then chuckled.

"Actually, I had a question," Alex continued.

"Well then, let's mosey down to my office," Beauregard said in his southern drawl. He handed the folder off to his secretary, then led Alex into the back. "Now," he went on once he'd taken a seat behind his desk, "what's put a bee in your bonnet?"

"Is there any way to know if someone has been buying up stock in Waverly Radio?"

Beau raised an eyebrow, but he nodded. He picked up the telephone on his desk and pushed one of the buttons along the bottom.

"Gene, get me the last two weeks of trading on Waverly Radio stock."

She said something that Alex couldn't hear, and Beau hung up.

"It'll take about fifteen minutes for Gene to get the information from Wall Street," he said. "In the meantime, why don't we talk about putting some of your money to work for you? Now I know the market's had problems in the past, but things are sturdy as a brick outhouse these days."

Alex grinned at the dichotomy of Beau's folksy speech patterns matched against his high finance knowledge. In this case, however, Alex wasn't too sure what he was talking about. It was true Alex had more money than he ever thought possible, but his bank account bounced between five hundred and just over a grand on a monthly basis.

"I'm not sure I'm the right candidate for your services, Beau," he said. "I thought you needed serious money before dipping your toe in the market."

Beau looked at Alex as if his hair had suddenly caught fire.

"Well, I don't know how people do it where you come from," Beau said, "but where I grew up, twenty grand was a lot of money."

"Twenty thousand?" Alex scoffed. "Where would I get that kind of scratch?"

Beau's mouth actually fell open at that.

"From the account Andrew Barton set up for you," he said as if it were a self-explanatory answer.

Before Alex could wrap his mind around that, Beau opened his center desk drawer and pulled out a notepad.

"The account was opened in your name three years ago by Andrew," he read. "After you came to see me the other day, I queried the bank to see what you had to work with and as of Monday, you had twenty-two thousand, three-hundred, ninety-eight dollars and eighty-seven cents."

Alex felt his mouth hanging open and quickly shut it. Three years ago was right around the time Alex first met the Lightning Lord. He didn't start working for Barton Electric until nineteen thirty-five, which was only two years ago.

"You didn't know." Beau said, reading the expression on Alex's face.

"I wasn't even working with Andrew three years ago," Alex protested.

Beau laughed at that, shaking his head.

"Well, you'll have to take that up with him," he said. "But there's certainly enough money there to put together a portfolio for you. I'd recommend putting about a third of your cash into the market and keep the rest liquid for a year or two. After that, we'll evaluate the portfolio and see about investing more."

"I'm sure that's great, Beau," Alex said, still trying to sort out what just happened, "but I think I need to talk to Andrew first."

Beau smiled and sat back in his chair.

"Take your time," he said. "I'll be here when you're ready."

Alex was about to respond when the door opened and the secretary came in. She put a piece of paper on Beau's desk, then turned and left. Beau thanked her as she went out, then picked up the paper and scanned it.

"This is your stock change information," he said. "According to this there was a bunch of movement out of the stock last week on Friday."

"That's when the news broke about Fredrick Chance's death," Alex supplied.

"Makes sense," Beau said, reading down the page. "The stock continued to fall off a little bit day by day until yesterday."

"What happened yesterday?"

"Looks like someone bought a large block of Waverly stock. If this is right, it's about seventy percent of what's available for sale. If I had to guess, someone is making a play to take over the company."

"You said they bought up seventy percent of what was available," Alex said. "Why didn't they buy all of it?"

"Because they didn't need to," Beau said. "You only need to have fifty-one percent of a company's stock to have full control over it."

"So," Alex said, his mind working a full speed now, "whoever bought the shares yesterday must have enough stock already to get to fifty-one percent."

"Maybe," Beau said. "They might not have that stock themselves. Sometimes these kinds of moves are made by a small group who have enough stock to take control when they put their shares together."

That wasn't good news. Alex had thought that all he had to do was track down whoever had the rest of the stock and he'd have his killer. If it turned out to be a group, it would add more suspects to his list instead of taking one off.

"How much stock was bought yesterday?" Alex asked. "I mean compared to all the stock Waverly has."

Beau checked a couple of numbers on the page, then did some math in his head.

"I reckon it's about seventeen percent of all Waverly stock."

"So if someone, or a group of someones, want to take control of Waverly, they would have to have thirty-four percent of stock between them, right?"

"That's it exactly," Beau said with a nod.

"Thanks for that, Beau," Alex said, standing. "I need to go take another look at my suspects."

"Don't forget to talk to Andrew," Beau said, rising as well. "And then come back and see me," he called after Alex's retreating form.

Alex rode the elevator back up to his office, going over the Waverly case in his mind. For the first time since he'd taken it on, he felt he was making progress. He was pretty sure everyone involved in his case had some stock in Waverly, not to mention their board of directors, and he'd have to check out all of them. Luckily he was pretty sure Lillian would give him the information on who had how much stock. Once he knew that, his primary suspects should be obvious.

You hope, he thought as the elevator doors opened.

As excited as he was, Alex had to push the Waverly case out of his mind. When he reached his office, the clock on the wall showed a few minutes past nine. People would be out at their jobs, and it was the perfect time for him to check out the list of houses he'd obtained from Manhattan Land and Building. There were only five of them, but they were spread out all over the city, so it was going to take him the rest of the morning and probably a good part of the afternoon to run them all down.

"Better get started," he said, as he passed into his office waiting area.

He went down to his office and pulled out the folder on Waverly, transferring the notes from his conversation with Beau into it. As soon as he was done, he put that folder aside and pulled out the notebook he'd used the other night with Sorsha, copying the addresses of the five houses into his flip notebook.

On his way out, he left a note for Sherry on her desk, then hung the 'Closed' sign on his front door and headed downstairs to catch a cab.

Alex mopped his brow with his handkerchief while he leaned backward to stretch out the muscles in his lower back. He'd been walking for hours, checking out one house and then another. Since all of the homes were in residential areas, he found himself walking long distances in order to find a cab to take him to the next location. The spring weather had turned warm and by the time he'd realized it, it was too late to use a climate rune. They would keep you at whatever temperature you started at and now Alex was too hot for it to do anything useful.

As for the three houses he'd seen so far, they were normal, regular, everyday houses. The kind of places anyone might live. None of them were anything like Hathaway House; most were smaller and less grand. They were also very unlike each other. One was a three-story in the Victorian style, while another was a basic single-story, two-bedroom number, and the last was a wide house with a small upstairs over one part.

Alex had knocked on all of their doors and found no one home. Looking in the windows revealed that they were mostly empty, and one was obviously having some work done inside, but nothing appeared out of the ordinary. He'd walked the small lawns of the homes and even talked to some of the neighbors, but so far, he'd come up empty. All the neighbors knew was that the previous owners had sold quickly and moved away. He was starting to think this was a dead end.

"Except that all these houses were bought under aliases," he reminded himself. Looking down at his notepad, Alex searched for the next address. It wasn't anywhere near his current location, but he could see a sky crawler rail a block over.

Before he put his notebook away, his eyes drifted to the name beside the address.

"Rhea Curren," he read, then shook his head. "Reoccurring. There is no possibility these people aren't up to something."

Reassured that he wasn't on a wild goose chase, Alex tucked his notepad into his shirt pocket and headed off toward the sky crawler station.

The house bought by Rhea Curren turned out not to be empty. In fact, as the cab drove up, Alex could see a team of workmen carrying tools and building materials inside the house through a hole in the side wall. It looked like they had made the hole to expedite their work.

"Go down two more houses," Alex told the cabbie as the car started to slow. He wanted the chance to observe the workers before he talked to anyone.

Paying the cabbie, Alex got out of the cab and crossed the street. He turned and walked past the construction, not seeing anything suspicious. The workmen looked like workmen, and everyone seemed to be busy.

Feeling more confident, Alex crossed the street again and approached a heavyset man in overalls.

"You can't be here," the man growled before Alex could speak. "This is private property."

"I just need to speak to whoever is in charge," Alex said. "Won't be a minute."

The man glared at Alex for a long moment, then scoffed and headed inside through the hole in the wall. He'd only been gone a few seconds, but Alex felt the hair on his arm stand up. Without moving, he shifted his eyes, glancing around. At first nothing seemed amiss, but as he watched, he realized the men coming out of the house to pick up more materials were all watching him. They were trying to be subtle, but they weren't very good at it.

There's no reason for them to be this suspicious, he thought. *This must be the right place.*

The whole scene reminded him of that time a bunch of Nazis were pretending to be workmen at Andrew's Brooklyn tower. The memory gave him chills.

Alex took a slow breath and then let it out. So far, these roughnecks hadn't done anything but stare, and they couldn't know he was on to them. The last thing he wanted was a fight, especially since his 1911 was in his vault along with his knuckle duster. He did have his flash ring, but he'd used two of its four runes and hadn't replaced them. Still, two flash runes were more than enough to make a run for it, if it came to that.

The tension in the air seemed to be growing with every passing moment and Alex was grateful when a large man in coveralls with a bald head, massive shoulders, and the stub of a cigar between his teeth strode out of the house. He had the kind of no-nonsense look Alex expected from bouncers in low-rent bars, and the man's presence seemed to ease the pregnant atmosphere. The other workers returned to their tasks, moving quickly, though some of them still threw Alex furtive glances as they went.

"You the guy asking for the foreman?" the bald man growled as he approached.

Since Alex was the only one present who wasn't one of the workmen, the question struck him as a bit odd, but he nodded in reply.

"Alex Lockerby," he said, handing over one of his cards.

The bald man glanced at it, then handed it back.

"None of my boys have warrants," he declared. "So if that's everything, I've got work to do and no time to waste."

"You misunderstand," Alex said as the man began to turn. "I represent a client who would like to buy this property."

The bald man actually laughed at that.

"Then they should hire an agent, not a private dick."

"Well, that's the problem," Alex cut in quickly. "He couldn't track down the owner, Miss Curren, so he hired me to do it."

"Well she ain't here," Baldy said, still half turned away from Alex.

"But you work for her. That means she pays you." Alex looked at the hole in the side of the house and the considerable piles of materials in the yard. "For this kind of work, she isn't paying you in cash, she'd have to give you a check, and that means you know her address."

The big man turned back to face Alex, a nasty smile spreading across his face.

"Sure," he said. "I know where my employer lives, but my clients don't like people nosing into their business. So I keep my mouth shut; better for business that way. Now, I've got nothing more to say to you, and you being here is slowing my boys down, so leave, before I have to have you thrown out."

Alex knew a losing hand when he saw one, so he tipped his hat and headed back to the sidewalk.

Whatever was going on with Manhattan Land and Building and the real estate buyers with the fake names, Baldy and his crew were in on it. A legitimate company might have withheld the name of their employer in the name of privacy, but Alex had mentioned Miss Curren by name, and the big man hadn't flinched. Whoever bought the property might have wanted to conceal their name when dealing with Manhattan Building and Loan, but now that they owned the house, there wouldn't be any pressing need for secrecy.

Unless there is, he thought.

He dismissed that idea as soon as it came. If the buyer were truly that paranoid, they'd have used a different alias with Baldy. Either Baldy didn't know the person who was employing him, which wasn't likely, or he did know them and he knew that Rhea Curren was a pseudonym.

When Alex reached the end of the block, he looked around for the best direction to find a cab. He was somewhere in the mid ring, south of the core, and although he could see Empire Tower, his chances of catching a ride might be better in another direction.

Pausing to light a cigarette, he caught sight of someone ducking behind a large hedge in one of the yards. Alex stood, puffing on his cigarette for a moment, watching the hedge out of the side of his eye. Whoever had jumped behind it didn't reappear, but he saw two pairs of work shoes underneath another part where the hedge had been trimmed, off the sidewalk. That meant at least three people were following him, no doubt sent by Baldy to teach Alex a lesson about poking his nose in where it didn't belong. The only reason the men hid themselves here was that Alex hadn't gone far enough from the construction site for them to have plausible deniability.

Alex searched the horizon again, but this time he wasn't looking for likely cab sites.

"That ought to do," he said, looking at the roofs of several industrial buildings off to the west. He turned left and began walking quickly along the residential sidewalk. His tail wouldn't have much cover in this area of small homes and picket fences, so Alex doubted they'd try anything. The industrial area, however, would be exactly their kind of place to jump him.

Alex walked a little faster, pushing himself. He needed to put enough distance between himself and his pursuers so he could open his vault before they reached him.

At this point Alex was in a slow, calculated foot race, and if he figured wrong, he might end up dead.

19

EVEN ODDS

Alex turned the corner of a block of mostly industrial buildings, slipping into a jog as soon as he was out of sight of the men pursuing him. He passed a diner from which he wouldn't order water, then a shop selling work boots. Beyond that was a tannery, and Alex covered his nose from the smell. After the tannery, there appeared to be an abandoned machine shop.

Perfect, he thought.

Now all he had to do was disappear around the corner before his tail saw where he went. They'd spend at least five minutes checking out the diner, the boot shop, and the tannery before they reached the alley between the tannery and the empty machine shop.

He'd just ducked out of sight when he heard an exclamation back down the street. Alex was tempted to listen, but he couldn't spare the time. If they'd seen where he went, he'd have less than a minute to get his vault open.

The area between the tannery and the abandoned shop turned out to be an open field that served as a loading area for the shop. It was now a forest of weeds, growing up through the ground with a long cement loading dock running along the machine shop, with large, boarded-up doors behind it.

Alex didn't give the location any more than a passing glance, as he turned to the blank wall to his left and quickly drew a chalk door. The vault rune was already in his hand, and he stuck it to the wall and lit it with his lighter. As the heavy metal door melted out of the sturdy brick, Alex held his key ready, shoving it into the lock as soon as it appeared.

He could have simply entered his vault and pushed the door closed behind him, but he needed to know who Rhea Curren was, and this was his best chance to find out. Stripping off his suit coat, he dropped it on the floor as he pulled open his gun cabinet. His Colt 1911 was in his shoulder holster that hung from a peg. Moving quickly, Alex pulled on the holster, then withdrew the pistol and pulled the slide back to check that the barrel was empty. Satisfied the weapon wasn't loaded, he grabbed a magazine from the shelf at the bottom of the cabinet, sliding it into the handle and releasing the action to push a round into the chamber.

Returning the weapon to its holster, Alex grabbed an extra magazine and slipped it into the holster's elastic pocket under his right arm. The last thing he grabbed was his knuckle duster, slipping the fingers of his right hand through it as he closed the cabinet with his left.

Scooping up his suit coat, he did a quick head check outside his vault. It wouldn't do to get ambushed as he left. Finding the little loading dock empty, he stepped out and shut the vault, slipping into his suit coat as the heavy steel door melted into the brickwork.

"That doesn't go anywhere," a gruff voice growled. "Skip it."

Alex hadn't considered that his personal gang of roughnecks might pass by his hiding place. That was actually pretty smart of them, wrong though it was. In a similar circumstance, he might skip this dead end as well. He considered calling out or making a noise to attract their attention, but before he could, another voice spoke up.

"It don't go too far," it said. "Let's check it."

Alex moved to the far side of the weed-bound lot and put his back to the wall. He wanted to be able to see everyone who came through the alley while giving himself enough room to react if they did something unexpected.

As he watched, three men emerged from the wide alley that served as a drive for the loading area. The men wore work clothes and heavy boots with flat caps on their heads. They were all heavy men, not fat but thick, with the general large frame hard-working men developed.

The man nearest to Alex was shorter than the others, with a baby face that was marred by a thick scar running from his right ear, across his cheek, and down to his chin. He grinned when he saw Alex, causing the scar to bow outward.

"There you are," he growled in a high-pitched voice that belied his stocky frame.

"Took you long enough," Alex said, leaning casually against the wall with his arms crossed across his chest. In that position his knuckle duster was hidden in the crook of his left arm.

"You should'a run when you had the chance." This came from the same man that had urged them to skip the loading yard. He had a black mustache that made him look like a henchman extra in a Roy Rogers picture, with overalls and a plaid shirt.

"Now why would I do that?" Alex said, trying to project as much confidence as he could. He was relatively sure he could take these guys with the aid of his knuckle duster, but he always had his pistol and even his flash runes to fall back on if things got nasty.

"He thinks because he dates a sorceress, he's safe," the third man said. He was tall and blond with massive hands that he flexed as he walked. "I say we teach him otherwise, boys."

Blondie reached behind his back and pulled a two-foot length of lead pipe from the waistband of his trousers.

"That wouldn't be the same pipe you used to kill Lucius Briggs," Alex asked. "Would it?"

"Shut up," Overalls sneered before Blondie could respond. He pulled a heavy folding knife from his pocket that must have been a foot long when open and locked. Mustache, on the other hand, pulled a large revolver from his trouser pocket. From the look of it, Alex guessed it was a .44 or .45.

That's really going to hurt, Alex thought. Shield runes could slow bullets down enough so they wouldn't penetrate, but it still felt like getting kicked by a mule.

As much as the thought of the .45 bothered him, Alex was much more worried about the other two men. He was too used to fighting proper thugs who came armed with guns and fists. There were several variations of the common shield rune, and Alex knew them all. One was designed especially to stop knives. He'd used that one three years ago when he'd helped apprehend the ghost killer, but that was only because he knew Duane King attacked his victims with a knife. He hadn't seen any reason to use one since.

As for Blondie and his pipe, Alex could have used a low impact shield rune. They were great for stopping fists and bludgeoning weapons, but a high velocity round like Mustache's .45 could get through them.

What this meant was that Alex's shield rune would stop the bullets, but wouldn't do much to stop the other two men. He wavered momentarily with simply pulling his pistol and putting Blondie down. The problem with that was that his friends would probably run, and Alex needed information. He'd have to play this smart and hope for the best.

"So," he said as the workmen stalked toward him. "What's your boss so afraid of? He behind in his permits?"

"He don't like people snooping around," Mustache said. "He wanted us to let you know that you're not welcome."

The men moved closer, now less than ten feet from Alex in a semi-circle around him.

"I hate to tell you," Alex said, uncrossing his arms and letting his knuckle duster hang loose in his hand, "but I don't care what your boss thinks. I go where I want and a group of miscreants like you isn't going to dissuade me."

Overalls cursed and stepped forward, preparing to rush him.

That was Alex's cue.

He dropped to one knee and dropped his chin to his chest while holding his knuckle duster over his head. With a simple touch of his thumb, he activated one of the flash runes on the butt end of the weapon and blinding white light suddenly filled the loading area.

The three men howled in pain and rage as their vision was temporarily burned away. Normally, Alex would have trouble seeing in the first few seconds after he set off a flash rune; the light was simply too bright, even with his eyes closed. This time, however, with his head lowered, the brim of his fedora kept the worst of the light from affecting him.

When he opened his eyes, he found Overalls only a few steps away, waving his knife blindly back and forth. Stepping to the side, Alex waited for the man to swing away from him, then stepped in and drove his knuckle duster into Overall's side. The impact rune and the numbing rune both went off and Alex heard the man's ribs crack before he went down in a heap.

Overalls moaned in pain and clutched his side as he curled himself into a ball in an attempt to ward off any future blows.

"Allen!" Blondie yelled, hearing Overalls groaning.

Considering him the most dangerous of the three, Alex rushed at Blondie. The pipe-wielding man must have guessed that his buddy Allen was down, because he immediately lashed out with the pipe, swinging it at the level of his chest.

Alex should have seen it coming, should have anticipated the blow, but he didn't. By the time he saw it coming, all he could do was turn so he took it on the back instead of on his left arm.

The lead pipe landed with a solid thud and Alex staggered forward, seeing stars. Instead of trying to hold his footing, Alex let himself fall to the ground. Behind him Blondie pressed his advantage, stepping forward with another vicious swing, right where Alex would have been if he'd remained standing.

"Got you," he yelled, swinging again a bit to the left. "I got you."

For his part, Alex planned to roll away from Blondie, then stand, but when he tried, his back spasmed in pain and it was all he could do not to groan and give away his position.

Blondie and Mustache would be blind for another fifteen seconds or so, but then their vision would start returning. Alex needed to move. Taking a deep breath, he gritted his teeth and forced himself to roll, ignoring the pain. When he got far enough away from the pipe-wielding ape, Alex stood up slowly.

The blond builder was still swinging wildly, hoping to get in another lucky blow, but this time his trajectory had turned him away from Alex. Without hesitation, Alex stepped forward and drove his knuckle duster into Blondie's lower back. Roaring in pain, he tried to turn, but Alex was ready. Slamming his fist across the big man's jaw, he knocked him cold. Blondie spun around like a slow-moving top, then collapsed to the hard dirt of the lot.

Alex took a deep breath that made his back muscles twinge. The only man left standing was Mustache and he had the .45. That was something Alex could deal with.

"Mike! Alan!" Mustache called out, blinking his eyes furiously. "Sound off, did you get him?"

"They sure didn't," Alex responded, speaking a bit louder than normal to spook the other man. It worked like a charm when he fired wildly in Alex's direction. "Maybe you're ready to tell me who Rhea Curren is. I mean really, since I know that Rhea Curren is a made-up name."

Alex decided to wait until Mustache's vision returned, the .45 would hurt if he got hit, but the psychological value of shrugging off Mustache's shots would be worth it.

Just as Mustache's blinking began to slow, Alex heard the crunch of old leaves behind him. There wasn't time to do anything but react, so Alex threw himself forward, turning away from the sound as he did so. It almost worked, but Alex felt something pinch his side and rake across his ribs.

He knew what had happened, even before he turned all the way around. When he first looked back and noticed he was being followed, there were four men, not three. Obviously the fourth man had been left as a lookout, but the sound of his friends in trouble drew him in.

Alex staggered, struggling to keep his balance. Falling now would be a very bad idea. Clutching his left hand to his side, he spun all the way around to confront the fourth man. He was younger than the others with a flat face and buck teeth, revealed by his lip, turned up in a snarl. Buck teeth clutched a hooked knife that would have done Alex serious hurt had he not heard the young man coming. Blood dripped from the tip as Bucky recovered from not killing Alex, and he lashed out with the knife again.

This time Alex knew the blow was coming and he stepped back as Bucky slashed, taking himself out of range of the wicked blade. As soon as the nasty hook-point went by, Alex darted forward, lashing out with the knuckle duster. Bucky might have been young, but he was quick, leaning aside to take his head out of range. Unfortunately that also brought his shoulder right up to Alex's blow.

The force rune went off and Bucky screamed as his clavicle cracked. That took the wind out of the man, and he collapsed into a weeping and moaning heap. Before Alex could even step back, Mustache's gun boomed and a slug hit Alex in the back. The impact hurt, but it hit right where Blondie had bashed him with the lead pipe.

Alex swore and staggered forward as his back spasmed with pain.

"That's enough of your tricks, scribbler," Mustache growled. "Get your hands up and turn around. Slowly."

Alex did as he was told and found Mustache standing about five yards away, holding the hand cannon in both hands. Tactically it was a good position, close enough for accurate shooting but too far away for Alex to rush him. For his part, Alex bided his time while the pain in his back began to ebb.

"Who told you about us?" Mustache demanded, waving the gun for emphasis. "How did you know about the house?"

"Why do you care?" Alex fired back.

Mustache fired, clipping Alex in the leg. It didn't hurt so much, but he went down on one knee because of the impact.

"Now you know," Mustache gloated. "Your protection runes won't help you. I've got spellbreaker runes on this gun, so you'd better answer my questions."

Alex resisted the urge to laugh. Spellbreakers were primarily used to disrupt sorcery, but there were a handful of runes they would affect. Alex had used them to remove the escape runes tattooed on Duane King's arm, and a spellbreaker might be able to disrupt the life transference rune, but simple constructs like shield runes were immune to their effect.

Letting a slow grin spread across his face, Alex stood up.

"Oops," he said.

Mustache fired again, clipping Alex's neck. It stung like the dickens, but Alex managed not to flinch.

"I guess your boss isn't as smart as he thinks he is," Alex said, touching his wounded right side. He winced just at touching it and his hand came away bloody. Bucky had got him pretty good with that hooked knife, but it wasn't bleeding too badly. "So," Alex continued, "who are you and your friends working for?"

Mustache glared at him with pure hatred.

"How would I know?" he growled.

"Then what are you doing in that house?"

"Building out the cellar. The owner thinks it's too small."

Alex had to admit, that didn't sound terribly nefarious, assuming Mustache was telling the truth. He looked back up as Mustache raised his gun and fired again. This time the bullet hit Alex right in the forehead.

Stars exploded in Alex's vision and he felt himself fall backwards. The impact stunned him, and he heard Mustache making a run for it, leaving his friends to whatever mercy he expected from Alex.

Shaking his head to clear it, Alex laid on the dirt looking up at the sky for a long moment. Not for the first time, he thanked his shield rune for keeping him alive. Last year such a shot would have killed him easily, but that was before Alex discovered the real power of linking runes.

Most runes were very temporary magic, but there were ways to extend their durability. In Alex's office his strongbox had a pass rune that he only had to replace every six months or so. That was thanks to its being carved into the surface of the steel box. His new shield rune worked the same way; it was one rune but carved into a block of solid steel in Alex's vault. With his vault permanently open, the link between the rune and Alex's body would work from any distance, and it would protect his entire body. He still wasn't sure what its limits were, but so far it was holding.

With a groan, Alex rolled onto his right side and forced himself into a sitting position. Blondie was still out, but Bucky and Overalls were conscious. He guessed a little pressure on Bucky's broken clavicle would convince the kid to give up everything he knew.

Just as Alex started to push himself to his feet, he heard the sound of sirens in the distance. Someone had heard the gunshots and called the cops and that meant there wouldn't be time to force answers out of anyone. With a sigh of resignation, Alex fished out his rune book and walked painfully over to the spot on the wall where he'd previously chalked a door. Since none of the conscious construction men were facing his direction, he opened his vault and passed inside right as the sound of screeching brakes announced the arrival of the police.

20

REBUILDING

The heavy steel door melted away, leaving the cool gray stone of the vault behind. Alex made the mistake of leaning against it while his body ached. The support of the wall let his mind drift until he realized he was in danger of falling asleep.

Gasping, he pushed away from the wall and staggered back. He wasn't sure how long he'd been there, but he knew he was bleeding down his pant leg, so he turned and began shambling toward his medical room.

He hadn't cleaned it since he'd hit his head on his own vault floor, so the burned remnants of his shirt and the empty potion vials Iggy used were still scattered around his sink and instrument tray. Alex had a momentary thought of limping to his phone and calling his mentor, but Iggy was working on the construct to save Sorsha.

"You'll have to do it yourself," he said out loud.

That wouldn't be as much of a problem as it sounded, since when Alex had put in the medical room, Iggy had given him a few days of intense first-aid training. Alex even remembered some of it.

Removing his rune book and his pocketwatch, he struggled out of his bloody suit jacket and tossed it into the hamper by the door. His vest and his shirt followed once he'd managed to undo all the buttons.

Moving to the mirror, he examined the wound. Bucky's knife had punched through his side right above the rib cage. By a sheer miracle of luck, Alex had turned away from Bucky's slash, putting the hooked point on the far side of the knife. If the young man had managed to catch Alex with the hook, it would have peeled his side wide open. As it was, the blade dragged along his ribs, leaving a shallow cut running perpendicular to his side.

"Not too bad," Alex said, hoping he was right. He tried to turn, to get a better look at the puncture, but his back spasmed in pain.

Cursing, he walked gingerly to the cabinet against the back wall. Reaching up slowly to open it, he took down a small vial of bluish-green liquid and removed the cork stopper with his teeth. Spitting the stopper into the sink, he tipped the vial up and swallowed the cloyingly sweet liquid in one go.

Immediately, Alex felt a warm numbness in his gut that began to creep outward. The potion would stop his muscles from spasming and dull the pain from his injuries, but he would need to be careful. Not feeling pain meant he could cause further injury to himself and not even know it. Resolving to move slowly and not put too much stress on his back, Alex focused on what came next.

The cut in his side was still leaking blood, but he didn't seem to be in immediate danger of bleeding to death. Thinking back to Iggy's training, Alex remembered that he needed to start the deep part of the wound healing before sealing the surface damage.

He took a washcloth from a shelf by the sink, then ran the water until it got hot and held the cloth under the stream. Squeezing it to remove most of the water, Alex ran the cloth carefully around his wound, removing the rapidly drying blood. He sat in the little chair that stood under the linen shelf and repeated the process with his leg. When he stood again, he stripped off his undershorts and tossed them after the rest of his bloody clothes. He'd have to deal with them eventually, but now wasn't the time.

Returning to his potion cabinet, Alex took down a round bottle marked *Internal Restorative*, followed by a bottle with a dropper in the lid labeled, *Tissue Mend*. The round bottle, he opened like the pain reliever before it, then chugged it down, barely able to resist the urge to gag. When he was finally finished, he gasped, panting like a racehorse who'd done a mile and a quarter.

Alex felt a pinch in his side and gritted his teeth; restorative potions always stung like a thousand bees, even through the pain killer. It would take five or so minutes for the restorative to finish its work, so Alex moved to the examination gurney and laid down carefully on his good side.

Focusing his attention on the pocketwatch, Alex kept himself awake by watching the motion of the tiny second hand as it went around. After seven minutes, just to be sure, he set the watch aside and unscrewed the dropper cap on the little bottle. Squeezing the dropper's bulb, he siphoned up some of the liquid from the bottle, then began dropping the golden liquid along the cut in his side. Everywhere the liquid touched his skin, it sizzled and the wound was drawn together.

Alex knew from experience that this was incredibly painful, but the potion he'd taken earlier kept most of it from affecting him. Moving slowly from the furthest edge of the cut, he proceeded along its length to the puncture, which closed up after three drops of the *Tissue Mend* solution.

He waited another five minutes to be sure the potions had done their jobs, then pushed up and off the gurney and moved back to the mirror. From what he could see, the wound was completely closed, though it left an impressive scar behind. There were potions that could have sealed the whole thing and left nothing, but those required more medical knowledge to use than Alex possessed.

"Women are impressed by scars," he said, quoting an old axiom, then he sighed. "At least it's not on your face."

Satisfied with his work, Alex placed the empty vial and the bottle in the sink, then returned the dropper bottle back to the cabinet. He wasn't excited about the next part of his treatment, but it had to be done. If he tried going out or even working at his desk, his battered muscles and joints would get worse, or he could be permanently injured.

Reaching up, he removed a large beaker filled with purple and black liquids that were disinclined to mix. As Alex examined it, the two liquids seemed to move and swirl in the bottle all by themselves. A neatly printed paper label was stuck to the angled side of the beaker, reading *Soft Tissue Restorative*. Printed below the name was a warning not to drive or sign legal papers within three hours of consumption.

Walking slowly and deliberately, so as not to exacerbate any injuries he couldn't feel, Alex made his way across his vault. After his accident, he'd been tempted to give Sherry her own key to the vault. As he walked, naked, across his great hall, he was glad he hadn't. With his luck, Sherry would choose that exact moment to come in, no doubt with Sorsha in tow.

Alex passed by his reading area and entered the brownstone hallway. To his left was the opening leading to his kitchen and to his right was the little bedroom he'd built for himself. Since he'd left his pocketwatch sitting on the gurney in the medical room, he turned into the bedroom and pulled back the covers of the bed.

"Here goes nothing," he said, holding up the beaker with the restorative. Using small movements, he began to swirl the liquid inside. As he moved, spinning it faster and faster, the contents began to react. The purple liquid glowed with a pinkish light and the black ooze became somehow blacker. After a few moments of this, the beaker flashed and the cork was blown out of the top, followed by sparks that looked like miniature shooting stars. The light subsided and the liquid inside was now a deep rich purple, the kind of color Alex had seen worn by royalty in paintings.

With a sigh, he sat down gently on the bed, then he tipped the beaker up and chugged the potion until it was gone. This one tasted like black currant jam, so Alex had no trouble swallowing it. He quickly set the beaker on the little table beside the bed and laid down. Reaching for his covers, Alex was barely able to pull them up and over him before his vault faded away into blackness and he knew no more.

Every part of Alex's body hurt when he finally managed to claw his way back to consciousness. He lay there in his vault bed, looking up at the gray ceiling with no idea what time it was. The *Soft Tissue Restorative* would have taken care of his back and any bruises he might have acquired, but it was a fairly basic potion and that meant it exacted a toll for its healing. That toll was usually several hours of unconsciousness while the potion directed the body's processes to the healing. Iggy called it the magical version of the conservation of matter and energy.

All potions required extra rest from the body in return for their miraculous gifts, but more powerful alchemists could brew the potion so that it would take that toll in small chunks over the course of weeks. Unfortunately, Soft Tissue Restorative did the bare knuckle brawling kind of healing, fast, effective, and painful, so alchemists brewed it to take its required rest right up front.

With a groan, Alex pushed through the pain and forced himself up into a sitting position. It was after one when he'd patched himself up, so there might still be time to get some work done. The first thing he had to do was get down to the hall of records and they closed at five.

Alex stood, but staggered immediately as a wave of dizziness and nausea washed over him. Taking several deep breaths, he cleared his head and stepped into the hallway.

When he reached the medical room and checked his watch, the time was twenty-five minutes after four. Even if he were already dressed, he'd never make it to the hall of records in time to do anything.

Time to tag in some help, he reasoned.

Heading back into the great room, Alex moved to his writing desk and picked up the telephone there. A moment later the operator connected him to Lockerby Investigations.

"Where you been, boss?" Sherry's chipper voice greeted him.

"Sleeping off a healing potion," he answered, seeing no reason to lie.

"A couple of construction roughnecks jumped me, but don't worry. I'm okay. Did you find out anything about the Waverly trust?"

"Sure did," she said in a voice that positively glowed with pride. "The trust hasn't been amended since before Tommy's mother Lula died. Right now there are only two beneficiaries, Tommy and his father."

Alex smiled at that, wishing he had his notepad to write that down.

DAN WILLIS

"That's great, doll," he said. "Listen, I hate to do this to you, but I need you to run over to the hall of records and look up some building permits."

The sound of Sherry scribbling on a notepad came through the receiver.

"Whose permits am I looking for?"

Alex closed his eyes and pictured the house under construction he'd visited earlier. There was a sign posted in the front yard with the name of the construction company on it. He hadn't paid particular attention to it at the time, because he assumed the workmen were just workmen, now he struggled to bring the mental image into focus.

"Dobosh," he said at last. "Dobosh Construction."

Sherry asked him to spell it, then promised to leave right away and hung up.

Alex pushed the hook down on the candlestick phone, then released it and waited for the operator. This time his call was to Arthur Wilks.

"Tommy Waverly is your man," he said when the insurance man picked up his phone.

"You think he killed Fredrick Chance?"

"I do," Alex said.

"Can you prove it?"

"No," Alex admitted, "but I think you can. When Mr. Chance was killed, it threw Waverly radio into disarray, and that brought the stock price down."

"I'm familiar with how Wall Street works, scribbler," Wilks growled. "Without Fredrick Chance and his special rune, the company's value would drop significantly."

"Making them a prime target for a hostile takeover," Alex finished. "Recently someone bought up a large chunk of Waverly stock."

"But didn't you tell me that Lillian Waverly cut her husband off from the family money?"

"She did," Alex said, "but I've just learned the Waverleys have a family trust, one that Lillian is not a beneficiary of. Even if she knows that account exists, she doesn't control it."

"So you think Tommy killed Chance to drive the stock price down, then bought up as much as he needed, using an account Lillian can't control."

"That's it exactly," he said.

There was a pause, during which Alex could swear he could hear Wilks' mind working.

"All you need to do now," Alex said quickly, "is have your firm subpoena the trust's records and you'll be able to prove that Tommy is the one trying to buy out Waverly Radio and take over."

"That does sound like an awfully good motive for murder," Wilks admitted, somewhat grudgingly. "Tommy gets his company, his autonomy, and his manhood back in one fell swoop. I like it."

"Check the trust's bank records and I suspect you'll like it even more," Alex assured him.

"All right," Wilks said. "It'll take weeks to get those records, but you've given me enough reasonable doubt that I won't have to cut the Waverlys a check any time soon. I do want you to keep digging, though. Just in case this doesn't pan out."

Alex didn't see any reasonable way this wouldn't pan out, but he'd seen surer cases fall apart, so he agreed.

Hanging up the phone with Wilks, Alex shivered. He was still completely naked and vaults were naturally cool. As he returned to the medical room, however, he wondered if he ought to solve more of his cases in the nude. It was strangely liberating.

He chuckled at the thought, but liberating or not, he needed clothes. He had five suits, and the others were hanging in his wardrobe in the brownstone. Instead of grabbing his pocketwatch, however, he grabbed the hamper from his medical room, picked up his shoes, and carried them to his workbench in the great room.

Dumping the hamper out, Alex found two button-up shirts, a suit coat, suit pants, a vest, two ties, a pair of socks, and a pair of his undershorts. All of them were covered in dried blood, most of the large garments had holes, and one of the shirts was burned.

Alex laid out the garments on the top of the workbench, moving to the next bench when he ran out of room. Once everything was in place, Alex pulled out a drawer under the workbench top and took out a hard leather case with a large red cross on it. This was his 'Fix It' kit.

The kit was closed by a heavy brass snap and once Alex popped it free, the top pivoted back one-hundred eighty degrees. Inside were several small tools, a sharp chisel, a small ball-peen hammer, a sewing kit, a clean rag, and a bottle of cleaning solution. Behind the tools was a thin wooden divider about an inch thick that contained rune paper.

Taking the rune box out of the kit, Alex pulled the stack of papers out as a group and then moved down the line, setting a minor mending rune by each piece of damaged clothing and a standard mending rune by the burned shirt.

Burns took more energy to mend because they needed to regenerate some of the destroyed fabric.

This done, Alex set a cleaning rune aside, then returned the stack of loose runes to the wooden box, and the box to the kit. He reached for his lighter, which he carried in his pants pocket, before remembering that he wasn't wearing pants. He sighed and headed back to the medical room to get it.

When he returned, he went down the line, lighting the restoration runes, pausing with each one to will it onto the damaged area. In less than two minutes all of his garments were in pristine, if dirty, condition.

Next, Alex picked up all the repaired garments and tossed them into a pile in the middle of the table, then added his blood-soaked shoes. He bent down and pulled a metal wastebasket out from beneath the table, setting it up on top, next to the pile of clothes. With everything in place, Alex stuck the cleaning rune to the pile of clothes and lit it. The rune blazed to life and the pile of clothes began to rustle and move. A dark fog seemed to evaporate from the top and began to coalesce into a cloud of inky black particles.

In the old days, Alex would never have used a cleaning rune in his vault. The black particles were the dirt and grime from his clothes, compressed into a concentrated form. If they touched anything, they'd pop, expanding back to their original size and staining whatever they made contact with. Now, however, he was ready. When he wrote the cleaning rune, he linked it to a rag in the bottom of the garbage can. Eventually the rag would fill up with the dirt and gunk from his clothes, but all Alex would have to do then was replace it with a new rag and burn the old one.

As he watched, the stream of black particles flew out from the gaps between the pile of clothes, swirling into a line that moved invariably to the metal can where it dropped down through the open top and disappeared.

When the process finished, Alex stowed the can back under the bench and returned his 'Fix It' kit to the drawer. Separating his clothes, he began to dress, then returned his gear to his pockets. He hesitated when he got to his shoulder holster, but after the day he'd had, Alex slipped it over his shirt, then donned his suit coat.

"All right," he said once he was ready. Pulling his watch from his vest pocket, he saw that it was already after five, but that didn't mean he was out of options. "The day's not done yet," he said, snapping the cover closed on his watch, "and neither am I."

21

THE BUILDER

Alex headed to his office, then down the little hall to the waiting room. It was almost six, but Sherry was there, sitting at her desk and compiling several pads of notes into several client folders.

"You feeling better?" she asked when she looked up.

"I'm a bit stiff and sore, but no permanent damage," he said. "What did you find out about Dobosh Construction?"

Sherry looked around her desk, eventually settling on a notepad next to the telephone.

"They were founded last year by a man named Aaron Dobosh," she read. "They do new building as well as renovations, but based on their current list of permits, most of their business seems to be remodeling." She tore a page from the notebook and handed it to him. "This is the list of building permits they currently have."

Alex took the list and scanned it. He wasn't surprised to find all five of the houses Sorsha found at Manhattan Land and building on it, but there were a half-dozen other properties on the list as well.

"Was there anything in the permits about what kind of work they're doing on these properties?" he asked.

"I didn't actually see the permits," she admitted. "I got there so late, they didn't have time to pull the permits, but they had a master list of the properties that they showed me."

Alex nodded, looking at the houses he didn't already know. Like the other five, they were all over the city and none of them seemed to be near each other. There didn't seem to be any rhyme or reason to it, but it was possible some of these houses weren't involved with whatever was actually going on.

Only one way to find out, he thought.

"Call around to the cab companies and see if I can rent a cab for the evening," he said. "I'll need it for a couple of hours at least."

"Why don't you rent a car?" Sherry said.

Alex was taken aback for a moment.

"Can I do that?"

"Of course," she said as if that should have been self-evident. "I'll call a car service and have them pick you up downstairs."

Alex stood there for a long minute, then he chuckled.

"Okay," he said. "I'll go get my kit."

Two hours later, Alex watched as his driver pulled up to the fifth house on his list. So far, the four houses he'd visited had been empty, standing cold and dark in the fading light. He'd gotten out of the car and walked around each one, but he couldn't find any evidence of habitation or construction at any of them. With the driver of his rented car waiting for him, he couldn't exactly break in and search any of those locations.

Unlike the others, the fourth house was aglow with light and the windows were fogged over, indicating the house was heated.

"Stop here," Alex said.

"Yes, sir," the driver said as he eased the car up to the curb. He was an older man with a saggy face and droopy eyes that reminded Alex of a Saint Bernard, and it was clear he had years of experience driving, since he handled the car with expert ease.

Alex got out and made his way up the walk to the door, rapping smartly with his knuckles.

"Yes?" a middle-aged woman asked as she pulled the door open.

Alex plastered a smile on his face and took half a step back so he wouldn't appear threatening.

"Sorry to bother you, ma'am," he said, "but did you recently have work done on your home?"

The woman looked surprised and a little defensive, so Alex pressed on.

"My wife and I are thinking of having some work done on our place, but we want to make sure the builder is up to the job. They're called Dobosh Construction, and they said they did work for you."

As Alex spoke the woman visibly relaxed and by the end, she was smiling.

"Yes," she admitted. "They rebuilt our kitchen."

"Did you like their work?" Alex asked.

"They did a wonderful job," she said. "We'd recommend them."

"Could I see the work they did?" he pressed.

The woman hesitated, but then stepped back, allowing Alex to enter. She showed him to her kitchen and pointed out the work that had been done. Alex didn't know anything about homes or remodeling, but whatever Dobosh Construction had done seemed professional enough. After a few minutes of polite conversation, Alex excused himself and headed back outside.

His theory was that Dobosh Construction was a front for something else, but the fact that they had managed to remodel a kitchen so well that the homeowner was proud of it didn't fit that narrative. Front companies didn't need to hire skilled workers because they never actually did any real work. He didn't doubt that they were up to something, but he had to readjust his thinking. Whatever their game was, it had come up after they became a construction company.

"Where to now?" the driver asked as Alex got back into the car.

Alex gave the man the last address, then leaned back in the seat, shutting his eyes as the car smoothly accelerated away from the curb. He was still tired and sore from the healing he'd undergone, as well as the frustration with this case. He must have dozed, because what seemed like a moment later, the driver spoke up.

"We've arrived," he said.

Alex thanked him and got out again. He'd expected that the last address would be a dark and empty house like the first four. Even a lit and lived-in house wouldn't have surprised him. What he wasn't prepared for, however, was the blackened, charred husk of a building.

Clearly there had been a fire, and the house was a total loss. A few blackened timbers still stood, trying and failing to reach straight up toward the sky. A fireplace and chimney of crumbling brick occupied one side of the destroyed structure, but it was one of the few recognizable bits remaining.

Alex considered getting back in the car and heading for home, but someone had murdered Lucius Briggs, over whatever all this was, and Lucius deserved his best effort.

With a sigh, Alex shut the car door and trudged up to the pile of rubble that constituted the remains of the building. Nothing stood out as he circled the burnt wreck. He could see the steel frames of beds, twisted into barely recognizable shapes by the heat of the fire. A range stood in what remained of the kitchen, blackened and broken. It was everything he expected from a burned-out home.

He was about to turn away when he noticed something in the grass. Since the sun had gone down, Alex pulled out his lighter and knelt down, flicking it to life. The tiny flame wasn't much of a light, but it didn't have to be. A wide swath of the grass had been trampled by the movement of many people. At first, Alex reasoned it must have been the fire brigade, come to put out the fire, but he dismissed that idea. That would have only been a dozen or so men, but this looked like more, or maybe a smaller number going back and forth many times.

The image of the construction site he'd visited that morning sprang into his mind. There had only been a few men on the site, but they had been moving back and forth from their pile of supplies to the hole in the house wall.

Turning toward the house, Alex followed the trampled grass. It ended at a set of brick steps that would have originally accessed the kitchen's back door.

Mounting the steps, Alex surveyed the wreckage of the kitchen. He didn't need the tiny flame from his lighter to see what was amiss. A large area had been cleared of debris, exposing the ground under the kitchen floor.

DAN WILLIS

The ground and a large square frame.

As Alex approached, he could see what looked like a cellar door set into a metal frame. Based on the shape of the destroyed kitchen, he doubted it had existed before the fire.

Leaning down to expose it to the glow from his lighter, Alex found the door to be made of thick boards that had been banded with steel. A heavy padlock hung from a ring that connected to the metal frame that ran around the door.

"Whoever put this here doesn't want anyone messing with it," he observed.

Alex was tempted to try picking the lock, but he'd need better light and more privacy for that kind of work.

Standing up, he released his lighter, snuffing the tiny flame, and returned it to his pocket. Now he knew what Dobosh Construction had done at this house, and he had a pretty good suspicion what they were up to.

Striding quickly back to his rented car, he bade the driver to take him back to the office.

When he returned to his office, he found it dark and empty, but that was to be expected. Sherry would have gone down to the terminal level, crossed to the security station and ridden the private elevator up to his apartment. Alex almost never used his apartment, and he didn't really think about it much, but now, with Sherry in it, he felt like his ability to move around had been hampered. That was ridiculous, of course, and he couldn't rationalize why he felt that way, but he did.

Closing and locking the office door, Alex moved to the back hallway, ending up in his map room. He'd spent the better part of two days chasing all over the city looking at houses and something about it bothered him.

Alex crossed to the sideboard that held his box of tin compasses and the drawer full of finding runes. The center drawer held blank notepads and he took one out; tearing off several pages, he dropped them on the table, then began copying one address from his list to each notepad paper. When he was finished, he added the address from Hathaway House and tossed it on the table as well.

Over the next hour, Alex mapped out each house on his map, then crumpled the corresponding paper into a ball, and set it in its proper place. When he was done, he had a group of papers that ran all the way around the south side of the island. Most of them were separated from the others, making each appear to be alone, disconnected from the whole. There were two that stood within a block of each other, but that was it.

Alex circled the table, stroking his chin as he went. He didn't know what he was expecting, but he thought something about the way the houses were arranged would spark some thought, reveal some hidden clue. Now that he looked at them, though, they just looked like balls of yellow paper on his black and white map.

He felt like something important was eluding him but the more he walked, the less certain he became.

"What am I missing?" he growled, stooping down to view the map edge on. From that perspective the papers seemed to be a jumbled mess. He thought about circling the table again, but couldn't see how that would help.

He stood, and the papers shifted with his perspective. It almost looked like they were resolving into a pattern rather than being random points on the map.

Alex felt the hair on his arms stand up.

The map of Manhattan Alex used for his finding runes was held up by a large dining table, capable of seating ten people. To make it easy to move around the table, the chairs had been removed and stacked against the back wall. Grabbing one, Alex put it at the foot of the table, then climbed up on it.

From the higher angle, the pattern resolved itself. The properties from Manhattan Land and Building and from Dobosh Construction were laid out in a rough circle. There were two buildings that didn't fit the pattern. One Alex recognized immediately as Hathaway House, but the other he didn't know. Both of these properties were inside the larger circle but with only two points, they didn't have any discernible pattern.

This felt like progress; Alex took out his notebook and made a rough sketch of the circle and the two points.

"Now what?" he asked himself as he stepped down from the chair.

Reaching for the unknown house in the middle of the circle, Alex unfolded the paper and read the address. He remembered going by the place — it was a row house done in an old style. This was one of the buildings from Manhattan Land and Building's records, and he hadn't noticed any construction there.

"What's so special about you?" he muttered.

After a moment, Alex left the map room and headed down the hall to his vault. Passing into the great room, he headed for his library and searched his bookshelves until he found a slim volume covered in black leather. A silver embossed title ran across the cover, *New York Registry of Historical Buildings*.

Opening the book, Alex paged to the section on Manhattan, then ran his finger down the list of addresses until he found the one for the unknown building. Unlike Hathaway House, this building didn't have a name, but it had been built during the Civil War to house recuperating soldiers. Its claim to fame was that several Union Generals had stayed there during their recovery after the war.

Taking the book, Alex went back to the map room. He searched each of the other properties but none of them were listed. Only the two buildings in the middle of the circle were historical.

That made no real sense. The circle of homes seemed to indicate a pattern, but they appeared to have been chosen at random. Alex sighed and tossed the black book on the table.

Whatever the realtor and the builder were up to, he didn't have enough information yet to figure out what.

"I need more data," he said, rubbing his eyes. It wasn't particularly late, but Alex felt like he'd been awake too long.

Resolving to have Sherry dig into Dobosh Construction some more, Alex returned the chair he'd used to its place along the back wall.

Dig.

The thought hit him like lightning. The construction crew he'd seen were expanding a cellar, and the burned-out building had a cellar installed after it burned down.

"What are they looking for?" Alex wondered as he leaned over the map again. The answer was obvious: the digging men were looking for something buried under the foundations of the houses in the circle. It couldn't be something valuable; there were too many houses involved for that.

Or could it?

"Maybe they haven't found whatever they're looking for yet," he postulated.

But what about the two in the middle? he thought. If there were four in the middle, that would make more sense — with four points on a map, you could draw lines between each set of two points to indicate a hidden location, but not with just two.

"That's what they're looking for," Alex said, snapping his fingers for emphasis. He ran his finger around the edge of the circle of paper. "Somewhere under these houses is the location of the other two points, and once they find them, they'll be able to pinpoint the final location. That's what they're looking for."

He slammed his hand down on the table hard enough to make some of the paper balls roll.

"It's a treasure map!"

22

DUMPLINGS AND LIGHTNING

When Alex reached the first floor of the brownstone, he found Iggy out in the green house, sitting among his orchids. He wore his smoking jacket with a snifter of brandy and a smoldering cigar sitting, forgotten, on his side table. His look was pensive, but his eyes were glazed over as he stared at an orchid with white petals and deep purple highlights.

"Iggy?" Alex said. He repeated the entreaty when his mentor failed to respond.

"Eh?" Iggy said, rousing himself from whatever state of contemplation he'd fallen into. "Oh, it's you, lad. I'm sorry, I came out here to relax. Apparently it worked a bit too well."

"I've been working on the Lucius Briggs murder," Alex said, barely managing to keep the excitement out of his voice, "you'll never guess what I found."

Iggy drained his snifter, then stood, picking up his cigar.

"First things first," he said as he exited the greenhouse into the kitchen, "did you arrange everything with Barton?"

Alex's excitement vanished. He'd been so worried about Sorsha that morning that he made an effort to bury himself in his cases and it had worked. A bit too well, as it turned out.

"Barton is out of town until tomorrow," Alex explained, rehashing his conversation with the sorcerer's valet.

Iggy sighed and nodded.

"That's probably good," he said, shutting the insulated door to the greenhouse. "I finished the transference rune about an hour ago, but I'm completely drained. I should probably go over it again in the morning, make sure everything is where it's supposed to be."

"Why don't we go over it now?" Alex suggested. "Together."

Iggy shook his head at that.

"Right now, I need a distraction and some food," he declared. "I'm not in any condition to review a complex construct. Besides," he added, "we need to tell Sorsha what we've been up to. She has to agree to all of this, you know."

Alex hadn't thought about that. His plans to restore Sorsha's life energy were well thought out and earnest, but he hadn't actually involved the sorceress in any of it.

"I'll call her and we'll grab something to eat at the Lunch Box," he said, heading for the telephone. "We'll let her in on our plans then."

A minute later, Alex heard Sorsha's voice over the telephone. She sounded as tired as Iggy.

"I can't face another one of your greasy spoons," Sorsha said when Alex proposed dinner at the Lunch Box. "Take me someplace nice."

Alex could certainly do that, especially after finding out how much money was in his secret bank account. The problem with that was Iggy. It was very unlikely that someone would recognize him as Arthur Conan Doyle, but it wasn't impossible, especially if he appeared in a tabloid photo alongside Sorsha. He needed a place fancy enough for Sorsha's sensibilities but not so fancy that it attracted hungry tabloid photographers.

"I know the perfect place," he said after a moment's thought. "Put on something slinky and Iggy and I will pick you up. How long do you need?"

"Give me ten minutes," she said, then hung up.

Alex chuckled. It had always taken Jessica at least half an hour to get ready to go out, back when they were dating. There were definitely advantages to being a sorceress.

He turned to find Iggy standing right behind him, with a stern look and a raised eyebrow.

"What happened to you today?" he asked.

"How...?"

"You used an Internal Restorative potion," his mentor explained, "they leave a bluish tinge on the skin for a day or so. Now, tell me what happened."

Alex shrugged.

"I got stabbed...a little."

Iggy's look was not amused, and he insisted Alex detail the entire experience along with pulling up his shirt to show the remnants of the wound.

"You did a pretty good job of it," Iggy grudgingly admitted at last. "You'll have a scar, of course, but that hardly matters on your side."

"And yet I sense you're still upset," Alex ventured.

"Of course I'm upset," his mentor growled. "Stab wounds can be tricky; you never really know how deep they are. You might have lost enough blood to pass out while you were getting your shirt off in that medical room of yours. Then where would you be?"

"Dead, I expect."

"Precisely," Iggy declared. "I know you didn't want to bother me in my rune work, but from now on, you tell me when you get stabbed or shot or get hit hard enough that you're coughing up blood. Understand?"

Alex put on a serious face and saluted.

"Yes, sir," he said. "Now, you might want to put on your suit coat, because we're got to pick up Sorsha."

"Where are you taking me?" Sorsha asked once the three of them were in the back of a taxi. Alex had requested something slinky, and the sorceress hadn't disappointed. Her dress looked like it was made of silver fish scales that glittered and shimmered as she moved. It had a high collar that moved down in a triangular shape, running under her arms, and leaving her shoulders bare. It clung to her form like a second skin. A small handbag made of the same material completed the outfit, though Alex noticed she was also wearing the necklace he'd given her.

"Someplace nice," he answered as the car pulled up in front of the Lucky Dragon restaurant. "I hope you like Chinese."

Sorsha's face actually split into a bright smile and she nodded.

"I adore it," she said, "but how are you going to get us in?"

She nodded, indicating the line of well-dressed people standing beside a colorful hostess in an embroidered dress.

Alex chuckled as he paid the cabby.

"I called while Iggy was getting dressed," he said, "asked them if they could provide a private dining table for Miss Kincaid and party. They were only too happy to accommodate me."

"Name dropping, Alex?" she said, with an insincere smirk. "How gauche."

The hostess must have been told to keep watch for them, because before Alex had shut the taxi door, she hurried across the sidewalk to them with a broad, welcoming smile. A minute later, Alex was holding out Sorsha's chair in one of the Lucky Dragon's private dining rooms.

The room had a curtained entrance on one wall, with a large salt-water fish tank along the back with dozens of brightly colored fish darting around the rocks and plants inside. A big round table stood in the middle of the room, big enough for six people with a lazy susan permanently mounted in its center.

Just as Alex sat, a small army of people appeared through the curtain. They moved around the table with the precision of dancers, placing china, silverware, napkins, and glasses as they went. They were followed by girls in embroidered dresses of black and gold, who filled glasses with water, set bowls of rice on the table, and placed a half-dozen appetizers on the lazy susan. The whole process took less than a minute, then with a gracious bow, the last of the women disappeared through the curtain.

"Okay," Sorsha said, beaming at Alex. "I'm impressed."

A short, dignified man in a tuxedo appeared next, walking them through the menu and taking orders. When he finally left, Iggy brought the conversation to the business at hand. First he removed a small brass lamp from his medical bag. It looked like a tiny version of Alex's multi-lamp, though without the four sides, and a round glass chimney. Using his gold lighter, Iggy ignited the wick in the lamp, then lowered the glass over it, changing the light to a pale green color. It also highlighted several runes on the glass that became visible, glowing with the light.

"Now we won't be overheard," he said, putting his lighter back into his vest pocket and turning to Sorsha. "Alex tells me your life energy is still depleting at an accelerated rate," he said.

Sorsha gave Alex a dirty look, then sighed and nodded.

"May I see it, please?"

Sorsha took the watch out of her handbag and turned it so Iggy could see it. Alex felt his gut tighten as he saw the red hand; it was pointing to seventeen minutes past the hour.

Iggy stroked his mustache and nodded.

"Well, there's good news," he said at last. "Based on what Alex has told me about the drain on your life energy, it looks like the drain isn't accelerating any more."

"I don't see how that's good news," Sorsha said, her voice small.

"It means that we don't have to keep fighting against an ever-increasing rate of drain," Alex said.

"It took you three days to make that rune to transfer life into me," she said. "Even if you started right now, I'd be dead before you finished."

Iggy grinned, forcing the ends of his bottle-brush mustache up.

"That's where these come in," he said, reaching into his pocket. He took out his green rune book and slipped three loose papers out of it, laying them down on the table.

"They're beautiful," Sorsha said, looking at the complex and colorful runes. "What are they for?"

"It was Alex's idea," Iggy said. "I'll let him explain."

Alex quickly walked Sorsha through his thought process, reminding her of Bradley Elder's plan and how this rune would be even more direct.

"As I recall," Sorsha said when Alex finished, "Mr. Elder's head exploded when he lost control of the flow of magic. I still have nightmares about it. So, how do you propose to keep that from happening to me?"

"Bradley Elder didn't have any way to regulate the flow of magic," Alex explained. "That's why he used electricity and then converted it — he knew how to regulate electricity."

"And since I know how to regulate the flow of magic, you think it will be safe for me?" Sorsha guessed.

"You'll control the flow of life energy into your body by using your watch," Iggy said, indicating one of the three constructs on the table. "Keep an eye on the red hand and try to position it at six o'clock. If it starts to move forward, use the crown to move your watch hands backward until it returns to six, then advance it a bit to keep it there."

"And the reverse if the red hand moves backward toward noon," she said, nodding as she understood.

"All we're waiting on now is for Andrew to come back from wherever he's disappeared to," Alex added.

Sorsha looked at him, confused, and Alex explained about the sorcerer's mysterious retreat. When he finished, Sorsha rolled her eyes at him and gave him a playful slap on the cheek.

"You can be quite the idiot sometimes," she said, reaching into her sequined purse. When her hand came out, Alex felt exactly like a fool. Sorsha held a small clamshell made up of two pieces of round, concave metal joined by a hinge and kept closed with a friction clamp. Alex had never used one, but he knew that inside, one half held face powder and the other, a small mirror.

It was a makeup compact.

He'd seen her use one previously, when Alex warned her that the target of a German poisoner wasn't an international conference, but rather the New York six.

Opening the compact, Sorsha placed it on the table, flat so that the mirror pointed up, and quickly spoke a few deep, echoing magic words. As soon as the echoes died away, silver light began to emanate from the little mirror and another moment later, the image of Andrew Barton appeared over the glass.

"Sorsha," he said, a roguish smile touching his lips. "To what do I owe the pleasure?"

"Andrew, I..." Sorsha stopped suddenly. She clearly didn't want to tell her fellow sorcerer about her problem, but hadn't thought that through. "I need your help," she said at last.

"You know I'm always available to a fellow sorcerer," he said. "Why don't we meet in my office on Friday and we can discuss it."

Sorsha blushed, not wanting to press, but she had no other choice.

"I'm afraid I need to see you now," she said. "I wouldn't ask if it weren't extremely urgent."

Barton raised an eyebrow at that, but didn't object.

"I suppose I can cut my trip short," he said, clearly not liking the idea. "Do you want to meet at my office?"

"Can you meet me at the Lucky Dragon?" she said. "It's a Chinese restaurant on the north end of the core."

"Is Alex with you?" he suddenly asked.

"As a matter of fact, he is."

Barton snorted and shook his head.

"I should have known; this has the feel of one of his last minute revelations. All right, I'll be there in a few minutes."

With that he waved his hand and the image above the mirror disappeared.

"What did he mean, one of my revelations?" Alex protested once Sorsha put away her compact mirror.

"Oh come now, darling," she said, patting him on the cheek in the manner of a parent explaining something to a child. "You have to admit, you do have quite the flair for the dramatic."

Alex looked to Iggy for support, but his mentor was suddenly fascinated by the movements of the fish in the giant aquarium.

"You'd have made a good sorcerer," Sorsha added.

Alex opened his mouth to protest, but right then there was a tremendous boom from the direction of the street.

"Case in point," Sorsha went on with a widening smirk. "That's going to be Andrew."

"You don't explode when you teleport," Alex pointed out.

"Whenever Andrew appears in public, he likes to make sure everyone knows who he is by appearing out of a lightning bolt," Sorsha explained.

Alex chuckled at that, wishing he had that ability, which, ironically, was exactly Sorsha's point. That made him laugh out loud.

The curtain to their private room was whisked aside by the hostess, whose eyes were as big as saucers. She quickly bowed and Andrew Barton strode through the opening like he owned the place. He wore a tan three-button suit with a matching bowler hat and carried a cane of some exotic, multicolored wood. A mischievous smile played across his lips and Alex noticed a tiny arc of energy at the tip of his pencil mustache.

"Well, here you all are," he said, raising his voice so that the now-silent restaurant could hear. Then he turned to the hostess and thanked her. For her part, the girl jerked the curtain closed and fled back to her post in terror.

Alex and Iggy rose as Barton made his way to the table.

"Sorsha," he said, taking her hand and kissing it. "Always a pleasure. Alex. Dr. Bell," he addressed the men in turn before sitting down. "Now," he said, taking a dumpling from the plate of appetizers on the lazy susan, "Why doesn't Alex tell me what's going on here and why I had to rush right over?"

Alex looked to Sorsha, but she spoke first.

"I'm dying, Andrew," she said. "Some very dangerous runewrights from an organization called the Legion put some kind of curse on me and it's been draining my life energy. Alex and Dr. Bell have a way to stop it, but we need your help to do it."

Andrew didn't respond right away. He appeared to be staring at Sorsha and his eyes closed into a squint. If Alex had to guess, he was bending all his sorcerer's senses on Sorsha, trying to see if she was telling the truth.

"Has Malcom examined you?" he asked, referring to Malcom Henderson, the sorcerer who specialized in healing magic.

"That wouldn't do any good," Iggy said. "The curse is an especially potent runic construct that's been written in such a way as to make it impossible to safely break it."

"It's called a Gordian rune," Alex added.

"You're sure about this?" Andrew asked, looking at Alex, who nodded.

"I can see that your power has faded," Andrew said to Sorsha. "If I didn't know better, I'd say you weren't a sorcerer at all."

"You should try it from my end," Sorsha retorted.

Andrew turned back to Alex.

"Tell me this plan you have," he said.

Alex spent the next ten minutes explaining everything in detail, only stopping when the waiter brought in their entrees. When Alex finished, Andrew just sat, looking intently at him.

"All right," he said at last. "I can cast the spell to draw magic energy, but it will take me about ten hours to do it."

"Thank you, Andrew," Sorsha said, relief plain in her voice.

"But," Andrew went on, "before I do anything, I want the truth."

"What truth?" Alex asked, pretty sure he knew the answer to that one.

"I've known plenty of runewrights in my life," Andrew said. "Some very talented ones too. But nothing I've ever seen comes close to the two of you." He moved his finger between Alex and Iggy. "Alex wants to try to duplicate that stunt Bradly tried to pull, but instead of transferring magic, you're going to convert magic energy into life energy. Sure, makes sense. But then you," he pointed at Iggy, "you just come up with the rune to do it in a day? No runewright has that kind of knowledge. No runewright has that kind of power. So if you want my help, you're going to tell me everything."

Alex looked to Iggy, but his mentor only shrugged.

"You want the long version or the short," Alex said.

Andrew took another dumpling from the bowl and sat back in his chair with a smile.

"There's plenty of food and this place won't close for hours," he said. "Tell me everything."

23

THE ANCHOR

"Do you have any idea what we could do together with what's in here?" Andrew demanded, an angry light flashing in his eyes as he looked up from the Archimedean Monograph.

Alex did know and he said so. They sat around the kitchen table in the brownstone as the Lightning Lord paged through the infamous rune book.

"As soon as we get Sorsha's problem sorted out, I want to go through this page by page with you," Andrew went on. "I don't understand the rune theory, of course, but the written descriptions fire the imagination." He looked up suddenly, pointing to a handwritten note in one of the margins. "Did Francis Bacon really write this?"

Alex chuckled and nodded.

"You'll find notes in there from Ben Franklin, Rene Descartes, and DaVinci as well."

Andrew let out a breath and shook his head.

"I know several historians who would part with a sizable portion of their own skin to read this."

"The same people that are trying to kill Sorsha want the Archimedean Monograph desperately," Iggy said. "If anyone found out that you'd held it in your hands, they wouldn't hesitate to use their curse to extort the secret from you."

Andrew gave Iggy a hard look, then a smile spread across his face.

He smiled like a kid on Christmas and Alex sighed. He'd already connected Barton's relay towers to Empire tower by creating a short hallway that ran parallel to his great room, connecting it to Barton's office at one end and adding cover doors to the other. The hall needed to physically join to his vault proper, but Alex managed that with a tiny vent at the top of the hall, which came out behind his bookshelves.

"We can go through the book after Sorsha's safe," he said.

"You realize, if you marketed some of this, you'd make a fortune," Andrew said.

"Think of all the mischief a criminal mind could do with something like this," Sorsha pointed out.

"We could keep anything we made secret," the sorcerer said, sounding very sure of himself.

Iggy and Alex shook their heads in unison

"Once other runewrights know something is possible," Iggy said, "they'll figure out how to do it for themselves," Iggy said. "It's best if we keep most of these things a secret."

Andrew sighed and shook his head.

"All right, I'll get started on the spell to draw magic for your runes and we'll meet in my office in the morning." He closed the Monograph and handed it to Alex. "But once this is over, I still want to work with you on what's in here."

"All right," Alex said.

While Iggy returned the Monograph to his bookshelf, Alex escorted Andrew and Sorsha up to his vault and through to his office. Once Andrew was gone, Alex offered Sorsha his arm.

"Can I walk you home?" he said with a serious expression.

"You mean to the other side of this room?" Sorsha snickered, looking across the great room to the closed door that led to her flying castle.

She took his arm and he led her toward the door.

"I'm going to bed," Iggy announced from behind him.

"Wait a minute," Alex called over his shoulder.

When he reached the door, he opened it for Sorsha, then promised to pick her up in the morning.

"So what's so urgent you want to talk about it now?" Iggy said once the sorceress was gone.

Alex shifted mental gears and began telling Iggy all about the strange homes and the treasure map. Instead of getting excited, however, Iggy's face shifted to a scowl.

"I know that look," Alex said. "What's wrong?"

"Well," he began, "if you're right about using Hathaway House as a triangulation point, then why would they murder Lucius? Or try to buy the house in the first place? All they'd need is its location, and they could get that off any map."

Alex chewed his lip. Iggy was right; the only thing they would need to triangulate was the location of the house.

"Maybe they need something in the basement, or under it."

"I don't like that theory either," Iggy said. "Some of the houses you looked at are relatively new. How did someone from the past manage to bury clues to a hidden treasure exactly under where those houses would be built?"

That didn't make sense either.

"Then what are they doing under all those houses?"

Iggy gave him a wry smile.

"You're assuming again," he said. "As far as you know, there are only two houses where whoever's behind this is interested in basements."

That was true. Alex had only seen two houses where basement work had occurred, the one under construction and the one that had burned down.

As the realization sank in, Alex groaned. He'd eaten well at the Lucky Dragon and now he wanted to go to bed.

"I'm going to have to break into a few houses tonight, aren't I?"

"Only if you want to know what those rogues are really up to," Iggy chuckled. "As for myself, I'm going to bed."

He turned and made his way toward the brownstone door.

"Don't get stabbed again," he called over his shoulder as he entered the short hallway and disappeared.

"Right," Alex sighed.

A waxing gibbous moon bathed the rural street in pale light as Alex made his way along the row of darkened houses. He wore his trench coat with the collar pulled up, both to ward off the chill of the night air and to hide his features. It wasn't likely that anyone would look out at the street at this hour, but it didn't pay to take chances.

Since his goal was to break into houses, he couldn't hire a car for this outing. On that score, he needed to hurry, since the cabs would stop running after midnight.

Quickening his pace, Alex turned the corner at the end of the block. The first house across the street was a snug two-story number with an attached garage and a copper birdbath in the front yard. It was separated from the next lot by a tall hedge that was already greening up from its winter dormancy, providing the house with privacy. They needn't have bothered, of course, since the next house down the block didn't exist.

It had burned down the previous week.

Alex crossed the street, then moved past the hedge, turning into the yard of the incinerated house. For a long moment he stood still, watching for any sign that the property was being watched. Dobosh Builders knew he was on to them, and he wouldn't put it past them to put a man on all their properties at night.

Five minutes later, Alex was satisfied he and the house remains were alone. He hugged the hedge, moving along until he was parallel with the destroyed home, then crossed the yard to the opening in the rubble that he knew would be there.

The heavy trap door was exactly where he remembered it, secured to the floor in what used to be the house's kitchen. The heavy padlock was also still there.

Alex knelt down by the heavy door, pulling his hinged ball flashlight from the right pocket of his trousers. Keeping the flashlight low, Alex squeezed it, sending a bright circle of light over the padlock. The lock was heavy, with a large keyhole in the center, which meant it wasn't new.

He smiled at that. The new pin and tumbler locks took time to pick, but old locks could be opened easily with a police issue skeleton key. Opening the little leather wallet that held his picks, Alex selected the smaller of the two skeleton keys inside and opened the padlock.

Putting his pick wallet away, Alex removed the lock and pulled up on the trap door. Beneath it was a dark hole that smelled of fresh dirt and curing cement. Alex pointed his flashlight into the hole, revealing a sturdy ladder against one side and the barest hint of a floor below. From the look of it, the basement they'd dug was six or seven feet down.

He glanced around to make sure no one had come to investigate the glow of the flashlight, then pocketed the heavy lock and climbed down into the basement. When he reached the bottom of the ladder, Alex's heels clacked down onto the concrete floor. The ceiling wasn't quite tall enough for him to stand, so he dropped to one knee and shone the flashlight to get a good look around.

It didn't take long.

The entire basement was a square with wooden supports holding back dirt walls and a slab of concrete for a floor. It was also entirely empty.

"What the devil?" Alex said. "Why dig this and lock it up then leave it empty?"

He turned his flashlight on the floor and leaned down, but after a full five minutes of searching for seams, cracks, or secret doors, he was forced to give up. It simply made no sense.

"Unless..." he said, reaching into his trouser pocket for his chalk. He quickly made a door on the wall, then opened his vault. Given the height of ceiling, the door was a bit short, but the magic handled it without a hitch. A minute later, Alex was back in the tiny basement with his kit bag. He strapped on his oculus and lit the silverlight burner in his multi-lamp.

Playing the light over the concrete floor, Alex saw very little save a couple of hand prints near the ladder. That was to be expected with such a new construction, so Alex moved on to the ghostlight burner. This time when he shone the lamp around, the little space bloomed with light. In the exact center of the floor, someone had written a very complex rune.

Two hours later, Alex stepped up to the back porch of a large wooden house with dark-blue painted walls, elegant shutters, and a yard that had once been quite picturesque. The back door was heavy and strong, with a gleaming, new, modern lock set in it.

Alex didn't bother with the picks for this door; after all, he already had the key.

Pulling out the ring that Ethel Briggs had left him, Alex inserted the key and stepped inside Hathaway House. There wasn't much to be seen with the lights off, but Alex didn't turn them on. He didn't need nosy neighbors calling the police.

Squeezing open his flashlight, he made his way along the back hallway, opening doors until he found one with stairs that went down.

The basement of Hathaway House was enormous compared to the tiny space under the burned building. To Alex's right was a coal-fired boiler and an empty coal bin under a metal chute. Clearly the boiler had been converted to work on a boiler stone.

Off to the left, the basement ran along the entire length of the house. Alex could see stacks of chairs and neat piles of storage boxes. Turning that way, Alex played his flashlight around as he went. Dust covered every surface, so he checked the floor. An obvious path had been made along the aisle by someone who had no intention of hiding his presence. Judging by the amount of dust removed, it was either one person returning multiple times, or a group of people.

Following the tracks, Alex came to a spot where the floor hadn't just been cleaned of dust by the passage of feet, but had actually been mopped. The flagstones that made up the floor were almost pristine as they gleamed in the flashlight's beam.

"This is it," he said, setting the flashlight down and opening his kit. This time he knew what to expect, so he didn't bother with the silverlight. Another complex rune about four feet across bloomed into existence as Alex pointed his multi-lamp at it. As he pulled out his notepad to copy it down, he noticed that this one wasn't the same as the one in the burnt house. In fact, they had very little in common.

When he finished, Alex sat down on one of the storage boxes and stared at the rune. It looked familiar, but he couldn't place it. Pulling out his drawing of the first rune, he compared the two, but still couldn't make any connection. He had a feeling that he ought to recognize them, but nothing came to mind.

There was one thing in his mind that was certain, however.

"The Legion is behind this."

It was almost one in the morning when Alex made his way to the map room in his office. When he arrived, he found the door ajar and the light on, but that wasn't a surprise; he'd used the phone at Hathaway House to call Iggy, telling his mentor to meet him here. Opening the door, Alex was greeted by pungent cigar smoke and the aroma of fine whisky.

"Since you woke me up for this, I thought I'd help myself to your good Scotch," Iggy said. He stood on the far side of the map table in his smoking jacket over a white shirt with open collar. and trousers.

"Sorry about that," Alex said, shutting the door behind him. "But I think this might be way more important than it seems."

"Well," Iggy said, leaning close to the map and the paper markers. "Color me intrigued. This," he indicated the papers on the map, "isn't a very interesting pattern. What did you discover while you were out?"

"I think the Legion is behind this," Alex said, fishing out the drawings of the runes he'd made. "I found these in the basements of Hathaway House and the one that burned down." Alex indicated the two properties on the map table.

Iggy picked up the papers and scrutinized them, each in turn. While he was at it, Alex followed his mentor's example and poured himself a Scotch.

"Well," Iggy said after Alex had drained and refilled his glass, "These aren't whole runes, they're anchors for something bigger."

"Those are very complex for anchor runes," Alex noted.

Iggy chuckled at that.

"Complex for one of mine, yes, but the Legion isn't as skilled as you and I."

"How so?"

Iggy put the papers down and pointed at the few components they had in common.

"I think they're using these to link the anchor to the main rune."

Alex stared at the construct for a long minute, then he saw it. Instead of simply linking the construct to the central rune, they'd bound it together and used a match rune to connect it. It was like going around a building the long way to get to the door, but it would work.

"So what are they doing?"

"Haven't a clue," Iggy said, picking up the runes. "But we do know that this rune is here," he placed one paper next to Hathaway House, "and this one goes here." He placed the second paper next to the burnt house. "I suspect that if we want to know what they're up to, you'd better have a look in these other basements."

That was not the answer Alex wanted, but it was a job he could handle. He was about to suggest they go to bed and take it up in the morning, when another thought stuck him.

"Iggy," he said, staring down at the map. "What if this is a pattern?"

His mentor glanced down at the yellow balls of notepad paper, then back up to Alex.

"How so?"

"What if this isn't a complex construct," he said. "You said it yourself, the Legion doesn't have our knowledge, our expertise. They don't have the Monograph."

"So?" Iggy said. "They knew how to make that Gordian rune. They might not know what we know, but that doesn't make them stupid or inferior."

"I'm not suggesting that, but what if this," he described the rough circle of papers with his finger, "what if it's a giant rune?"

Iggy stroked his mustache and considered the idea.

"If that's the case, then each of these locations would be a node in the rune, and these," he indicated the two runes Alex had drawn, "represent the effects that happen at those locations."

"So what rune is it?" Alex asked, searching his mind in a vain effort to place the indistinct outline.

"That's not the question you should be asking yourself," Iggy said, looking up. "This construct covers a third of the island. If this is a basic rune, then how are they going to power it?"

Alex felt his blood run cold.

"Sorsha," he gasped. "They haven't just been draining her power, they've been pumping it into this."

"That's my guess," Iggy confirmed. "And, in the morning, when we give her access to virtually unlimited magical energy…"

"It's going to give the Legion even more power for whatever," he waved his hand at the map, "whatever this is."

Iggy puffed on his cigar and nodded.

"We can't postpone linking Sorsha to Andrew's spell," Alex said, a prickling fear beginning to run up his spine.

"No," Iggy agreed. "We're pushing it as it is. We have to go ahead or Sorsha will die."

"But what about the Legion?"

Iggy blew out a plume of smoke and gave Alex a fiendish grin.

"Even basic constructs are skittish things," he said. "And one that's been deconstructed into so many parts is bound to be inherently unstable. Give it a little push and it will blow up in the Legion's face."

Alex nodded, understanding.

"But how will we know where to push?"

"You'd better get busy and find out what that rune is," Iggy replied. "As soon as we know, we'll figure out a way to send the Legion a message they'll never forget."

24

ENCHANTING

Sorsha lay in her massive bed listening to the sound of her alarm clock ticking. It was all she'd managed to do since she'd gone to bed. Normally an evening with Alex and Dr. Bell at a fancy restaurant would have been eminently satisfying, but this felt like the last meal of a condemned man.

With a sigh, she sat up and switched on the table lamp beside her bed. The clock beside it showed that it was after four in the morning. She wasn't due to meet Alex, Andrew, and Dr. Bell until seven, and lying in bed wasn't doing her any good. Growling in frustration, she cast off her sheet and blanket, swinging her legs out of bed. Her fur-lined slippers were on the floor below and she felt around for them, eventually getting them on her feet.

As she stood up, her tired brain told her to take a hot bath and come back to bed. Even an hour or two of sleep would be worth it at this point. As she turned toward the bathroom, however, she caught sight of her writing table against the wall by the glass doors that led out to her private balcony.

Changing her direction, Sorsha moved to the table, then pulled out the gilded chair and sat down, switching on the desk lamp. A stationery set sat on the desk, complete with an inkwell and her favorite fountain pen, so the sorceress opened the center drawer and drew out a sheet of her best stationary.

Taking the pen, she began to write. She addressed the letter to Carolyn Burnside, her personal secretary and confidant. Carolyn had been her office receptionist a few years ago, but Carolyn and Sorsha got along so well that Sorsha had promoted her. Sorcerers tended not to have very many real friends; it was a hazard of the job. Most people clung to her like barnacles on a steam ship, using their association with her to further their ambitions. Carolyn was different. It was what made her indispensable.

Sorsha paused in her writing, not knowing how to go on. When she'd started, it had been a list of instructions about how to maneuver her castle out over the Atlantic in the event of her death. The spells holding it up would begin to degrade the moment she died, so certain things would have to be done to ensure the safety of the city.

With a sigh of resignation, she put her pen back to the paper and continued in a flowing hand. She'd learned proper handwriting as a youth and she prided herself on her skill.

Alex always prints, she thought, *and his notes are so messy.* Her thoughts turned suddenly to the tall, rugged private detective and his thoroughly charming ability to irritate her. The ghost of a smile crossed her lips when she thought of their first meeting. He'd been afraid of her, but that was most people's first reaction to meeting a sorcerer, yet he'd stood his ground. He even stood up to her. That was a very rare quality in Sorsha's experience, and it was what had drawn her to him in the first place.

Of course Alex could also be quite infuriating at times. She still got angry when she remembered Dr. Bell's words, declaring that Alex had used up most of his own life sending her falling castle into the sea. It had taken a long time for her to forgive him for that. Then there was the time he had the unmitigated audacity to lie to her under the influence of a truth spell.

She snorted and shook her head at the memory of that. Only someone with supreme confidence and a quick mind could have pulled that off, and Alex had. It was one of the reasons she loved him.

And she did love him.

The feeling had come on sort of gradually, so she had trouble pinning down the moment when she'd first realized it. If she were forced to choose, she'd have to date her realization to the dance they'd shared in the Emerald Room. Of course pictures of them had shown up in the tabloids the next day and ruined her mood. It seemed like something was always doing that when it came to Alex; he'd do something to make her angry, then be charming and get her to forgive him.

"If you live through today, you really need to have a long talk with him and sort all that out," she said out loud. "Now stop thinking about Alex and finish your letter."

She put pen to paper again and wrote more directly to Carolyn, thanking the woman for her service and companionship. Her will already had a large provision for her as well as Sorsha's other personal staff, so she left that part out, focusing instead on personal details and messages she wanted Carolyn to deliver to her staff and employees.

When she finished, Sorsha signed the letter, then put it in a heavy envelope and addressed it. Her hand shook at the last bit when she recalled why she was taking the time to write such a letter.

Closing her eyes, she centered herself. She didn't want to die any more than anyone else, but she'd lived long enough to know that worrying about things that were out of her control was a waste of time. And, of course, there was Alex. If anyone could find a way to keep her alive, to break the curse those Legion bastards had put on her, it would be him.

She would just have to have faith.

A wave of weariness washed over her, and she struggled to keep her eyes open. It had taken her about half an hour to write the letter, so there was still time to get some rest. Rising, she left the letter on the little table by her bedroom door where Carolyn would be sure to see it, then made her way to her bed and fell asleep the moment her head hit her pillow.

Alex woke ten minutes before his alarm was set to rouse him. As he sat up, worry about the day came flooding into him, the same as it had yesterday and the day before. He'd held Dr. Kellin, and by extension, Jessica in his arms as she died, and he had no desire to repeat the experience with Sorsha.

Whether or not he wanted it, the possibility was very real. He'd rattled his brain for a way to break the draining curse on Sorsha. He'd thought he'd beat it with the life transference, but the Gordian rune overcame his efforts. Now he was down to his last idea and Sorsha was out of time. If the magic lifeline he and Iggy had created failed to stop the progression of the curse, Sorsha wouldn't live out the day.

He shuddered as that thought hit him.

He wanted to despair, but the words of Father Harry rose in his mind, "If you want something, roll up your sleeves and go after it. Give it everything you have, every ounce of energy, every bit of your faculties, and, when you've done your all, leave the rest in God's hands, trusting in His wisdom to aid you."

Alex never found it easy to have faith, but that was Father Harry's stock in trade, and the old priest didn't just say things like that, he lived them.

As Alex sat, battling his own terrible doubts, he took a deep breath and cleared his mind. Whatever happened today, it was out of his hands. That meant there was no sense worrying about it.

He stood and went to the little bathroom to shower and shave. In less than an hour they all would be meeting in Andrew's office, and then it would be in God's hands.

Fifteen minutes later, Alex descended the stairs to the brownstone's kitchen. Iggy was there, wearing his best tweed suit, without his jacket, and an apron while he fried some eggs in a pan.

"Are you ready, lad?" he asked as Alex came in.

Alex thought about that before he responded.

"As ready as I'll ever be," he said, moving to the china cabinet to get out dishes and silverware.

"You have the plate?"

Alex nodded even though Iggy's back was to him.

"I have several ready to go in my vault for just such an emergency," he said, setting the table. "They're all hardened steel, the strongest I could find. Did you double check the construct?"

"I did," his mentor responded. "Double, triple, and quadruple checked it. We're ready."

Iggy brought his pan to the table and dished out two fried eggs onto each plate along with two links of sausage. When he finished, he returned the pan and came back with a plate of toast before sitting.

"I've been giving your giant rune construct some thought," Iggy changed the subject once grace had been said.

Alex had been so focused, he'd forgotten about his strange visit to the burned dwelling and Hathaway House.

"And?" he said, when Iggy didn't immediately continue.

"I'm wondering why whoever did this bothered," he said.

"The Legion did it," Alex insisted. "Who cares why?"

"I understand you're a bit distracted this morning, but you need to focus and think," Iggy admonished him.

Alex took a deep breath and tried to clear his mind. When he and Iggy spoke last night, he'd wondered what rune the Legion was trying to use. If he could identify the rune, he'd be able to figure out what they were up to and try to stop it. Their motives were important, but he didn't see how he could make even a guess without knowing what the rune did.

"I don't mean to ask what they're trying to accomplish," Iggy said once Alex voiced his opinion. "I mean why make a giant rune in the first place?"

"We're assuming they have access to Sorsha's stolen power," Alex said. "Normally there wouldn't be any way to power a rune that size."

"That would imply that the only reason for doing it is because they could," Iggy said, "and that's a terrible reason to do anything."

"Maybe they needed a place to put all that stolen power?" Alex suggested. "Maybe they had to use it or it would blow up in their faces."

"Possible," Iggy mused. "But, if that's all it was, why buy houses for more than they're worth? Why intimidate Lucius Briggs and his wife, and when they resisted, why resort to murder?"

Alex was silent for a long minute while he chewed his breakfast.

"You're right," he said. "Whatever they're doing, it's very specific and they needed a giant rune to do it. They needed those particular houses to build their construct. But why make a giant rune in the first place?"

Iggy didn't answer and the two of them just sat, finishing their breakfast. Finally, Alex checked the clock on the wall. It was already half past six and he needed to pick up Sorsha in ten minutes.

"I think you're on the right track," Iggy said as Alex rose, taking his plate to the sink.

"How so?"

"The Legion is powering their construct with the power they're stealing from Sorsha."

"So, whatever this is, it's a crime of opportunity?" Alex guessed.

"Oh, I don't think so," Iggy said, rising. "If I were a betting man, I'd say that the Legion has been planning this for some time."

"They couldn't have known Sorsha would be there at the National Rune Research Lab," Alex pointed out.

"No," Iggy admitted, "but they had that Gordian rune already made and ready to use."

Alex hadn't thought about that. It was awfully convenient that someone from the Legion had that rune on their person. Then there was the matter of the houses bought by Manhattan Land and Building — some of the purchases went back six months.

"They were planning this all along," he realized. "Sorsha was a target of opportunity. If she hadn't been there, they'd have used their Gordian rune on some other sorcerer."

"That's about the way I figure it," Iggy said, hanging up his apron and picking up his suit coat.

"So why do they need a giant rune?"

Iggy grinned at him.

"The same reason they needed to siphon the power from a sorcerer," he said, "to make the construct do more. Whatever that construct is, they need it to be much more powerful than it normally would be."

Alex was about to point out that empowering a standard rune didn't require making the rune bigger; all you had to do was use better materials. Before he could point that out, another thought accord to him.

"The Legion doesn't know about major linking runes," he said, following Iggy out into the foyer, then up the stairs. "That means it's a cinch they don't know about using materials like hardened steel to hold a rune. That's why they made it bigger."

"Just so," Iggy agreed.

"So I need to figure out what construct they're trying to use," Alex said. "Once I know that, I'll know what they're up to, and how to shut down their rune."

"I suggest you get on that as soon as we're done with Sorsha," Iggy said.

Sorsha paced back and forth in front of the simple wooden door on the right side of her massive foyer. The door looked out of place among the opulence of the room. It was a simple, basic door, with a brass knob and a heavy steel bolt right above it. She had undone the bolt so that the door could open, but actually opening it was beyond her power. The door had runes on it that denied her entry.

When she'd had her full power, it would have been child's play to blast the door into splinters, but now, all she could do was wait and nervously pace.

She was tempted to check the time, but the thought made her stomach queasy. The watch did more than tell the time, it would show her its little red hand, the one that measured how much life was left in her. It was a revelation she could do without at the moment.

The handle of the plain door rattled and turned, and a moment later the door swung inward. She knew to expect Alex, but a burst of relief washed over her when he stood, revealed in the opening.

"Thank you," she said before he could even speak.

Alex's face, which had worn a look of stern resolve, melted into the half-smirk he usually wore in her presence, and she relaxed even further.

"Don't worry, sorceress," he said, offering her his arm. "We're all ready for you."

She suppressed a shiver as he brought to mind what was about to happen, then took his arm, stepping through the door into his vault. It was an impressive magic, Alex's vault, and one of the few things she couldn't do. When Alex had first shown it to her, he took no small amount of pride showing her around. It didn't bother her. She'd taken a great amount of pleasure showing off to him by pulling things in and out of her dimensional pocket, after all.

Alex led her from her castle door over to the left where Dr. Bell waited for them. He stood beside a large frame which had been mounted on the vault wall. Inside the frame was a square metal plate that had been polished to a gleaming sheen. Etched into the surface were fine, cobalt-blue lines forming an intricate pattern that branched out from a central circle to three smaller ones, laid out as an equilateral triangle around the central rune. Sorsha didn't know the language, of course, but that didn't stop her from appreciating the intricate beauty of it.

"This rune will take the energy produced by Andrew's spell and convert it to life energy," Dr. Bell explained, shifting into the professorial voice he used when elucidating a point. As he spoke, Alex rolled up the sleeve of her blouse, exposing her right arm. "We've already attached linking runes to the construct," Bell went on. "Now we'll attach one of them to you."

Alex held up a folded rune paper, illustrating Bell's explanation, then set it on her forearm.

"You know how this works," Alex said, pulling his cheap squeeze lighter out of his suit coat pocket.

He should get a better one, she thought.

"Now hold still," he said, oblivious to her thoughts. He squeezed the lighter to life and touched its flame to the paper. It rushed into a minor conflagration and she felt heat on her arm. Before the flame could burn her, however, it vanished, and she felt the tingle of magic on her skin.

Alex touched her exposed arm and closed his eyes for a moment.

"The link is good," he pronounced after a moment.

Sorsha suppressed a shiver and smiled.

"Now, I need your watch," Alex said.

Sorsha retrieved the little round device and dropped it into Alex's open palm without looking at it. Alex took another rune paper and folded it tightly, placing it on the back of the silver body of the watch. This time, when he lit the paper, she felt something, like an awareness of the watch's presence.

"There," Alex said, handing it back. "Now you can use the watch to increase or decrease the flow of life energy. Once we get Andrew's spell connected, of course."

Sorsha crossed her arms, gripping her biceps and trying to control her breathing. It sounded easy enough, but that didn't make her any less scared. She swept an appraising eye over Alex and Dr. Bell, but saw no signs of doubt or fear.

"All right," she said, after drawing a trembling breath. "Let's go see Andrew."

25

THE SECOND CHANCE

Alex put his hand on Sorsha's as she gripped his arm. He could tell from the desperate hold she had on him that she was nervous. Truth be told, they all were, but unless Sorsha asked for comfort, the rules of polite society wouldn't let anyone mention the tension in the room. Even Andrew Barton, the Lightning Lord himself, wore a worried look when the doors of his private elevator swept open, revealing his cavernous office.

Everything in Andrew's office was as Alex remembered it with one exception. Off to the left side, against the sorcerer's wall of photographs, there was what looked like a short Doric column, complete with a decorative capital and fluted sides sitting atop a heavy plinth. Atop the marble decoration, a reddish-brown spell hung in the air, spinning like a tiny galaxy. As Alex looked at it, minuscule flashes of bright yellow light moved inside the spell, spiraling out from the interior to ride along the trailing edges. A glass box sat on the floor beside the column, and looked to be the exact size to sit atop the capital and cover the spell.

"Sorsha," Andrew greeted his fellow sorcerer with a nod.

"I wanted to thank you for doing this for me," she said in response.

"Alex didn't have any real idea what he was asking you to do, but I know, and I'm grateful."

Alex raised an eyebrow at that. He knew this would be a major spell, even for the Lightning Lord, but he didn't look as if it had taxed his abilities.

"Think nothing of it, my dear," Andrew replied. "I was happy to help."

"Is there anything we need to know before we connect your spell to the rune construct?" Iggy asked.

"I don't think so," Andrew said. "I did as you instructed. The spell draws magical energy from the universe and holds it inside. Sorsha should be able to draw energy into your construct as soon as it's connected to her."

"We've already taken care of that," Alex said, holding up the last linking rune. "All that's left is the spell."

Andrew looked at the paper for a long moment while the room went quiet.

"Well," he said, reaching out to pluck the paper out of Alex's hand, "we might as well get it over with. Dragging things out won't help."

With that, he strode to the swirling spell and pressed the rune paper into its side, causing the flowing eddies of magic to swirl and distort around it. Alex saw a tiny spark fly from the sorcerer's thumb, igniting the paper.

Alex felt the rune reach out, searching for its twin, now locked in place to the steel plate in his vault. With a snap only he and Iggy could hear, the rune made contact, forming an ethereal bridge between the Lighting Lord's spell and Iggy's construct. Power pressed forward, trying to escape the rune, but it was met with resistance. The other side of the magical bridge ended with Sorsha, and it kept the power in its place.

"I can feel it," Sorsha gasped. "It's like a pressure against my skull."

"Try letting a tiny trickle in," Iggy said. "Don't overdo it."

Sorsha nodded, then turned the tiny crown of the silver watch. Alex felt the power flow over the link and into his vault. A moment later Sorsha shivered, and a wide grin spread across her face. She still held Alex's arm and he could feel her grip relax, losing its desperate need for connection.

"This feels...incredible," she said, her grin becoming sensual.

"That's enough for now," Iggy said, a firm, no-nonsense edge in his voice.

Sorsha actually pouted, but then she turned the dial back and Alex felt the flow of power cease.

"Now, let's see that watch of yours again," his mentor said.

Iggy had stolen a glance at Sorsha's watch when he'd linked it to his construct. The little red hand had pointed to seven minutes past the hour. That had chilled Alex to the bone, though he'd kept his mouth shut at the time.

Sorsha handed the watch to Iggy, who peered at it for a long moment. Once he'd finished scrutinizing it, his face broke out into a wide smile.

"Ten minutes after the hour," he announced. "You've managed to move the hand two minutes with just a little energy."

"Should I do more?" she asked, sounding eager.

"Yes," Iggy said, handing the watch back, "but remember to take it slow. I shouldn't have to remind you what happened to that Bradley Elder fellow when he pulled in too much power too quickly."

The sorceress made a face but nodded as she moved the watch crown gently. Alex felt the power begin to flow through the linking rune again. After a full five minutes, Sorsha rotated the crown back and the flow diminished.

"Now what does it say?" Iggy asked, not bothering to hide the smug smile spreading across his face.

Sorsha took a deep breath, then looked down at the tiny face. A moment later her face split with a wide grin.

"It's pointing to twenty-eight minutes past," she gushed. "It worked."

"Of course it worked," Alex said, pretending to be offended by her statement.

Sorsha ignored him, accepting hugs from Iggy and Andrew. When she finished, she turned to him, looking better than she had in months, and pulled him into a fiery kiss. Alex kissed her back, letting his imagination follow the chain of promises that kiss was making.

When they finally broke apart, Sorsha tried to take a step back but stumbled, causing Alex to grab her to keep her from falling.

"I'm sorry," she said. "I'm suddenly a bit dizzy."

"I think that's quite enough excitement for now," Iggy said in his take-charge, medical voice. "Miss Kincaid needs to rest and recuperate after absorbing so much energy. Alex, will you escort her to the brownstone, please. She'll be staying in your room for the next few days."

Sorsha gave Iggy a probing look, but the one he gave her back stopped her from objecting.

"To my knowledge," he went on, "this kind of transference has never been done before. I want to keep a close eye on you until I'm sure you're not in any danger."

"I have people who can do that at my home," she said.

"Yes, but they're not me," Iggy said. "You can sleep in Alex's room, and he'll move into his vault for the time being."

Alex wasn't thrilled about that, but at least his vault bed was comfortable.

While they had been talking, Andrew picked up the glass covering and dropped it down over the spell. When it touched the base, there was a flash of magic and the glass vibrated for a moment.

"There," he said, stepping back. "That'll keep anyone from disturbing the spell. Now I've got work to get back to and it sounds like you've got some convalescing to do." This last was directed at Sorsha.

She stepped forward and hugged the sorcerer again. When she finished, Alex offered her his arm once more and escorted her to the elevator. He wasn't thrilled that she'd be under Iggy's watchful care for the next few days. That kiss had made some very specific promises, and he was looking forward to collecting.

His thought process must have been showing, because Iggy stepped up behind him.

"I believe you have some casework to do," he said in the most unsubtle tone of dismissal Alex had ever heard. "I suggest you figure out what our friends are up to as soon as possible."

In the rush of excitement over Sorsha, Alex had quite forgotten about the Legion and their strange giant rune.

"Right," he said as the elevator car descended back to Empire Station.

When Alex reached his office, he found Sherry waiting for him with an expectant look.

"What's the good word?" he asked.

"I've got three potential clients for you," she said, holding up a small stack of folders.

Alex was always excited to hear about new clients, but he had to find out what the Legion was up to. That was his highest priority.

"Anything Mike can work on?" he asked. Mike Fitzgerald was his apprentice, helping Alex by using the finding rune to locate lost treasures and pets. Recently, Alex had been teaching him how to write more and more complex runes. Now the little man was finally beginning to take some of the rune creation load off Alex.

Sherry cocked her head to this side, something she did when she was thinking, and put a finger to her lower lip.

"Well," she said, sounding like she wasn't ready to commit. "There was a man in here who thinks his wife is having an affair while he's at work. I suppose I could have Mike follow her if she leaves her house."

Alex thought about that. Cheating spouse cases were fairly simple, but they could turn ugly at the drop of a hat. Cuckold husbands could take the news in stoic stride or explode into towering rage. Still, this husband already expected an affair, so it was probably safe.

"Call the husband," Alex said. "Have him put a tracking stone in his wife's purse tonight, then have Mike set up in a diner near the house and watch his map. If she leaves, he can use the compass to follow her."

Sherry gave him a smile and a wink.

"Will do, boss."

"I've got something I have to work on," he said, turning toward the back hallway door. "I'll be in my office."

He started toward the door, then stopped and turned.

"One more thing," Alex said, tugging the silver flash ring off his right ring finger. "Give this to Mike. I don't think he's going to find trouble on this job, but if something does come up, you tell him to set off a flash and get out of there. No heroics."

Sherry took the offered ring and nodded.

"You need to make me one of these, too," she said, only half joking.

Alex laughed at that, feeling some of his pent-up tension releasing.

"I'll give it some thought," he promised, then headed to his office.

When he sat down behind his massive desk, he immediately wondered what he was going to do. Clearly the Legion was up to something, something big. None of that would matter, however, if Alex didn't figure out what they were up to in time to throw a monkey wrench into their plans.

What he needed to do was get into the basements and cellars of the other houses. He was positive they all had them and that he'd find a bit of the deconstructed rune in each one. Problem was, there were a dozen houses to check, and he'd have to break in to all of them. That meant he'd have to wait until dark.

Alex reached for his pocket watch but the intercom on his desk interrupted him.

"Yes?" he answered.

"Arthur Wilks is on the phone for you," Sherry said, her voice distorted by the little speaker.

Alex sighed. He thought he'd finally finished with the insurance man's case.

"Put him through."

Alex released the intercom key and put his hand on the handset of his cradle-style telephone. When it rang, he picked it up quickly.

"Lockerby," he said.

"Try again, scribbler," Wilks' gravelly voice came at him down the wire.

"Are you saying Tommy isn't our boy?"

"That's exactly what I'm saying," the insurance man growled. "He copped to buying up the extra stock with money from his trust, but his alibi for the night of the murder is solid."

"Miss Masterson, his nurse, had the night off," Alex said. "She could have easily driven him in to town and back. She is his girlfriend after all, maybe she did the deed herself."

"There's only one thing wrong with that theory. Masterson was in Jersey visiting her folks all day. I even took a ride out there to check and two of the neighbors remember seeing her."

"Tommy could have driven himself," Alex said, then hurried on before Wilks could object. "He has access to the money in the family trust. It's a cinch he's already taking the polio cure. He might be able to walk on his own by now."

"He is taking the cure," Wilks said. "I called around and he's getting it from an alchemist in the city named Linda Kellin."

"Did she say how long he'd been buying it from her?" Alex asked.

"No," Wilks said. "Something about patient privacy."

Alex remembered very well Linda's fight to walk after her long incarceration in an iron lung. It had taken almost a year before she could walk without crutches. It was unlikely Tommy had had access to the cure for that long.

He sighed and pinched the bridge of his nose. He really didn't have time for this.

"If it's not Tommy, then I've got nothing," he admitted. "No one involved with Fredrick Chance had any motive to kill him, not his coworkers, not his wife, and certainly not Lillian. I'm afraid this is shaping up to be a simple accident."

"If that's the way it is, I'll live with it," Wilks said, "but I want to be sure. I spent all damn day yesterday running down the Waverly kid's alibi. The least you can do is check into Lillian's."

Alex ground his teeth. He didn't want to spend the day digging into Lillian's alibi of having gone to the opera. Dozens, if not hundreds, of people would have seen her. Running that down was a waste of time.

"Remember, Alex," Wilks said. "You owe me."

"All right," Alex growled. "I'll double-check Lillian Waverly's alibi. But if I don't find anything, this case is going to have to be a tragic accident."

"I have to write the check tomorrow anyway," Wilks replied, "so be sure to get me your report by five."

DAN WILLIS

With that, the insurance man hung up. Alex had a momentary thought of banging his head on the table, but he resisted it. Instead, he pulled out his notes on the Waverly case and paged back through them. According to Lillian, her alibi was that she'd gone to see a performance of the opera Die Walküre on the night Fredrick died. Alex had checked and that opera was playing at the Majestic currently. What he hadn't done was actually go down there and ask around.

With a frustrated sigh, Alex closed his notebook and pressed the key to the intercom.

"I've got to go out to run down some things. Hold the fort till I get back."

The Majestic was one of the most opulent theaters in the city, though it wasn't on Broadway proper. When Alex had been looking into the Dolly Anderson murders, he'd heard about the Majestic and that its wealthy patrons often enjoyed the fact that the theater was on a side street. Without other theaters to either side, making a grand entrance at the Majestic was simplicity itself.

For his part, Alex pulled up in a cab and strode into the theater's front lobby. Since it was early in the day, most of the lights were out and no one manned the concession counter or ticket booth. He followed the sound of someone vacuuming and came across a pretty young girl in her twenties. She directed Alex to the theater manager, a balding, heavyset man in a white shirt with rolled-up sleeves.

After hearing Alex's request, the manager sent Alex to the stage where a half dozen stagehands were hauling furniture and bits of scenery around. He spotted a well-muscled young man with wavy hair and an infectious smile hauling what looked like a marble pillar with deceptive ease.

"That's quite impressive," Alex said, walking up to the young man as he set the pillar down.

"Not really," the young man said. "It's made of balsa wood and it's hollow inside."

"Are you Ricky Hughes?"

The young man looked surprised but then nodded.

"That's me, what can I do for you?"

"I understand you worked here a week ago Thursday." Alex said.

"That's right," Ricky said with a nod. "I'm in charge of the private boxes on the south balcony."

Alex asked what, exactly, that meant.

"I take tickets and escort people to their seats," he said. "I also make sure no one gets up on the balcony who isn't supposed to be there."

"Do you remember a Mrs. Lillian Waverly being here that night?"

"Lil?" he asked, then nodded before Alex could respond. "She was here. Her box is the third one back from the stage."

That pretty much confirmed Lillian's alibi. Ricky knew her well enough to call her Lil, and he said she was here. Still, Wilks wasn't going to like that answer, so Alex decided to press a bit.

"Was there anything unusual about her that night?"

Ricky thought about that for a moment, then shrugged.

"Weird stuff happens every night," he said. "But Mrs. Waverly stayed in her box all evening, then left with her friend."

Alex was in the act of putting his notebook away, but he froze.

"Friend?" he asked.

"She had a guest join her," Ricky said. "That's not unusual though. Mrs. Waverly almost always has guests with her."

"Who was this guest that Lil had?"

Ricky looked thoughtful, then shook his head.

"She wasn't anyone I knew," he said, "and I know all the regulars. She did have a ticket for Mrs. Waverly's box though, so I showed her there when she arrived."

"They didn't come together?" Alex asked.

"No," Ricky said. "The guest was actually pretty late. I think she got here right before the intermission. Anything else?" Ricky said. "I've got to get back to work. The stage has to be ready for tonight."

"No," Alex said, putting away his notebook and pencil. "Thank you, Ricky. You've been a very big help."

26

WHEELS WITHIN WHEELS

Two hours later, Alex pulled up the collar of his suit coat as he headed along Runewright Row. He'd been up and down the row, looking in on friends he hadn't seen in months, asking questions and picking up a few supplies he needed. While he'd been there, a light rain had started to fall, but these were runewrights, so they'd simply activated barrier runes and gone on with their work.

Alex had a bubble of rainproof magic around him as well, but his had the added effect of keeping out the chill the rain brought with it. Clutching his paper bag full of blank flash paper and several exotic inks, he made his way carefully along the sidewalk until he could catch a cab.

He turned and glanced back along the row, to the line of carts and stalls where his less fortunate brothers and sisters sold their wares. Only a few years ago, the row was a bustling avenue of cramped carts barely long enough to contain everyone. Now, as he looked through the drizzling rain, he could see large gaps between the carts, and everyone seemed to keep to themselves.

On some level Alex blamed himself for that. A year and a half ago, a large number of the runewrights who used to work there were killed when the Happy Jack Rune Factory burned to the ground. The owner of the factory, Carlton Maple, had set the fire to cover up his crimes, and to kill Alex with any luck. Alex had ended Carlton's luck, but he'd been unable to save more than a few dozen of the over two hundred people that worked there.

The rain began to pick up as he looked back at the men and women of the row, rendering them fuzzy and indistinct. Alex imagined he could see dark shapes, filling in the gaps in the row. Specters of those he couldn't save.

He knew it was only his mind playing tricks on him, so he gave them one last look, then sighed and turned away.

He took a cab back to his office. There were far too many runewrights in proximity to the Row, so he didn't dare travel through his vault. By the time he got off the elevator on the 12th floor of Empire Tower, it was a bit after two.

"Hiya, boss," Sherry's chipper voice greeted him when he opened the office door. "How did it go at the opera house?"

"Good," he said, somewhat noncommittally. "I think I know who killed Fredrick Chance and why they did it."

"Should I put a call through to Mr. Wilks for you?" she said, reaching for the phone.

"I'll take care of that," he said, feeling suddenly weary. All the late nights he'd been having were finally catching up to him. "You can call down to the lunch counter and get me a sandwich, though."

"Mike wants to see you," Sherry said as Alex opened the door to the back hallway and stepped inside. The hall was short with four doors in it. Three doors were on the right-hand wall, with large windows looking out into the city on the left. The fourth door stood against the back wall, opposite the door Alex used to come in, and that door led to his vault.

The first door along the line led to a large office with a heavy table in the middle of it. Alex used that as his map room. At the far end, the third door led to Alex's private office, and the middle door led to a meeting space with a conference table. When he first moved into this office, Alex intended to use it as a file room, or perhaps a place to put things he didn't want in his vault. Now it served a new purpose.

Opening the second door, Alex stepped inside. The conference table had been pushed against the left-hand wall and now stood laden with runewright supplies. There were pots of ink, jars of exotic powders, stacks of different kinds of paper, and boxes of quill pens, fountain pens, and pencils. On the right side of the room was a large drafting table, exactly like Alex's, where his apprentice Mike Fitzgerald now sat.

Mike was a short, wiry man with slicked-back hair and a mustache that reminded Alex of a blond caterpillar. When he heard the door open, he looked up from his work with a broad smile.

"Alex, you need to come see this." He indicated the rune he was working on. "I think I'm really gettin' the hang of this."

Alex set his bag of supplies down on the conference table and crossed to where Mike was working. On the table was a near perfect example of Alex's climate rune. There were a few minor defects, but not enough to prevent it from working.

It was good work and Alex said so. "You wanted to see me?" he added.

"Oh, yeah," Mike said, dismounting his stool. "I had a question about the map room."

He headed for the door and out into the hall with Alex in tow. Alex couldn't imagine what kind of question Mike would have about the map; he'd used it hundreds of times over the last year to track down everything from lost dogs to wedding rings. When Mike opened the door, however, Alex understood immediately.

Almost two dozen crumpled-up papers were strewn randomly around the map.

"I don't know what you're doing here, boss," Mike said, "but I didn't want to disturb anything. I just wanted to know if it's okay to use the map?"

Alex nodded.

"Don't worry about this," he said. "It's something I'm working on for a case. It won't affect the map at all."

Mike smiled and nodded.

"Good," he said. "I'm tired of using the one in my kit bag. I like the big one."

Alex was glad Mike was happy, but the map had reminded him of the Legion and their giant rune. He needed to find out what they were doing and stop it.

"If that's everything, Mike," Alex said, "I've got some calls to make."

"Sure thing, boss," Mike beamed. "I won't ask now, but I eventually want to know why you were marking out a big finding rune on the map. That's got to be one interesting case."

Alex stood in the doorway, his mind racing.

"What did you say?"

Mike looked startled and shrugged.

"I was wondering what the big finding rune is for." He pointed at the papers on the map for emphasis.

Alex rushed to the table and squinted down at the papers. They looked like they might form a pattern, but they didn't look anything like a finding rune.

"What makes you think this is a finding rune?" he asked.

Mike chuckled.

"I admit it took me a while to figure it out," he said, walking around to the part of the table farthest from the papers, "but when I stood here, I finally saw it."

Alex circled the table to stand behind Mike. As he went, the papers resolved themselves into a shape he knew very well.

"I'll be damned," he said, then he slapped his apprentice on the back. "Thank you, Mike. You're a genius."

"I am?" he said, more confused than before.

"I'm going to need the map room for a while," Alex said, pulling out his notebook and leaning down over the papers. He didn't hear Mike's reply, or the door closing after him. He was focused on the map and all other thoughts had been driven from his mind.

Hours later, the sandwich Sherry had ordered Alex sat, untouched, on the sideboard that held the box of finding runes and the spare compasses. A full notebook of papers littered the floor and Alex had added over fifty to the map. These latter ones he rolled into tubes and used to show how the nodes of the giant finding runes were linked.

He didn't actually know, of course, but he was pretty sure he'd worked it out at last. Thanks to the two basements he'd visited the previous night, Alex had a rough idea of how the Legion had deconstructed their rune. Since they didn't seem to have access to major linking runes, they'd used anchor runes as a kind of one-way gate to pass the magic from node to node. It was crude and horribly inefficient, but it would do the job.

"Can't fault the Legion for lack of imagination," he said.

A wave of hunger and exhaustion suddenly washed over him, and he had to grab the edge of the table to keep from swaying. Looking up, he caught sight of his waiting sandwich and grinned.

"Bless you, Sherry," he said.

"What's that?" Sherry's voice startled him.

He turned to find her standing in the open doorway to the map room. When he didn't speak, she went on.

"I'm sorry to bother you, but Mr. Wilks is on the phone for you."

Alex looked up at the clock and cursed. It was already a quarter past five. He sighed, looking forlornly at the sandwich, then pushed himself away from the table.

"I'll take it in my office," he said, stepping around her and out into the hall.

When he reached his office, he had just enough time to slump down in his chair when the phone rang.

"I thought you were going to have this wrapped up by five," Wilks angry voice assaulted him after he picked up the receiver.

"I wrapped it up hours ago," Alex said. "I got a little sidetracked."

"Well?" Wilks demanded. "If you've figured it out, who killed Fredrick Chance?"

"It was Lillian."

"I thought Lillian had an ironclad alibi," Wilks said, clearly playing devil's advocate.

"She does," Alex said. "But she did it nonetheless."

The line was silent for a long moment.

"I don't suppose you can prove that?"

Alex considered that and shrugged, despite Wilks not being able to see him.

"I think so. When are you going to give them the insurance check?"

"Tomorrow morning at nine," Wilks said.

"Do you still have any old pals at the Central Office?"

"A few," Wilks hedged.

"Okay," Alex said, pulling out his notebook. "Give them a call tonight and tell them this." He rattled off a few instructions, then promised to meet Wilks over at Waverly Radio in the morning.

"Are you sure about this?" he growled when Alex finished.

"Trust me, Arthur," Alex assured him. "This will work."

Wilks gave him a noncommittal growl and hung up.

Alex put his head down on his desk, but as he felt sleep trying to overtake him, he started up into a sitting position. After a moment to think, he reached for his phone again and dialed the brownstone.

"Iggy," he said when the line connected. "How's Sorsha?"

"She's resting comfortably. Her control of the flow of magic is getting more precise all the time. She is still physically exhausted, though I suspect that's the after-effects of having her life energy drained."

Alex smiled in relief.

"What did you need, lad?" his mentor asked.

"Can you come over to my office? I've got something here that you really need to see."

"You're sure about this?" Iggy said, circling the table for the third time.

Alex, who had his mouth full of sandwich, just nodded.

"It's incredible," Iggy went on. "I wonder how they even conceived of such an idea."

"They must have been planning this for years," Alex said through a bite of ham and cheese.

"Don't talk with your mouth full," Iggy admonished. "But you're right, this is not something they pulled out of thin air."

"You were probably right about powering it being the problem," Alex said, after swallowing his bite of sandwich. "They got lucky with Sorsha, so they put their plan into action."

"I suppose we can guess what they're searching for," Iggy chuckled.

Alex hadn't thought about it, but as far as he knew, the Legion wanted the Archimedean Monograph more than anything.

"Do you think that rune has enough power to punch through your protection runes?"

Iggy shook his head.

"I shouldn't think so. But to be safe, I'll move the monograph inside my vault until you figure out how to stop this construct from working."

"I thought we were going to find a way to make it blow up in their faces."

"As enjoyable as that would be," Iggy said, "if this rune blows up, it could take a sizable chunk of the city with it. Best find a way to make it fail instead."

Alex ground his teeth. He hadn't thought of that. Poorly written runes could explode, but they usually didn't do serious damage because of their size. A rune big enough to encircle a good part of lower Manhattan was another matter.

"All right," he said, not bothering to hide the disappointment in his voice. There were several ways he could disable the rune, assuming he guessed right about how it was constructed.

"The first thing I need to do," Alex went on, "is go to bed."

Iggy raised an eyebrow.

"That doesn't sound like an efficient use of your time."

Alex shrugged.

"I'm dead on my feet," he admitted. "Besides, I won't be able to break into any of the Legion houses until it's dark, and I don't want to mess around with their giant construct while I'm exhausted."

Hostile Takeover

Robert Benjamin left his post as a security guard in Empire Station promptly at six. He was an athletic man of average height with dark hair that he wore slicked back, and he strode with purpose across the station to the stairs. A half a minute later, he emerged on the street and hailed a cab.

He gave the driver the address of an inner ring house south of the park and sat back as the driver accelerated into traffic. Robert's hands trembled a bit and he folded them in his lap, taking a deep breath to calm his nerves.

"You shouldn't be nervous," he whispered to himself.

He shouldn't be, but he was. Almost a year of work would come down to a few minutes of implementation. It was both thrilling and terrifying.

By the time the taxi arrived at the neat house, Robert had mastered himself again. He paid the driver and then waited on the sidewalk for him to drive away. Once he was sure he was alone, he turned and headed up the walk that led to the house. It was a large structure, done in the colonial style with a covered porch running around the front and one side of the building. There were three stories and lights burned in almost all the windows despite the sun's not quite being down yet.

As he mounted the stairs to the porch, Robert pulled a heavy ring from his pocket and used it to knock on the bare steel plate that had been set into the center of the door in place of a knocker. The moment the ring touched the plate, a purple rune appeared, and the door unlocked with an audible click.

Stepping forward, Robert entered the building's foyer, shutting the door behind him.

A passingly attractive woman of middle years sat in a chair on the far side of the foyer. When Robert approached, she stood up.

"Why are you here, Journeyman?"

"I have news for the master."

She ran an appraising eye over him, then nodded and indicated a door to the right.

Robert thanked her, though he didn't mean a syllable of it. Journeyman Cline was a pretentious bitch who thought herself so much better than anyone else. Robert hadn't known her long, but he hadn't seen anything that convinced him that she was even competent.

He passed through the indicated door and found himself in a well-appointed study, with a large desk in the center and bookshelves all around. A hunched old man with a short beard sat in a comfortable-looking corner reading a book under a floor lamp. When Robert shut the door behind him, the man looked up.

"Ah," he said, once he'd peered over the top of his book, "it's our new recruit. How are you settling in?"

"Very well, Master Simons."

"And what name are they calling you this time? As I recall, you were Benjamin Robertson in D.C."

Robert blanched a bit, then answered.

"It's Robert Benjamin this time, sir."

Simon screwed up his face at that.

"I keep telling our people to come up with better names," he insisted. "But the Legion wasn't founded on a penchant for naming things."

"No, sir."

"Speaking of Legion business," Simons went on as if Robert hadn't spoken, "what have you to report about our troublesome detective?"

"That's just it, sir," Robert said. "I'm having a hard time tracing his movements."

"Have you checked the logs?"

"Of course, Master. Every time Lockerby uses the security elevator, they're supposed to log it, but either they're not doing their job, or Lockerby is getting in and out of the building some other way."

Robert had been worried that this report would earn him a reprimand, but Master Simons steepled his fingers in front of his chest instead.

"What about his sorceress girlfriend?" the master asked. "Could she be teleporting him around?"

"I thought that too, at first," Robert said, "but then I remembered the spike rune. I'd be amazed if she could get out of bed at this point."

Simons nodded and chuckled.

"You're right, young man." The master's smile suddenly vanished and his face grew pensive. "In fact, I'm amazed she isn't dead yet. I wonder if young Lockerby or his mentor have figured out some way to keep her alive?"

"That's not likely, though," Robert said, thinking better of it once the words were already out of his mouth. "I mean, sir, that if they'd found a way to stop the spike, the rune wouldn't be receiving any more power."

"Also true," Simons said, setting his book aside and rising. "You've done well, young Benjamin. Now come with me. I think it's time we tested the spike's link to dear Sorsha."

The clock in the foyer read two-forty-seven when Alex finally came stumbling into his room in the brownstone. After his nap in the afternoon, he'd managed to visit four more of the Legion's houses before he was exhausted.

Sorsha lay in his bed looking serene, beautiful, and asleep, so he crept to the door and headed downstairs. As he'd predicted, Iggy was awake, sitting in his reading chair with a pulp novel and a glass of cognac.

"How did it go?" he asked.

Alex shook his head.

"The Legion's rune wasn't laid out the way I thought," he said. "I couldn't find a good place to try to disrupt it properly."

"You'll have to go back tomorrow," Iggy said with a sigh. "We can't let those blighters get away with whatever they're up to."

Alex nodded, sitting down in his chair and leaning back.

"I think..." he began but the desire for sleep pulled at him. "I think I managed to foul the rune," he mumbled. "I used a link that should keep it from working the way they intended, but grounding it, or out-and-out breaking it would be..." he yawned, "would be better."

"You're not making a lot of sense," Iggy said, turning back to his book. "Go get some sleep and you can try again tomorrow."

"Right," Alex mumbled, forcing himself to stand. "Tomorrow."

27

NAVIGATING THE WARREN

Despite how late he'd retired, Alex arrived early at the offices of Waverly Radio in the morning. He was so early, in fact, that he ended up sitting in their front office reading the paper for half an hour. As he expected, Lillian was the first of his guests to arrive. It was her company, after all.

She wore a dark blue dress with a black jacket over it and a pair of polished heels that matched the dress. A string of glistening pearls hung around her neck, complementing the makeup that made her look flawless. What Alex didn't expect was the frown that twisted her lips when she saw him.

"I suppose you're here to sign off on Arthur giving me the insurance check?" she said. "Did you hear?" she went on before Alex could answer. "That sniveling bastard bought up all the stock. Now he owns enough of the company that he can throw me out on my ear. Oh, he'll love that, the despicable creep."

Alex did know that Tommy Waverly had purchased a bunch of Waverly shares, now heavily discounted thanks to the company's fortunes.

"At least it won't do him any good," Lillian fumed. "With Fredrick gone, we've only got a few weeks left before the sharks start circling."

Alex waited until she gave him a look that clearly indicated she was done and expected him to have something to say.

"You've run this company very well," he said. "I'm sure there's someone out there who'd be happy to have you on their management team."

Lillian gave him a patronizing look.

"You can't really believe that?" she said, motioning for him to follow her as she headed for the elevator. "You're too smart. The people I've beaten in negotiations would have too much pride, and all the rest think I got what I need by being a wanton."

Alex could believe that. Lillian might be pushing forty, but she still had her looks. There were probably quite a few people who would assume she'd slept her way to the top.

A few minutes later and they were in Lillian's massive office.

"Take a seat," she said, waving at the area with the fireplace and the couches. As Alex headed that way, Lillian turned to the bar. "I need a drink," she declared. "Do you want one?"

Alex declined but before he could sit down, the door opened, and Arthur Wilks entered the office.

"Oh, good," Lillian said, moving to the insurance man and taking his arm. "I'm eager to get this unfortunate business done with."

"Not so fast, Lillian," Tommy Waverly's voice came from the door.

Alex looked on from where he sat, leaning back on the couch with his legs crossed. Tommy's wheelchair emerged from the doorway, pushed by the beautiful Irene Masterson.

That's tempting fate, he thought as he stood up. He didn't know if he'd have to restrain Lillian, but he wanted to be prepared.

"That's rich," Lillian sneered. "Bringing her here. Why are you here, by the way?" She put emphasis on the word 'you,' meaning Tommy.

Her philandering husband jerked his thumb at Wilks.

"This insurance monkey called to let me know he'd be making the payment today," he said. "Since I'm now the majority shareholder in Waverly Radio, I figured I should be here to make sure none of it goes missing."

Lillian bristled, but regained her composure before she exploded.

"It's going to be a check, Thomas," she chided, in the manner of a schoolmarm who caught a student daydreaming. "There won't be any loose cash for you abscond with."

"I didn't need any money from you to buy this business right out from under your nose, now did I?"

"No," Lillian said, "only Daddy's money."

Tommy looked like he wanted to get up out of his chair and strangle his wife, but he, too, mastered himself.

"It doesn't really matter how I got a majority share," he said with a sneer, "what matters is that I have it. And as majority stake holder, I'm going to fire you right now."

Alex expected Lillian to explode at that, but instead, she laughed.

"It takes a vote of the board to fire me," she said, "majority stake or not."

"Well then," Tommy said, steepling his hands under his chin, "I guess I'll have to wait."

It looked like he was about to go on, but the door opened again and a slender woman in a black dress entered.

"Katrina," Lillian gasped. "What are you doing here? You should be at home."

"That's my fault," Alex said, striding across the room to Fredrick Chance's widow.

"I don't mind, Lillian," Katrina said as Alex approached and offered her his arm. "I don't think I could stand the house for another day."

"Alex," Lillian said, her eyes hard and boring into him. "Why did you bring her here?"

"Let's go sit by the fire and I'll tell you."

Alex led Katrina and Lillian over to the couch where Arthur Wilks was sitting, and waited while the women sat.

"Can we get on with this?" Tommy demanded. Irene had rolled him next to one of the padded chairs where she took a seat.

"Yes, Tommy," Alex said, giving him a nod, "an excellent idea."

On cue, Arthur Wilks reached into his briefcase and pulled out a long, rectangular book.

"I'm sorry I kept you waiting, Lillian," he said as he opened the cover of the check book. "But I had to be sure the conditions of your policy were met before I could issue you payment."

"I understand, Arthur," Lillian said in a weary voice.

Wilks was paging through the book, but he stopped and began searching his pocket for a pen. Not finding one, he picked up his briefcase again.

"While I'm filling this out," he said, "I'll have Mr. Lockerby give you his report on the death of Fredrick Chance."

Alex was ready for this, of course. He'd set the whole thing up with Wilks when they spoke on the phone. Usually, Wilks would write out a check for a client at his office, then drop it by, but taking his time writing it here gave Alex time as well.

Time he intended to use wisely.

"I must confess," Alex said, stepping in front of the hearth, "when I first examined Mr. Chance's office, I suspected foul play. I couldn't prove it, of course, it was only a feeling, so when Mr. Wilks asked me to investigate, I jumped at the chance."

"I'm sure we're all thrilled that a man's death made you so happy," Tommy growled.

"The problem I ran into," Alex continued as if Tommy hadn't spoken, "was that no one involved would benefit from Mr. Chance's death, and you all had alibis."

"You knew that when you came to see me," Lillian said. "What took you so long to tell Arthur?"

Alex gave her a sly smile.

"Just because someone claims to have an alibi, that doesn't mean they actually do," he said, "so I checked on your alibis."

"And?" Tommy sighed.

"And they all held up," Alex admitted. "So I called Mr. Wilks and told him Callahan Brothers Property would have to pay out on the insurance policy."

"Well, thank you," Tommy said, drawing out the word 'thank' in a sarcastic tone. "Now that you've wasted everyone's time with that story, is the check ready?"

"Not quite," Arthur said. "It'll take a moment for the ink to dry."

"Oh, good," Alex said, clapping his hands together. "I haven't gotten to the best part yet."

"There's more?" Katrina asked. She sat, huddled in on herself as if expecting a physical blow. Clearly all this discussion about her husband's death was weighing on her.

"Yes," he answered. "I'm afraid there's a great deal more. You remember I said that my instincts were telling me that Mr. Chance was murdered, but I couldn't prove it?"

"Yes," Lillian said, sipping her drink. "You did mention it a minute ago."

"Well, something about this case kept bothering me, so I decided to check all your alibis again." He paused, looking from face to face around the room. "Would you like to know what I found?"

"I think the ink on that check is dry enough," Tommy growled. "I don't want to hear any more of this gumshoe's ramblings."

"I found out that none of your alibis hold up, Mr. Waverly," Alex said, turning to Tommy. "Does that surprise you?"

"That's nonsense," Lillian said.

"Really?" Alex asked. "You said you were at the opera when Fredrick Chance died."

"And so I was," she insisted, a bit of passion creeping into her voice. "Dozens of my friends, people I know, saw me."

"Yes," Alex said, "they did see you, but I was a bit surprised to learn that none of them spoke to you. You arrived, went right to your private box, and didn't speak to anyone until the show was over."

"Lillian always has to warm up to social situations," Tommy chuckled. "I hate to admit it, but I don't see how that proves anything."

Alex gave Tommy a conspiratorial smile, then went on.

"In order for you to understand why your wife's alibi doesn't hold up, I'll have to tell you a bit of a story. You see, I only knew two things about Waverly radios when I got Mr. Wilks' call; one," Alex held up two fingers and began ticking them off, "Waverly radios got fantastic reception, and two, if they got too hot, that pretty Bakelite casing would crack."

"Everyone knows that," Katrina said in a small voice.

"Yes, but when I asked Lillian about it, she said they were exploring ways to make the radio casings more durable."

"So?" Lillian said, a confused look on her face.

"So you then showed me how you used Mr. Chance's rune to enhance the radio receivers." He turned to Wilks. "They use this great big wooden board inlaid with a conductive metal, and then they put the regular receivers into slots in the board. Once they're all in place, they use the rune, and it changes all the tubes in the board at once."

"Fascinating," Wilks said, "but what does that have to do with Lillian's alibi?"

"That's the interesting part," Alex said, addressing the whole room again. "You see, in the same room where they enhance the receivers was another board, only this one didn't have slots for radio receivers in it, it had oddly shaped rectangles. Now, I didn't realize what it was at the time, but it had to do with making the radio shells more durable. Those rectangles were the exact shape of Waverly's new compact tabletop model. Lillian here," he pointed to her, "was trying to use the same rune trick to make the Bakelite stronger."

"My husband didn't have a rune like that," Katrina said. "If he did, he'd have told me."

"No," Alex agreed. "Fredrick Chance didn't have a rune like that, but obviously someone did." Alex addressed Lillian again. "And that someone is the reason your alibi is worthless."

"I must confess, Lillian," Tommy said with obvious glee in his voice, "I'm interested to know who this mysterious accomplice is?"

"Officer!" Alex yelled toward the door.

The door opened and a uniformed policeman escorted in a slender young woman. She was pale with a small, perky nose, full lips, and brown eyes that tended toward a honey color. Her hair was light brown and cut in a bob that reminded Alex of Sorsha. The clothes she wore were of good quality, but there was fraying at her cuffs. Clearly she had fallen on hard times.

"Her," Alex said, pointing. "Allow me to introduce Tess Avery."

"Who?" Tommy and Katrina said in unison.

"Tess is the one with the rune to fix Lillian's Bakelite problem," Alex explained.

"How did you find out about that?" Lillian hissed.

"I was curious," Alex explained while the policemen led Tess over to one of the overstuffed chairs. "When I questioned Ricky Hughes, the usher at the Majestic Theater where you saw Die Walküre, he told me that a guest joined you for the show. He said they showed up right at the intermission and that you left together once the opera was over. I wondered why you didn't mention her to corroborate your alibi when the police first talked to you?"

"Everyone's trying to solve the Bakelite problem," Lillian growled, giving Alex a venomous look. "I had to keep Tess' identity a secret. Speaking of that, how did you find her?"

"You left a ticket for her at the box office," Alex said. "They had her name. Once I knew that, I went over to Runewright Row. I couldn't be sure she was a runewright, so I asked around, and you'll never guess what I learned." Alex turned to Tess. "Tess here is an expert with disguise runes. She's so good, she worked for several magicians until the money ran out." He turned back to the room. "Disguise runes are expensive to make, after all."

"What does that have to do with me?" Lillian demanded, anger starting to creep into her voice.

"It means your alibi isn't worth a plugged nickel," Alex responded. "It would have been child's play for Tess to create two disguise runes, one to make her look like you so she could go to the opera on time and establish your alibi. That would give you time to kill Fredrick Chance, then return to the opera wearing the second disguise rune, the one to make you look like Tess."

"Lillian," Katrina gasped, her eyes as wide as saucers.

"No!" Lillian shouted. "It isn't true."

During this exchange, Tommy Waverly laughed uproariously.

"What do you find so funny, Mr. Waverly?" Alex asked. "It took quite a lot of work to poke holes in your wife's alibi. I was able to destroy yours in just over an hour."

If this revelation bothered Tommy, he didn't show it. He shook his head and grinned.

"I would love to hear how you conceived a way for me to roll my way to the factory from Long Island to kill Fredrick," he said. "To say nothing of getting up to his office with the elevator turned off."

"Your husband here," Alex said, turning to Lillian to capture her attention, "told me that you cut off his access to the money from the business."

"He was spending it almost as fast as it came in," she said, casting Tommy a dark look.

"And when he heard there was a new cure for polio, you refused to give him the money."

Lillian looked down, then met Alex's gaze.

"I might have been a bit spiteful on that account," she admitted.

"You also know that when Waverly's stock crashed, your husband bought up enough stock to put him in control of the company."

Lillian shot her husband a look of pure venom and nodded.

"It sure was lucky that Tommy managed to convince the family lawyer to let him dip into the trust just in time," Alex said. "That got me wondering, what if Tommy didn't convince the lawyer this week? What if he did it, say, a year ago?"

"You have no proof of that," Tommy said, his easy expression still firmly in place.

"Sure I do," Alex chuckled. "You see, I knew the woman who invented that polio cure, and the best place to get it is from her daughter, Linda Kellin."

At the mention of Linda's name, Tommy's easy look evaporated like so much steam.

"Since Linda is a friend of mine, I called her and asked about her polio cure business, and what do you think I found?" Alex turned to the young nurse who had been sitting quietly and not making eye contact with anyone. "It turns out that Miss Irene Masterson, here, has been buying the polio cure from Linda for thirteen months."

"Does..." Lillian gasped. "Does that mean Tommy can walk?"

Alex smiled and nodded.

"Linda assures me that after a year, your husband should be able to walk normally." He turned back to Tommy. "So you could have easily taken the train to the city, climbed the stairs up to Fredrick's office and shut the flue to his heater."

DAN WILLIS

"I might have," Tommy growled, "but I didn't."

Alex favored him with a smile.

"I didn't say that you did," he reminded him.

"It has to be one of them," Wilks said. "Whoever shut that flue had to do it when Chance's back was turned. He never would have turned his back on a stranger."

"You..." Katrina's voice wavered. "You don't think that I..."

"No," Alex said, kneeling down before the stricken woman. "No," he repeated. "I know that you didn't kill your husband. Despite his faults, you loved him."

"Well, if she didn't kill him," Lillian demanded, "then who did?"

"She did," Alex said, standing and pointing to Tess Avery.

"What?" the runewright woman demanded. "I didn't even know him."

"And I believe that," Alex said. "But you knew *of* him. You knew that Lillian wanted desperately to acquire your rune, but you were holding out for more money. Money Lillian didn't have because what she did have was going to pay for that exclusive rune owned by Fredrick Chance."

Tess looked at him, shocked.

"How would killing Mr. Chance improve my fortunes?" she asked. "Without him, the whole company might go under. That's not going to convince Lillian to buy my rune."

"She has a point," Lillian said.

"Let the man talk," Tommy added, his self-satisfied smile returning.

"I know Lillian tested out your rune to see if it worked," Alex said to Tess. "That's why there was another board in the room where they enhance the receivers."

"So? We tested it. Why does that make me a murderer?"

"Because," Alex said, "when Lillian showed me the process, they weren't exactly hiding Fredrick's rune. I got a pretty good look at it. Enough that I'm relatively sure what it does. I bet you got a good look, too."

"And if I did?"

"You're a very skilled runewright, Miss Avery," Alex said, looking down at her. "I bet you figured out how the receiver rune worked, and that's when you hatched your plan. Lillian had invited you to the opera, no doubt to try to convince you to compromise on your price. You also knew, from the gossip around the shop, that Fredrick Chance worked late almost every night."

"She couldn't have killed him," Lillian said. "Arthur was right, Fredrick wouldn't have let her into his office after hours and he certainly wouldn't have turned his back on her."

"And you're right," Alex agreed with a nod. "But you're forgetting about Miss Avery's skill with disguise runes. She made one of you, and she wore it the night she drugged Mr. Chance and tampered with his heater."

"That's why you were late arriving to the theater," Lillian gasped.

"You can't prove that," Tess spat at Alex.

"I beg to differ," Alex said, reaching down and snatching Tess' purse out of her lap.

"Give that back," she shrieked, but as she tried to stand, Alex shoved her back in the chair. Before she could rise again, the policeman put a restraining hand on her shoulder.

"Let me go" she demanded, clawing at the policeman's hand.

Alex opened the purse and easily found Tess' rune book. It was a screw-post book almost exactly like his. Tossing the purse back into Tess' lap, he began paging through the book. A moment later he found what he was looking for.

"I said that I got enough of a look at Mr. Chance's rune to understand how it was put together, but if I was to try to recreate it, it would be substantively different." Alex turned to Lillian. "You still have some of Mr. Chance's runes left; would you be so kind as to get one?"

Lillian nodded and rose, walking to her desk. She took out a key and, after unlocking it, took out a stack of rune papers that had been clipped together. When she returned and held the stack out to Alex, he simply put the paper he'd taken from Tess' book beside them.

"They're identical." Lillian nodded, her eyes beginning to water.

"Yes," Alex agreed. "There's only one way Miss Avery could have reproduced Fredrick's rune so precisely. She took one from his office after he was dead."

Katrina shrieked with rage, lunging off the couch in Tess' direction. Warned in advance that this might happen, Wilks grabbed her and pulled her back on the couch. Lillian immediately put her arms around the stricken woman, pulling her into a protective embrace.

"With both runes that Lillian so desperately needed, and Fredrick out of the way, Tess could move in and take over as Waverly's resident runewright," Alex said, looking down at Tess. "She could squeeze Lillian for everything she could get, and maybe even negotiate for a piece of the action."

"That sounds like motive for murder to me," Tommy said.

Alex turned to Arthur Wilks.

"You think this will be enough?" Alex asked, holding up the rune from Tess' book.

The ex-police-detective-turned-insurance-man nodded grimly.

"Put her in handcuffs," he growled at the policeman who was still holding on to Tess, then he turned to Alex. "I'll go call that lieutenant friend of yours at the Central Office."

28

STRUCTURE

"Well, that was entertaining," Tommy Waverly said as Arthur Wilks disappeared into the hallway. "But now the insurance man is gone, and I believe he still has the check."

"Don't worry, Mr. Waverly," Alex said. "I've got a few more things that should hold your interest."

"Can I go?" Katrina Chance asked, casting a dark look at Tess Avery. "I think I'd rather be home."

Alex followed her glance.

"I'm sorry," he said, turning to the officer standing guard over the handcuffed woman. "Officer, would you please escort Miss Avery down to the lobby to wait for Lieutenant Pak?"

The big cop nodded, then grabbed Tess by the arm.

"Let's go, you," he growled as he physically hauled her out of her chair.

Alex waited as everyone watched the policeman hustle her out of the cavernous office and into the hall.

"I should have done that earlier," Alex said to Katrina. "But I did ask you here for a reason beyond knowing that your husband's killer will be brought to justice."

"Isn't your job done now, Alex?" Lillian said.

"My job for Mr. Wilks? Yes," Alex said. "But Mr. Chance's death isn't the only thing plaguing Waverly Radio, now, is it?"

Lillian looked confused, but before she could voice that, Tommy spoke up.

"That's not really any of your business, though," he said, "is it?"

Lillian's confusion turned to confidence. Her soon-to-be-ex-husband's words had the effect of making her interested to hear what Alex had to say.

"I'll admit there are some issues," she said in one of the biggest understatements Alex had heard this year.

"Let's be frank, Lillian," Alex said, starting to pace around the outside perimeter of the couches. "If you don't find someone to recreate Fredrick's rune for you very soon, Waverly will lose its advantage in the market. Then, of course, there's that rune of Miss Avery's. The one that solves your case cracking problem."

As Lillian listened, her left eyebrow arched incredulously, and a slow smile started to spread across her face.

"You said before that you recognized what Fredrick was doing when you saw his rune for a moment," she said, her voice accusatory. "Are you saying that you can make one yourself?"

"I believe I can," Alex began, but Tommy cut him off.

"None of that matters," he said to Lillian. "The next time the board meets, Waverly won't be your problem."

Lillian's eyes narrowed and she took a deep breath, but Alex jumped in before she could retort.

"I wouldn't be so quick to dismiss other people's problems, if I were you."

Tommy snorted derisively.

"The way I see it, Mr. Lockerby, the only person you should be pitching your services to is me. I hold all the cards here."

"That's true," Alex admitted. "At least until your wife cleans you out in the inevitable divorce."

Tommy's face hardened into a mask of anger, but Alex pressed on.

"Come now, Mr. Waverly, let's not play games; you've freely admitted to having an affair with Miss Masterson, not only to me but to Arthur Wilks. Unless you can prove that Lillian was unfaithful first, and I'm betting you can't, she's going to clean you out in the divorce. You'd better hope there's still some money in that family trust of yours, because all that stock you own is going to belong to her." He jerked his thumb at Lillian.

Tommy's anger turned to chagrin while Irene looked down, blushing to the roots of her hair.

"Is that why you brought me here?" he demanded. "To threaten me and insult Miss Masterson?"

"Hardly," Alex replied. "I came here to make you an offer." He looked between the pair of them. "You two can tear each other apart and leave this company a smoking hole in the ground, and Lord knows I won't stop you."

"Or?" Lillian prodded when Alex didn't go on.

"Or, I can solve all your problems."

Tommy snorted again.

"That would be some trick."

"I hate to agree with him," Lillian said, "but he's not wrong."

"Here's what I propose," Alex said. "First, Mrs. Chance."

Katrina looked up at him, startled to hear her name.

"I have the knowledge and the skill to reproduce your husband's rune, but that would take me time and effort that I'd rather not spend. Instead, I would like to buy the rights to use Fredrick's rune from you."

"Buy?" she said, a sudden burst of hope in her eyes.

"I'd be willing to pay you twenty-five percent of whatever I make selling the runes, less the expenses involved in writing them."

"I thought you were a detective," Lillian interrupted.

"Actually," Alex said, not taking his eyes off Katrina, "I have a side business providing runes to Barton Electric and Homestead Brewery, so I'm already set up to do this kind of thing. More importantly, I can actually write Fredrick's rune, something most runewrights in the city can't do."

"I don't know what to say," Katrina said, looking lost. "I don't have my husband's head for business." She looked to Lillian and the latter nodded.

"From where I sit, it's a good deal," she said. "You'll still own the rune and Alex will pay you a quarter of whatever he makes selling it."

"I guess that's okay with me," Katrina said, still unsure.

"Good," Alex said, turning to Tommy. "Now for you."

"What about me?" he blustered. "According to you, I'm finished in this business."

"Would you like to get out of your problem with your skin, and most of your stock, intact?" Alex said with a wink and a roguish grin.

"I think I have a say in that," Lillian cut in.

"Hear me out," Alex said.

"Okay, Mr. Lockerby," Tommy said, crossing his arms. "Impress me."

"How about I get Lillian here to go easy on you in the divorce."

Lillian snorted but didn't speak.

"How easy?" Tommy said, focusing on Alex.

"You give her that stock you bought this week, her apartment in town, and everything that goes with it, including her personal accounts...and that's it."

"I'd lose control of the company," Tommy objected.

"You fight it out in court, that's going to happen anyway," Alex posted out.

"No judge will give away a family company to an outsider," he pushed back.

Alex hesitated, then shrugged.

"You hope."

Tommy leaned back in his wheelchair and Alex could hear him grinding his teeth. Alex took the opportunity to glance at Lillian, who was staring daggers at him. Clearly she'd figured out Alex's game. That didn't surprise Alex; Lillian was a savvy businesswoman, but he was surprised that she appeared to be angry.

Turning back to Tommy, Alex found him still focused inward, running Alex's proposal through his mind.

It was time to sweeten the deal.

"Don't forget, Tommy," he said, "once you're divorced, you'll regain control of the family accounts and the family stock. That means as Waverly Radio grows and prospers, as a shareholder, so will you."

Tommy tried to hide it, but he clearly liked that idea.

"I could go for that," he said at last, though the look on his face said he almost choked on the words.

Alex acknowledged him with a nod, then turned to Lillian. Her sour expression hadn't improved, and now she sat with her arms crossed.

"You're a real bastard, Alex," she said with no trace of self-consciousness. "Do you know that?"

Alex put his hand over his heart with a wounded expression on his face.

"For giving you back your company and making sure you stay president?"

Her look hardened, and she shook her head.

"All you've offered me is what I already have," she said. "With your runes, I'll be able to keep Waverly going, at least until someone else figures out how to make enhanced receivers. If I take Tommy to the cleaners in the divorce, the company will crumble to nothing before it's over. I'd be left with very little beyond the satisfaction of destroying him."

"Oh, things aren't as bleak as that," Alex said, trying and failing to suppress a smirk. "You see, when I realized that you were trying to solve the problem of your beautiful Bakelite radio cases cracking when they get hot, I did the same thing Tess Avery did."

"You figured it out," Lillian gasped.

Alex nodded.

"So you see, I'm not only offering to put Waverly Radio back where it was," he said, "I'm going to give you crack-proof cases as well. That ought to allow you to increase your market share, and that will give you the money you need to expand. To take the Waverly brand national."

Lillian's eyes were jumping from side to side as if she were speed reading a long document. Alex looked back at Tommy and found the man's eyebrows raised as he ran through the possibilities himself.

"Fredrick was barely able to keep up with the demands of this factory," Lillian said suddenly. "How are you going keep up with factories all across the country?"

Alex had already thought about this, so he was prepared with an answer.

"With all due respect to Fredrick, I know a few tricks that he didn't," he explained. "My runes won't do one hundred receivers at a time, they'll do a thousand. That kind of volume will let you create the receivers here, where you can keep the rune a secret, and then ship the enhanced receivers to as many factories as you want. And I can do the same thing with the radio cases. You make them in a central factory and then ship them where they need to go."

A half-smile spread over Lillian's face, and she locked eyes with her husband. For his part, Tommy looked annoyed, but shrugged almost imperceptibly.

"All right, Alex," she said. "It seems you have a deal."

"Excellent," Alex said. "Have your lawyer write it up, exactly as we agreed."

"One thing," she pushed back, "all of this is contingent on you showing us that you can deliver on what you promised."

"Fine," Alex said, "put that in the contract as well. I'll conduct Mrs. Chance home and take a look at her husband's rune book, then I'll make the rune for you." He reached into his shirt pocket and pulled out his red-backed book. "This one will harden up your radio casings," he said, taking out a folded paper and handing it over. "You can test it out with that board you used for Tess' version."

Lillian stood and stepped close to him, talking the paper with a languid smile.

"If this works, I'm going to be a single woman again soon," she said, so low Alex could barely hear her. "You don't happen to be unattached, do you Alex?"

Surprised by the question, Alex cleared his throat.

"Not at the moment, no."

Lillian winked at him, then tucked the rune paper into her pocket.

"Pity," she said.

Instead of going to his office, Alex rode the secure elevator up to the offices of Barton Electric. His mention of the company earlier to Lillian and Tommy had reminded him that he needed to talk to Andrew. Since it was still relatively early, he figured he had a good shot to speak with the sorcerer.

"Come to check up on my spell?" the man asked when Alex stepped off his private elevator. Barton was tall and thin, clad in an expensive silk suit that was such a dark shade of red it looked black, but shimmered when he moved. When Alex had first met the man, he'd worn a handlebar mustache with ends that resembled lightning bolts. In the years since, however, he'd gone with the much more fashionable pencil mustache. He stood behind his massive marble and steel desk with several blueprints spread out before him.

Alex knew better than to ask what the man was doing. When Andrew got excited, he could, and would, go on for hours.

"I went to see Beauregard Mayweather the other day," Alex began.

"Oh, did he get you set up with an investment account?" Andrew asked before Alex could finish.

"I didn't have time then," Alex explained. "I was on a case. He did, however, tell me that I have an account, started by you, that has twenty Gs in it."

"Really?" Andrew said. "I had no idea that arm of the company was doing so well. It might be time to visit the main office and give out some performance bonuses."

"The company?" Alex began, but stopped himself. This was the very rabbit hole he wanted to avoid. "Never mind. According to Beau, you set up that account in thirty-four. That was right after we met."

Andrew stroked his chin for a moment, then nodded.

"That sounds about right," he said. "What about it?"

"I didn't work for you then. I didn't start working here until thirty-seven, so why did you open an account in my name, and where did the money in it come from?"

Andrew laughed, but when Alex failed to even smile, his face got serious.

"Did I forget to tell you?" he asked, more to himself than to Alex. After a moment of consideration, he shook his head like a dog getting water off its back. "The account is for your stake in my mining company," he said, as if that explained everything.

"Stake?"

"From that idea of yours about using my traction motors in mines."

Alex remembered that very well. He'd figured out that Andrew's warehouse foreman, Jimmy Cortez, had stolen the motor right off the loading dock to tunnel into the basement vault of the American Museum of Natural History.

"I took that idea and ran with it," Andrew went on. "Naturally, I allotted you a five percent stake in the business as a finder's fee…for bringing me the idea."

Alex tried doing that math in his head, but it quickly got away from him.

"That seems awfully generous."

Andrew put on an overtly innocent look at that, then grinned.

"Well, to be honest, I had hoped to show you how profitable working for me could be. It probably would have worked, too, if I hadn't forgotten to tell you about it."

"So that's really my money?" he asked.

"Of course it is," Barton said, laughing again. "Now that you know, I suggest you go back to Beau and have him help you invest."

That was actually a good idea, but it would have to wait. Alex had too much on his plate right now.

He thanked Andrew, then made an excuse and headed back down to the terminal. So far it had been a pretty good day: he'd caught Fredrick Chance's killer, secured an income stream for his widow and children, and kept the Waverlys from destroying each other.

"You deserve a good cup of coffee," he told himself as he headed for Marnie's coffee bar. In the years since Alex sent her to work for Andrew, Marnie's workplace had grown from a cart, to a counter, to a full-blown bar with half a dozen people working at it.

Alex got his usual and one for Sherry, then spent ten minutes talking with Marnie before heading up to his office.

"I brought coffee," he said as he carefully entered, so as not to spill anything.

"Alex!" Sherry cried, making Alex almost drop his burden.

When he looked up, his secretary wore a frantic look, but she didn't move from behind her desk.

"What is it?" he demanded, hurrying across to put down the coffee cups. As he did, he saw that she'd laid five of her tarot cards out on her desk. There were three touching in the middle with one card above and one below.

"I've been going crazy," she said. "I couldn't find you. When I called over to Waverly, they said you'd already gone."

"Easy," he said, taking her hand and looking her in the eyes. "I'm here now, so why don't you tell me what's going on?"

"Dr. Bell called," Sherry said, getting her breathing under control. "He wants you to come to the brownstone right away. It's Sorsha. He didn't say what, but I could tell something's wrong."

Alex had an impulse to turn and dash for his vault, but something in the back of his mind reminded him about the cards on the desk.

"You did this after Iggy called you?" he said, pointing to the cards.

She nodded, then sat down but didn't speak.

"What's it say?"

"It's not good," Sherry began, pointing to the lone card on the top of the pattern. The picture showed a robed man with an infinity symbol over his head. "This is the Magician, he represents resourcefulness or inspired action, that's you. And this," she pointed to the card on the bottom, a woman with a crown of stars, "is the Empress."

"That's Sorsha," he guessed.

Nodding, she touched the three cards in the middle of the pattern.

"Between you is the Tower, the Nine of Wands, and Death."

"That last one doesn't sound good."

"Death is inverted, though," Sherry said. "I think in this case it represents cleansing or renewal."

"You mean getting rid of that curse rune," Alex said, his fingers tingling with excitement.

"I think so, but the Tower represents destruction and ruin."

"So I know what happens if I fail. What about that last card?"

"The Nine of Wands," Sherry said. "It represents perseverance, a test of faith."

"So, if I'm going to save Sorsha from destruction, I have to cleanse her, and the only way to do that is through a test of faith."

"That's how I see it," Sherry said.

"All right," Alex said, draining his coffee in one gulp. "I know what I need to do, so I'd better get to it."

He turned and headed for the door to the back hallway, but Sherry reached out and grabbed his arm.

"Be careful, boss," she said. "The Tower is suspended between the two of you; if you're not careful, you could bring the Tower's ruination down on yourself."

29

THE ANCHOR

When Alex burst through the brownstone's vault door, he found Iggy sitting in Alex's reading chair with his nose in the Archimedean Monograph. Sorsha lay in the bed, next to him, covered with a sheet. Her eyes were closed as if she were peacefully asleep, but her face was wet with sweat and as Alex watched, her brow furrowed and she stirred but didn't wake.

"What's wrong?" Alex demanded as Iggy set the Monograph aside on the night table.

"The curse rune is accelerating again," he said. "Everything was fine at first, but then last night the drain became pronounced. Sorsha had to start pulling more and more power from Andrew's spell."

"But why is she like this?"

Iggy sighed.

"She put herself into some kind of trance about an hour ago," he said. "The amount of power she's drawing has to be massive and she's starting to experience transfer toxicity, like you did with your escape rune. The trance is helping her deal with the pain."

As if to punctuate Iggy's words, Sorsha moaned and rolled her head back and forth. Despite the warmth of the room, Alex felt a chill. His brush with transfer toxicity left his arm physically burned, and the thought of Sorsha trying to hold that off made him queasy.

"What can we do?" he asked, unable to tear his gaze away from the struggling sorceress.

"I was hoping you would have an idea or two," Iggy said in a serious voice. "I've been going through the Monograph, but this kind of power transfer is something it only hints at. There isn't much about transfer toxicity either, only some theoretical musings about it. I suspect I understand it better thanks to my medical background."

"And what is your medical background telling you now?"

Iggy looked at him with a steady gaze, shaking his head slightly.

"This is beyond anything I've ever seen," he admitted. "It's similar to burn victims, but if I were to use dream syrup to put her in a coma, who knows what would happen? She might not be able to fight against the rune curse."

"Meaning she'd die."

Iggy nodded.

"I hate to admit it, but I'm out of ideas."

Alex sighed, keeping his eyes on Sorsha. Seeing her, still struggling in her sleep, pinched at his insides like someone twisting a knife in his guts. For as long as he'd known her, Sorsha had always been a sure, commanding presence. Even when she'd been shot or wounded, she never lost the air of quiet control. Now it was all she could do to cling to life, and it was a battle she was losing.

"I might have an idea," he admitted. "It will take me a couple of hours to get everything together." He turned to Iggy at last. "Can you keep her alive till I get back?"

Iggy clapped him on the shoulder and nodded.

"I'll do what I can," he said. "But hurry all the same."

"Right," Alex said, then he turned back to his still-open vault door, pulling it closed behind him.

An incessant buzzing assaulted Alex, firing synapses in his brain that threatened to split his skull open. Cursing, he struggled to master his throbbing head, grabbing it with both hands as if he could squeeze the pain back inside.

Forcing his eyes open, Alex wished he hadn't, as the magelights of his vault burned his retinas. They were certainly bright, but it felt like he was looking at the sun, forcing his eyes closed again.

Taking a breath, he made another try of it, focusing on the faux fireplace opposite the reading chair where he sat. The source of the horrible noise turned out to be the electric alarm clock from his vault bedroom. Apparently in an act of supreme self-flagellation he'd moved it from its usual environs and placed it on the reading table next to the chair.

He slapped at the offending appliance but missed the button on top, causing him to try twice more before the sound mercifully ceased.

With the noise dealt with, Alex put his hands on the arms of the chair and tried to push himself up into a standing position. The pain in his head, which he thought was unbearable, exploded and his vision dwindled down to a single point, as if he were deep inside a long dark tunnel. Sinking to his knees, Alex pitched forward onto his arms and lowered himself until his forehead touched the soft rug he'd used to cover the cold stone.

"Get up," he growled to himself after a full minute. "You aren't meeting some Indian raja."

Taking a breath to focus himself, Alex pushed up to his knees, then, giving the throbbing in his head a chance to subside, he stood.

Even in this condition, Alex knew that there was something important he needed to be doing. The presence of the alarm clock told him that. If there was something he needed to remind himself, he would have left himself a note. Checking his pockets, he found nothing... which left only one place, his writing table.

Walking gingerly so as not to jostle his aching head, Alex made his way to the slanted table. When he got there, he didn't have to look for the note. A large sheet of thick paper had been pinned to the cork row across the top edge of the slanted board. Written across it in thick lines was one word, "Sorsha.'

Alex's headache evaporated in an instant as a far more painful reality came flooding back. She was dying, maybe already dead, and he was worried about a headache. Turning to the typewriter on his roll-away table, Alex pulled a single sheet from the rollers.

Reading it, his face broke out into a fierce grin, then he put the paper down and picked up the candlestick phone next to the typewriter.

"Bickman," Alex gasped when Andrew's valet picked up. "I need to talk to Andrew right now; it's an emergency."

The proper sounding Brit asked Alex to wait, then, a few minutes later, Andrew Barton came on the line.

"Alex?" he said, then went on before he could get a reply. "What is Sorsha doing? She's drawing an awful lot of power through that spell."

Alex explained what was happening quickly, then immediately got to the reason for his call.

"Do you have a Zoetrope?" he asked.

There was a pause on the line before Andrew answered.

"You mean that moving picture toy kids were playing with a decade ago?"

"That's it."

"Alex," Andrew said, a surprised note in his voice, "why would I have something like that?"

"Never mind," Alex rushed on. "How fast can you get to the RCA building in Rockefeller Center?"

"I've teleported there before," he admitted, "so very quickly."

"All right, get over there and go to the fourth floor of the RCA building and ask for the office of Jared McNamara, he's the head of their tabletop radio division. He has a Zoetrope in his office. Get it from him and don't take no for an answer, then teleport back to my office. I'll meet you there."

Andrew agreed, then hung up.

It would only take him a few minutes to get the Zoetrope, but Alex had preparations of his own to make. He moved to the secretary cabinet where he kept his kit. Taking the bag down, he removed his multi-lamp and inspected the runes on the glass and around the bottom. Satisfied that they were in good order and not in need of a touch up, he set the lamp aside and removed the amberlight burner.

Unscrewing the cap, he took a bottle from a nearby shelf and refilled the little reservoir.

Satisfied that his equipment was prepared, Alex returned everything to the bag, then moved to his rollaway cabinet. Kneeling down, he pulled out the top drawer where he kept his supply of written runes, ready for when he needed to refill his book.

The drawer was divided into slots and organized into major, minor, and standard runes. He quickly riffled through the stacks of prepared runes, pulling four major runes and two standard from inside.

Tucking the runes into his shirt pocket, Alex shut the drawer and stood. Satisfied that he was as prepared as he could get, he picked up his kit and headed for the door to his office.

"Boss," Sherry exclaimed when he entered the waiting room a few moments later. Her expression warred back and forth between relief and concern. "Are you all right?"

Since he hadn't looked in a mirror recently, he assumed he looked a fright, but that didn't matter.

"I'm good," he said. "I think I've got a way to save Sorsha but I'm waiting for—"

There was a soft pop and Andrew Barton appeared in the center of the room. He looked a bit green, but recovered quickly.

"Sorry it...it took so long," he said, as he stood up straight. "I had to convince your Mr. McNamara to part with his toy." He held up the Zoetrope so Alex could see it.

The idea of McNamara standing up to a sorcerer must have been a sight to see, but Alex didn't have time to ponder that.

"Follow me," he said, leading the way along the back hallway.

"You going to tell me why I paid some fussy radio guy a C-note for a child's toy?"

"You'll see, now keep up."

Alex hurried down the hall, then through his vault to the brownstone door. It had been almost exactly two hours since he'd left Sorsha

DAN WILLIS

and he hesitated as he took hold of the doorknob. Despite his growing apprehension, he turned the knob firmly and pushed the door open.

"Alex," Iggy gasped as he stepped in, "thank God you're back."

He sat on the edge of the bed, mopping Sorsha's brow with a damp cloth.

"She's exhausted," he said, rising. "Please tell me you have something. Sorsha can't hold on much longer."

"Maybe he'll tell you," Andrew said, coming through the vault door behind Alex.

"Just watch," Alex said, not wanting to take the time to explain it.

He moved around the bed and shoved the reading chair out of the way, pulling the side table over in its place. Setting the lamp and the candlestick phone on the floor, he opened his bag and took out the multi-lamp.

"Here," he said, handing Iggy and Andrew each a pair of yellow pince-nez spectacles. "Put these on."

As they complied, Alex clipped the amberlight burner into the lamp, then lit it. When he closed the oval door, the light that shone out of the crystal turned a rusty brown color and objects viewed through it began to flicker and swim. Alex took out his new oculus, strapping it around his head before twisting the outer ring. This brought a yellow lens into the field of view.

As soon as he looked at Sorsha, the shifting images of rune nodes erupted out of the sorceress' chest, spiraling upward toward the ceiling until they faded away.

"What am I looking at?" Andrew asked, turning his head this way and that.

"Amberlight," Iggy explained. "It's trying to show where the runic elements of the curse were written, or possibly where Sorsha spent most of her time after they were put on."

"How can you tell what it means?" the sorcerer asked, twisting his head about as he tried to bring the smeared image into focus.

"We can't," Iggy replied, "but I think Alex might have figured something out."

"Let me have the Zoetrope," Alex said, holding out his hand. Andrew passed it over and Alex held it up so that he could see the slits in the curved surface of the toy. Giving it a spin, he moved the edge of the toy so he could see the flickering images of the Gordian rune. As the spinning Zoetrope covered the runes, the images slowed down and became clear, exactly like the image of the galloping horse.

"I can see the pieces," he said, his voice hoarse.

Iggy walked around the bed and reached into Alex's shirt pocket, pulling out his flip notebook.

"Can you see the beginning or the end of the construct?" he asked.

"I think so," he said. "It looks like the first part is something like Arlo Harper's blasting rune."

"So we were right," Iggy said.

"Why is that significant?" Andrew asked.

"Because," Iggy said, "if we had tried to break the construct or shut it away in a vault, it would have blown Sorsha to bits."

"Can it still do that?"

"Yes," Iggy said, "but now that we can see what we're dealing with, we should be able to break this evil construct."

"Not break," Alex said with a fierce grin, "cut. According to the story, Alexander the Great didn't untie the knot, he cut it."

"And you're Alexander the Great in this case?" Andrew asked.

"Well," Alex said with a distracted grin, "maybe not Alexander the Great, but hopefully Alexander the correct."

"I've got the first rune down," Iggy said, jotting notes in Alex's book. "What's next?"

Alex moved through the construct slowly, taking his time. With Sorsha struggling to stay alive, he wanted to hurry, but hurrying had its own risks. If he mistakenly activated the blasting rune, everyone in the room would be dead.

Well, he mentally amended, *probably not Andrew*.

One by one, Alex read out the runes that made up the draining construct. It was a great deal like Iggy's own life restoration construct, but far less elegant. To Alex it looked like a house built by an incompetent carpenter, all jagged edges and odd angles.

Doesn't mean it won't kill us if I make a mistake, he reminded himself.

"Okay," Iggy said, reading the list of runes in the Gordian mess out loud. "This is poorly put together, but that works to our advantage. If you've given me these correctly, we should be able to break the construct at any place where the individual runes are joined."

"But how do you keep it from exploding?" Andrew asked.

Alex reached into his pocket and pulled out a pair of linking runes, holding them up.

"That's what these are for," he said.

"What are you thinking, lad?" Iggy asked.

Alex put the linking runes on the table next to the lamp and pulled the rest of the runes from his pocket.

"First," he said, laying down a temporal restoration rune, "we deconstruct the rune so we have access to it. Then I'll use the linking runes to get rid of the blast rune."

"How?" Iggy asked.

"I"m going to link it to the anchor rune," Alex said. "That's how they're syphoning Sorsha's power away, so I'll link the blast rune to it."

"That way, when we break the rune, the blast will go back to the Legion," Iggy said, nodding along as he grasped what Alex had in mind.

"Your evil runewright group?" Andrew asked.

"Later," Alex and Iggy said at the same time.

"What about their giant finding rune?" Iggy asked. "Will this stop it?"

Alex shook his head.

"I don't know, but there's no time to worry about that."

He picked up the temporal restoration rune and pulled back the sheet covering Sorsha. The rune spiral visible under the amberlight emerged from a spot roughly around her sternum, so Alex set the rune paper there.

"Doing this might cause the rune to collapse," he said, squeezing his lighter to life. "So I'm going to have to move fast."

"I'll hold the child's toy for you," Andrew said, picking up the zoetrope.

Alex touched the flame to the rune paper and the rune surged to life, glowing with red and gold lines. White sparks cracked and fizzed, dropping off the pulsating rune and floating down to where the invisible Gordian rune waited below.

As the first spark touched Sorsha, the rune exploded into a shower of light like a miniature firework. Glowing embers drifted down, but as they got close, they began to curve as if they were pulled into the center by the presence of the Gordian rune.

The sparks flashed and Sorsha gasped as the rune erupted outward, spiraling into existence exactly as the ghost images had under the amberlight. Like the former images, they were smoky and indistinct.

"Child's toy!" Alex called and a moment later Andrew spun the Zoetrope and held it into Alex's field of vision. "A bit higher," he said, starting to sweat.

When the rune finally came into focus, Alex found the blasting rune and followed it back to where it joined the next rune in the pattern. Because of the way the Gordian rune was structured, there was a small gap between the two, probably made by the time the runewright took between writing each of them. It wasn't much, but it was enough.

Taking the paper for one of the linking runes, Alex carefully folded it in half, then quarters, then eights. The paper was too fragile to fold any further, but he hoped it would work as it was.

Moving as fast as he dared, he held the paper in the gap between the runes.

"Don't breathe," he said, moving his lighter toward the paper slowly. When the flame touched the flash paper, the rune flared to life and took hold.

"Is it working?" Andrew asked.

"Well, it didn't explode, so I'm going to say yes," Alex said, trying to find a gap between the anchor rune and the runes on either side.

"Was that a possibility?" the sorcerer asked.

"Please, Andrew," Iggy said. "If it is a possibility, your bothering Alex won't help."

Alex folded the second linking rune and held it in the pattern, moving and rotating it as he tried to get it into the gap between two constructs. This time when he lit it, the rune fluctuated for a moment before it adhered to the pattern.

"That should do it," Alex said at last. He tried to sound confident, but his voice didn't carry it, and he came off sounding scared.

"You'd better hurry then," Iggy said. "Sorsha's pulse is getting irregular."

Alex took the last rune paper and folded it in half. The rune on it was an obliteration rune, one Alex had learned from the Monograph. Despite its ominous name, the rune only did one, very specific thing — it broke apart active constructs.

The rune popped into existence as Alex lit the paper, pulsed once, and the Gordian rune shattered. Alex grabbed Sorsha's hand and held his breath. A pulse of magical energy hit him as the temporal restoration rune began to collapse, followed by the pressure of the blasting rune as it tried to expend its energy.

Alex had figured it all out, calculated how to see the Gordian rune, how to open it up so he could manipulate it, and how to disable the blasting rune inside it, but all of that was theory. If he was wrong about even one of those things, Sorsha was a dead woman.

"You aren't wrong," he whispered, then the blasting rune exploded.

30

THE HOUSE OF PIGS

Time seemed to flow like molasses as Alex watched in growing horror. He felt the energy blaze inside the blasting rune before it burst. A wave of magical force erupted from the rune and slammed into him like a wave, knocking him away from Sorsha and onto the floor. He landed hard on his elbow but, much to his surprise, he wasn't dead.

Ignoring the pain in his arm, Alex scrambled up to his knees in time to see the blurry construct he knew to be the blasting rune flare with light. His ears popped as pressure pushed out from the rune, but it seemed unable to actually explode. Whatever was holding it back couldn't hold the rune for long, however.

Before Alex could do anything but gasp, the rune expanded, swelling from within.

And then it was gone.

Drawn away by the linking rune, the massive explosive force was sent through space to wherever Sorsha's stolen power had gone. The pressure in the room vanished and the oppressive weight of the magical energy drained away.

"Did it work?" Andrew asked. He'd clearly felt the magical pulse, but wasn't sure what to make of its absence.

Alex got cautiously to his feet and adjusted his oculus. All traces of the draining construct were gone. He couldn't tell if Sorsha was able to draw on her magic yet, but at least she wasn't losing any more of her life.

"Sorsha?" he said, reaching out for her.

Before he could take her arm and feel for a pulse, Sorsha sat up suddenly, her eyes wide. She gasped, then screamed, and her eyes began to glow a deep sapphire blue.

Alex stepped away from her, intending to ask Iggy what was happening, but the question never left his lips.

Someone screamed but it wasn't Sorsha. Alex had the momentary feeling of being somewhere else. He saw fields of snow stretching off in all directions, then some kind of underground hallway, but cut from solid ice and glowing blue from refracted sunlight. The passage seemed to go on for a great distance, then Alex stood in front of an enormous, armored door. It was made of some dark metal with brass hardware and gold pin-striping all around. A handle like a ship's wheel occupied the center of the door and it spun around of its own accord, finally coming to a stop with a booming, metallic clang.

As Alex stood, transfixed before the door, it began to swing open. A wave of inexplicable dread washed over him. He wanted to leap forward, to put his shoulder against the massive door and force it closed again, but he was powerless to move. The door swung open, but whatever Alex expected to see revealed inside, he was disappointed. The interior of the vault was entirely black. Not dark because of the lack of a light source, but as black as the unknowable depths of the ocean or the furthest reaches of outer space.

Alex was certain that what waited for him inside the black vault was nothing less than death itself, and as he was pulled inside, he realized that the voice he'd heard screaming was his own.

Iggy jumped when Sorsha screamed, but his medical training kicked in.

"Help me hold her," he said to Alex. Before he took even one step toward the sorceress, however, Alex howled like a wounded dog and clutched his head with both hands. His back arched and he spasmed for a moment before crashing down on the floor in an unmoving heap.

"Get down!" Andrew yelled, suddenly grabbing on to Iggy's arm and pulling him to the floor by Alex.

Iggy landed hard, but he wasn't as old as he used to be, and nothing seemed to be damaged. As he opened his mouth to protest, Andrew held up his right hand and the air between him and the sorceress rippled just as Sorsha threw out her arms, shattering the bed.

Bits of batting and wood and torn bedding pelted the invisible barrier Andrew had raised and when it settled out of the air, Sorsha was gone.

"What the devil?" Iggy demanded, pushing himself up to his knees.

"Sorcery Psychosis," Andrew said, finally lowing his hand.

"I've never heard of that," Iggy said. "Help me, here."

Alex lay in a heap a few feet away, and Iggy pulled him over on his back.

"I understand what happened to Sorsha," Andrew said, kneeling down next to Iggy, "she absorbed too much magic when that rune was broken, but what happened to Alex?"

Iggy ground his teeth. He should have found out what Alex did to the Legion's giant finding rune.

"That group of evil runewrights," he explained as he checked Alex's vitals.

"The Legion," Andrew confirmed. "Alex told me about them after that mess in DC."

"They're the ones that put that infernal rune on Sorsha."

"Did they do something like that to Alex?"

"No," Iggy growled, holding Alex's eyes open to inspect his pupils. "The fool did this to himself. He figured out that the Legion was using Sorsha's stolen power to fuel a giant finding rune, but it was spread out all over the city. We wanted to disrupt it, but it was too spread out, so Alex tried something else."

"Is he okay?"

Iggy sighed.

"I can't say. We need to move him to a bed. The closest one is in his vault."

"Allow me," Andrew said. He made a motion with his hand that Iggy associated with women calling a small dog to jump into their laps, and Alex's unconscious body rose off the floor.

"This way," Iggy said, opening the cover door to Alex's vault. He moved along the short hallway to the door on the left, then pushed it open.

Andrew followed after, floating Alex in through the door, then onto the bed.

"Is there anything we can do for him?" Andrew asked.

Iggy shook his head, sitting on the edge of the bed. Alex was alive and he didn't seem to be in any kind of physical distress, he was simply unconscious. He might be stunned, or he might be in a coma, only time would tell.

"No," he said in answer to Andrew's question. "There are some things I can try, but it's best to wait and see if he comes around on his own. Tell me about what happened to Sorsha. I've never heard of Sorcery Psychosis."

Andrew chuckled darkly.

"It's not exactly something we advertise. It's usually something that only happens when a sorcerer first gets their powers. They take in too much power and it puts them into a kind of trance."

"Isn't that dangerous?" Iggy asked. "Shouldn't you go after her?"

Andrew nodded.

"It is dangerous, and I've been listening for her ever since she vanished."

Iggy give him a confused look, and the sorcerer went on.

"There's no way for me to know where Sorsha went," he explained. "If she uses enough magic in one place, however, I can track her."

Iggy thought through Andrew's explanation, but something still bothered him.

"Sorsha came into her powers years ago, so why is she going through this psychosis now?"

"It's like a drowning man," Andrew said with a shrug. "When he finally manages to come up for air, he gulps down all of it he can get. Based on what you told me, that Gordian rune had been draining Sorsha's magic for months."

Iggy nodded.

"So the moment the rune broke, she drew in all the magic she could."

"It didn't help that she was still connected to my power spell," Andrew added.

Iggy hadn't considered that.

"What can she do with that much power?"

Andrew started to answer but cocked his head as if he heard a noise.

"I guess I'll go find out," he said. "Sorsha's doing something."

He suddenly winced and covered his ears.

"Something big."

With that, he took a deep breath and disappeared with soft pop.

"Good luck," Iggy said to the empty air.

Sorsha could feel her life slipping away. The power she was desperately pulling through Andrew's rune simply wasn't enough to fill the voracious hole in her chest. The more she pulled, the more it ate. It was all she could do to keep drawing the power she needed to keep her alive... and she was tired.

So very tired.

Despite her need to maintain concentration, her mind began to wander. People and places from her life began to flash before her mind's eye in rapid succession and a wave of nostalgia flowed over her. She was surprised at how many of her friends had passed since their acquaintance.

I wonder if I'll get to see them when I die? she thought.

She had always been afraid of death. It was a rational position, after all. No one really knew what happened when you died. You might simply cease to exist.

As she drifted, floating in a void of exhaustion and memory, the prospect didn't seem so bad. She had almost resolved to let go, to surrender herself to whatever lay on the other side of life, when someone punched her in the gut.

With a sound like a thunderclap, the void of her magical meditation shattered, and she found herself sitting up in bed. Her body felt as if it were burning as pure, sweet, raw magical power rushed into her. The hole in her chest was gone and the power surged through every joint, ligament, and synapse.

Vaguely she was aware that she was still pulling power through Andrew's spell, giving her a double dose as her own power flooded into her. The burning intensified as the magic swept away the decay of the last few months, but it didn't stop there. The power filled her, filled her to bursting and she laughed as it exploded away from her, shattering the bed and leaving her hovering in the air.

The act of destroying something felt good, but it left her wanting. She had almost died. She had almost died, and someone had done that to her.

Rage replaced her joy as she searched her memory.

Why is it so hard to remember? she thought.

A moment later her mind provided her with the information she sought, and she raised her hand and teleported.

An instant after that, she stood on top of the Chrysler Building, looking south along the island. The Legion had been stealing immense amounts of power from her and she could feel it, out there in the city. Much of it was gone but there was enough left. With a trembling hand, she summoned it, willing the power to burst its containment and rise up into the sky.

At first, the hint of her vanished energy eluded her, slipping away like an eel in the water. She bared her teeth in an animal snarl.

"I am Sorsha Kincaid," she yelled into the semi-darkness of sunset. Her voice boomed through the air and echoed back from the ground. "I command the power of the universe," she spat. "I WILL NOT BE DENIED WHAT IS MINE!"

Windows on the observation deck below her shattered at the sound of her voice pitched low, filled with magic.

She reached out again with the power that filled her, throwing the magic outward like an extension of her arms. She felt the faint tickle of her stolen power and she seized it. Instead of trying to free it, she instead infused it with more power, focusing it into a single blast, an impact that shattered whatever had been used to contain it.

"RISE," she commanded.

At first she thought it hadn't worked, but a moment later a pure column of blue light rose from somewhere in the south side inner ring.

A tingle of excitement ran through Sorsha and she smiled. She focused on the distant beacon, closed her eyes, and vanished.

The street where Sorsha appeared looked like any residential street, though this being the inner ring, they were larger and nicer than most of the rest of the city. The beacon of blue light had burned itself out, but Sorsha didn't need it anymore. This close, she could feel the residual traces of her stolen power. It was coming from a large colonial style building with a wrap-around porch. Part of the roof was missing, and bits of furniture were lying in the yard, some still on fire.

Two men stood by the door staring at her, and Sorsha realized she was hovering in the air. A quick look down also revealed that she was naked; whatever clothes she'd been wearing having burned off during her initial burst of magic. She felt no shame. The people who had stolen her power were insects, crawling bugs next to the radiance of her power. But if these insects were going to feel her wrath, they deserved the whole treatment.

Waving her hand down from her shoulders to her knees, Sorsha summoned clothes to her body: a navy-blue corset top with silver wire woven into it and a long, silver skirt that flowed as she hovered above the ground.

A bullet hit her in the arm, and she cursed. It hadn't penetrated her skin, but it hurt like a particularly large bee sting. Turning back to the porch, she found one of the young men shooting at her with a semi-automatic pistol. Another round slammed into Sorsha's leg and she winced, but the flattened slug fell away without doing damage.

The sting of the impact dissipated quickly, but the spot where the slugs had actually touched her burned long after. She could smell a strange, caustic tang in the air, like the aroma of powdered chlorine.

"Spell breakers," she hissed.

Lashing out with her left hand, she turned the unfortunate gunman into a frozen statue. She clenched her hand when she was done and the statue shattered, exploding into a million pieces of gory red ice. The second gunman ducked inside the building and slammed the door behind him.

Sorsha dropped to the ground, setting her bare feet on the cement walk that ran from the street to the front door. Before she reached the porch steps, she pointed at the door and it burst.

Immediately a hail of bullets swarmed out of the opening. Sorsha was hit over a dozen times, but while the bullets stung, they didn't wound. She touched the silver necklace at her throat, the only thing to survive whatever happened to her clothes. Alex had given it to her. He said it would keep her safe.

Sorsha faced the open door and passed through, walking an inch above the floor. Inside there was a large, open receiving room to her left and a kitchen straight ahead. At least a dozen people had taken cover behind furniture and tables, leaning around to fire at her.

"How dare you," she growled in her sorcerer voice. "How dare you use your filthy little magic to try to kill ME." This last word boomed like dynamite exploding and sending several of the gunmen scurrying for better cover.

Someone was screaming, giving orders to the gunmen. Sorsha caught sight of an older man with gray hair and a short beard.

"*And he asked him, What is thy name? And he answered, saying, My name is Legion: for we are many,*" her voice boomed, quoting the Bible verse that Malcom Jones had let slip.

Much of the gunfire stopped and the grey-haired man stared at her with horror in his eyes.

"Time to finish your quotation," she announced. "*Now there was there nigh unto the mountains a great herd of swine feeding. And all the devils besought him, saying, Send us into the swine, that we may enter into them.*"

She looked around at the stunned faces, raising her arms over her head.

"I hereby grant your wish," she said, her voice almost a scream. "I cast you into swine."

All around the room the men and women of the Legion convulsed, dropping to the ground, writhing in agony. Sorsha turned her eyes to the grey-haired elder, who'd managed to only drop to one knee. His eyes met hers, then he grabbed his own forearm and vanished.

Sorsha cursed him for a coward, but he was gone.

All around her, the sounds of terrified pigs erupted. Several tried to make a break for the opening where the front door had stood, but Sorsha flicked her hand, sealing the opening with a sheet of ice. Satisfied that her tormentors couldn't escape, she waved her hand over herself again. This time her skirt went from silver to white and her blouse blossomed into patterns of red and gold flowers. She'd worn this during a trip to Hawaii, years ago, but hadn't put it on since.

"And now," she said turning back to the pigs. "It's time for a little luau."

She raised her hands and the floor opened up beneath the pigs, filling with dirt that began to pull the swine down. Terrified screams filled the house as Sorsha summoned two balls of fire to her hands. Fire wasn't her preferred element, but that didn't mean she couldn't use it.

"You were always pigs," she shouted over the din, "but now you'll make excellent bacon."

"That's quite enough of that, young lady," a male voice boomed.

With a snarl, Sorsha turned, looking to find out what insolent fool she'd missed. Instead, she saw a man in an expensive suit with glowing yellow eyes. She raised the fireball in her right hand, intent on striking him down, but before she could complete the action, the man reached out and slapped her.

Sorsha staggered under the blow, and the fire went out. Anger surged through her and she came back swinging, but the man simply struck her again, much more forcefully this time.

She dropped to her hands and knees, as her vision wavered. Sorsha shook her head, but she couldn't seem to clear it. Finally the swimming floorboards stabilized and she looked up.

"Andrew?" she asked, confused at his appearance. "What's going on? Did you just hit me?"

The sorcerer offered her his hand and pulled her to her feet.

"I'm afraid I did, my dear," he explained, "but I simply had to spare you a very mortifying case of indigestion."

31

WHEELS WITHIN WHEELS

Sorsha sat at the kitchen table of the inner ring home she'd attacked. Andrew had made her a cup of tea and she let the warmth of the cup seep into her hands without drinking any. He'd told her what had happened when the Gordian rune had broken, but she still had trouble believing parts of it.

At least until a policeman ran into the kitchen in hot pursuit of a pig.

"How are you doing, Miss Kincaid?" a familiar voice asked her. She looked up to find Police Captain Callahan standing next to her. "Do you mind?" he asked indicating the next chair.

"Please," she said, "join me."

He sat, placing his hat on the table.

"Mr. Barton has explained what happened here, but..."

"It doesn't make a lot of sense, does it?" she admitted.

Callahan chuckled at that.

"Not really, no," he said. "It would help if you could turn these pigs back into people."

Sorsha made a face at that. Sorcery was more like an art than a science. Alchemy and rune magic were very scientific, but sorcery worked on how the sorcerer thought and felt.

"I'm sorry," she said in a tired voice. "I wasn't in my right mind when I transformed them. I"m afraid there's no way to get them back now."

Callahan sighed.

"I was afraid you'd say that. We'll get the pigs rounded up and then I'm sure the government will want to study them."

"What are you going to tell the neighbors?"

"That the couple who lived here had a falling out," he said. "The wife took off and the husband turned a bunch of pigs loose in the house as revenge." He stood and put his hat back on. "Don't worry, they'll buy it."

Sorsha nodded. It sounded like exactly the kind of salacious story the neighbors would believe. She felt ashamed. She'd effectively killed over a dozen people in a fit of magical insanity and, if Andrew hadn't come when he did, she would have eaten them.

The thought made her sick, and she clutched her mug tighter.

"Mr. Barton says he'll teleport you out of here whenever you're ready," Callahan said. "But I'd rather you did it sooner. The more people who see you here, the more tongues there are that can wag."

Sorsha nodded again and stood up.

"Thank you, Captain," she said. "You've been very kind."

"Think nothing of it, ma'am," he said.

Lloyd Morrow, Master of the Legion, tried hard not to fidget in his chair. He sat with his legs crossed, trying to present an image of calm and serene control...but he wasn't feeling that.

In front of him was a chessboard that had been forgotten in the last half hour. Lloyd doubted his opponent, Dale Torrence, would make another move since he was hopelessly pinned down.

Dale was the kind of man who thought himself smarter than everyone else, and he hated to have that assertion challenged.

None of that mattered now, of course. They hadn't spoken since word came that communication had been lost with the Manhattan chapter house. Rupert Simons had taken over that operation several months ago, and now no one there could be reached by phone. The Legion had a few operatives in the area, but they were proving difficult to reach. All Lloyd and Dale could do was sit and wait for news.

Almost on cue, a young woman came hurrying into the Sanctum of the Masters. She wore a simple yellow dress and her sandy blonde hair was pulled up behind her in a ponytail.

"Master Simons has arrived," she said without preamble or formality.

That got Dale's attention.

"He's used an escape rune," he gasped.

There could be no other explanation, of course. For Simons to be here, when he was in Manhattan less than an hour ago meant things in New York must have gone badly indeed.

Behind the girl, the outer door was opened by another young initiate. He paused, holding the door open, but lowering his head so that he looked at the floor. A strange thunking sound came next, then a man shrouded in a long cloak entered. He grasped a heavy cane in a gnarled hand and seemed to be having trouble maintaining his balance. The hood of the cloak was up, casting his face in shadow, but Lloyd could hear whoever it was breathing heavily.

He and Dale both stood, more out of a need to better see the strange figure than for politeness or habit.

"Who are you?" Dale demanded as the figure approached. "Where is Master Simons?"

"Shut up, you fool," Simons' voice emanated from under the hood.

"Rupert?" Lloyd asked. "What...what happened?"

Simons limped up to a chair on the far side of the chessboard and turned to face his peers.

"I'll tell you what happened," he growled, his voice sounding like he was talking through a mouthful of food. He reached up and pulled the hood from his head.

Dale and Lloyd gasped in unison. The man was unrecognizable. The right side of his face had been transformed, with heavy, thick skin and deep-set eyes. In the center of his face, where his nose ought to be, was the snout of a pig, and two upward-curving tusks jutted out from his lower jaw.

As Lloyd observed him, he noted that the hand that clutched the wooden cane was deformed. Where he'd once had four fingers, there were now only two, as if his index and middle, and ring and pinky had fused into a single digit each. And, when he sat, Lloyd saw a hoof in place of the man's right foot.

"In the name of God, Rupert," Dale said, awe and horror in his voice. "What happened in New York?"

"Sit," he grunted. "I doubt there's anything left of the Manhattan chapter house," he said once Lloyd and Dale had taken their seats.

"How is that possible?" Lloyd asked. "The finding construct was perfect."

"Yes, it was," Rupert said. "This was done to me by the sorceress, Sorsha Kincaid."

"Impossible," Dale said, staring hard at Rupert. "You and I both know that she should be dead by now."

"He's right," Lloyd added. He hated to validate Dale's superior opinion of himself, but facts were facts. "Even if Miss Kincaid managed to survive this long, she'd be weak as a kitten."

"Look at me!" Rupert yelled, slamming his cane down on the floor. "Do you think I'm lying?" He looked between his peers, as if daring them to object. "I saw her with my own eyes. She tore open the chapter house and turned everyone inside to pigs. She was practically bursting with magical power. If I hadn't activated my escape rune, I'd probably be just so much bacon right now."

Lloyd didn't want to believe Rupert's story. It went against everything he understood about magic. It was absurd.

And yet here sits a man I've known for over a decade, he thought, *and he's been half-transformed into a pig.*

"How could that sorceress bitch have bested our withering rune?" Dale demanded. Apparently he was having a harder time coming to terms with the evidence of his eyes.

"She didn't," Lloyd guessed.

"Do you want me to take off my shirt?" Rupert fumed. "Give you a better look?"

"No," Lloyd said. "I don't mean to question your report. Undoubtedly Sorsha Kincaid has regained the use of her magic, but I don't think it was she who broke the withering rune."

"Why do you think that?" Dale enquired.

"We know that sorcery is fundamentally different from rune magic," Lloyd explained. "Sorsha would have had to understand rune magic on a truly impressive level to break apart a Gordian rune."

"Ah," Rupert said, nodding his grotesque head. "You suspect the perpetual thorn in our side, Alexander Lockerby."

"Sorsha is his girlfriend," Lloyd pointed out. "He'd be well motivated to cure her."

"You're suggesting he found the book on Gordian runes," Dale suggested. "Learned how to unravel them."

"To the best of our knowledge," Rupert said, "there is no way to take apart a Gordian rune. They're supposed to be inviolate."

"I think you hit the nail on the head, Rupert," Lloyd said. "'To the best of our knowledge.'"

"Are you saying this…this…private detective knows more than we do?" Dale sputtered, his voice on the edge of outrage. "That he possesses more knowledge than all the Legion?"

"Yes," Lloyd said, looking around at his companions. "I think it's obvious. Alexander Lockerby has the Archimedean Monograph."

The silence around the table in the aftermath of Lloyd's declaration was profound, and each man looked at the others, as if waiting to see who would speak first.

"That's how he met the sorceress," Dale said. "She came to him when the government ordered her to look for it."

"And Lockerby's knowledge is well beyond someone his age," Rupert added. "Some of the things he's been able to do rival our own power."

"I think he and the sorceress found the Monograph and decided to keep it," Lloyd said, surer of his supposition.

"No," Rupert said after a moment. "I think you're half right. According to our research, Lockerby was quite the up-and-coming detective before that cursed sorceress met him. It was said of him that his finding rune was the best in the city."

"You think he found the book before he met Sorsha?" Dale asked.

"No," Lloyd said, catching Rupert's train of thought. "He means that Alex got that finding rune from his teacher."

"Dr. Ignatius Bell," Rupert growled, saliva leaking out of his deformed mouth. "He's the one who found it, and that means he still has it." Rupert lunged to his feet, sending the little table and the chessboard flying. "It's time the Legion paid the doctor a house call to take what is rightfully ours."

"Easy, Rupert," Dale cautioned. "Lockerby has proved a dangerous foe in the past. If you're right about his mentor, then Dr. Bell is likely to be equally formidable. If not more so."

"Do you see what that bitch of his did to me," Rupert wailed, holding out his three-fingered hand. "The doctor and the private detective must answer for this outrage."

"Easy, my friend," Lloyd said, standing as well. "You're both correct. Lockerby, Dr. Bell, and the sorceress must all be made to pay for what they've done, but they are also wily and dangerous opponents. We must be cautious. We must watch and plan, choose our moment. Only then will we have any chance of success."

Rupert snorted and slammed his cane down on the floor.

"So be it," he growled, not happy, but mollified. "We will wait...for now."

Consciousness slowly seeped back into Alex's synapses, his awareness rising gradually as if it feared being seen. As the ceiling of his vault bedroom came into view, Alex realized his consciousness had a damn good reason to be scared, as the mother of all headaches threatened to screw his eyes out of their sockets from the inside.

He groaned and covered his eyes, but even the groan hurt his head.

Struggling to throw off his blankets, Alex pushed his feet over the edge of the bed and let them dangle for a long moment. The last thing he remembered was breaking the Gordian rune that was killing Sorsha.

That did work, he wondered, *right?*

Even the act of thinking to himself hurt, and he groaned again.

"Ah," Iggy's voice assaulted his eardrums like a sledgehammer. "I see you're finally up."

"Sshhhh," Alex shushed him.

He couldn't see Iggy, but he knew the old man had a massive grin on his face.

"Drink this," Iggy whispered, pushing a glass into Alex's hand.

Not even stopping to wonder what it might be, Alex put the glass to his lips and drained it. At once his body went cold and a numbness fogged over his brain. He wanted to shiver, but the effect happened too quickly; he didn't have time. The fog in his brain melted away and the chill exited his body with his breath.

Carefully, Alex opened one eye, but no stabbing pain assaulted him.

"Thanks," he said, opening the other eye. "What was that stuff?"

Iggy gave him a wry smile and waggled his eyebrows.

"Something Charles and I have been cooking up," he said with a tremendous amount of false modesty.

"Well, it works," Alex said. "How long have I been out? Where's Sorsha?"

"Easy," Iggy said, holding out his hand as Alex tried to rise. "Your head may feel better, but you're not better. You need to take it easy. To answer your questions, you were out for a couple of hours and Sorsha is fine. Andrew brought her back, but she burned through a lot of magical energy, so I sent her home to rest."

"She burned through magical energy?" he said. "What?"

Iggy chuckled darkly, then told Alex what had happened once Sorsha teleported away. Alex almost laughed when he learned that she couldn't change the former Legion members back from being pigs. Normally he'd find such a fate horrific, but the Legion had tried to kill Sorsha by condemning her to wither a bit every day.

They deserve whatever happens to them, he thought.

"I need to check on Sorsha," he said out loud.

"She's resting," Iggy said, more emphatically this time. "You can talk to her in the morning."

Alex was absolutely certain that was bad advice. If Sorsha thought he hadn't been concerned enough about her welfare, she'd make him pay for that lack of judgement.

"All right, I'll leave her be," he lied. "It's still early enough that I could call Ethel Briggs."

"Like Sorsha, you need some rest," Iggy said. "You can call Mrs. Briggs and anything else you need to do in the morning. Now, tell me what you did to disrupt the Legion's giant finding rune."

"I told you," Alex said, "I couldn't figure out how to disrupt it."

"But you did something to it, didn't you?"

"Of course," Alex said with a grin. "I found the node where they linked the construct back to whatever map or compass they were going to use to locate whatever they were looking for."

Iggy groaned and put his hand over his face.

"Tell me you didn't link yourself to the outgoing part of the rune."

"Of course I did," he said. "And a lucky thing I did."

Iggy splayed his fingers enough to look through them.

"And?"

"And I know what the Legion is after."

Alex described his disjointed vision to Iggy.

"So they're looking for a special vault under a field of ice," Iggy said.

Alex nodded.

"And you could only see darkness inside it."

"It was more than just darkness," Alex said, recalling the vision with a shiver. "It was malevolent, evil. Whatever's inside that black vault is something far too dangerous to fall into the hands of the Legion."

"Like the Monograph itself," Iggy said. "All right, I want you to write down everything you can remember while it's fresh in your mind. After that, I want you to get back in bed and stay there. You've experienced a large shock to your system, and I don't want you overdoing it. I'll come back and take a look at you in the morning."

Alex nodded.

"Write everything down and go back to bed," he repeated.

"Gotcha."

Iggy gave him a tired smile, then turned to leave.

"You gave me quite a scare tonight," he admitted. "You and Sorsha both. I'm going to take my own advice and go to bed."

Alex watched him go and waited until the cover door to the brownstone shut, then he got slowly to his feet. Whatever Iggy had given him was blocking the pain in his head, but his body ached like he'd gone a few rounds with Joe Louis.

Rolling his shoulders, he left the bedroom and made his way to his drafting table. He pulled a blank notebook from his rollaway cabinet, then set it on the table.

He sat, but instead of turning to his drafting table, Alex pivoted to the rollaway cabinet. The clock still sitting across the room on his reading table said it was a bit after nine, so he picked up the candlestick phone, and fished his notepad out of his pocket.

"Hello," he said when the call connected. "I'm trying to reach Ethel Briggs; this is Alex Lockerby."

"Hello?" Ethel's hesitant voice greeted him a moment later.

"It's me, Mrs. Briggs, Alex Lockerby. The men who killed your husband are...well they're not dead, but they didn't escape justice."

He took a deep breath and told her everything. He couldn't be certain that the man who killed Lucius was at the house when Sorsha turned everyone into pigs, but Ethel deserved closure, so he kept his doubts to himself.

"Thank you, Alex," she said when he finished. He could tell from her voice that she was crying. He'd given her a certain amount of satisfaction, but that wouldn't bring her husband back.

"I'll leave the key to Hathaway House with my secretary," he told her in closing. "Come by and pick it up whenever you're ready."

She thanked him, and he wished her well before he hung up.

Alex sighed as he looked at the phone. He might not be able to bring Lucius back, but he could make sure the men in league with the Legion didn't get away.

"Get me Lieutenant Pak," he said when the police operator answered his next call.

When Danny came on, Alex told him about Dobosh Construction and Manhattan Land and Building. It was possible that not everyone there worked for the Legion, but that was something he'd let the police sort out.

Satisfied that he'd done all he could, Alex hung up the phone and turned back to his drafting table. The blank notepad still sat there on its slanted surface, waiting for him to write out his icy vision of an evil vault.

He closed his eyes for a moment and swiveled all the way around in his chair. When he opened his eyes a moment later, he was facing the new door on the back wall of his vault. The one that led to Sorsha's flying castle. According to Iggy, Sorsha had retired to rest after her experience with the Legion. It was the sort of thing a normal woman would do.

But Sorsha is far from normal, he reminded himself.

Making up his mind, he set down the pencil he'd picked up and walked across the vault to the door. For both modesty and security reasons, the door locked from both sides. If Sorsha had engaged the bolt on her side, he wouldn't be able to open it, but he took out his pocketwatch just the same, and released the runes on his side.

Taking the doorknob in his hand, he turned it and pushed the door, grinning when it opened freely. He wanted to go through, to make sure the sorceress was okay, but walking around a woman's home uninvited was highly improper. Resolving to leave the door ajar, Alex returned to the drafting table and started writing out the vision he'd had.

He reviewed the jumble of disjointed images and feelings at least a dozen times, making notes of each separate piece, and trying to remember how they fit together. After what must have been two hours, he finally sat back, satisfied that he'd reproduced his experience exactly.

"Finished?" Sorsha asked.

Alex turned to find the sorceress sitting in his reading chair drinking his twelve-year-old Scotch. She'd turned the chair around to face the drafting table and she sat easily with her legs crossed. Her clothes consisted of a pair of silk pajamas in a light shade of purple, and matching slippers.

"I didn't want to bother you," she said when Alex didn't speak. "You looked very intense."

Alex nodded at that, swiveling his chair around to face her.

"Iggy wanted me to write out..."

"Write out what?" she asked as he struggled to find a way to explain this to Sorsha without making himself sound like a reckless idiot. Since he couldn't come up with one, he told her the whole story up to the point that Iggy sent him to write everything down.

"That's some experience you had," she said when he finished. "We're going to have to go through that vision of yours in depth. I wonder if Miss Knox might have some impressions about it?"

"You know what," he said, giving her his most charming grin. "I don't want to talk about that right now." She smiled back at him and Alex felt himself relax. For the first time in months, she looked healthy and strong.

"But you will tell me eventually," she said.

It wasn't a question, but Alex nodded anyway. He stood, crossing the floor to Sorsha, who stood to meet him. When he reached her, Alex pulled her into a fierce embrace.

"I was worried for you," he admitted.

"*You* were worried?" she replied, putting emphasis on the word 'you.' Then she hugged him again. "Thanks for saving me."

Alex chuckled.

"You're welcome."

He finally released her, and she stepped back.

"Now," she said, her take-charge voice firmly in place. "I believe Dr. Bell ordered you to get to bed once you were done writing everything down."

Alex nodded, actually feeling a bit tired.

"May I see you home?" he said, offering her his arm.

She took it and allowed him to lead her to the still-open door to her castle.

"You know," she said once they reached it. "I destroyed the bed in your bedroom right before I teleported away earlier."

"I've got two more," Alex said. "No need to worry about that."

"But I do worry," she said, a sly smile creeping onto her lips. "You let me use your room while Dr. Bell was looking after me." She stepped through the open door to her castle, still holding his arm. "It's only fair that I return the favor."

Alex worked very hard not to smile, and he gave her a serious nod.

"You're right," he said, stepping through the door to join her. "It is only fair."

32

THE ALLIANCE

When Iggy returned to Alex's vault bedroom to check on him, he found the room empty. Since Alex's secretary was currently sleeping in his Empire Tower apartment, that only left Sorsha's bed for Alex to occupy.

Iggy wasn't happy about that. He had no objections to Sorsha, or to relations between consenting adults, but he hadn't been lying earlier. Alex had done something very foolish by connecting himself to such a massive and powerful construct. The repercussions of that act might not be seen for days, months, or even years.

He was going to have to keep a very close eye on his protégé and watch for potential danger signs.

In addition to checking on Alex, there was a second reason Iggy had invaded Alex's sanctum. Two sorcerers had managed to teleport away from the brownstone earlier that evening. That shouldn't have been possible. The only explanation was that Alex was still using the old security construct on the cover doors to his vault. With the two doors in Empire Tower not properly secured, a sorcerer could not only teleport into the vault, they could go right on through into the brownstone, and that simply would not do. He only had two of his new security constructs written, but if he fixed the doors to Alex's apartment and office, that would plug the leak. He could deal with the brownstone door later.

Updating the two runes took only a minute, but as he was crossing the vault again, he noticed the two new doors Alex had installed for Sorsha. One led to her castle and one to her office in the Chrysler Building. He'd forgotten about those, but they would have to be secured, too, assuming Alex intended to leave them in place. Then, of course, Andrew Barton wanted doors that would link his office to his power towers and who knew how many doors that would end up being.

"I'll show Alex the new security rune and let him take care of it," Iggy grumbled.

He turned back toward the hallway that led to the brownstone, but paused when he saw the notepad on Alex's writing desk. Moving over to it, Iggy scanned through the handwritten account of Alex's vision.

"At least he was thorough," Iggy said, a note of approval in his voice.

With a sigh, he put the notes back, but he couldn't bring himself to leave. He couldn't get Alex's actions out of his mind. He'd been too reckless, stupidly reckless, at a time when things seemed to be spiraling out of control.

For the first time in a long time, Iggy needed help.

Gritting his teeth as he made up his mind, Iggy turned to the back wall of the vault. This was where Alex's main vault door opened when he summoned it in the field. The sturdy gun cabinet stood to the left of that space, and Iggy focused on the blank wall to the right. A single chalk line was there, in the shape of a door, except this chalk door wasn't for one of Alex's doors.

Alex had drawn the door there himself, right after Moriarty had opened his own vault in that exact spot.

Iggy walked up and inspected the chalk line. There wasn't anything particularly interesting or unique about it, so Iggy took a heavy steel ball out of his pocket and proceeded to pound on a spot in the center of the chalk door.

"I know you're in there," he called out in a loud voice. "I think it's past time you and I had a little tête-à-tête."

When nothing happened for several minutes, Iggy pounded again.

"I know you keep a pretty close eye on Alex," he said. "I don't believe you can't hear me."

"Of course I can hear you," a cultured British accent erupted from the stone. A moment later a vault door appeared, and with a loud click, it began to swing open.

Iggy stepped back, returning the steel ball to the pocket of his smoking jacket lest he appear armed. As soon as the door was open, he could see a massive space behind, with natural light streaming through floor to ceiling windows, illuminating bookshelves and furniture and even the standing skeleton of a fearsome-looking dinosaur alongside a stuffed mammoth.

Almost as soon as the amazing view appeared, it was blocked by a man. He was average height, with an athletic build and long hair he'd tied behind him. His smoking jacket was purple instead of red, but other than that, it was identical to Iggy's.

"Good evening, Dr. Doyle," he said with a broad smile on his clean-shaven face. "I knew we'd have to meet someday, but I wasn't expecting you at such a late hour."

"Well, you know my name," Iggy said, somewhat belligerently. "Who are you?"

"I'm afraid I'm not at liberty to say," he said. "Alex told me that you called me Moriarty. I must confess that tickles my fancy rather more than you know."

Iggy ground his teeth. He was quite sure he'd seen this man, or his likeness, somewhere before, but the memory eluded him.

"So why have you summoned me so vigorously?"

Iggy sighed, then looked the man straight in the eyes.

"Do you have Alex's best interest at heart?" he asked. "Or is Alex just another errand boy to be used and discarded, like that blackguard, Paschal Randolph?"

Moriarty returned Iggy's level gaze, then let out a sigh of his own.

"I could make many excuses about Pash," he said, "but none of them would convince you. What I can tell you is that Alex is vitally important to the future of the world. Not only him, there are others as well," he added when Iggy looked skeptical, "but Alex is the key. I need him to help the world survive what's coming."

"So you say," Iggy challenged.

"I understand you're in the habit of reading the paper and then discussing the news with Alex over dinner," Moriarty said. "Did you happen to read today's paper?"

Iggy shook his head.

"Today was a bit busier than usual."

"If you had," Moriarty admonished, "you'd have learned that Hitler marched his army into Austria this very morning. The Austrians didn't even put up a fight. Now Austria is officially part of the Third Reich."

That news chilled Iggy. The Nazi government had been proclaiming their desire for unification with Austria for months, but that hadn't seemed real.

"The trouble I warned Alex about is starting," Moriarty went on. "I'll admit, I need Alex, and you, to be ready to help stop the world from careening into darkness. So, yes, I have Alex's best interests at heart."

He gave Iggy a steady look as if to punctuate his words.

"Why do you ask?"

Iggy sighed. He didn't want to tell this mysterious stranger about Alex's personal business, but something had to be done. He took a deep breath and told Moriarty about Sorsha and the Gordian rune, then about the Legion's giant finding rune. When he finished, the man simply nodded.

"We knew some of that," he admitted.

"Did you know that it was Alex who defeated both the Gordian rune and the giant finding rune?"

Moriarty shrugged.

"Why is this significant?"

"Because," Iggy said, "unless I'm very much mistaken, Alex is in terrible danger, and I'm going to need your help to save him."

THE END

You Know the Drill.

Thanks so much for reading my book, it really means a lot to me. This is the part where I ask you to please leave this book a review over on Amazon. It really helps me out since Amazon favors books with lots of reviews. That means I can share these books with more people, and that keeps me writing more books.

So leave a review by going to the Hostile Takeover book page on Amazon. It doesn't have to be anything fancy, just a quick note saying whether or not you liked the book.

Thanks so much. You Rock!

I love talking to my readers, so please drop me a line at dan@danwillisauthor.com — I read every one. Or join the discussion on the Arcane Casebook Facebook Group. Just search for Arcane Casebook and ask to join.

And Look for Alex's continuing adventures in Hidden Voices: Arcane Casebook #9.

ALSO BY DAN WILLIS

Arcane Casebook Series:

Dead Letter - Prequel

Get Dead Letter free at www.danwillisauthor.com

Available on Amazon and Audible.

In Plain Sight - Book 1

Ghost of a Chance - Book 2

The Long Chain - Book 3

Mind Games - Book 4

Limelight - Book 5

Blood Relation - Book 6

Capital Murder - Book 7

Hostile Takeover - Book 8

Hidden Voices - Book 9

Dragons of the Confederacy Series:

A steampunk Civil War story with NYT Bestseller, Tracy Hickman.

These books are currently unavailable, but I will be putting them back on the market in 2022

Lincoln's Wizard

The Georgia Alchemist

Other books:

The Flux Engine

In a Steampunk Wild West, fifteen-year-old John Porter wants nothing more than to find his missing family. Unfortunately a legendary lawman, a talented thief, and a homicidal madman have other plans, and now John will need his wits, his pistol, and a lot of luck if he's going to survive.

Get The Flux Engine at Amazon.

ABOUT THE AUTHOR

Dan Willis wrote for the long-running DragonLance series. He is the author of the Arcane Casebook series and the Dragons of the Confederacy series.

For more information:
www.danwillisauthor.com
dan@danwillisauthor.com

facebook.com/danwillisauthor
tiktok.com/@danwillisauthor
twitter.com/WDanWillis
instagram.com/danwillisauthor

Printed in Great Britain
by Amazon